LAND OF NEBRA

THEIR NEW HOME

CHEECOWAH JACK

ISBN   978-1-970160-32-1 Ebook
ISBN   978-1-970160-14-7 Paperback

This is a work of fiction.
Names, characters, places, and incidents either are the product of the author's imagination or are used fictitiously, and any resemblance to actual persons, living or dead, events, or locales is entirely coincidental.
The content in this work of fiction is not intended to diagnose or treat any illness or injury or be a substitute for medical advice.

The Land of Nebra Series takes place in a time 35,000 years ago.
There is no intention from the author to imply a religious theme or content.

The EC Publishing LLC books may be ordered through booksellers or by contacting:

EC Publishing LLC
116 South Magnolia Ave.
Suite 3, Unit F
Ocala, FL 34471, USA
Direct Line: +1 (352) 644-6538
Fax: +1 (800) 483-1813
http://www.ecpublishingllc.com/

Ordering Information:
Quantity sales. Special discounts are available on quantity purchases by corporations, associations, and others. For details, contact the publisher at the address above.

Printed in the United States of America

Contents

Acknowledgements

Dedicated to and written for, children, to help them learn and grow.
Enjoy and have fun.

Author Notes

One of my greatest difficulties, doing this book, is the fact that indigenous language uses first person speech. The ancient languages does not transfer well into American English. In order to convert this story to modern American, the writing styles and language format had to be changed.

The problem is that the translation sometimes loses some of the "heart, love and compassion of the stories. I have done my best, please forgive me if any of the feelings are not as strong as the original, after translation.

My dear wonderful friend Sue Vetter has tried with all of her considerable expertise and heart to help me convert all these stories and legends into more modern, proper text format. Sue has also shown me and helped to teach me some of the editing terms and rules used in English writing. She is a wonderful teacher and friend. I am so grateful for everything you have taught and shown me.

I would like to thank Mark, you are like a true bother to me. You helped give voice and relay a lot of the stories to English. I was able to keep and marry the old and new together.

You will find words such as, "Peoples." First persons speak converted to English of trees, animals, plants, and any group of living things as peoples or the word family. For example a group of trees were believed to be a family. But if it talks to you, it would say its peoples did whatever. A group of humans would also be a peoples. You will find words like "beings;" they are normally spirit form, such as Angels, other worlds, or non-human, unless it says human beings. Sometimes a being can be living, but it would not be human. I have purposely kept the old speech in this book.

I have spent many years finding out stories, and history from Indigenous people and loved the ideas and the way they speak. This book series is not history just idea's from myths and legends from Indigenous history. The

Medicine stories are told in this story, the way storytellers told them to me, including wording.

Translation help with book.

Buka is a circular room built on top of a pyramid. It was believed to contain energy from flowing out upon the world.

Chukwah is a spiced cocoa drink talked about in old legends.

Here is a little fun, try pronouncing Technockrowsee, Tech-nock-row-see.

Tech – Technology.

Nock- Knocking over or turning over.

Row- is running or rowing your boat fast away.

See - is hoping you keep your eyes in the process.

CHAPTER 1

Lemurian Continent

35,000 years ago there was a beautiful island in the Pacific Ocean. It was long and wide like a shape of the great whale. This is the island of Lemuria. It was a clear beautiful day here on the island. The sounds of the animals and birds filled the rainforest. The tall trees formed a thick canopy overhead.

It was cool and welcoming to the twins as they skipped down the path towards the berry bushes. They felt happy at being alive and excited to see what this new day will hold for them.

As they walked the path they saw to the berry bushes up ahead. Kaylah said, "Wow, look at all those red and blue berries!"

"I think they grew over night," Kalub said.

"While I pick the berries, you go over there and gather our paper-bark, so we can make the paper we need for school, please," Kaylah said.

"Alright, but don't pick them all, because I am hungry too," Kalub said, as he put another handful of berries in his mouth. He bent over pulled out his machete from the side pocket of his knapsack. Swinging the knapsack over his shoulder he began walked down the path to gather the paper-bark.

Kaylah was daydreaming about the fun she imagined they will have this winter in school. They will be seven years old this year. She was looked forward to meeting new friends and learning new things. She picked the berries and placed them into her hand woven basket. Her mother taught her how to make last year during the survival training. She was startled to hear her name being called.

"Kaylah! Kaylah, come over here, by the bushes."

"What?" coming out of her dreamy state. "By the bushes? Which ones?"

Kaylah looked around the area to search where the voice might have come from. She walked to the area and had to pass throw a thick group of bushes to the other side. Kaylah saw her old friend and teacher, Black Panther. He was sitting down waiting for her.

"Oh it is you my friend what words of wisdom do you have for me this day?"

"I have something very important to tell you," said Panther.

"Oh how great! Are you going to tell me another story or have more wonderful lessons for me?"

"No little one, there is trouble coming. The animal council have felt it, and some have seen it. It is the bad sky people again. They have come back once more. Our scouts have seen bad things."

"Bad sky people? What are bad sky people?" Kaylah asked.

"The bad sky people, from the ancient ones war, my child. It happened long ago, before you were born," Panther said.

"What is war? My people live in harmony with everything around us. As she raises her arms and swings them around trying to show panther everything. We are taught to have peace, love for everyone and joy, Panther. Honest we do." Kaylah stopped turning and looked at Panther, then nodded her head.

"Yes, today you are my child. My ancestors speak of a time when there was no peace in the world. The bad sky ones came and brought weapons of war. Both peoples killed nature and each other as well.

"War is killing each other?" Kaylah took a deep breath, "This can't be true! How terrible!"

Panther nodded his head and spoke, "There are signs of the danger again, here in our home land. It is coming little one, you need to prepare."

"Prepare, how do I need to do to prepare for killing people and all nature?" Kaylah asked.

"The bad sky people are returning again they do not know how to live in peace. They don't understand how to live in harmony with nature. Their hearts are darkened with power and greed. They know your energy crystals have great power my little one."

Kaylah interrupted, "Energy crystals? Are you talking about our fire, healing, and wisdom crystals?"

Panther nodded again and continued, "They need your crystals for their machines. I heard the men talking by the great volcano. They need the crystals and gemstones to make their," pausing to think of the right words to speak. "Non spirit people. They are called drones. They are here trying to destroy your world again.

I've heard them talking and they are planning to make the mountain lava cover our land and take your crystals."

Panther stood up and looked at Kaylah, while giving her a final warning, "Look after your crystals Kaylah. Hide them away! Look after your crystals! Put away your gemstones! Keep your knowledge a secret at all cost! This is my warning."

Then he bounded away into the rain forest.

"Wait!" Kaylah looking puzzled, "I have so many questions?" Looking out into the rainforest where her friend had gone. She thought to herself, "None of this makes sense. War? Non spirit people? What could this all mean?" She shook her head and returned to the berry bushes and returned to picking. She put a handful into her mouth to enjoy the sweetness and refreshing taste, which brought some comfort to her thoughts of what she just heard.

* * *

Kalub was cutting the bark from the paper-bark tree. He knew the special way of cutting it so it does not harm the tree. He carefully placed each piece into his knapsack, so they would have enough for the coming schoolwork. His friend Grandfather Snake slithered down the tree next to him and surprised him.

"Good Morning-sss, young Kalub-sss," Grandfather Snake said.

"What?" He looked around and saw Grandfather Snake. "You surprised me. Welcome Grandfather Snake, do you have any words of wisdom for me today?" Kalub asked.

"Kalub-sss, your fire-sss is going-sss to be very-sss dangerous-sss."

"What do you mean the fire is dangerous?" Kalub asked.

"The bad sky ones-sss put things sss In zheee fires-sss."

Kalub asked, "The spirit gave me a vision about the fires. I saw the fire from the great volcano come out and spread across our island. Are you speaking of this?"

Grandfather Snake nodded his head and spoke, "You-sss need to learn to hide-sss little one-sss. Hide-sss, from the bad sky ones-sss, who want to hurt-sss you-sss."

"Why do they want to do that?" Kalub asked with a puzzled look on his face. "We are a peaceful people; we use love and live in harmony of the nature around us."

Grandfather Snake did not reply to Kalub. He had a lesson to teach only and had not time to answer questions. "You must learn-sss to hide yourself, like this-sss."

Kalub watched Grandfather Snake slither up the tree and disappeared.

"Wow!" Kalub spoke. Then before his eyes Grandfather Snake reappeared very close to Kalub.

"Wow, that is great! Can someone as young as me, learn to do something as great as that?" Kalub said.

Grandfather whispered, "Yes-sss little one. It is why I have come-sss. Learn-sss now to feel-sss yourself. Allow-sss yourself to be the nature around you, as though you are a part-sss, of my forest-sss, my little one. Feel-sss yourself a part of everything around you."

Kalub listened hard to be sure he understood each step and did each one as he was told. He allowed himself to feel the trees all the way down to their roots, and allowed the sounds of the nature to become part of him. Then he breathed deeply and felt a warm blanket of wind surrounding him. He took a few steps toward the path, then turned around and asked, "Grandfather Snake like this?"

Grandfather Snake answered, "Very-sss Good-sss! You need-sss to use this lesson very soon. Practice many times-sss, so you can be safe-sss."

"Safe? Safe from what?" Kalub asked.

Without answering Grandfather Snake disappeared back into the forest.

Kalub, now very puzzled thought to himself, "How and when is the Volcano going to spit fire? What is war? I don't understand what Grandfather Snake is talking about. Who are the old ones and what does all of this mean? What was Grandfather Snake talking about now? Why was he talking strange things like this and not answering my questions?"

With his thoughts swirling around in his mind, he finished collecting all the paper-bark. His tummy started to grumble and he thought, "I am hungry, those berries sure tasted good."

He grabbed his knapsack and headed for the path. He saw the berry bushes in the distance and started walking towards them.

As he walked he saw a young monkey playing in the trees. He stopped to watch the monkey. The monkey was playing with a coconut. The monkey saw Kalub and stopped playing and climbed to a low branch to talk to him.

"Come Kalub. Come and play with me," monkey said.

Kalub loved to climb trees in the rain-forest. Today though he knew he had to work and return home quickly.

"No Monkey I can't play today. I must take the paper-bark to mom. We have lots to do before we start school."

"It will be long time before we get to play again Kalub. Come and play." Monkey said.

"I will come tomorrow and play monkey," Kalub said.

"Bad peoples are here near our village. It is too dangerous to play very soon. Come and play now Kalub. Tomorrow we might not be able to," Monkey said.

"To dangerous? What do you mean?" Kalub asked.

Monkey knew Kalub would not come play today, so he climbed back up the tree and throw the coconut down at Kalub and disappeared.

Kalub looked up the tree confused, but shook his head and continued on the path to the berry bushes. He sat down, picked a few berries and ate them. He looked around for his sister hoping she was finished, so they could go back and play with the monkey.

Upon seeing her, he said, "Blessings my sister, I am finished. These berries are sweet today," as he shoveled another handful in to his mouth.

Kaylah saw her brothers' mouth was covered with berry juice. She let out a little laughed and thought to herself. *Thank goodness I know berry speak.*

"Yeah, they are good." She walked over to Kalub and sat down with him and picked a few more berries. She put some in her mouth and some in the basket.

Something really odd happened while I was working. My old friend Panther came and spoke to me about some old ones war. Then he told me about how I should protect my crystals and gemstones. No stories, no ideas, just warning. Really strange, don't you think?" Kaylah said.

"Really? That is strange. I had something happen to me also. I was cutting the paper-bark when Grandfather Snake told me about an old ones war and warned me about the fire. I don't understand what war is."

"War has something to do with killing each other," Kaylah said,

"Killing each other? Why would you do something like that?" Kalub asked.

"That is what Panther said," Kaylah said.

Kalub shrugged his shoulders and raised his eyebrows up and down. Grandfather Snake taught me not to be seen. Want to see?" Kalub tilted his head and watched her with a playful eye for her approval.

"Would I ever! That would be amazing, if you could!" Kaylah said.

With a large grin upon his face, Kalub remembered what Grandfather Snake showed him. He felt the warm blanket of wind swirling around him again. He stood up, then took a few deep breaths and stepped away from the berries bush as he disappeared.

"Wow! How did you do that?" Kaylah turned and looked around the area.

"You just have to feel the earth and be one with everything. You know, just feel everything, like we do naturally. As you focus on it, feel it wrap around you like a blanket. Then just breathe deeply, and take three steps," Kalub said,

"Kalub that is great! How can you be seen again?" Kaylah asked.

"Be seen? Ah, well, I don't know, can't you see me now?" Kalub asked.

"Not yet I can't," Kaylah said.

"Uh-oh, Well this is not good." Kalub said with worry in his voice. This was not turning out the way he wanted it to.

* * *

Toma was a wild elf that lived on the island. He loved the twins very much. He knew they were more than just special. He had become their teacher and friend.

They had just turned three when he first appeared to them on that wonderful day long ago. They had been trying to climb a tree to get a closer look at the playing monkeys. Kaylah had gotten her leg caught between the branches, when he showed himself.

He remembered their little heart-shaped faces and bright crystal blue eyes. Their eyes were so bright and full of the wonderment of life. He could not say no. Even though he knew it was against all the laws to show yourself to the humans. He knew the adult human would kill him if they found out, and his own people would punish him greatly.

In spite of all this, he decided to helped this very special humans. In the short time he knew them, they had learned so much about life.

These two were true Lemurian they have the blue sheen almost a sparkle to their silky tanned skin. This is always how you can tell a true Lemurian.

But their heart was different. It was full of love, and the joy of everything around them. He was leaning against a tall tree looking upon the twins as they learned a new lesson. He could not help himself and started to laugh.

Hearing the laugher she looked around. She knew this laugh she has heard it so many times before, Kaylah yelled out. "Toma! Where are you this time?"

"Over where the standing peoples are," Toma whispered.

Kaylah put down her basket full of berries and walked to the trees and started to look around for Toma.

Kalub felt the area to find him. He ran over to the trees, looking around then found him.

He was wearing his leather pants and green woodsy shirt that allow him to be hidden in the rainforest.

Kalub grabbed the back of his green shirt and yelled out, "I got him this time! Tickey tack, tickey tack, one, two, three, I see thee!"

"Where are you Kalub? Why can't I see either of you," Kaylah said as stopped walking, stomped her foot and crossed her arms.

"Because Kaylah, your brother is being tricky. He does not stop his deep breathing, and being one with his surroundings. Although my dear Kaylah, I know a way for your to be tricky too.

Just close your eyes half way. Make them see what's not there by shifting your eyes. Just put them out of focus." Toma said.

"What? I not tricky! I need to breathe normally and stop being part my surroundings? That is not fair. I didn't know!" Kalub said.

Toma laughed harder which brought tears to his eyes. Kalub stood with his stubborn stance and wonderment of the lesson. Toma loved to watch these twins learn and grow. He was truly proud of how much they have learned in their short years they have lived.

"Now I can see you both! Kaylah said. But you look kind of funny. Kind of like, you are in a fog or you have a mist around you. This is such a great new lesson!" Kaylah said.

"Like this Toma?" Kalub breathed normally and stopped focusing on the nature around him. He looked at his sister to break his connection because he knew she was grounding for him.

"Good job both of you!" Toma said putting aside his laughter, and wiping his eyes. "Now do you think you are ready for your next lesson today?" He said as he beamed love at the twins.

The twins yelled in unison, "Yes! Yes! We love your lessons!" They started jumping up and down, clapping their hands.

Toma took a deep breath, his eyes changed to sadness as he remembered his vision the night before. He looked at the twins and said, "This might be the last lesson we have together. The twins stopped jumping and felt sadness overcome them.

"Why? You have been our teacher and friend for a long time. We would truly miss you," Kaylah said.

There are events coming that are not of harmony and love. This story is for another time. "Today," as his eyes brighten and the smile returned to his face, "You both need to disappear, then go to the rock field, and find me one garnet, one emerald and one piece of fluorite," Toma said.

"We can do that!" the twins said in unison.

Kalub took a deep breath, felt his surroundings and with the wind around him, walked towards the rock field, happy with his new gift.

Kaylah breathed deeply, thought of her surroundings and took three steps.

Toma was standing by watching and said, "Nope, not quite my little one."

Kaylah was disappointed and tried again.

Toma said, "Would you feel your surroundings, instead of thinking of your surroundings. Then just take three steps Kaylah and you will do it."

"Do I need to do all that?" Kaylah asked.

"You must connect, and be a part your surroundings. To feel the trees, to be part of all that is around you, that is the key" Toma said.

Kaylah nodded her head with a new understanding and started again. She breathed deeply again, felt the earth, trees, and all her surroundings, then took three careful steps forward. She felt her skin start to tingle. Then a warm blanket formed around her shoulders. Then she knew in her heart, she was doing it and smiled a big smile. She clapped her hands and shouted, "I did it!"

Toma in a joyful voice said, "Well done my little one. I knew you could do it."

She skipped down the path following brother to the rock field.

When Kaylah arrived at the rock field, she looked around for her brother.

He was looking around in the distance for his stones.

Kaylah found what she thought was a garnet then walked over to Kalub's area to look for the green emerald stone. The emeralds always like to hide in other stones.

Just a little ways they saw a man made cave of dirt, and stones. It was deep enough to enter and find all the stones they needed.

They both went inside and saw a few good chunks of emeralds. So they each chose a good one and put it in their pockets.

Fluorite was everywhere around the rock cave. Nobody really cared about these kinds of rocks and just left them lying around.

Kaylah picked up her favorite yellow and purple piece.

Kalub found a purple and green one.

The fluorite is very pretty with the many layers it has inside.

The layers reminded Kaylah of dreamtime.

Kalub found a piece of garnet as big as his first finger.

He is very happy to find a nice large piece to put with his emerald he found.

As they were coming out of the cave, they felt their skin tingle and a shiver went up their spines. They looked around for what might have caused this and saw a sky-ship off in the distance. As they searched the skies, they saw many sky-ships and thought, "This is strange." As they were watching the action up in the sky, Toma came quickly to where they were standing.

Toma could feel the evil sky-ships around. He sent love to the area where the twins were standing and smiled at them. He knew as long as they held their invisibility they would not be seen.

"Very good you two." To these kind words the twins turned their attention back to Toma.

"My sweet Kaylah that in your hand is a ruby. The other red stone a garnet."

"But how can you tell the difference? They are both red and both could be shined up?" Kaylah asked.

"Very good! I am so proud of your learning so much about the stones. Even though they look similar, they are very different. Toma picked up a nice size garnet that beamed of energy and handed it to Kaylah and said, "Put this in your right hand Kaylah. Now hold the ruby in the left hand."

Kaylah did as she was instructed and felt them both. "Oh my, the ruby is hotter, and the garnet feels cooler. Aw!" She opened her hand and looked at the stones more closely. Kaylah spoke up, "The ruby looks more pink!"

"Very good Kaylah," as Toma's smile grew.

"We believe that the ruby has special powers to protect us. It comes from the red color of our volcano. So there is fire in the stone from the living fire, like (Pele) herself.

Now we are going to tie them together, like this," Toma said. He took out of his hip pouch, a piece of sinew string. Then he tied the garnet, fluorite, and emerald, together to make a bundle.

As Kaylah searched, she felt a piece of garnet calling her to it. She lovingly picked it up and placed it in her left hand and felt the energy to be sure it was right.

The twins carefully tied their stones together like they were shown by Toma.

Kalub looked up at Toma and asked, "Why, if the ruby is living fire like our volcano, how come we are not using that energy? Like Pele herself? What is this for?"

Toma winked at Kalub and said, "The ruby is very special, that is true. The garnet also has protection and it can forewarn of danger, as well.

Fluorite will help strengthen and protect you for the future. This is a part of something I have for you."

"Why do we need so much protection Toma?" Kalub asked.

"I have seen into the future my dear little ones. Elves know more about energy, future happenings and other things, then most humans. Nature is alive and we live as one with her. We have many gifts, just like you two," he pointed to each of them as he spoke. "Now it is time to come with me to my village."

The twins held Toma's hands as Toma instructed and said, "Think of my village, breathe deep and feel you are there. The twins did as they were instructed. They all stepped forward together into his village away from the bad sky-ships.

"That always makes my tummy do flip-flops," she said as she rubbed her tummy.

Toma's village was completely hidden under the canopy of trees, deep in the rainforest. Humans rarely travel to this part of the island. If they did they would get a feeling of dread and leave the area.

Toma lived in the largest wild elf village on the island. There was a large round gathering hut in the center of the village. It was made of poles, with stretched animal hides around it, to cover the walls. There were patterns of animals and symbols drawn on hides to tell a story.

On the hide had many round open areas, which made nice windows. It looked like they could be opened or closed. The door was so large you could stretch your arms out as you went through, and still have some room. The grass roof looked like emeralds, yet it was woven grass mats.

Kaylah said, "I always love seeing the roof of your homes Toma. The woven grass mats sparkle like an emerald, which makes me smile."

They walked they saw the spirit house it was smaller than the gathering hut and was placed in the east side of the village. It was also rounded and it could hold a few people. It also had animals drawing on the hides. It looked like a story painted on it too.

The hides were stretches around the poles to make the walls and block out the light. There was a large rock pile near it with stacks of wood.

As she looked around she saw similar round smaller wooden huts with gold sinew fibers wrapped around them. They were also round with the same emerald woven grass roofs. They were all hidden in the trees around the area.

Toma guided them to the edge of the village. There were many big green leafy plants by Toma's little hut. It could not be seen by the large gathering hut.

He pulled back the deer hide door that has strange painted designs on it. He held it open for them as they stepped through.

"Come in and sit down I have something for you," Toma said with a knowing smile.

They stepped through and saw a nice wooden table with two chairs. Just off of the door area, in the back of the hut is a soft bed with quilts on top. Near the table against the wall there were many books on shelves with wonderful crystals and stones lying on the shelves in front of the books.

The kitchen was small, with a cook stove, and sink. There were many large pots and pans that looked too big for Toma to lift. There were many herbs gathered together and tied, that hung from the ceiling to dry.

As they looked around his home, Toma shuffled through a trunk near his bed, and pulled out two decorated knapsacks. Each one of them was personalized for each twin.

Kaylah had two beaded feathers on the front. The flap was beaded with pink, green, and purple stone beads.

Kalub had a tree beaded on the front of his with blue, green and gray stone beads around the flap of his.

Each of them had a pocket one side and a holder for a machete of the other side of the knapsack. Toma walked over to Kalub and Kaylah and handed them their special knapsacks.

"These are very special knapsacks I have made them with elf energy. They will carry heavy loads, yet they will be as light as one small stone. You must keep these stones we collected today in your new knapsacks. The time will come very soon that you will need to hide many of your personal things. The thing you place inside can be it large or small. Size or weight does not matter. You will need to place love into your knapsacks to keep them activated. Remember our friendship and me. You can do that, yes?"

They nodded their heads that they would and said, "Thank you Toma," together.

But how do you know this Toma," asked Kalub.

Toma smiled and nodded a knowing nod and then took their hands. With a whoosh they were back at the berry bushes, with their special knapsacks. They looked around, but Toma was nowhere to be seen, he was gone.

"Wow!" Kaylah said. "These are such special gifts."

Kalub looked at his knapsack and saw the special pocket on the side.

"I don't know Kaylah. But they sure are wonderful." He smiled looking at the berry bushes then picking up his new knapsack. He stretched it wide open and started to shake the berries into the pack to see how much he could put into it. Even though he kept filling it, the berries on the bottom still formed a small layer.

Kaylah asked, "What are you doing?"

Kalub said, "Just a light snack for later."

She looked over at him smiled and thought, "My brother," and laughed loudly.

"What?" Kalub asked.

"Oh nothing, just thinking." Kaylah said.

Kaylah bent down and picked up her survival knapsack and without thinking puts her new knapsack into her survival knapsack and finds that Toma knapsack seem to shrinks effortlessly. She put her knapsack on and picked up her basket full of berries and started towards home. She called back to Kalub, "Hurry!"

Kalub noticed what the special knapsack could do. He picked up his machete and put it into his survival knapsack full of paper-bark and put it into the new knapsack and followed.

In the distance they heard, "Come in now! It is getting dark!" Their mother yelled out.

"Coming," Kaylah, said." Come on Kalub, mother said."

* * *

The children reached their pyramid home. It was made from smooth cut rocks, which was made into a pyramid shape. There was a round ball that looked like someone cut the top off a pyramid and put a ball on the top. The front door was made of papaya wood.

There were a lot of fruit trees around their home. The coconuts were plentiful and still on the trees ripening.

They open the front door, which opened into a large living room. They felt things were not right as they enter. So they put down their survival knapsack by the door. She pulled out her new Knapsack that Toma gave her and leaned it by the door.

Kalub pulled out his survival knapsack and leaning his new one by the door.

As they heard, "Hurry you two, get in here."

The twins rushed through the living room and opened the door to the kitchen and joined their mother.

"What is going on" asked Kalub? You feel angry mother."

"Good noticing Kalub, and yes I am. You two were seen doing energy work by your auntie today. She called and told me you were talking to the trees and you Kaylah were petting a panther? Is this true?"

"Well, I was not petting it, I was talking to him."

Her mother gave her that look.

"Yes mother, but he wanted to tell me something important. He was telling me."

"ENOUGH" mothers voice rang out. "I have warned both of you about using your gifts! You know it attracts those that hate. It is taboo to use your energy outside. People will think you are cursing them or something even worse, upsetting the natural order of things, and everything under the heavens. I repeat again, Never, use your gifts outside this house, do you understand?"

"Yes mother," they both said together in low sad voices.

"Mother," Kalub pleaded, "Why can't we talk to the animals when they talk to us?"

"Enough, it is taboo until you are in school, and that settles it."

Kalub bows his head sadly and said, "Sorry Mother."

"I know about the other peoples, but we can't ignore nature either," Kaylah protested.

"I know something is going on with the volcano," Kalub added. "The Snake told me it was smoking, he continued. There was a sky-ship that went over the other day. The Snake said he saw something being put into the volcano."

Kaylah added, "Does this have to do with the earth changes? Or is this about the old war thing?"

Feeling very flustered by the twins questioning, she rolled her eyes not desiring to tell her children the full truth about what was going on. She believed they were too young, she reasoned with herself.

Then she spoke up, "Enough, "No more! No more questions, you two," pointing her finger at the twins, "You need to stick to your studies and not worry about rumors."

Kalub quietly said, "They are not Rumors! Cause the snake told me so."

Mother said, "What did you say? She gave Kalub a warning look. "Did you even get the berries I sent you for?"

"Yes, I have some really sweet ones here Mother," Kaylah said, as she passed the basket to her mother.

"Good job Kaylah. Did you get our paper-bark?" Mother asked.

"Yes Mother," as he handed her the many good size pieces of paper-bark from his knapsack

"Very good," trying to sound cheerful again. "Now you must go up to your Buka and get ready for evening studies," Mother said.

"But mother," asked Kalub.

"Now," she spoke sharply.

Kalub said, "Yes Mother, I am sorry."

They left the kitchen and clicked the door closed before they hurried over to their new knapsacks. They pickup them up, and hurried to the door that led up to the spiral staircase up to their Buka. It was a long walk when you have short legs. They could hear the sounds of the house as they climbed up the stairs.

The Buka was the very top, round ball part of the pyramid that is said to stop energy flowing outside.

Kalub and Kaylah knew differently, the energy worked much better in their round Buka. They tried it out one day. Kalub was outside their home and Kaylah was inside. They passed an energy ball right through the Buka with no trouble. Kaylah's energy ball was small when she throws it to Kalub outside. When Kalub caught it, it doubled its size. It was fun to experiment.

They knew Father arrived home when they heard talk and stopped on the stairs to listen.

"Good day at work Bayon?" their mother asked.

"Sure if you call the earth changes, total destruction of what we know as civilization, with massive pole shifts, a good day." Their father said.

"What are you talking about?" their mother asked.

"You know a lot of people are talking about the earth changes. How the ocean is rising, and the temperatures are acting up. It is becoming winter in summer and summer in winter. Some are blaming it on the Atlantains. Saying they are building some kind of a weather device or something.

They have been spotted over the volcano last weekend. I think most of it is just scare tactics to keep us here, on the island. The government is now putting orders into place. They said that our influence in the global world would bring disasters.

So we are not allowed off the island anymore to help the primitives that we are already in touch with. All of our borders will be closed within days.

"Although the Atlantains are preparing for the same thing, yet they are leaving their island and starting to influence other cultures. Can you imagine? Breaking the laws of harmony?"

"Like I was saying, you know Dayna at work and I were talking about something her child told her."

As he took off his coat, and put it on the back of the couch, and continued speaking.

"You know Dayna's child is like ours, special. Anyway, her child said that he heard from a snake that there was an attack on our volcano a few days ago. I told her that Kaylah dreamed that the earth shake was coming, with a large wave of cold water. Dayna said, her son Jai dreamed the same thing."

"Oh dear Creator could it be true?" gasped their mother. She did not want to believe any of this.

"Well yes, it is looking like it could be," said Bayon.

He walked over and sat down on the couch and motioned his wife to join him. She sat down by Bayon to listen.

"Maylah my dear, It's just a matter of the earth peoples. They are not as advanced as we are. They are what we might call primitives. If we took our modern knowledge to them they would call us Gods. We would bring too much advance knowledge and they would not understand it properly."

He paused then continued, "We can never leave this island. Never! We would destroy the balance of nature." They heard their father say.

Maylah does not want to believe what she is hearing, so she stood up and said, "Well, it is almost dinner time. We will talk more about this later."

She stood up and hurried back to the kitchen. Bayon watched her go. He was sad that his wife refuses to believe what was going on in the world. He stood up and followed to help her prepare the evening meal.

The twins knowing that talk was over. They finished climbing the rest of the stairs and went into their Buka. There are three rooms in the round Buka. One area for Kalub and one for Kaylah. There is a bathroom that separates the two rooms. In the main play room, there is a Blue Crystal reaching up from the floor, almost touching the ceiling.

"I ponder what that was all about?" Kalub asked.

"I don't know, It sounded like we are in for troubled times. With what my friend said about the bad sky ones war coming back, and the large wave of water.

Kalub interrupted, "Don't forget the volcano spitting out fire."

"Oh yeah, that too. Well maybe Toma was trying to tell us something. Maybe we should start thinking about what we should pack if we had to leave," Kaylah said.

"Leave? Why would we have to leave? We are safe here in our Buka with our Blue Crystal in the center of our room, Kalub said.

"Yeah, maybe, I just don't know Kalub, I feel something is coming, and soon." Kaylah said, as she turned and walked into her room.

* * *

When dinner was ready the twins could heard their mother calling up the stairs to come and join them.

The table was filled with wonderful flavors of food. As the food disappeared off the table, Bayon spoke up. "Well children tomorrow is the big day. It is the Blue Crystal ceremony. Are you both ready?"

Kaylah and Kalub looked at their father. They had forgotten about the big ceremony with everything they learned today. They nodded her head and smiled excitedly.

"That is good." Bayon smiled back at them. It is a great honor to be asked to join. Your mother will bring you to town and I will meet you there. It is time for your evening studies. I would like you to work on your reading before going to bed, Alright?"

The twins said, "Alright father." They stood up and put their bowls in the sink. They lovingly rub noses with their parents and went to their Buka. They worked on their schoolwork then took their showers and got in to bed.

CHAPTER 2

Blue Crystal Ceremony

From their Buka they heard their mother calling upstairs, "Hurry we do not want to be late."

"Coming," Kalub and Kaylah spoke together.

"Hurry up Kaylah it is almost time!" Kalub fidgeted in the chair.

"Your long hair is very tangled Kalub, I am almost done, I have one more knot then a braid,"

Kaylah said, as she pulled the comb through the last knot, and braided the last section.

"Ouch!" Kalub fussed.

"There I am finally done!" Kaylah sighed.

"Good, I am glad that is over! Now that you pulled most of my hair out! How do I look?" Kalub asked.

"I did not pull your hair out, you just had a lot of tangles! Your big blue flowered sarong looks really nice," Kaylah said. "How do I look Kalub?" as she turned around waiting for an answer.

"I love your purple flowers on your sarong. I think you look nice with your long hair braided down your back. Don't forget your Flower Lei for your hair Kaylah," Kalub said.

She picked up her flower Lei and said, "Let's go! Mother is waiting for us."

"Kalub reached under the chair he was sitting on, I found my other sandal! I am ready," Kalub said as he put it on.

They bounded down the stairs and greeted their mother. The twins saw their mother wearing her formal sarong with large purple flowers. Her long braided black hair is carefully beaded with gemstones and clay pattern beads. She is tall with tanned skin with just sheen of blue.

Kalub loved his mother's face that always shined. Her eyes sparkled crystal blue. Her tanned skin is always soft like a blanket of love.

Kaylah asked, "How do we look mother?"

Their mother took a step back, smiled while gazing at her children. Their crystal blue eyes beamed back at her for approval. She thought to herself, "They are so beautiful, they have doe shaped eyes, that are crystal blue, and holds the mischievousness and knowledge that was beyond their years. Their little heart-shaped faces, with full lips that holds their small white teeth. They have the tanned skin which has a sheen of blue, like their mothers. They are shorter, and muscular in stature, just like their father.

Then she said with a smile, "You both look wonderful, good job. It is time for breakfast," as she turned and went into the kitchen. She puts the cereal and their bowls of fruit on the table. She poured their milk and sat down to wait for them.

"Mother, would you tell me again what we need to do at the ceremony. I know it was something about our star home," Kaylah asked.

The Blue Crystal was brought from the Crystal planet, from the star system of Pleiades. Our ancestors came and made our home here. We helped the people of earth remember Creators love and harmony. Some of our people became crystals and stayed behind on the crystal planet. But others like us did not. Some of us can create energy naturally. In our long lineage we know that some of us do not have the gift naturally.

Instead we must teach them how to touch and flow their energies like your father. The people who have the natural gifts are asked to help in the re-energizing the great Blue Crystal on the Autumn Equinox. Our positive energy flows through and around the crystal. In doing this we also re-energize ourselves. It is the balance of harmony, to give and receive. You will learn to control your energy when you are at school.

Our Crystal heals, protects, and is a part of each of us. We stand around the Blue Crystal, with pure heart energy. When the ceremony begins, all the children will circle around it and the adults will circle in behind them making a second outside ring.

The children will walk?" she paused to wait for her children to answer.

"Ah, Sun-wise!" said Kaylah.

"Yes, Very good Kaylah, their mother said. Children are the most powerful. They have the purity of heart. This is why they must be closer to the crystal. And we give to the crystal what?"

"Love!" Kalub and Kaylah said in unison.

"Very good, now put your bowls on the counter it is time to go." Maylah said.

The children got up and place their bowls in the kitchen sink and hurried back to the living room.

"Let's go, we need to be sure we can find a place to park the sky-ship," their mother said.

"Alright mother, we are ready," they said excitedly.

* * *

It was a clear day when they walk outside to their sky-ship. This is the first time Kalub and Kaylah are allowed to ride in the sky-ship. The sky-ship is round with a pinkish tint to the metal. On the inside it has two seats in the front and one long seat in the back. There is a door on each side that effortlessly moves up and down to allow them to get in. The twins climb into the backseat and their mother gets into the front seat to pilot the sky-ship. The sky-ship lifts off the ground and they are on their way.

Kaylah presses her face against the window, amazed at what she sees, as they fly over the tops of the trees.

Kalub recalls all the different paths they know very well, on the ground, but never saw it from the sky.

Maylah asked, "What is the name of that tree?" as she pointed out the window.

"That is Cedar," The twins singsong back.

"Good Job! What about that one?" Maylah asked.

"That is paper bark," Kaylah answered first.

"You children are very good," Maylah said. The town we are going to is called, Tattooma. It is far from our home, but we should be there in a little while."

The children replied excitedly, "Alright, Mother."

As Kaylah looked out, she saw the city, finally come into view. She saw many free formed sculpture buildings and the Blue Crystal, which was very large and towered above the city.

Maylah piloted the sky-ship towards the east; she flew around the area until she found the right place to park and said, "Alright, we are here children. We have to stay together there will be a lot of people here so stay close to me please."

"Alright," Mother don't worry," Kalub and Kaylah, they said together.

"Worry? Hm mm, today worry is my middle name," she said in a whispered, as she forced a smile.

Maylah pushed a button and the doors slide open as they got out.

Kaylah held her mothers hand as she looked around.

Kalub walked on her other-side, but rejected the hand she offered. I'm a big boy now," he thought to himself. "I don't need to hold your hand."

There are white mud walls and stairs leading down towards, a moving walkway. Kalub and Kaylah jumped down the stairs and waited for their mother at the bottom. They started to enter the area where the moving walkway was located.

Kalub looked at the moving walkway and got scared. Their mother encouraged them to step onto the moving walkway.

"Come on now this will be fun," Maylah said.

The children followed her but their balance was not as steady as hers.

There were many people on the moving walkway, who were also crossing over to the street towards the park.

Kaylah pointed north to a high building of beautiful white polished stone with black pillars and asked, "Mother what is that building?"

"That is the Library, you will be allowed in after you start school," mother said.

"It is really big, does it have a lot of books in it too?" asked Kalub.

"Oh yes, it would take you two life times to read all of them," mother answered.

"Wow!" the children said.

"Do you see children?" as Maylah pointed out what each area was, "The parking area is there, in the east. Over there in the south is where the government offices are. Do you see the horseshoe shaped tall building?"

The children nodded.

"That is where your father works. Over in the west where we cannot see, are our hospitals and medical centers. If you want to become a doctor this is where you would study and work. Do you see the long buildings by the horseshoe building over there in the north?"

"Yes," the twins nodded their heads.

"All of this is the school area. This is where you will start and finish all your education."

"Mother what kind of stone is on the streets?" Kaylah asked.

"That is a mixture of volcanic rock and our dark rich earth. This mixture is made into mud blocks, then dried and laid down in this artistic pattern to make this road," mother said.

The twins look at each other and said, "Wow."

They continue to move toward the park as they look around at the sights. They were filled with amazement at the tall beautiful buildings and the beautiful paved streets below.

They reach the end of the moving walkway and again Kalub is scared. It looked as if it would suck him up into the rollers ahead. So he decided to jump across it and sure enough he made it. Kaylah followed his lead and jumped as well.

They walked to the park looking at all the beauty around them. Maylah saw her husband Bayon sitting on the park bench wearing his ceremonial sarong. His long black hair is braided with many braids, with gemstone and hand carved beads carefully placed in each braid. She loves his doe shaped blue eyes that shined love and peace. He was shorter than her. He was only 5'10 but has a muscular stature. The sight of him still makes her heart calm and knowing all is perfect in the world around her.

"Hurry now, there's your father." their mother said.

The twins looked up, on saw him, and took off running to join him. Bayon saw his lovely children in their formal dress, a sense of pride flowed through him. When they reached their father they hopped up on either side of him asked, "Blessings father, are you ready for the Blue Crystal Day?"

"Oh yes, I love feeling the energy and you will too. I will be right here by the bench watching you," their father said and then he winked at them.

Their father stood up when Maylah came up to them. He held out his hands to hold hers and said, "Blessed be Maylah."

Maylah reach for his hands and spoke, "Blessed be Bayon," and then they rubbed noses.

"Well my children this will be our first year together, in re-energizing our great Blue Crystal. Are you excited?" Bayon asked.

The twins nodded their little head quickly and said in harmony, "Oh yes father."

"This is good. I am happy and proud you are here with us this year. Remember it is a great honor, and a true gift to be able to re-energize the Blue Crystal. You must be respectful to the elders and do as you are told," their father reminded them, as he adjusted Kaylah's Lei.

"We will father," the twins singsong back.

Kaylah looked around the area. It was a large spacious grassy area with trees that touched the sky. There is a large beautiful blue pond with a magnificent fountain in the center of the pond. There are ducks and geese floating lazily. Colorful birds and animals were everywhere. They are chattering to each other awaiting the ceremony to begin.

The big Blue Crystal was shining brightly in the center of the park. It stood manifestly above the building around it. All of the Lemurian's have gathered to participate in the ceremony.

Kalub saw many large flat stones suspended in the air around the park. He asked his mother "What are those strange stones things?"

Maylah replied, "They are special magnets and metal that carry voice, like your vocal cords. Our leader speaks into a device, which these stones, as you call them, amplify so everyone can hear him.

The twin's eyes grew wider but remind silence. Kalub said, "Thank you mother."

Over the stones they hear, "Blessed Be citizens of Lemuria. Welcome to the Blue Crystal ceremony celebration. Will all special children and the elders please come to the Blue Crystal at this time."

Kalub and Kaylah stood up from the bench and grabbed their mothers arm and jumped up and down saying, "It is time mother! It is time!"

Their mother looked down lovingly at her children and smiled and said, "Yes it is young ones, letting out a deep breath, and Lets go." She leaned over to Bayon, rubbed noses then stood up, walked to the Blue Crystal with Kalub and Kaylah happily traveled besides her.

All of the Lemurians stood in respect and honor, as they watch the special ones walk to the Blue Crystal.

The Announcer spoke, "All children must go sun-wise around the crystal. Your parents will be walking counter sun-wise. Reach out your hands, palms towards the crystal while you walk. For you first timers, a special warm blessing goes to you and your family. Remember to send loving thoughts to the crystal as she hums."

All became silent, even the chattering from the birds and animals. Everything seemed to have also become participants of the ceremony. The children walked side step in a sun-wise direction, around the crystal until their circle was complete.

The Nebra's wait until the lead person nods, which meant it, was time for them to start. They held hands and also walk fancy side step. Stepping sideways left foot crossing over the right, touching lightly with toe then hard on the heal of the foot. Then with the right foot crossing behind the left foot again touching lightly with the toe and heavy heal. And they repeated as they form their circle.

Soon everyone was around the Blue Crystal. It was so large you could not see the people on the other side. All of the people stopped and waited for the announcer and the Blue Crystal.

Kalub was standing next to an older boy who has long dark brown hair with bright red streaks. It was braided in many braids with a few gemstone beads. He was tall, skinny and tanned. He looked worried.

Kalub asked breaking the boy tension, "What is your name?"

"My name is Jai. What is yours?"

"Mine is Kalub. This is my first time." he said proudly. "Why do you feel nervous?"

"Oh well, I had a dream last night. But it was only a dream. First time? Well, all you have to do is send love, just remember good times." Jai said as he nodded his head towards the Crystal then fell silent again.

"I can do that." Kalub thought to himself.

The Announcer spoke, "It is time to Begin."

Just as the announcer finished speaking, the Blue Crystal started to hum, and started to glow a sky blue.

The children begin side stepping sun-wise and the adults on the outer ring also follows to side stepping counter sun-wise. They all raise their hands in front of them, palms facing the crystal and beam pure love.

The crystal glowed bluer with each step the people made. After one complete circle Kaylah noticed the Blue Crystal started pulsing out blue glowing rings of light, which filled the park.

Everyone could feel the peace and love it was sending out. The people watching filled their hearts with love and beamed it to the crystal as well. Soon the Crystal hummed louder and became a beautiful medium blue. This energy then flowed all over the island and out into the island chains of Lemuria. Everyone and everything is at peace.

Bayon from the park saw his family start to glow. It is the same beautiful blue color as the crystal. He is proud to see his children in the circle with their mother.

Bayon's ancestors were not from the Crystal Planet. Although they were from the same star system of the Pleiades. It was Bayon's great, great grandfather who married a crystal woman, after they landed on planet earth.

When their children were born that is what started a new race of people with a new energy called, Nebra energy. This union maintained their long-lasting friendship they had before they left their planets for earth. The new race of people born on earth, named themselves Lemurians, which means the first people of light.

Bayon falls into a trance like state, from the energy the Nebra's and the Blue Crystal illuminated. He closed his eyes and remembered sitting on his grandfather's lap.

He will never forget what his grandfather said that day. *"Bayon it is not a bad thing to be born without the gift of touching your energy naturally. In school you will learn how to touch the energy that we all have. Learn how to touch it and bring the energy forward. Do this Bayon and you will give hope to all the people you will touch throughout your life. You will teach the gift to many primitive peoples. You will be the proof that all people have energy and gifts waiting to be opened through love."*

* * *

Loud screams awakened Kalub and Kaylah from their trance-like state, as they circled the far side of the Blue Crystal.

Strange sky ships flew from all directions, straight toward the park.

The announcer shouted, "Atlantains! Run everyone, hide!"

Everyone ran in all directions to get out of the park and away from the

Atlantain's sky-ships. Some of the people ran and hid in the rainforest just on the edge of the park. The parents and children that could not get away in time, were frozen solid by an ugly green beam of light.

The beam shoots down from the bottom of the Atlantain's sky-ships. The unfortunate ones were lifted up and sucked through the ugly green cylinder disappearing in the underbelly of the ship.

Kalub and Kaylah look around trying find their mother. She was nowhere to be seen in the mass of people around them. Suddenly through the mass crowd of people, they saw their father.

Kaylah yelled, "Over here Kalub."

Kalub grabbed Jai's hand and said, "Hurry this way!"

It was difficult to run fast through the frantic people not knowing where to go.

They are pushed toward the pond away from their father.

Kalub jumped up and down to get their fathers attention, with no success.

Kaylah reached out and took her brothers hand. Kalub looked at her with a reassuringly smile. Just up ahead they see the ugly green beam coming towards them. They rushed away from the ugly green beam.

The crowd around them pushed them farther away from where they were trying to go. With more people lifted up into the green beam of light they found an opening they could sneak through without getting caught in the beam of light.

"Hurry Kaylah, this way! I see father in the distance!" Kalub said.

With the good spirits at their side, they find a small opening. It opened up long enough for the three of them to squeeze through. They bowed down forcing and wiggled their way through the herds of people. Some of the people stood frozen with a glow of green around them waiting to be lifted up. Others were trying to run towards the street where they knew they would be safe. But were being push back towards the outside ring of the park, where the one side of the park where the tall trees stood.

The children got away from the crowd of people, to where their father stood.

Bayon frantically looked around the park and the crowds of panicking people, as he tried to find his family. He finally saw his children through the crowds. Bayon watched as they worked their way through the crowds to get to him.

He hurried to catch up with them. Bayon swooped up his daughter, and swung her on to his back. He grabbed his sons hand, looked around one more time for his wife, although she was nowhere to be seen.

"Come on children this way," whispered Bayon. He knew they must get to safety.

He runs towards the horseshoe shape building that he worked at. Everyone in this area knows it is the place to go, if safety is ever needed.

The Atlantian sky-ships were everywhere picking up adults and the children in a cylinder of ugly green light.

They ran to the edge of the park hiding behind trees and bushes, while watching for the location of the sky-ship.

They were sweating and out of breath when they got to the edge of the street where a large group of bushes were. They stopped running and hid inside the bushes out of sight from the sky-ships overhead, to catch their breath.

Bayon swings Kaylah down off of his back, and said, "That was quite a ride wasn't it. Are you alright?" Putting on a reassuring smile.

"Yes father I am alright," Kaylah said.

Bayon turned to Kalub and Jai and asked, "Are you two alright?"

"Yes father," Kalub answered while he was bent over panting out of breath.

"Yeah I'm fine," answered Jai.

Bayon looked over his shoulder and saw through the bushes, the Atlantian sky-ship's. They were picking up the Lemurian's that looked frozen in fear and confusion. The ugly green beam of light sucked them up with the remaining people.

They started to fly over to the Blue Crystal. Some of them hovered around, and other sky-ships hovered over it, as if searching for something. In the distance was a large Atlantian sky-ship. It was as big as a blue whale, coming closer to the park.

Anyone close to the park could hear the loud hum it was making. Bayon and the children watched this massive sky-ship from inside the bushes. You didn't have to be a Nebra to feel the evil energy illuminating from this sky-ship. While the sky-ship inched closer to the Blue Crystal the smaller sky-ship's move aside out of its way.

Bayon whispered, "Children, this is a sight I hope you will never see again."

"Father, do you think mother is alright?" Kalub asked.

"This is a good time to use your powers," Bayon said.

All three children closed their eyes, taking a deep breath and slowly letting it out. They open their eyes and all three of them have big smiles on their faces.

"She is fine!" Kalub and Kaylah said at the same time.

Kaylah spoke, "Mother is helping many people hide."

"My sister is safe" Jai said.

"This is very good, your gifts worked even if the Atlantains disrupted the blue energy." Bayon said, with a smile.

They all turned back to see what the blue whale sky-ship was going to do next. The enormous sky-ship was directly over the Blue Crystal. Suddenly a red cylinder beam of light shoots down from underneath the sky-ship. The large red cylinder of light engulfed the Blue Crystal.

"The Atlantain's have come, not only to steal the Lemurian's, now they want the Blue Crystal," Bayon said in a whisper.

The Blue Crystal changed the hum as the red cylinder of light worked hard to pull the Crystal up onto the ship. The people hiding around the area that were watching, held up their hands up toward the Blue Crystal and sent love. The redder the cylinder became, the louder the blue the crystal hummed and glowed a deep cobalt blue. The cobalt blue penetrated the whole area with a protected beam so powerful that the few people in the green light were released and also fled to the surrounding area.

The love energy the Blue Crystal produces was so intense; it blasted the red cylinder back into itself. Red sparks flew from the underbelly of the sky-ship like fireworks. This experience left the sky-ship weak and vulnerable, it faltered several times, as it slowly flew away and out of sight.

The smaller sky-ship re-circle, they force the ugly green beam around the Blue Crystal and with all their might trying to lift it up.

The Lemurian's scrabbled their Protective Forces sky-ships for a rescue mission. The mission took longer than usual because they never imagine being attacked during the Blue Crystal ceremony. They hurried to the Blue crystal and fired shots at the Atlantis sky-ship's.

A few fell into the trees. Others out maneuvered them and began trying to search for more people to capture. The Protective Force makes a blue energy net around the park to capture the few remaining sky-ships.

More Lemurian's Protective Forces sky-ships are looking around the area. The Atlantain's decide they had enough and leave the area in victory.

Bayon and the children, each give a sigh of relief, and lowered their hands.

"My mother told me we are enemies with the Atlantain's, now I can see why." Jai said.

"They have been coming here for years to take our people and the blue energy crystals. They have never tried with their entire army of sky-ships. I just can't believe they tried to get past the Blue Crystal on this day! This is just unthinkable!" Bayon grows with anger, his energy started to go dark. This new energy coming from their father the twins felt was a sticky black energy.

Kalub and Kaylah felt their father's energy going evil like the sky-ship they just felt and grab his hands and scream in harmony, "Father NO! You are not allowed to do this!"

Jai yelled, "Get behind your father, and push all your love through him, aiming it at the Blue Crystal!"

Jai lunged forward and grabbed their father's feet. Jai in a commanding voice said, *As my grandparents have always said. I say it this time from me. Creator and the loving light set this darkness free. Allow him to feel the love! Return him to our ways. No darkness, no tainting can touch us now. In heart you shall be!"* Jai lets go and rolls over to his back shaking. "Who made me say that? What is going on?"

As the twins beamed their love through their father and out to the crystal. They felt the love return to their father as Jai let go. They all collapse to their knees.

A few minutes later their father said, "Thank you. It is this energy that they create is why we cannot live with them, they are without love, and it spreads out to all peoples close by."

As they look around and noticed people were either disorientated or sending love to the Blue Crystal. Suddenly the Blue Crystal turned to the Lemurian blue light then slowly goes dim, and goes silent.

"Who are these Atlantain's, Why would they do this?" Kalub asked.

"I can answer that," Jai said as he looks over to Kalub's father for permission.

"Alright, go ahead," Bayon said.

Jai spoke up, "Atlantis and Lemuria are bitter enemies. Atlantis believed they should be the only ones with power. They don't look at energy as a gift. Greed and power is what they lived for. They hurt the earth, and they make slaves out of the primitives around them and make them work in the mines. They take away the primitives lands to make their land more powerful. They want our Blue Crystal and the Nebra's power, Mother told me this."

Bayon nodded his approval towards Jai and pointed across the street to the horseshoe building made of white granite then spoke, "We need to go to my workplace, we will be safe there."

"Mother showed us where you work father." Kaylah said proudly.

"Hold my hand Kaylah we need to run. Do not stop until we get to the front doors." Bayon said in a low calm voice.

Kaylah takes her father's hand and they all ran across the street. They pass the tall pillars and the paintings that were painted on the walls. They passed many doors and archways until they get to the horseshoe building.

The front door of the building has a large double door with designs over the top. There are two great carved pillars one either side of the door.

One side reads *Peace*, the other side reads *Harmony*. They all stopped to catch their breath. Bayon reached out and opened the door to allow them safe entry.

"The Atlantain's are gone. Why did we have to run?" Jai said out of breath.

"They may not be gone yet. They could come back to the park and try again," Bayon answered.

The children look up at the high ceiling with wonderment in their eyes. The front part of the building has many cubicles with desks. There is a long hallway leading to the back of the building. To the right, are stairs leading to a second floor of the building with a sign that said *Authorize Personal Only*.

Jai looked up at Bayon to catch his attention and asked, "What do you do here?"

Bayon smiled and spoke, "We help people with many problems. We guide some of them in a healthy way of thinking, which we call the enlightening department. We teach primitives cultures to have an easier life style. We gift them with supplies and equipment."

Kaylah spoke up proudly "So everyone can know peace of mind, spirit and bring the joy of life to them again."

"Yes Kaylah, especially after today's traumatic events. People know how to come here for safety and communication. Let me show you where we take the traumatized people who come here," Bayon suggests with his hand beckoning them to follow.

"Wow! This is a big place! What are all these little areas with tables for?" Kalub asked.

Trying to break the tension Kalub and Kaylah had never felt before. "How do people know which space is theirs?" Kaylah asked.

Their father smiled, took a deep breath and said, "These little areas are called cubicles and the tables are called desks. Each person has a desk to work at and each area is given to a person. This is the greeting area. People here help others with their problems and guide them to the area or person they need. "Come now."

The children walked down the long hallway towards the backside of the building behind Bayon. They finally come to a large round tiled room. In the middle of the room is a waterfall cascading down on all sides and over huge rocks. Circling the waterfall is a clear blue pond with beautiful colored fish lazily swimming around. Around the edge of the pond is a nice sitting area where people can enjoy watching the fish while relaxing.

There are many large chairs and sofas around the room with small tables placed close by for people to place drinks, or books on them. Upon seeing the fountain they walked over and sat down on the ledge and looked down. They saw the beautiful fish swimming around. It children started to relax after the shock of the attack.

Jai spoke softly to the twins, "I saw this attack in a dream. My mother said it was just a dream and that I should not speak of it." He shook his head in disbelief then continued, "This will show her that not all my dreams are wrong! Won't it!"

The twins looked at Jai then nodded their heads in agreement.

Kaylah looked at Jai. "You should not be angry with your mother Jai. She may be trying to look out for you, or hoping it wasn't true. You should know that. I hear warnings too. So does Kalub. But sometimes I feel like the grownups don't want to hear or know about bad things. Our mother is so kind and full of love, except when we see what is coming. She taught us all of our survival training. Our mother is always full of patience. Well until lately. She just does not desire to hear."

Jai and Kalub nodded in agreement.

Then Jai spoke, "Yeah you are right I guess. My mother just does not want to hear. I wish she would listen, just once."

The twins felt his pain and were sad for him.

Kalub pointed out a fish that was trying to attack a fly in the weeds, to ease the tension he felt.

Bayon was looking out the long high windows that cover one long wall. He was watching for the Atlantain's sky-ship's, as he scanned the skies.

"It looks like the Atlantain's have gone," Bayon said more to himself then to the children.

In the distance they hear the large front door open. Bayon turned to the children and spoke reassuringly, "Stay here."

He quickly walked down the hall to find out who come in. It was his wife Maylah with many children and adults. With a sigh of relief he picked up his pace to reach her. Bayon reached out and embraced her with a long relieving hug, thanking the good spirits she was alive.

Releasing her from his strong embrace Maylah said, "Thank the good spirits you are safe. Where are the children?"

"They are in the relaxing room safe from harm," Bayon said.

Kalub and Kaylah heard their mothers' voice they got up from the fountain and ran out of the relaxing room, down the long hall calling to her. "Mother!" When they reached her they hugged her tightly.

Kaylah spoke up, "Mother, I knew you were alright!"

"I did too," Kalub spoke up.

Maylah asked, "How did you know that?"

Kaylah spoke up, "Father asked us to find you through our hearts and we did," nodding her head up and down.

Maylah looked up at Bayon with a shocked look on her face followed by a stern look.

Bayon got an "Uh oh," look on his face. He quickly forced a smile and motioned them towards the relaxing room. They all walked down the long hall and entered the relaxing room Jai saw his sister among the survivors. He quickly went to her side giving her a big hug.

"Maylah, over here," Bayon reached out for Maylah's arm and guided her over to the window and said, "I would have never guessed they could do that during the Blue Crystal ceremony. We had no warning!"

Maylah said in a low voice. "How many do you think they took?"

"We will not know until tomorrow after everyone reports in." Bayon returned his gaze out of the windows and saw another group of Lemurian survivors walking towards the building.

"Look!" Bayon spoke as he pointed out the window.

Maylah look out the window to see what Bayon was pointing too.

"Let's go see who survived!" Maylah spoke with relief in her voice seeing more people safe from harm.

Many people turned to looked towards Bayon and Maylah as they left the room and walked down the long hall. As Bayon opened the large front door to welcome the next group of survivors in. They straggling in as he counted the hot and tired Lemurians.

"Any ideas of when we can go home?" Maylah asked.

Well our sky ships are in the air working on clearing the area. I am sure they will let us know when it is safe." Bayon said. Please Maylah go and stay with the children, I will be right back," as he smiled at her.

"Oh, you have must work now? After what has happened to us all?" Maylah said as she shook her head in disbelief.

Bayon gave her the look of understanding he spoke softly, "Relaying information is very important to my dear. We all need to know how many people are safe."

She nodded her head, turned and walked back to the relaxing room. She saw Kaylah staring down the hall for her. When they saw her Kaylah waved her over to the fountain where Kalub and Jai were looking at the fish.

"Look mother there is a pink colored fish here in the fountain." Kaylah said.

"Yeah, and there is an orange and white one too. It is really big," said Kalub.

Their mother walked over to the fountain and looked at the fish with her children. They pointed out different kinds and asked her what each kind were called.

* * *

Bayon went upstairs to his desk, and sat down. He took a few deep breaths before he started entering the report about the attack, on his computer. He put the information in of how many people he knew where safe. There were seventy adults and over fifty children downstairs, which he was very thankful for.

He thought, *"We are the lucky ones. This could have been a lot worse. How did they get by the Blue Crystal? Our crystal is our best protection? Only the most pure heart can even stand close to it. This is the first time anyone has come when our energy is at its highest level. Oh dear Creator, what are we going to do now? With more children taken, we will be more vulnerable to Altex. He must be using our people against us, to get past our protection."* Pausing and shaking his head at the thought, *"He just must be using them."*

The reports started to come in from all over Lemuria. They all read the same on his computer; Atlantain's sky-ships have kidnapped children and adults, from all over the islands. Bayon leaned back in his chair to think of what he is going to do.

He pictured his dear friend Magoose in the front part of his mind. He remembered his heart-shaped face with brown doe shaped eyes. Bayon remembers his wonderful jade neckpiece that he wears and the beautiful feathers that were braided into his hair.

He connected telepathically to Magoose," *Magoose the next shipment is going to leave for the home lands of the Mayans, in a couple of days. I am afraid this will be the last shipment my friend. Today the Atlantain's attacked us with a mighty force. They took many children and adults. They even attempted to take our Blue Crystal but they failed luckily."*

Then a beep comes out of his computer, which brought him back to his office. Bayon looked over and reads, "All Atlantian sky-ship's have left the Island chains. So far they have taken 534 children 320 adults and we are still counting. It is safe to go back to your homes. Repeat it is safe to go back to your homes."

Bayon continued to think to himself, "534 children! That is a lot of children to be missing."

Magoose answered telepathically, *"We knew something like this would happen, my dear friend. After the attack of the Chinkutic people and the forced agreement that those poor people had to sign. We all know Altex is on the move again. We know he has taken over Egypt, and the surrounding islands. This evil Atlantian must be stopped. It is difficult to believe Altex would try to take the great crystal though. It is buried deep into the earth. It would be as if he would try to carry a pyramid back to his main base,"* Magoose laughed.

"Don't worry Bayon; send your special children to us. We have added protection around our area here in the mountains. We will take good care of them, and train them for their life's work."

Bayon telepathically spoke, *"They are only six Magoose."*

Magoose answered, *"Young enough to simulate into our culture. They will be able to learn their special abilities with us. It is important to keep them safe."*

Bayon thought, *"You are right I know but, how am I to send them away to you. Maylah will not release them easily. These are truly difficult days we live in Magoose."*

Magoose answered, *"Yes my dear friend, these are difficult days we live in. But your children are truly gifted. They are an important part on the great wheel. We have talked many times about what I have seen in your children Bayon. It is important to keep them safe. Your island is no longer safe. This is only the beginning of the attacks. Norah and I will guide them and be sure they never forget you. It is good that Creator is always watching for us. Keep your faith my dear friend. It will all work out well for your children."*

"Thank you my dear friend. I know you are right. They will be arriving in the next shipment. Now I have to convince Maylah." Bayon said.

He got up from his desk and went back downstairs to the relaxing room where everyone is waiting for news.

He announced, "It is safe for us to return to our homes now. The threat is over. There is Protective Forces helping all those that have been separated from their families. Go to the main pathway in the park, for more information.

All of the survivors leave the building with too many questions and not enough answers. Bayon waits until every survivor has left the building, then he guides his family to the exit.

"Wait here, I will be right back," as Bayon checked to make sure there was no one left behind. He returns to his family and said, "It is time to go, we will have our Protective Forces sky-ship's in the sky guiding people out of the city."

"Alright father," the twins said.

"Are you sure it is safe?" Maylah asked.

"I just got the report and it said it was. Why what do you feel?" asked Bayon.

"Right now?" Maylah asked.

"Yes, right now." Bayon replied.

Maylah felt around the area and said, "A lot of confusion and pain out there. I feel the Atlantains are at bay, but I don't think it is over."

"No, I don't feel it is over at all." Bayon agreed.

Their father pulls out a device from his pocket and aims it towards the parking lot. Their sky-ship flew right out of the parking lot and landed in front of them.

"Woo.., How did you do that?" asked Kalub.

Bayon looked down at his young son, smiled and said, "I have a few gifts too you know."

Maylah giggled and winked at Bayon and said, "Sure you do."

They all laughed and got into their sky-ship.

He pilots his sky-ship to the main pathway in the sky and finds a small space for them to join with the others. The sky is really crowded now. The Protection Forces sky-ships are guiding all of the people out of the city.

"I didn't know there where this many people who could fly!" Kalub said.

"Look at those sky-ships they have the Blue Crystal painted on them." said Kaylah.

"Those Kaylah are our Protective Force's sky-ships. They are helping us leave the city safely." Their father said.

"Oh," Kaylah said.

* * *

They flew out of the city and headed back home flying very low to the tops of the trees. Bayon kept an eye out for Atlantain's sky-ship's that might be hiding in the canopy below.

"Over there father, Look! There is one of those bad sky-ships!" Kalub screams, and bounced up and down and pointed in the direction of the sky-ship.

Their father started to push buttons instinctively in the sky-ship and climbed higher. He yelled back at the children, "Hold on tight!"

Their sky-ship rolled sideways and Bayon turned the sky-ship back towards the enemy. He pushed a button that shot a red laser beam light from their sky-ship. It is a direct hit and the Atlantains sky-ship bursts into flames and falls into the forest. They see a large black cloud of smoke coming out of the trees.

Bayon turned the sky-ship level and pushes more buttons then pulls a microphone out of the dash and speaks into it. "One Atlantain's sky-ship down co-ordinates 162 degrees, just over 2 meters from Big Momma. There is lots of smoke out here."

A voice through the speakers came back, "stay there, we will be with you soon."

The twins giggled at hearing their father technical terms.

From the speakers they hear, "5 minute arrival stay close."

"Wow father, you were great! How did you learn to fly like that? I want to learn!" Kalub exclaimed.

"It is part of my job Kalub. We have to prepare for everything that might come. We have a few minutes let's go and look at the volcano." Their father said.

Bayon flew his sky-ship towards the sacred volcano. He pilots his sky-ship very close to it and flew around it so the children could get a bird's-eye view of Pele the sacred volcano. The children saw the red-hot lava and steam rising out of the center of the volcano. It was very rocky and nothing they could see grew close to the top. They could smell the sulfur in the air. It was amazing to see the volcano up close.

"Mother, My tummy doesn't feel good," Kaylah spoke up.

"It is alright Kaylah. The first time I rode with your father, my tummy did not feel good either. We will be home soon," her mother said with a smile. She passed back a piece of mint candy to both of them and said, "This should help," and smiled at Kaylah.

"Thank you mother," as Kaylah put the candy in her mouth.

The Protective Forces arrived and Bayon flew them around the thick black smoke from the Atlantains sky-ship he had shot down. The protective force flew into the canopy and out of view. Bayon pushed more buttons and they were off again towards home.

Kaylah spoke, "What is the Big momma?"

Kalub giggled at hearing it again.

"It is a code name for our volcano," Bayon said. "You see we call her Pele the Goddess of the volcano, but we nicked named her Big momma."

Kalub and Kaylah giggled again and said together, "That is funny father, big momma, just funny," and began laughing hard.

Their mother joined them in the laughter and soon father did too.

* * *

They arrived home safely and their mother spoke, "Go on up to your Buka and I will start dinner," Maylah said.

"Alright mother," they spoke in unison, they hop out of the sky-ship and went into the house. In their Buka they noticed their families blue crystal was not glowing as strong as it normally does. They walk over to it and send it love as they learned in the park. The glow from the crystal did not get stronger. So they went back downstairs and into the kitchen.

"Mother, our crystal is not glowing like it used to," the twins said in unison.

"What? Are you sure?" their mother asked.

"Yeah," shaking their head, "We are positive mother," Kalub said.

"I will go up and see what I can do. Bayon will you watch the dinner? There is something wrong with our crystal," Maylah asked.

"Sure I will Maylah," Bayon said.

Their mother went up the stairs to the Buka with the twins. She notices the blue crystal had a dimmer glow to it, She exclaims, "Oh my Goddess," she puts her hands on it then feels for her energy and beams her love into it.

The blue crystal started to grow a little stronger but not enough for their safety. She smiles at the twins to reassure them and said, "See it is better now, we will just have to keep giving it love." She turned around and went back downstairs with more worry then hope.

As she approached the kitchen Bayon asked, "Is it alright?"

"No, not really, I think something is out of balance from the ceremony." Maylah thinks for a moment and the answer comes to her. "We did not get to finish the ceremony. I fear that we will not be granted the protection from the energy that we are used to." Maylah said.

Bayon looks up from the stove and says. "I know," pausing "The sky-ship today did not react the same way as I am used to. It should have turned faster. My computer at work was really slow too. I will find out tomorrow what the plan is," he says turning away from Maylah and finishes cutting the papaya.

"I don't want to worry the children Bayon. I want them to know it is still safe here." Maylah said.

"Well it really is safe here Maylah. We have plenty of protection around this area. We have many blue crystals here in the rain-forest. I don't want you to worry either," Bayon said.

"Yes you are right and we also have the healing crystals. I almost forget how protected we are here in the rain forest, by," pausing, "Big momma," Maylah giggles at the thought of calling the great Goddess Pele, Big momma.

Bayon looks up and smiled big as he finishes up the salad he is making.

* * *

That evening everyone was feeling better. They played guessing games for their schoolwork. Kaylah is better than Kalub at guessing the different herbs. Kalub is better at the mushrooms and birds then Kaylah.

They worked on reading the names of different trees and plants. They knew over five hundred different ones.

They remembered all the different ways to build a fire, and huts. They worked on the names of the each stone of the medicine wheel as well.

It was a fun night full of laughter. The twins go to bed with love and joy in their thoughts.

❧❧

CHAPTER 3

Finding Out Secrets

Kaylah was up early, ready to start a new day.

"Get up Kalub!" Kaylah said. "It is time to go play."

"I awake," Kalub said sleepily.

"I just don't know why the Atlantain's attacked us yesterday. Why would they want to hurt us?" Kaylah asked, and then walked out of the room.

Kalub shrugged his shoulders and got dressed.

By the time Kalub finished dressing he finds his sister in the play area braiding her hair and putting it up for the day.

"I am ready," said Kalub. "I've been thinking, maybe we are so powerful that we scare the Atlantain's. Maybe they are afraid we might take them over. So they are getting us first?"

"But we are peaceful people, I thought everyone knew that," said Kaylah.

"Well maybe we should write a letter to them and tell them that," Kalub suggested.

The children went downstairs for breakfast.

"Good morning," sang their mother.

"Good morning," Kalub and Kaylah sing-sang back.

"I am so glad you two are up early, I have a new list for you to gather today" their mother instructed. "We are almost out of rosemary. We could use some fresh berries for dinner as well." She paused and said, "You know what we look like. Our people are tall, lean and muscular. However the Atlantain's are heavier and taller and less muscular. And if all else you will know them by the lack of color to their skin. But trust me you will know them. Be on guard and watch for anything strange. If you see anything hide until you can make your way safely back home."

Kaylah asked, "How will we know their sky-ship's?"

Kalub said, "I felt the sky-ship before I saw it yesterday."

Kaylah said, "So if we keep our hearts open, we will feel them before trouble comes. Right mother?"

Mother smiled and nodded at them.

Kaylah said, "Oh I remember feeling something strange yesterday. I felt the smaller one has one child like us, but the big sky-ship had many children like."

"Stop! The fact you remember is good. It is time for you both to go outside and enjoy this sunny day. Let's leave yesterday as a lesson, and enjoy a new day full of wonderment," Maylah insisted.

The children nodded their heads in agreement. Kalub and Kaylah finished up their breakfast, put their bowls in the sink and hugged their mother.

Kalub spoke softly to his mother, "Mother why don't we just write a letter and tell the Atlantain's that we are peaceful people. We don't want to fight them. Do you think that will stop them?"

Maylah looked down at her son and smiled, "Maybe we should write that letter. You could get a little more paper-bark."

"Sounds good mother," Kalub said with a smile. "Don't worry, will be fine outside today. Toma will be close, he always is. I do hope he has another great lesson for us."

Kaylah picked up her handmade basket and Kalub swings his knapsack over his shoulder. They both leave the kitchen and hurry to the door.

"Come on!" Kaylah said waving her bother on as she started for the path.

"Coming!" Kalub hurried as he grabbed his survival knife.

* * *

The children skipped along the path into the deep rain forest where they loved to play and explore. A good way down the path, Kalub stopped and pulled Kaylah arm.

"Over here, look," as he pointed to some strange prints on the ground.

"What is it?" Kaylah asked.

"It looks like a strange animal track, maybe, well a" he raised his eyebrows and continued. "Well it could be a tiger elephant track?" Kalub said as he knelt and looked at the animal track more closely.

"Could be" Kaylah added, "or a horse with toes?" She questioned, more then asked.

The children looked at each other shrugged their shoulders and started walking down the path again. They were more cautious of their surroundings, to where they knew the berries were hiding.

Suddenly Kaylah stopped, "Over here Kalub, she whispered. Kaylah pointed to some strange animal dropping. I have never seen yellow and orange dropping before, and we know what lives in our forest. What do you think is going on?"

"I don't know, but look at this plant. It does not look or feel right." Kalub said." I bet Toma knows. Do you want to try to call him?" He looked at his sister hoping for an agreement.

Kaylah nodded her head and raising her hands with her palms towards Kalub.

Kalub raised his hands putting his palm on Kaylah's palm.

They raised their energy, and called out for Toma.

"Toma, come please! We need your help!" The twins spoke softly in harmony.

A small voice came from behind a nearby tree, "It is good to see you again my little ones."

The twins put their hands down as they hear the familiar voice. They turn around and saw their friend Toma leaning against a tree.

"So how can I help you today my little ones?" Toma asked.

Kalub said, "There are strange tracks and animal droppings over there!" as he pointed back in the direction they found them.

Kaylah spoke up, "The Atlantains attacked us yesterday at the Blue Crystal ceremony! And now there are strange plants growing over there by that tree." Kaylah pointed to the strange plant.

Toma felt worried and walked with the children to see the strange plant the children found. "Yes it is what we all feared. The Atlantains are back." He shook his head and clicked his tongue in disagreement to the fact. "This I need to know little ones. Does each of you still have our secret knapsacks?"

The twins nodded their heads that they did.

"I am not sure what my vision told me. But I do know this, a warning is coming and you will need our secret to carry your things. It looks like you will need them on your next leg of your journey," Toma spoke very clearly to be sure they understood.

"What kind of journey Toma?" Kaylah asked.

"This is the part I cannot tell you my friends. It is the secret knapsack that you will need. Keep it safe and secure."

The twins nodded their heads and Kalub asked, "What kind of animal make horse tiger tracks?"

"What is that strange plant Toma?" Kaylah added.

"The animal I am not sure of," Toma said in a matter of fact way. "But I am sure it is something created in their evil laboratories. The plant," taking a deep breath and a long sigh. "That dear ones is poison. It is one of the most deadliest poisons on earth. It only grows on one of the small island of Atlantis. It will start as a small plant and then chock out everything around it. This plant will destroy all the plant life on our Island."

Toma took out a pair of gloves and pulled the plant and its roots from the soil. He then puts it in his pouch that he wore on his hip. "I will need to go back to my village and show this plant to our elders. This poison could be very bad for our forest and needs to be attended to immediately."

The children nodded their heads that they understood. In a flash, Toma disappeared into the forest.

"I have never seen Toma look so worried before," Kaylah spoke softly to Kalub.

Kalub nodded his head in agreement and started walking slowing again towards the berry patch.

Kaylah followed close behind.

They walk a little ways up the path when they hear some strange noises up ahead. They quickly duck down and stepped off the path into a large elephant leaf brush. They saw strange looking men standing near a tree and heard they were talking.

The first man said, "Our mother sky-ship sure took a beating yesterday."

The second man said, "It sure did, and Altex is furious. I heard he whipped the men that failed.

The first man said, "Yeah, But we got a village full of little brats for him. He might be a little pleased."

The second man said, "Yes it will be fun to train those new one. I love watching them squirm, scream, and begging for mercy that will never come."

The first man said, "Well with all these plants we hid around this island. It should not take long before our little plants friends choke out all of their plant life."

They both laugh.

The first man said, "We have just finished hiding enough explosive last week around that volcano. So it won't be long before we send Willykat in his sky-ship to sink this horrible, stinking race.

As he finished speaking, he sees their sky-ship fly in and land with a great thump, near the men. A strange-looking man climbs out of the sky-ship. He was 7-foot tall, long yellow hair with deep green eyes. He is wearing a black jumpsuit, with a large belt that has strange objects hanging around it. His big eyes and a stern look that made the children shiver in fear.

In his low gruff voice he said, "It is time to leave the area. We can no longer hide here. The Lemurians are scouting all areas, hourly. The sky-ship is ready, so load up boys; we don't want to be stuck in this awful place."

The first man replies, "Yes Sir!"

Kaylah and Kalub peek through the bushes. They see the back-end of the sky-ship open up. The men line up in a straight line and march to the sky-ship You could hear their boots marching on the metal inside. The doors closed with a bang, which made Kaylah and Kalub jump. Up again it flew above the trees and out of sight.

The twins breathed a sigh of relief as they watch the sky-ship fly away. Kalub whispered, "I don't think it is safe anymore in our forest."

"Well they are gone now. So we should just hurry up and pick our thyme, berries, and get home!" Kaylah said.

They stepped back onto the path cautiously, as they look around for any more trouble. They quickly walked to the berry patch and took a deep breath. Soon they realize that a lot of the animal and birds are quieter and looking around, as if they were scared too.

Kalub said, "Everything is acting different since the ceremony yesterday."

Kaylah nodded her head in agreement. "I feel we best use our new trick, if the animals are this scared, maybe we should be worried too. Let's hurry and finish gathering.

Kalub said, "Alright."

They feel their surroundings then take a few breaths and moved a few steps away from each other. Then they look back to be sure they have done the trick right.

He said, "I don't see you, it must have worked right?"

Kaylah said, "I don't see you either, it must have. This should keep us safe, I hope."

Kalub said, "It will, Toma has never lied to us."

* * *

They go in different directions, to finish collecting the items on their mothers list. Time passed quickly for the twins, in their rain-forest home. They love gathering items for their mother. They both finish their task and Kalub yelled out to Kaylah, "I got mine!"

"I got mine too," Kaylah yelled as she walked to where she heard her brother's voice and they quickly find each other.

"Do you have a strange feeling that something is about to happen to us, soon?" Kalub looked at his sister for conformation.

Kaylah felt within herself and nodded her head and spoke, "I feel something is going to happen but I am not sure what it is. I think we better get home it looks like a storm is coming in fast."

Kalub spoke up, "I don't want to go in yet. I love the feel of lightning. It makes my hair stand on end."

"Yes, I do to love the way it makes me feel, brother."

Why is it so important for us to go inside when storms come?" Kalub asked.

Just for fun they begin to play with the energy of the coming storm. They begin making balls of colorful energy in their hands.

"This is fun, I am so glad we are special Kaylah, and we can attract the lightening energy from the storm. Kalub said.

"True, but we can also be hit by the lightning if we keep playing with it," Kaylah reminded him.

She stopped playing with her energy while Kalub was engulfed in his energy.

"It won't hit me," Kalub speaks back.

The clouds become very heavy and dark. The cloud opens up with the next strike of lightning and the downpour began.

"Come on Kalub, I don't want to get soaked." Kaylah waves to him as she started to run.

The lightning strikes a few feet away from Kalub. It hit the ground so hard it lifted him up off the ground breaking his concentration. He started to run before his feet touch the ground.

Kaylah, looked back just in time to see it, and laughed at the funny sight breaking her concentration and became visible.

Kalub catches up to his sister, knowing she saw what happened he smiled.

She smiled back at him still laughing.

They didn't stop running until they got to the front door.

The twins quickly catch their breath and find the rope and pull on it.

Attached to one end of the rope is a long lightning rod. They pull and pull on it until the rod stood vertically, high above their home. The children looked up at the lightning rod and give each other a long sigh.

They burst into laughter knowing the lightning did not bit them.

They opened the door and go inside the dry house still laughing quietly. They swing their knapsacks off from their backs and pour all the berries into the basket.

The twins scurry to the kitchen, to joining their mother.

"What did you two do?" mother questioned.

"Nothing mother," the twins say in harmony, staring at the floor, not daring to look into their mothers' eyes.

"Did either of you see a sky-ship?" mother asked raising her voice a notch because she knows they are not telling the full truth.

"Sky-ship?" the children reply.

"Did either of you see a sky-ship? Their mother asked sternly.

The children nodded their heads, yes.

"Did it look like the sky-ship's with the crystal on it?"

They shook their heads no.

"It was the bad men, they looked strange," Kalub said.

"How many men do you think there were?"

Kaylah spoke up, "There were many mother, and they all got into the back of the sky-ship and flew away. They said they hid something around our volcano and they planted poisonous plant around our island."

"Poisonous plants? Oh my, how do you know they were poisonous?" their mother asked.

"Toma told us, mother," Kalub said.

Their mother nodded her head. "Well if there is one sky-ship I am sure there are many more."

"Did you remember the berries?"

"Yes, but we could only fill our basket half way," the twins said at once.

"That is good, it is getting late in the season for berries," their mother said.

"The bad Atlantain's ate them all. Here is the paper-bark mother," Kalub said.

"I have your rosemary too, mother," Kaylah said.

"Very good job both of you. Please go up to your Buka and get ready for evening studies."

"But mother when is this earth change going to happen? Why were the strange men still on our island?" asks Kalub.

Maylah closes her eyes, takes a deep breath and shook her head no. In a soft voice she said, "I truly don't know, please go up to your Buka now. Give mommy some time to think."

Kalub and Kaylah walked out of the kitchen and opened the door to the long spiraling stairs to their Buka. They close the door behind them. As their short little legs climbs the spiral staircase they heard their father's voice. The twins stopped and looked at each other. They both sat down on the stairs, waiting for more news.

"Fathers home early today," whispered Kaylah.

"Yes, I bet he has something interesting to say to mother, whispered Kalub.

The children sat quietly listening to the storm outside and the sound of their father walking towards the kitchen. Suddenly the thunder, lightning, and pouring rain from the storm stopped.

"Kaylah did you do that?" Kalub whispered.

"Do what?" Kaylah whispered back in his ear.

"You know, make the storm stop."

Kaylah smiled and said "Quiet, I want to hear what father has to say" Kaylah whispered.

The children heard their father's footsteps stop and they heard their mothers voice say, "Bayon your home early today. Did you have a good day at work? Tell me about it please?" their mother asked.

"It is official none of the special children, or Nebra's can leave the island!" He sat down on the couch and motioned his wife to join him.

"What? What about our children? Why can't we leave?" she asked in a panic voice.

If we leave, the balance of nature would be destroyed." They heard their father say. "But, there is a sky-ship leaving tomorrow afternoon for the Mayan Lands. I know it would be very dangerous. I know you have trained our children well." With tears in his eyes he said, "I think we should talk about sneaking the twins and Dayna's child aboard and pray they live."

The twins sitting very quietly on the stairs look at each other with shock.

"But they are only 6!" mother shouts.

Their father added, "Almost 7. And besides Dayna's child is 10, almost fully grown. I think they will have a solid chance with Magoose's people. They are still young enough to become Mayan," their father said.

Kalub and Kaylah looked at each other and both of them have silent tears running down their faces, while they listening to their fate.

"Have you already talked to Magoose?" their mother asked, with silent tears in her eyes.

"I spoke telepathically to him. He said that he would welcome them in to their village with open arms." their father added, "Making sure the children will never forget us or our memory, he promised."

Their mother spoke, "I remember them when they came to visit us. Norah was a special lady with a kind heart. They are my babies. How can I just let them go?" mother was almost in tears.

"Do you want to hold them while we all die?" father said as a matter of fact.

"No, I don't like that choice either," she said.

"Then it's settled we will talk to the children tonight and prepare them for their future. You know honey, the Great Wheel turns in strange ways. We are only small pieces in the great wisdom. There is a reason for the twins having such great gifts, it does not just happen." Then he reached out to pull his wife closer to him while she cried in his arms. Maylah knows Bayon is a very wise man and she trusts his wisdom.

Kaylah grabbed Kalub's hand as they tip toed up the stairs with tears falling down their glistening cheeks. At the top of the stairs they hold each other in a long, loving embrace.

Kaylah said as they walked into their Buka, "We must face the facts."

Brother nodded, "I agree. One should never lie to oneself, but."

Arriving at their play area Kaylah said, "Isn't this kind of exciting?"

"Exciting? We are leaving home going to a faraway place, and we will never see our parents again! How can you say that's, exciting?" Kalub asked.

"Well no, not leaving mother and father, that is not exciting. But we do get to see the whole world and meet new people, who might accept us for what we are. I trust mother and father. They have always been there for us. They have taught us the right way to live and they always do what is best for us," Kaylah said.

"That will be exciting, I agree. I would like to be accepted, in spite of my gifts, but to never see mother and father again? I hope we can survive away from the only love we have ever known. This will be very hard and very sad." Kalub spoke to her telepathically more than verbally.

"I do feel the sadness too," she paused, "But I know we will be alright. Toma said he saw us needing our new knapsacks. Mother has taught us a lot about the herbs and hunting. I can even make my dress! Remember?"

Kalub hesitantly said, "Yeah, I remember, but I also remember my pants. I worked really hard on them, and they took me a long time to make. They became a skirt when I was trying to climb over that rock. Remember?" Kalub said in sarcastic tone.

Kaylah began to laugh at the memory and smiled. "Yes I remember. But we can do this! Mother taught us all the survival skills we need out in the new world. And Toma taught us special things too. Things we need to survive. We will be the only ones left in our family. You remember the dreams like I do. You saw the fire and the wave of water too. We will die if we stay, father is right you know."

Kalub remembers the vision and what the snake said. "Yeah I remember, and I know our dreams always come true. But it does not mean I like it."

"All we don't know is when," Kaylah said.

"Soon, too soon." Kalub said and walked to his room looked around to see what he wanted to pack for his life journey.

Kaylah went into her room and started sorting out what she needed, and wanted to bring. As they wait for dinner and the big news their father is going to tell them soon.

* * *

Maylah is in the kitchen cooking supper while Bayon helps. All the wonderful smells from their mothers cooking weaves through the house and up to the Buka. The great smells are just too much for the twins. So they stop packing their things, and walk down the spiral staircase into the kitchen.

Without being told they set the table.

Maylah and Bayon bring from the kitchen plates and bowls filled with delicious food. They all sit down at the table waiting for the feast.

Bayon begins the prayer, *Great Creator. Hear our prayers this evening. Bless our food and our lives with safety. Thank you for the gifts you have given to us. Thank you for the riches of your Earth and all that was sacrificed for our table. Blessed Be.*

Everyone also said, "Blessed be."

Bayon begins to pass around the bowls and plates of food. They enjoyed the food that was prepared. As he is admiring his children, he thought to himself, *"I wish I could see them grown."* Then he thought *"nonsense! Yet their energy work was more advanced than anyone had ever seen before. There is little the twins can't do, on an energy level. I do hope their energy is enough for what has to be done."*

He pushed his fears aside and started to speak, "It has come to my attention that your visions were indeed right my young ones. Your mother and I have decided to send you to a friend of ours, Magoose. He lives far way in a place called Zaculeu in the Maya country. They will not have anything like what we have. No phones, no communications, no bathrooms.

They live like we do when we play survival games. You should remember him from a few years ago when he came and helped you make your arrows, and then we went to his home. Do you remember?"

The Twins shook their heads in agreement at the memory.

"Each of you are allowed to carry one knapsack and tie on your sleeping roll. That is all."

"But," looking shocked, Kaylah said, "That is all? What about my books? What about all the teachings of our family? What about pictures? What about all my things?"

"I am sorry Kaylah, but only your survival gear will be allowed. This is all we can do for you." Their father looked down almost ready to cry himself. "And there is no promise you will even make it off this island. You will have to be very sneaky and not be seen by anyone. There will be no goodbyes, just leaving."

Kalub looked up at his father, "No worries father, I have found a new gift. My friend Grandfather Snake taught me about invis hum, inbilbly hum, well to make me not seen."

Father looked up surprised, "Really? Please son, show me."

So Kalub stood up, feels as one with his surroundings. Then takes a few deep breathes and feels the warm blanket of wind around is body and walked towards the wall.

"Oh My Goddess, Blessed be the Wheel of Time!" His mother spoke.

"Wonderful job Son! Well done!" his father said, clapping his hands with approval. "Now can you be seen again?"

A voice from behind him said, "Sure father" and Kalub appeared right next to him. He started to laugh when he sees his father jump out of his chair. "You see I can do it," Kalub said.

"Yes you sure can Kalub and I am very proud of you." His father said as he sat back down in his chair. "What about you Kaylah can you also do this?"

Kaylah spoke, "Yes father, Toma taught me."

Her father looked at her and said, "Always remember, both of you are from the same seed, different, Yes, although still the same. You have my gifts and your mother's gifts as well. You both come from the Star Peoples so you have much energy to share.

Remember to harm none unless there is no way out. It is time to prepare each of you, for tomorrow the wheel of life will turn for you."

"Father," Kaylah said, "Can you tell us about the ancient sky peoples war?"

"Where did you hear about this Kaylah?" Her father asked.

"My friend Panther told me a little about it before the Blue Crystal ceremony. Mother did not really want to talk about it." Kaylah said.

Their father looked passed them for an answer from their mother. But none came, so he took a deep

breath and said; "In the old days it was spoken we were the first star people on this new earth. The Atlantain's said they were the first civilized people. We both have the gift of using energy, but sometimes this energy would be used in bad ways.

There was a great war for power. The Atlantain's believe they should be the only ones with power. They believe this planet had to be their home because they destroyed theirs.

We on the other hand still have ours, even to this day. They are in the Atlantic Ocean side of the world. We are in the Pacific Ocean side of the world.

There are great landmasses that separate us.

There is a plate that connects both of our island chains together. We found in the last Great War that if one of us sinks, and then it affects both islands.

That is why the last war ended. It was not really a peaceful ending but an end.

We as a culture live to better our spiritual selves. To create harmony with our surroundings. We have wonderful music, and libraries for learning."

Kalub asked, "So why do they want to kill us now father?"

Bayon takes a deep breath and looking seriously at his children. He does not want to tell them the things he knows. But reasons with himself that they just need to know, at least the basics.

"Although once again, like before the Atlantain's capture our energy people and make them into slaves. They want our sacred blue crystal for their energy source, as you saw yesterday at the ceremony.

The Leader of the Atlantain's is called Altex.

Altex must have forgotten why we ended the last war, or does not care. He is ruthless! He is the one ordering the drones to get the specially gifted children. They have created a special type of human that has *non spirit*.

They are used to build, work, and kill. They are large men that stand 8-12 feet tall. They can feel energy from others around them, and they drain the life force out of anyone or thing that is not one of them. They are the ones called drones."

The twin's eyes are big as they listened to their father.

Kaylah said, "We saw those drones people today father. They were putting poison plants in our forest. Toma took some back to his village. They also wear black jumpsuits and have strange-looking box things on their belts."

"Oh my, this news is not good little ones. Did you see where they went?" their father asked.

Kalub spoke first, "They just got into their evil sky-ship and flew away."

Kaylah asked, "Father are there any nice Atlantains?"

"Yes child there are wonderful people who live there. They live just like us, with peace and love in their heart." Bayon pauses then said, "I believe you both should go to Magoose and Norah. You will both be safe in the Mayan lands.

The Mayans have special gifts that Altex, so far can't get through. You see if Altex finds you children, he will take you to his laboratory and there will be nothing we can do to stop him. Magoose and I have been working very hard to stop him for many years."

Bayon stood up and went to the desk by the door and pulled out some paper and a pen. Then He returned to the table and begun drawing a map.

"Come here and I will show you where you will be landing. You will land by a large lake. The camp will be a large oval camp with a few buildings around. On the outside edge of the camp they will have lanterns to light up the area." Bayon draws out the encampment on the paper so the children can see.

When you can get off the sky-ship, you will travel west from where you land. You will find a road just past the boundary lanterns. That road will take you north to a footpath. This footpath leads you into the jungle. You will see a big rock with a tree growing out of it. Magoose will be there waiting for you." as Bayon marked the area on the map.

Then continued, "There will be hundreds of Drones and a few men in charge of them in this camp. You must be careful when you get on and off the sky-ship tomorrow. These Drones are ruthless and will kill you on sight. The Chinkutic people have joined with Altex thinking they are safe. What they don't know is Altex wants the secrets to the Mayan protective energy so he can destroy them."

The children looked at their father with shock and fear in their little faces.

"You both must be careful! Do you promise?" Their father looked at them with the most serious face they had ever seen.

The twins promised and raised their right hand and said together, "We swear."

Kalub spoke up, "Father, can we write a letter to Altex and remind him of our connection and tell him we are peaceful people and we don't want to fight?" He looked at his father for approval.

Bayon looked back at Kalub with love and said, "Kalub, some people have so much darkness that they can't see the light. Atlantain's have fallen into a great darkness. I am sure a letter would not work at this time."

Kalub was disappointed that his father said his plan would not work.

Maylah spoke, "It is important my children, for you to understand that we will always be with you. We are of one blood, and one spirit. Through our connection of energy, you will always be able to feel us."

Kalub asked, "Even throw death?"

Maylah smiled and said, "Yes child, even throw death. For we are from the Crystal planet and the Pleiades. We will always have a home to return to. Your father and I are also gifted. So were your grandfathers and grandmothers. This is why you chose us. There are many ways to return home. But for you two it is time to prepare."

"Choose?" asked Kaylah.

"Yes, before you were born you choose to come and be with us," their mother said as she stood up. "Come with me Kaylah, It is time for us to prepare."

Kaylah stood and followed with her mother.

Kalub stood and followed with his father.

There was heaviness in the air with the knowing that this would be their last night together.

* * *

Kalub's father said as he is braiding his son's hair, "This is good work for your fingers, each strand of hair looks like this," as he showed him how to braid. "Now attach a bead every inch to show every 10 years of age. Well in your case you are special. I will use your years.

You are going far away son. I want you to have some special beads of mine that your grandfather and myself have both worn. It is a family tradition. I was going to wait until you were older, but now is a good time."

He puts a few beads in Kalub's hand to hold as he braids in the old beads. This red clay bead with the silver wrapped around it belonged to your grandfather. This green emerald with the ruby was his as well. I found this turquoise bead on one on my trips to the main land. I had the chance to meet one of the great elders. It was a special day to me. So I made this into a bead to remember my experience, now it is yours. We always add beads with each generation. So when you are a man you will find or make more beads to pass to your son."

"This is great father," said Kalub, "I will treasure them always."

As his father continued to bead and braid all of Kalub's hair into small braids all around his head, Bayon spoke, "Your grandfather came from the great stars of the Pleiades. We honor each other strengths and wise thoughts. We are not large people but we are the first ones called to help the weak.

Your Grandfather was a mighty warrior who saved many from the evil forces that attacked our home world. Because of this, you also carry the honor of your great grandfather. Your arrow is always straight and pure of intention, just like your grandfathers before you.

Beside the worrier in your heart, you also have the harmony of great love. This love can conquer all your fears and doubts. All you need to do is listen to your heart and follow it.

Always listen to your elders, they have great wisdom to share with you son. They have learned more lessons than you, so they have earned the respect and should be listened to. Through their lessons you can learn not to make the same mistakes."

When they were finished they went back to the Buka. "I also want to give you these arm cuffs. They were also your grandfathers. The gold is for heart, the emeralds are for healing the wounds, and the diamonds are to remember to be strong yet soft. Wear them with pride when you are a man."

Kalub smiled big and agreed that he would and tucked them away in his knapsack.

* * *

Kaylah's mother was bathing and preparing Kaylah and said, "I have given you the best that I know my little one. I have taught you to survive in the harshest of ways. I knew one day you would be on your own. I do hope you are not angry with me."

"Mother I am not angry with you," replied Kaylah. "I love you and father with all that I am. I am proud of all you taught me. I know I made a lot of mistakes, but you were always there to help, if I really needed you."

"Well my dear, this is something very special from your grandmother," her mother continued. "This is an ancient necklace of silver and crystals. It has pieces of the stars in it and a large blue crystal in the center to remind us of home."

"Home? But mother I thought this was your home?" Kaylah asked.

"Yes and no child. This is my home I am from Lemuria but our ancestors come from the stars. All Lemurian's did."

As her mother was finishing braiding her hair in a long braid that flowed down her back, She placed a special headband around her head, it was gold with long strands of silver wrapping the emerald stones securely every inch or so. The strands were six inches long. The front of the headband was diamonds that formed the Pleiades star system that were wrapped in gold.

Maylah said, "This my daughter was from your grandparents from your father's side of the family. I wore this when your Father and I were married. Please put this away in a special place, so that one day when you are ready to marry you can wear this and have a small piece of me with you."

Her mother was in tears and Kaylah turned around in the chair and hugged her and said, "It is alright mother, we will be fine."

"Magoose is a good friend of ours, he is very special and does love all of us," mother said.

"But mother I am worried about the elves. Do you think I could go and tell them about the, the earth changes?" Kaylah asked.

'I am sorry dear, but the government has put more guards up around the whole area. If they see you they will arrest you and we will have to go into court, and you would not be allowed every to leave this island with your brother. We just can't take that chance. But you can telepathically call them and talk to them can't you?" her mother asked.

"Sometimes", Kaylah said, "I will try tonight."

* * *

Their parents finished helping the children get ready for bed and tucked them in.

"Good night you two," their parents said and turned off the light and closed the door.

Kaylah got out of her bed and waited to hear the Buka's door close. Then she walked into Kalub's room. "Do you think all the little people will be alright?" Kaylah asked.

"I am not sure," Kalub said.

Kaylah said, "I am going to repack everything in my special knapsack that Toma had given me."

Kalub whispered, "Good idea."

They pull out their knapsack and carry them into the playroom.

Kaylah took out her night stones; she wrapped them up in a cloth so the glow was hidden. She looked around for her healing crystals, as well as her knowledge crystals and her other gemstones. She then tucked all her stones and crystals into her special knapsack.

They put in their survival knapsack and the things their parents packed. Then they added their special things they wanted to take.

When they finished up, Kaylah walked over to the Blue Crystal and placed her hands on it. Kalub joined her on the opposite side.

They both pictured Toma in their mind. *"Toma! Toma, Can you hear us?"*

There came an answer in their mind, *"Yes young ones I can hear you. You are up very late."*

"Toma the Earth Changes are coming! You must leave the island! Great Danger is coming!

We are leaving for the Mayan lands tomorrow" Kaylah spoke.

"This is very good news that you are leaving. Danger is all around this island at this time. Remember what we have taught you, and the stories. Carry them in your heart Kaylah and Kalub. Keep them close, and remember us," Toma telepathically said.

Kaylah whispered, *"We will Toma, please be safe and find a way off the island. Goodbye."*

Kalub whispered, *"Goodbye my dear friend."*

Toma spoke back,*" Goodbye my Friends and Good Luck."*

The twins went back and sat down on their chairs.

Kaylah whispered, "I do hope the little Toma and the little peoples will be alright."

Kalub whispered back, "They have a lot more knowledge then we do. Toma has more energy than we do as well. I know they will find a way off the island."

"Kalub asked, "Do you think the animals will get off the island to?"

Kaylah thought for a moment, "I think some will, the ones that work energy should be able to get off anyway."

Kalub took a deep breath.

"Kaylah," Kalub whispered, "I am scared to leave home."

"I know Kalub, so am I," said Kaylah.

Kalub whispered, "Do you really think we will, be accepted?"

Kaylah spoke, "I hope so."

Kaylah and Kalub went back to their rooms, and climbed back into bed. Soon after they fell asleep and dreamed of a new life far away from home.

CHAPTER 4

Going the New Land

Kalub and Kaylah awoke, to a new day and future. They are excited and feeling a little scared at the same time.

Kaylah put on her best buckskin skirt that she tanned and her best green bamboo shirt. She slips on her knee high moccasins that she beaded in the pattern of a feather.

Kalub puts on his best buckskin pants that he made. He found his best green bamboo shirt with the dark green fringes down the front. He looked around for his knee high moccasins with the heavy soles. In the empty room he looked under his bed. He found them and slipped them on. He looked under his dresser and end tables and found more of his crystals. He found his lost fire crystal in the corner of his closet he thought he had lost many moons ago. He goes into the play room to find Kaylah and sat on the couch.

Kalub broke the silence they are both feeling, "Kaylah did you remember all your crystals?"

"Yeah I have them and a few other things too," Kaylah said. "Don't forget your feather bedroll and our special blankets. We need to roll up everything."

"Yeah, I am doing it. I feel really sad though. This is the last time I will see my room, mother and father. I don't want to go, forever," Kalub said.

They hear mother and father downstairs getting ready for another day. Kalub and Kaylah picked up their sacred books and put them in their knapsacks. They look around their room for the last time scanning for anything else they might want or need.

They walked to the Blue Crystal and put their love into it. It spoke for the first time to them and said in a sweet voice. "Be strong of heart, little ones. Carry these pieces of the heart of your star home. Listen to your heart always, and remember your homeland here in Lemuria." Then two large pieces of the blue crystals broke off. As it fell towards the ground the children caught them.

Kaylah and Kalub looked at each other with shock and awe. They spoke back to the Blue Crystal in harmony, "Thank you." They beam more love into the crystal and Kaylah said, "Keep mother and father safe for as long as you can."

The Blue Crystal sent out a gentle hum that they know and loved. They looked at each other with more question, then they have answers for. They each bent down and picked up their special knapsacks. They turned around, and walked down the long spiral staircase into the kitchen. They found warm bowls of cereal and fruit waiting on the table for them.

The twins sing-song as they walk in, *"Good morning."*

Their Parents reply, *"Good morning."*

They hurry and sat down. They said thank you and ate it fast. They saw their parents waiting for them to finish their breakfast. They know father was ready for work.

The twins said together, "Thank you mother, we are done," and go to the sink and put their bowls away.

They walk to the living room and attach their survival knifes to their knapsacks and waited.

Their mother and father follow them.

They felt their mother tears and pride, as she stood there with her arms out stretch for one last hug. They go to their mother and hug her knowing, this would be their last. She kisses them on the forehead as their tears roll down their little cheeks.

Maylah notices the new knapsacks and asked, "Where did you get those?"

Kaylah said, with tears running down her cheek, "Toma made them for us. He said they would help us on our journey."

"What a wonderful gift. Eleven-made knapsacks are the most prized of all. I do hope you left the bathroom sink," Maylah said. She knew the secret but does not say anymore. She opened the front door for them.

They went to the door, look around to be sure no one was watching. They stepped to the side of the door, carefully looking around one more time; to be sure they can't be seen. The sky-ship is hovering low to the ground with the doors open waiting for their father's usual day at work. They did not feel anyone around so they climb into the sky-ship and hunched down very low and put a blanket over them, so no one could see them.

Then father came out and got in like he always did, and took off waving to Maylah, as he flew away.

* * *

It seems like a long time the twins stay out of sight, under the blanket. They peeked out from underneath and gazed out the window. They looked down and see a part of the rainforest they had never seen before. After a long time they looked out again and see a large light pink sky-ship

So they ducked down quickly so they would not be seen.

Their sky-ship hovered down and landed on the rain-forest floor.

"Stay under the blanket until I tell you it's safe please," Bayon whispered to his twins.

He looked out the window, "There were a lot of men out there, more than I have seen in a long time. No matter what children, you can't be seen until you are with Magoose." whispered their father.

The twin whispered back, "Alright father we won't forget."

The side doors of their sky-ship opened, and Bayon got out. He walked over to the light pink sky-ship that landed near theirs. The large door at the back of the sky-ship opened. The waiting men of men began to load it.

The lead man after checking the area to be sure all was loaded, walked over to Bayon and said, "Here is the list sir."

The ship's captain left his seat and came to the side door. He looked around to see if they were about ready to go. He motioned to one of the men.

"We're all loaded. Waiting for Bayon to finish the check list," said the lead man

"Very well, the captain said as he returned to his seat.

The Lead man and his assistant climb into their sky-ship and closed the door behind them.

Bayon looked around the area to see if anyone else is watching them. He walked over to his sky-ship and whispered to his children, "Alright, You can come out now, please be careful."

The twins come out from underneath the blanket. Bayon looked at his children and smiled and said, "Don't forget to listen to Magoose, he is a very wise man. He will guide you in the ways of becoming great energy people," their father said.

The children nodded their head with understanding as they stood in front of their father. There is a sense of pride and love on Bayon's face. The twins looked like two travelers ready to face the world.

Another sky-ship flew in and hovered down and landed. Dayna and her son get out of their ship and walked towards the pink sky-ship. She stopped her son, and grabbed him by the shoulders and said in a harsh voice, "Do as you are told!" Dayna's attitude left the twins in a shiver. Dayna's son didn't seem to care about how harsh her words were. He smiles at her and disappeared.

Dayna looked at Bayon and nodded to him that she was ready. They walked to the pink sky-ship to check the load. She made sure the basket were loaded, and cheeked the supplies she was in charge of. Then nodded her approval walked back to her sky-ship and flew away.

The twins seeing what just happened looked at each other and know what they must do. To say goodbye would be hard on them as well as their father. They grabbed each other's hand and walked to the pink sky-ship and they instantly disappeared.

Bayon watched Dayna's sky-ship fly out of sight then walked back to his sky-ship to say good-bye to the twins, but they were already gone. He took out his water bottle, and then walked back to the loaded sky-ship. He looked over the cargo hold to make sure the cargo is in order and secure. This is business as usual for Bayon. Before each shipment is released he shifts around crates and cheeks his list.

As he walked out of the sky-ship, Bayon whispered, "Goodbye my little ones and good luck.

As he stepped out of the sky-ship, from behind Bayon hears the twins voices, "Goodbye father, we will never forget you. We will love you forever"

Bayon smiled and kept on walking to the front of the sky-ship and told the pilot "all is secure, be safe. There are a lot of drones in the encampment this time. Just get the load off and hurry home. Altex seem to be everywhere," then he handed the pilot the list.

The pilot nodded and said, "Yes sir. I know about those drones. No one I want to cross that is for sure."

Bayon nodded and thought to himself, "You are carrying my life blood and the hope of our futures today."

The huge sky-ship rear doors closed with a thump. The sky-ship hovered up slowly, and then flew over the trees, into the blue sky and out of sight. The huge sky-ship traveled towards the mainland, Mayan country and a scary new adventure for Kalub and Kaylah.

* * *

Bayon walked to his sky-ship arguing with himself, "Did I make the right decision." As he climbed back into his sky-ship and flew off to work.

Bayon Telepathically sends a message to Magoose, *"My children have left the island and are out of danger for now."*

Magoose answered telepathically, *"They will be safe here, I am almost there. We will take good care of them."*

Bayon sent back to Magoose, *"Thank you my good friend, I know my children will be in good hands."*

* * *

Once they were over the water Kalub spoke up. "I did not know there could be so much water."

Kaylah went over to the window and looked out, "There really is a lot of water, and it is very blue. Do you see any land?"

"The boy came out of hiding and said, "There will not be any land until tonight." The twins turned around and saw a tall boy. He was tanned with the bluish glow to his skin. He had long dark brown hair, with bright red streaks in it that looked like someone poured liquid fire on top of his head. He wore plain leather pants, an old cloth brown shirt and plain slip on moccasins that covered his feet. He looked like he had come from a poor family.

Kaylah spoke, "Hi Jai."

"Hi Kaylah and Kalub. I am glad it is you we get to go with. Your father was great yesterday! Oh, this is my twin sister, Loora."

"Loora come on out and show yourself please," Jai asked.

Loora was very shy and did not speak but showed herself. She was also tall and almost too thin, with the tanned bluish glow to her skin like they all have. She had white hair with streaks of black in it. Loora had all the look of a true ancient Lemurian. She was wearing a plain tattered old leather dress with low cut moccasins that covered her feet. Her hair was short and cut in all different lengths and it looked like someone with a pair of scissors was in a hurry and did not care.

"Your hair is so pretty," said Kalub.

Loora spoke to his mind, *"Thank you."*

"Oh sorry," said Jai, "She can't talk."

Well that's odd Jai. Cause I heard her just fine," said Kalub.

"What? You can hear telepathically?" asked Jai.

"Yeah!" We both can," said Kalub.

"It is great to have friends that can understand us," said Jai.

Everyone agreed.

"Father never said you were a twin," said Kaylah.

"Oh yeah, I know that," said Jai. "It is because my sister is very different even from us." He thought how to say what he meant without saying the word that his sister hates so much. "Ah, Special one. She can't speak like we do, nor can she always control her energy. Mother said she is touched? She is just, really special."

"That is great!" Kaylah and Kalub said in harmony.

Kaylah walked back to the window and looked out. Then she spoke softly, "I saw a great water wave hit our island. Father said it might be true. What do you think?"

Loora spoke telepathically and said as a matter of fact *"Yes, it will. Only after the great volcano blows."*

Kaylah turned and looked at Loora with wide eyes, "What? You mean the people will burn then drown? That is horrible."

Jai spoke, "The other land will do the same and then they will both sink. Because of the balance. Either they both live or they will both die. They are joined together from the tectonics platelets in the sea. The scientist found that out during the last Great War. That is why they stopped fighting. But that was long ago and many people have forgotten the reasons."

Kaylah spoke up, "The panther spoke of the ancient sky peoples war. I never heard war or about other peoples, until last night."

Jai spoke up, "How old are you?"

Kalub spoke up proudly, "6 almost 7. How old are you?"

Jai smiled and said, "That is why you don't know, you are still at the age of survival. Next year you will start school and learn of the ancient things. We are 10 almost 11."

Kalub is almost insulted but nodded and said in a sarcastic tone, "Yeah, we would have started this Winter Solstice after our birthday." Taking a deep breath he changed his tone, and continued, "We do know how to read and write."

Jai smiled and said, "Don't worry I will teach both of you, with Loora's help, all about our history. Loora knows more than I do. She is really smart. She advanced faster than me in school. Mother said it was because of her being, ah, really special."

Loora spoke telepathically, *"I am not a 'Nebra' anymore! I am just me! Today I am just like you! Just different! I am free of the hatred from of other peoples. I will talk one day when I, hmmm, when I find my voice! And I don't need the special tutors either."* She was standing with her arms crossed in anger.

Kaylah walked over to Loora and put her arm around her and said, "Don't you ever think on it again Loora. We don't even know what that word means, and I don't think I want to know. We are all in this together, and we will be alright." Kaylah smiled up at her and nodded her head.

Loora felt her heart and was truly touched by Kaylah's words. All of her anger seamed to disappear. She bent down and hugged Kaylah and whispered telepathically, *"Thank you dear friend."*

Jai walked over to the girls and joined in the embraced and spoke, "You are right Loora, all the bad is behind us. Today is a new day with new friends," he smiled big and hugged them all.

Kalub spoke up, "Well I am getting hungry, and it should be around lunch time right?"

They all giggle at Kalub and Jai spoke up, "You my little friend are right! The time has arrived for us to search through our bags and see what we were allowed to bring. In doing so we will probably find things we still need. Let's get organized and find out what we all have."

The children made a circle around the large boxes. They begin to search their knapsacks.

Jai looked around and asked, "Ever wonder what is inside these boxes?"

Kalub spoke up, "They are just supplies for the Mayan people" father said.

"What kind of supplies?" Jai asked as he pokes around and looked into the baskets.

Kalub looked at Kaylah with a questioning look.

Kaylah spoke up, "Things like machetes to help them in the jungles. There is fruit, paper, clay pots and stuff they like. Father said it was to help them survive during the earth changes."

Kalub spoke up proudly, "Father works in the Department of Research, and helped the primitives. He helped the outside people become enlightened as well." Nodding his head as he spoke.

Loora thought to herself, *"enlightened? Yeah right, more like we controlled them by making them need us."*

Loora knew a lot more of her world then the other children. Her tutors were teaching her much more than just schoolwork. There is an uprising starting to build in Lemuria that the others did not know. The governmental politics are not as fluffy as the others think it is.

She knew of the others, the old enemies of her country. She even knew the name, Atlantis. Because she could not speak it was always safe for the teachers to talk in front of her. They did not know she was telepathic, and she never told them differently.

The Atlantain's are on the lookout for Lemurian's children and they want to destroy all of the Nebra's.

Only her brother knew of her special gifts, and he never told. She never told him about all the cruelty she suffered or the things she knew. It is best for her to keep silent, than to let him suffer the same as she. She knew that the "Nebra's" were beaten and treated differently. She would one day end up working as a spy for the government. A slave is what her teachers called her. And they taught her to obey! She also knew that Jai was just like her, but his abilities are not developed yet. She thought, "I am so happy to be away from that place. I can start again, in a new home."

"Loora, Loora!" said Jai.

She looked up and said telepathically, *"Sorry I was just remembering."*

They all nodded with understanding of missing their home.

Even in the telepathic world each of them had their private place. No one could ever invade it.

Kaylah felt Loora pain and knew it was not because she was leaving.

"Alright, let's see what we have to start our new life with," Jai said.

Kalub and Kaylah open their knapsacks and pull out their survival gear their mother and father put together for them. They keep their private things hidden.

It looks like we all have a good knife that is a good thing. We do have lots of rope, fishing hooks, string, and fire crystal. Oh nice, old timers matches, good one Kalub," said Jai.

"Father said when we get to Magoose's village; we can't use our crystals anymore." Kalub said.

"Why is that Kalub?" Jai asked.

"Because they don't have working crystals and modern things like we have. They are primitives, father told me."

"Oh," Jai continued. "We each have good pocket knives, mirrors, combs, tooth brushes, soap, towels, a plate set and cups, silver ware. This is really good; it looks like we have enough food for about a week. I am sure we can hunt and get more. What is that Kalub?" Pointing to the pyramid shaped stones.

"Oh, these are from the Mayans, they are called spear heads. Kaylah and I have learned to tie them on the ends of sticks and hunt with them." Kalub said.

"Really?" asked Jai. He is shocked at what he heard.

"Yeah!" Kalub said nodding his head. "And I know how to bend a stick and string it with this sinew and make what they call a bow. Then you use the sticks with these tied on to them and put these feathers on the other end to guiding them to make them fly straight. They are called arrows. The Primitives use them to hunt animals. And these are special ones for cleaning the hides. They are called, scrapers" Kalub said.

"Where did you learn all this?" asked Jai, not quite believing what he is hearing.

From our mother" Kaylah said. "She is a Survivalist teacher. She has taught us everything about making huts, sweating baths, collecting water, making drums, rattles, and how to kill and process the whole animal. Even how to watch the herd animals so we will know which ones not to harm, and which ones we can kill, to keep the balance.

We know the herbs for healing, and the herbs for eating. It is all we have been learning since we were tiny. Almost everything in our packs is just for surviving in the rainforest. I brought a few things along just for my own memories. I was not supposed to, but I did it anyway."

"You see," Kaylah reached into her knapsack and pulled out more things. "I have a small shovel for digging the herbs, and a small pot for preparing healing herb and one for cooking. We have everything we need. She put her things back into her knapsack. We use knapsacks that look like this, all the time when we do survival training. We have a special blanket that will keep us warm in winter, and netting for the bugs in summer. I sneaked a pillow in my feathered bedroll and my doll. I know Kalub has his Teddy bear in his," as she smiles over to Kalub.

"Hush, they will think we are babies." Kalub said, as he puts away his survival gear.

Jai giggled and said, "We are children! If we were adults we would not be here. What is a feather bedroll?"

"It is made from wool that we got from the primitives up north. The feathers are from geese, we get them during molting season," Kaylah said.

"I am really glad we have you two with us. We were not taught how to survive and we don't have survival skills. Mom told us it is not important for us to learn because we are, well special," Jai said.

The twins looked at Jai with wide eyed and said at the same time, "What?"

Kalub said, "You never had survival skills training? How could that be?"

Kaylah spoke up, "How will you feed yourselves? Or dress your children? Or even gather your healing herbs? How will you ever care for yourselves? How will you sew?"

Kalub piped in, "Or even hunt and tan your blankets?"

Jai spoke, "Well we are special. Mother would never allow us to be taught about those things. So instead we were taught out of books. Besides mother said we are only going to work for the government anyway. We will not need to know these things," he pausing and looked around, "Well we thought that anyway. We are all book learned, but we studied about that stuff. Besides reading is the same as doing it anyway. So we passed the written test with high scores. Besides it just silliness to get into school."

The twins nodded but still could not believe that they had not learned to take care of themselves.

"How did you get all that stuff in your knapsack?" asked Loora telepathically.

"Oh well, these are special knapsacks that our friend Toma gave us," Kaylah said.

Toma? Who is Toma?" Jai asked.

"He is our friend from the forest. He plays with us and helps us collect herbs and berries and stuff," Kalub replied.

Jai said, "Well I am with Kalub I am hungry. We can eat the survival bars, and water. That should fill us up, so we don't have to cook."

"I am afraid we can't cook anyway on this sky-ship," said Kaylah.

"Nope we can't" said Kalub smiling. "But we can have these sandwiches I made this morning before anyone got up." He pulled out a big goose out of his bag and a large loaf of bread. Then he pulled out sandwiches. He pulled out a knife to carve the goose, with a big smile on his face.

"How many sandwiches did you make Kalub" asked Kaylah.

"The whole loaf, cause I knew I would be hungry" as he giggled under his breath. "Here I got some grapes and berries too!" Kalub said.

As he put a large bunch of grapes and a bag of berries in the of center circle. "I also have a pineapple and 2 coconuts in my pack for Magoose and Norah," Kalub said.

The children were amazed at all the food Kalub had in his knapsack.

"Where did it all this come from?" Loora asked."

"Kalub looked at Kaylah and back at Loora and said, " From our kitchen of course."

Jai and Loora shook their head in disbelief. They all enjoyed their lunch, then put away their gear and decided to take a nap while they were safe from harm's way, at least for now.

Each of them knew that when the sky-ship lands it will not be easy or safe for them. No one really slept as they day dreamed of their home, their parents and friends they already miss, and the worries of the new land.

Loora sat up first and said telepathically, *"That was a waste of time."* She walked to the window and looked out. There is no more water; she could barely make out some, maybe trees. But way in the distance there is a large mountain.

Loora said telepathically to each of them, *"I think we are almost there."*

Kalub sat up and said, "I really miss home, with tears in his eyes."

Kaylah spoke, "It is going to be fine Kalub," as she wiped her face with her shirt. "We have our home in our heart."

Kalub nodded his head in agreement.

They all got up and looked out the window.

Kalub said, "It is ugly land out there. What kind of place is this?"

Kaylah said, "It has strange-looking trees too."

Jai spoke up, "That Mountain looks dark and mysterious."

"Glad we passed that mountain. I wouldn't want to cross it," Kalub said.

They all nodded in approval.

"Do you know where we are going?" asked Jai.

"Yes," said Kalub. "I remember father talking about Magoose's village being called Zaculeu. It is by those dark mountains and there are lots of rivers flowing from them."

Kaylah spoke, "I know it is not too far from where the sky-ship will land. There are two villages near each other. The sky-ship will land not far from a large lake, as mother calls it. We saw the map last night. We were told to go west when we leave the sky-ship then go north towards the mountain to find Magoose.

He is supposed to meet us by a big rock with a tree growing out of it. It is just to the west and north from where we land. I guess father checked it out before he sent us."

The sky-ship started to make funny humming sound and then a big clank sound.

"It is time!" Kalub spoke up. "We need to grab our knapsacks and get great to get off this sky-ship. We can't be seen for any reason. Father said, if we are caught they will kill us. The Chinkutic people hate outsiders. They have an agreement with the Atlantain's. The drones are watching for anyone sneaking around sky-ship's, and trying to enter or get off."

Kalub and Kaylah put on their knapsacks just as they felt their tummy's sink and the cargo door started to open. They became invisible before the sky-ship landed. The door began to open wide. Kalub and Kaylah held hands and jumped down from the sky-ship and ran west in the moon lit night. They traveled to the west side of the camp. Then they walked up a hill to the path and waited quietly for Jai and Loora.

Jai and Loora held hands but did not have a clue where west is so they quickly jump away from the sky-ship and ran towards the moons direction hoping to find the path. Jai and Loora looked around for any sign of Kalub and Kaylah. They quietly walked to the edge of the darkness and looked back at the sky-ship.

Jai speaks telepathically, *"Are you sure we should do this? We could go back to the sky-ship and go home."*

"NO!" Loora said. *"I am not going back, I am free now! Let's look around for the twins, they have to be here somewhere."*

Then quietly walked to the west without really knowing it and climbed the hill to the path. Once they were in the darkness and far enough away from the drones they reappeared and started to quietly call for Kaylah and Kalub.

Kaylah had her night crystal in her hand and it glowed very softly in the dark, "Over here," she whispered loud enough for them to hear.

Loora and Jai felt warmth of relief come over them at the sound of her voice and walked over to the glow of the night stone.

The children decided to talk telepathically to each other so they would not be heard. *"Look at all the drones!"* Jai said, as he pointed back behind them.

The children looked back at the sky-ship and saw the large half-moon circle with lanterns all around the camp. It gave them plenty of light to see the army of drones that are unloading the sky-ship.

The order was given and the drones lined up shoulder to shoulder to be sure no one could escape the sky-ship. Then the huge army of drones marched to the sky-ship in rows. The first row would pass the boxes and creates, then hand it to the next row, as they started unloaded the sky-ship. The supplies were being stacked high. They saw men with whips in their hands standing outside the row of drones waiting to do harm if one slowed down or stopped.

"If we were sleeping we would never have gotten off that ship. Never!" Loora spoke to them telepathically.

The children all nodded and turned back around to see where to go next.

"We can't get to the north path with all those drones, what will we do?" Kaylah asked.

The drones were everywhere, scanning everyone checking for permits. Their scanning devices had a red laser beam that was attached to their knees, waist and forehead. The children were still invisible and spoke telepathically, as the look around. Kalub saw a narrow pathway that lead north.

"See that path over there, it looks like it bends north ahead of the drones," Kalub said. He took his compass out of his pocket and checks the direction.

"Yes it does, it goes north. That is the path, follow me," Kalub said.

Kalub lead them. They made their way carefully through the jungle on the narrow path. The children had traveled only a short distant when Kalub looked ahead. He saw knotted tree limbs and vines hanging over the path, blocking their passage. Kalub stopped and took off his knapsack.

"What are you doing Kalub," asked Jai.

"Look ahead," Kalub said, as he pointed up the path. Kalub pulled out a large machete from his knapsack.

"How did you get that big knife out of your little knapsack?" Jai asked.

Kalub showed his machete with his two little hands *"Jai, the Mayans call this a machete,"* Kalub said.

Kalub swung his knapsack back over his shoulders and looked up at the moon. *"Father timed our escape just right. He knew we could have the full moon to light the way."* Kalub said, with a smile as he reappeared for a few seconds.

"What are you going to do with that big knife?" Loora said telepathically.

"Having invisible bodies don't work. We can't just think our way through vines and limbs. Remember we are only a part of our surroundings, we can't just go through stuff!" Kalub felt flustered at the older children lack of knowledge.

"Alright, but what are you going to do with the knife, I mean the machete?" Jai asked.

"You children really don't know a thing about survival do you?" Kaylah stated.

"Nope, You see this machete, Its going to cut through that thick jungle, and I'm going to do the cutting. Just watch and learn. Come on we've got to go before they find us," Kalub said.

They walk down the path, with Kalub is in the lead until he gets to the vines blocking the path.

Jai took the machete in both of his hands and attempt to cut away the limbs and vines. He finds it very difficult and clumsily swings it, like a cave man and almost cuts himself.

Kalub said," *Give it back please, I will teach you later."*

Kalub with his machete in both hands started cutting away the limbs and vines. He swung the large blade like he was born with it in his hands. Kalub cut the jungle away until they come to a clearing. Far away he saw in the moonlight, more drones lining both sides of the path.

Kalub sighed and pointed up the path and asked, "N*ow what do we do?"*

Kaylah telepathically spoke, *"Let's just keep going here in the jungle maybe we can find a place to cross."*

"What about the drones?" Loora asked.

"If they look our way, we'll just have to stop and stand behind a tree," Jai suggested.

As the children travel just off the path into the jungle one of the drones saw movement and shouted, "Over there!" all the drones looked their way. The children stopped behind a large tree.

The drones used their red light to scan the area and only found a cub. One of the drones fires a red beam at the cub and killed it. "It won't be bothering us anymore" one of the drones laughed.

They all went back to their post and stood again like well-trained soldiers.

Kaylah looked at Kalub with fear in her eyes and asked telepathically, *"Now what?"*

Kalub looked around and said, *"This way."*

They kept walking even more quietly until they found the footpath they were looking for.

"There it is!" Kalub said.

"But what about the drones?" Kaylah asked.

Jai spoke telepathically, *"We are allowed to use energy to protect ourselves or others, Right?"*

Loora telepathically spoke, *"Yes but we can't just cross between those drones! They will kill us!"*

Jai spoke telepathically, *"No but we can levitate."*

Kalub spoke telepathically, *"What is levitation?"*

Jai answered, *"It is when you raise high off the ground and walk."*

Kaylah said, *"Fly? You think we can fly cross? Are you joking?"*

"Do you have another idea?" Jai asked.

Kalub spoke telepathically, *"I don't know how to do that. But I am small enough that I can crawl under the red light things on their knee."*

"That is too dangerous" Kaylah spoke.

Just as they were starting to argue, seven large jaguars came running down the path to attack the drones. All the drones went running towards the jaguars and in the disturbance, the children quickly crossed the path and walked up the foot path towards the rock.

"Lucky for us those jaguars attacked," Jai said.

"I don't think that was luck," Kaylah said feeling sad about the jaguars that were killed during the attack.

"Quick let's get up this path! Those drones will be back," Kalub said.

The children started to climb quickly up the hill, they were still invisible. No one could see them. They hurried until they saw another line of drones up ahead.

"Now what?" Kaylah asked.

"I don't know, but there is the big rock with a tree growing out," said Kalub.

"Yeah but how do we get to it," asked Jai.

The children left the path and walked through the jungle to get around to the back side of the large rock. They could see a tall old man wearing a gold colored cape from a fabric the children had never seen before. He wore buckskin pants and had many long colorful feathers braided into his hair. Around his neck he wore a silver and jade necklace. He has a cloth shirt, which is mostly hidden under his cape. The old man turned and looked up at the rock with the tree growing out of it.

The children could see that he was wearing arms cuffs made of silver with jade stones imbedded in the silver. In his hand was a beautiful walking stick.

One of he drones walked up to the old man and asked, "What are you doing here Old man?"

"I have come to wait for our supplies," said the old man.

"They will not be ready until morning," snarled the drone.

Kalub and Kaylah recognized the old man as Magoose. They ducked down and went up the path away from the drones to wait for him.

Loora using a different part of her mind spoke to Jai. *"Do you think we can trust him?"*

Jai answered, *"Do we have a choice? Unless you want to go back."*

Loora looked back remembering the sky-ship and home, and shuttered at the idea of going back. She held her mouth shut and shook her head, "I will not go back. Let's follow." Loora knew she never wanted to go back. She made the commitment to herself that whatever comes that she would trust Magoose. *"She would do anything but go back! That would not be a choice that would be torture."*

Magoose knew the children were close, so he turned around and went back up the path. The drones did not follow or notice the children.

Magoose caught up with the children and spoke quietly, "Do you think it is safe to use a night crystal in a strange land? Do you not think that others could not see this night crystal? There are many enemies that would love to steal it from you and kill you for it."

Kaylah quickly put her night crystal away and said, "Well I guess I did not think of it like that."

"Hum, I guess little ones need more training for your new home," Magoose said.

"Phew, that was close, said Jai."

Kalub whispered, "Are we safe yet Magoose?"

"Almost Kalub, Magoose spoke quietly."

They all walked quietly until the moon almost touched the mountain ahead.

Magoose found a nice opening in the jungle. He motioned to the children to stay. He pulled out his tobacco from a small pouch on his hip, as he walked around the opening and sprinkling tobacco around in the traditional sun-wise direction. Magoose sang a prayer song quietly as he walked. When Magoose finished the circle, he walked over to the children and told them to start making camp for the night.

Jai and Loora just stood there not knowing what to do. While Kalub and Kaylah go into the circle and dropped their knapsacks and went to work.

Kalub went to the outside of the circle and collected small pieces of fire wood. while Kaylah lifted the flap of her knapsack and took out her little shovel and started to dig a small fire hole in the center of the circle.

Kalub brought the first armload of wood and looked at Jai and stated, "I could use some help."

Jai nodded his head and followed Kalub. He was happy to help. "This way was very different than what the books said. The boys brought armloads of firewood into the circle.

Kaylah motioned for Loora to join her at the fire circle she has finished digging.

Loora walked quickly to Kaylah's side hoping to learn something about this new way of life.

Would you pass me over some small sticks so we can start a fire?"

"*Sure,*" Loora said. She went to the woodpile and brought Kaylah a handful of some small sticks.

"Thank you," Kaylah said with a smile. She then showed Loora how to start a fire with a fire crystal and soon the fire was going and the grate was on.

Kalub and Jai joined, Kaylah and Loora at the fire. Kaylah show them how to set up the pots on the fire so they would not fall. She began to put some of the food into the pots.

Kaylah asked Magoose, "Is there a stream we could collect more water close by?"

Magoose said, "Yes, little one, not far from where we are now. Crystals are not safe to use this close to the drones. Although it is wonderful to show your friends how to use your fine tools."

Kaylah spoke, "I am so sorry. I did not realize we could not. I mean we are alone and so I, it would be alright.

Magoose looked at Kaylah and said, "We must be very careful around those nasty drones."

Kaylah turned back to the fire, feeling she let her family down by not thinking ahead and felt very sad.

* * *

It felt good to sit around the fire. It was not really cold yet, but it felt nice to take the chill off the air. Magoose sat on his blanket near the fire, watching with pride at how must the children knew about setting up a camp. The little ones were really trained like their father told him. It was nice to have the help with camp and even better to relax after the long trip, to meet the sky-ship. Magoose was curious about what other surprises the children might have brought from Lemuria.

Before long all the pots were boiling with meats and vegetables cooking away. Kalub took the left over goose and berries they had earlier, out of his knapsack. Kaylah made a pot of Chukwah, which was now ready to pour.

Kaylah said to Magoose. "Magoose, I don't have an extra cup for you, do you want a bowl?"

Magoose pulled from his pouch a cup and handed it to her and said, "I am always prepared young one," then winked at her.

Kaylah and Loora poured the Chukwah into every ones cups and then sat down around the fire.

Magoose spoke, "This is wonderful Chukwah Kaylah. It is perfectly spiced and the dark brown cocoa, has a wonderful smell and the honey makes it sweet, just like I enjoy it. Good job."

Kaylah upon hearing this, it brightened her spirit and said, "Thank you Magoose. I have a year's supply of the dried spices, I collected all by myself. Mother taught me the spices and gave me her recipe. I don't have milk that we need for the complete recipe. Maybe when we get to your village I can add some."

Magoose smiled and nodded his head.

Kalub spoke, "I remember that voice from a few years ago, when we were little. Remember? He taught us about how to feel the Earth and nature too."

Magoose laughed, "You are still little."

Kalub looked at Magoose and replied, "Father said I am a man now! And I need to learn wisdom and the great wheel with you. So I will become a great man."

"I remember you too. You came to our home a long time ago," Kaylah said.

Magoose nodded in agreement and smiled.

Jai spoke up, "That's impossible, no primitives are allowed in Lemuria. Our government does not allow -no- such thing."

"Oh yes, they speak the truth," Magoose said. "I was in your home world a few years ago. I saw the beautiful building that holds your music. I saw your libraries, and schools, too. I walked your city and saw running water coming from the cities gardens, and the fountain that flows in the middle.

The Blue Crystal that comes from your star home, the crystal planet. Oh yes, I was there. And I was happy to return to my home too.

I do not like your round shaped sky-ship's that fly over heads of people and makes my stomach do circles. But my wife," he stopped to remember, "Well she did enjoy your sky-ships. Strange woman," He smiled with the memory of their trip.

Kaylah broke the silence, "Yes and we went to your home too, with father. You live in the great Pyramids with the high steps that I could not climb."

"That we do young one, that we do," spoke Magoose.

"My name is Magoose, and you two are?" pointing to Jai and Loora with his walking stick.

"Ah, I am Jai and this is my sister, twin sister Loora."

"Nice to meet you two. Bayon told me you were coming with his children. Said you were also," he paused with a questioning look, "Special also?"

Jai spoke up, "Yes we are, but we would rather be just normal."

"Hmm I see, but special is normal, if you know how to use it. I was told neither of you were trained in your gifts. Is this true?"

Loora telepathically spoke to Jai, *"Don't tell him everything, he may not be trust worthy."*

Magoose spoke up, "Oh yes, I am trust worthy. But I am special also."

Loora looked at the old man, she scooted backwards almost leaving the circle. Upon realizing she didn't know where they were or where to go. She thought rather loudly, *"How can this old man know what I say? He is just a primitive."*

Jai spoke up, "How did you hear her?"

Magoose just smiled and winked at them. "I might not be as -primitive- as you might think."

Loora and Jai looked at each other and then back at the old man and paused before Jai asked,

"What did you do earlier before we came into the circle? You know with the stuff you put on the ground?"

Magoose was surprised that he did not know, and then tilted his head and spoke, "I was purifying the circle, and calling to the power of the directions, which is also called, putting protection around us. So that we will be safe here in the jungle. The stuff as you called it, is tobacco."

"Directions?" Jai asked.

Kalub pipes up, "Yeah. the animals in the 4 directions, I know about that."

Kaylah spoke up, "Yeah and there is colors too, mother told me."

Jai looked surprised and asked, "How do you two know about this? How do you always know how to do everything?"

"It was part of our studies" Kaylah spoke.

"It has everything to do with the Great Wheel," Kalub said.

Magoose was also surprised at the young twins. "My, my, I am very impressed you two. Knowing so much at such a young age. Your parents have taught you both very well."

Kalub and Kaylah smiled proudly.

"I am glad you like it Magoose. I... well we... have studied hard. It is hard to remember what mother called the basics. She tested us all the time, to be sure we could remember" Kalub paused. "Mother said it was very important to know the primitive cultures so we could work with them later in life.

Kaylah pipes in, "One day she said we would be working with father in helping the people."

"Well she did a good job. What animals and colors are there in the directions you two?" Magoose pointed at Kaylah and Kalub.

"Um", Kalub spoke, "Well I know there is a large bird in the um, East, that is it." In the East."

Kaylah piped up, "It is yellow like the sunrise."

Kalub said, "There is a Jaguar in the south too."

"That is a good start," said Magoose.

Kaylah said, "Fire," she remembered, "Fire is in the South."

Loora spoke telepathically, *"Water is in the west."*

Magoose looked surprised at Loora and said, "Well done, Loora. This is a good start all of you. Because of Bayon, I have seen many villages throughout this large continent. I have found that every primitive culture has the Great Wheel. However I found out that each culture is different, in their ideas of animals, colors, and about the Great Wheel. I will teach you our culture. Hopefully, you will learn many different cultures as well."

Jai asked, "Why is this even important? It sounds like a lot of old timer's stuff that does not matter anymore. The Great Wheel is not helping our parents, or our friends."

Magoose nodded his head. "I understand your loss, but the Great Wheel does matter. The Creator of all things made this Great Wheel. It is the cycle of life, the beginning and the end of life as well. If the wheel grinds to a stops all life will be gone. It is not just a belief, it is a fact. When people forget about the wheel of life, then bad things will happen to the planet. Do you understand that Jai?" Magoose asked.

"That is what is said yeah. I guess I just don't believe."

Magoose nodded his head, "Do you believe in the seasons, Jai?" asked Magoose

"Of course. What does that have to do with the Great Wheel that will destroy everything and everyone when it stops?"

Magoose laughed and said, "The seasons are part of the Great Wheel. This Great Wheel is not destroying everything; it is the choice of humans that is destroying everything. Humans are causing the Earth Changes not the Great Wheel."

He looked around at each of them. "Humans have choices and through these choices they are causing the weather to change, the waters to rise, and the air is no longer clean. It is the human's actions that is forcing the wheel to change."

Kaylah spoke up, "Oh you mean the Atlantain's right?"

"No Kaylah, I mean all humans," Magoose said.

Magoose starts to draw the Great Wheel in the dirt. He drew a large circle in each direction, and three smaller circles between each direction. Magoose spoke, "This is the start of the Great Wheel of life. This wheel even went as far back as the cave-apes. There is much more to this, but for now we need to learn this first."

Jai looked at the circles Magoose drew and questioned Magoose, "I have never seen anyone draw this before. Does everyone know about this?"

"Cave-apes," Kalub laughed and started jumping around like an ape.

Magoose locked his eyes on Kalub and said, "Learning time, not play time Kalub!"

He turned back to Jai and said, "No. Only very few can understand the fullness of the Great Wheel. Only the few that are special like you four," pointing his stick at each of them.

Jai looked up with a question, but then looked back down pondering what Magoose said.

Loora spoke telepathically, *"Magoose are we really part of the Great Wheel?"*

"Yes Loora, you are a very important part of the great wheel."

"Important? Us?" Loora asked telepathically.

"Yes each of you are," Magoose paused to think, "Each person on earth are little lights of energy."

The children became a little confused at Magoose's words.

Magoose breathed deeply a few times to gather his thoughts. Then spoke, "You see all of you are special, not because you can use the energy of the Great Wheel, but because you are a part of the Great Wheel. Each of you holds the power of each direction and you can use it with your hearts intentions. Each of us, every living thing is a part of the Universal Life Force, the Creator. You were called special all your young lives. This is true. Although so is everyone else. The difference is you know how to use your gifts, and they do not."

Kaylah spoke up, "Almost? I thought you said everyone does."

"Let me explain, every living thing from the Creator has a spirit, the key is spirit young one. There are things you have never seen, or even know about in this world yet, little Kaylah. Do you remember the men back there unloading the sky-ship?" Magoose asked.

"Yes," they all said and nodded their heads.

"Those dear ones, are Drones. They were not made by Creator, they were made in test tubes and laboratories. They do not have the spark of spirit. At least not a whole one anyway. They are not from Creator. Living peoples, and tribes, have a spirit, or what we call live force. This is one of the great secret of the Great Wheels teachings." Magoose said.

Kalub piped up, "Father said they would kill anything that has life force, except their Masters. Is that right?"

"Oh yes little one that is correct. They are owned and programmed from the time of their birth to only obey their masters and to hate all humans with special energy. The Great Wheel of life has always been, and it will always be. Even far in the future, man will try to change it, and then hate it. Then re-change it, and hate it again. This is the way man has lived since the beginning and will live in the future. There will always be a few like yourselves, that will understand the Great Wheel and work with it to understand why they are here and why they are special."

"What are the small circles Magoose? Asked Kaylah.

"These are the moons of the Year. These tell you what season we are in. It helps us keep up with the year and month you were born and when the next great timed event will happen. There is much more to the Great Wheel of life. In fact there are thirty-six stones, it would be too much for you to learn at this time."

Magoose paused and smiled. "Instead I would like to start with just the basic four directions. This is what my people believe. It is spoken that a long time ago Creator put four guardians on the four corners of the earth. Each guardian has a job of holding energy in their direction. For my people the animals on our wheel is the Monkey in the north. The Quetzal bird in the East. Jaguar is in the south, and the Whale is in the West. All four animals are powerful, and have great medicine.

The East is where we start our Wheel and walk around it sun-wise. The Quetzal has the abilities to see clearly and has the gift of far sightedness. The Quetzal helps the human children to see clearly through the different levels of life. With the help of Quetzal we can see into the spirit world, and hear the voices of the ancestors that have walked before us.

In the South is the place we believe Jaguar lives. He has the ability to use stealth, to survive and teach this energy to the human children. Jaguar helps bring growth and trust into our hearts. Their arrows will fly true when we walk beside him. With Jaguar as our guide, we will learn to trust what we feel and grow in the ways of energy.

Whale lives in the West. She has great knowledge of healing from living in the oceans depths. One of her greatest lessons for us is to look with in. The Whale flows on the waves as she breathes in and out . She is able to understand the energy, flow, and movement of mother earth, and the people, even though she is blind. She is the holder of the keys to dream-time, with ancient knowledge, through the use of sacred breath.

In the North we believe Monkey lives there. It is the place of tones and vibrations. With monkeys knowledge of the jungle and her kinship with the human children. She can teach us survival and music from Mother Nature herself. With her ease and grace of moving through the jungle she will help the human children to move with ease and grace through their life. She teaches us how to keep our spirit bodies clean and teaches us to purifies ourselves with the herbs and vibrations. By watching Monkey we have learned healing herbs and medicine. We know which ones we can eat and which ones we cannot. What plants kill, and which plants cure.

So you see each direction has a gift of power to teach us. Each one helps keeps the balance of harmony of creation."

"Magoose, is the law of harmony still a law today?" Jai asked.

"Oh yes, most people have forgotten it. Tomorrow will be a long day of walking; now it is time to rest."

The children nodded their heads. They pull out their bedrolls and laid them down near the fire. They climbed into their bedrolls, each slipping into their dreamtime with the animals guiding their path.

❧❧

CHAPTER 5

Learning to Trust

Magoose wakes as the first light of day is awaking. He stretches and looked at the sleeping children with a smile. He closed his eyes and connected to his wife, *"Good morning my dear Norah."*

Norah answered, *"Good morning my dear husband. Are the young ones awake yet?"*

"No, it is still early for them. They had many adventures, and a long day yesterday. It will be a long day this day as well. It is best to allow sleep to heal their tired bodies." Magoose said.

"Are they special as we thought?" Norah asked.

"Oh yes, dear wife. Kalub and Kaylah were trained very well in their survival skills. The other two have much energy just fearful to use it. They were not allowed to learn survival skills and watch the little ones closely," Magoose answered.

"This is good news my husband. Please start the fire while I will make all the preparations here at home," Norah said.

Magoose picked up some sticks and pieces of wood that is left over from their fire last night. He waved his right hand over the sticks, and igniting the fire. He stood up and walked out of the circle. He waved his hand to reseal it as he walked towards a small stream and washed.

As he began to walk back to the camp, he thought to himself, *"What lessons should I start today with? They need to fit into our culture. The Great Wheel will help them fit in. Fit in? I ponder if they really can fit in. Their energy is so strong they will have to become, medicine people. Yes, I think that is what I will do. Train them as medicine people."*

He walked back to the circle and waved his hand to re-enter the camp. He found pots full of cornmeal ready to be placed on the fire. He goes to the fire and started their morning breakfast. There are bowls of fruit and a small pot of Chukwah. There are large bowls with hot water for each of the children and a nice towel for drying. He walked over to each of the sleeping children. He placed the large bowls with a towel near each of their sleeping places, so they can clean up.

As the breakfast is almost ready, the wonderful smell started drifting throughout the camp and slowly wakes the children up. Magoose poured himself a cup of Chukwah, to start his day. He began to drink when he heard the rustling of Loora.

She is surprised to see the bowl of water placed near her pillow. She sat up and rubbed her eyes. She then nudged her brother to wake up and started her clean up by washing the dirt off her face.

"What?" Jai said in a sleepy voice.

Loora spoke to him telepathically, *"It is time to wake up!"*

"Yeah, yeah, I am up." Jai also looked surprised to see the bowl of water.

"Hush Monkeys! I am tired!" yelled Kalub as he sat up rubbing his eyes.

"They are trying to tell you Good Morning Kalub." Magoose said.

Each one of the children climb out of their bedrolls, cleaned up and rolled up their bed.

"Do not throw out the water; we will need it to put out the fire," Magoose told the children.

Each of the Children nodded to him that they understood.

Magoose poured each of them a cup of Chukwah, filled small bowls with hot cereal, and served each of them a bowl of fruit.

The Twins in turn thanked Magoose, as they were being served.

Hurry up now, the sun is awake, ready to smile upon us." Magoose said smiling.

"Magoose this Chukwah is sweeter then what I make," Kaylah said.

"Aw yes my little one. I always put a little more honey and cacao in mine" Magoose replied.

The children finished up their breakfast and cleaned their dishes with the water from their morning clean up bowl.

Magoose pulled out his small bag. He reached in and took out a pinch of tobacco. He sprinkled it around, and in the fire. Then sang a prayer song." *Thank you great fire for coming and helping us this night.*"

Jai asked Magoose as he was pouring his water on the fire. "Why did you do that?"

Magoose looked at him and smiled, "You did not get burned last night did you? And to my recall the fire allowed you warm water and a full tummy right?"

Jai looked at him and shrugged his shoulders and thinks, "Non sense."

"Be careful Jai, the fire has a great energy also, just like you. It is important to honor all things, or they might bite you later," Magoose said. He used is hands pretending to be a snake trying to bit him, with a knowing smile.

Jai gave Magoose a disgusting look, poured Loora's bowl of water on the fire, and put his knapsack on.

Kalub and Kaylah poured their bowl of water on the fire and said, "Thank you fire." Just in case Magoose is right, they don't want to be bitten. They walk back to their knapsacks pretending to be a snake biting each other. They secure their things and put on their knapsacks.

Magoose smiled at the little twins with great approval. Then he tapped his walking stick four times on the ground. Instantly the morning breakfast dishes and baskets disappeared. Everything was clean, as though they were never there.

"What happened to the large bowls? And the dishes? And, and all the stuff?" Kaylah asked, with a surprised look on her face.

"It is just energy child, it comes and it goes." Magoose said with a knowing smile.

Kalub looked up, Magoose, "Can I do that some day?"

Magoose smiled "In time, I am sure all of you can. Now go, and stand outside the circle."

They walked to the outside the circle and waited. Magoose walked sun-wise around the circle. He clapped his hands four times at each of the four directions and said thank you. When he was finished he walked over to the children and said, "This way."

* * *

The Kalub, Kaylah, and Loora, just stood glued to the jungle floor. They were spellbound by the sounds each element is making as it was released. The sound was like a voice of sweet music. The vibration hums in their spirit made each of them remember the Blue Crystal ceremony. The children awaken from their musical trance by the remembrance.

They stare at each other with puzzled expressions, when Jai broke the silence.

Jai said, "That felt like the Blue Crystal energy, but different."

"Oh I hear and feel many tones and vibrations," said Loora telepathically.

"It made me feel happy and safe," Kalub added.

Kaylah nodded her head in agreement.

Loora said to the children telepathically, *"Just energy? He said we could do this kind of energy? What does he think we are? Gods?"*

Kalub just shook his head in disbelief and said, "I don't have a clue, Loora, but I want to learn."

They all agreed they wanted to learn. Then they remember they were supposed to be following Magoose. They remembered which way Magoose pointed his walking stick, and ran in that direction to catch up to him.

* * *

Magoose slowed his pace a little knowing the children were lagging behind. He understood they had never seen this kind of energy work before. He thought to himself, *"It is good, they need to know what is expected of them, besides a few tricks, its nothing compared to what they will do."* he smiled a big smile.

Magoose used his energy to feel for the children as they walked up behind him. He turned around and greeted them with a big smile. He knew he must keep close track of them in the jungle. This place is not forgiving of mistakes.

Kaylah saw the high trees that creates a canopy over their heads. As they walked, Magoose pulled branches away from the path, to allow the children to walk through. They stepped over rocks, and climbed over old tree stumps. It is a hard trek for their short legs. They looked around and saw they were heading towards the scary mountains in the distance.

Kalub spoke up, "Where are the animals Magoose? I don't feel any animals here."

Kaylah spoke up, "Yeah and the trees are not talking either."

"Everything is dead here, except for the noisy birds, and whatever is making that strange sound." said Kalub.

"I don't want to live where there is no life," said Kaylah." Magoose I want to go home. I would rather die than not to touch or feel nature. It means a lot to me," Kaylah said, as the loneliness started to full her up she started to cry.

His eyes went soft and he stopped walking. "It is the energy children. The energy is different here. It is not like home. This is how you got past the drones last night. Your energy is different from what they were trained for. But there is a new group being trained that will find you. They have taken the special children and adults off Lemuria and made them into slaves."

Loora gasped, *"Oh no, my friends, is that what happened to them? I thought they just went to work for the government."*

Magoose looked at her with sad eyes and said, "I am sorry, many children were taken by the by force by the Atlantain's. They are called missing children. I have been doing work with Bayon for many years, trying to find them. The Atlantain's need other races because they have damaged themselves. The cells that allow them to make children are broken. And of course they want to control the world too.

Now it is time to shift your energy to match the trees here. They have been talking to me as we were walking. Now wipe your eyes little ones, and find your center," Magoose said.

"My center?" asked Jai.

Magoose looked at him and said, "Where do you find your energy when you want to use it?"

Jai answered, "I don't know, I just do."

"You can't -just do- anymore Jai, You must know." Magoose touched his solar plexus to show what he meant.

"You are not a tiny child anymore, throwing around energy as you please. It is no longer allowed. Everyone sit please." Magoose asked.

"No longer allowed? We were *never* allowed to just use energy!" Jai shot back with anger. As Jai and the children sit down around him.

Magoose continued to speak. "Here above your belly button is your energy center. From here we get ready to use our energy. It is not in motion yet, just prepared." Magoose rests his hand above his belly button to show them. "Above this is where we use our energy. Our energy flows upwards and out from our solar plexus. This energy then goes through our heart and out to where we need it to go. We store energy here below our belly button. Does everyone understand this?"

The children nodded as they followed Magoose's directions and felt around for their energy in their bodies.

"Now," Magoose said, "I want you to feel your energy and make it rise to your solar plexus. Right here Kalub," Magoose put his hand on his solar plexus, "You must focus. Now, send this energy out through your heart center and over to a tree. Feel the tree, really feel it from the roots to the limbs and leaves."

"Yeah, I do feel the tree Magoose," Kaylah said, "And she is singing."

Loora spoke telepathically, *"They are all alive, I feel it too."*

Then a memory started to happen, Loora feels the pain of her past, and she starts to shake.

Magoose was waiting for Loora to open up. He knew she had a lot of pain in her. He got up and went to her side. He put his hands on either side of her head. He takes his spirit into her mind to connect with her memories.

Magoose and Loora see the horror of her past. As she was three years of age she remembers using this energy and they started to beat her. The male she called father beat her until she went silent and has never spoken again.

Magoose thinks to himself, *"My dear child, I understand why you speak no more. Today you will be healed."*

Magoose steps into her memory and physically stops the male from hitting her. Magoose then whispers to Loora "Keep screaming, but this time let the whole world hear you."

Then Loora did scream. She screamed so loud the jungle vibrated from the sound. Loora begins to slow down her screams. Everyone around could hear her start to calm down.

With this memory, Jai remembers his sisters' scream from long ago. He started to cry and rock back and forth holding he knees where he sat. The pain in his heart for his sister is almost too much to bare.

Kaylah walks over to Jai and sits next to him sending him as much love as she could and then holds him tightly

Magoose inside Loora's mind tells her, *"You are free forever from all of your beatings. Today is the first day of the rest of your life. All you must do is follow me out of your memory."*

Loora was hesitant, and thinks to herself, *"Follow? How do I follow?"*

Magoose reaches for her hand inside her memory and said, *"Walk with me out of your memory. All you have to do is follow me."*

Loora listened to the voice of Magoose and leaves the memory behind her.

Magoose, still in her mind, said, "Build a bubble around this memory Loora. *Trust in yourself.*"

So Loora brings up as much trust she could find within herself. Then she put the memory in a blue bubble. Then she made the bubble smaller, until it became very tiny bubble and sent it out through the top of her head.

They opened their eyes together and Magoose said, "It is gone now. It is safe to speak to us, and to feel all that is around you. Life is safe today my little child. No more pain, no more tutors, no more harm."

Loora began to cry, Magoose kisses her forehead then stands, walks over to the rock and sat down. He waits for the tears to heal the oldest twins pain. As the pain lifts from Loora's heart she put her arms around her brother.

Jai puts his arms around his sister to comfort her until all the pain was gone.

After a time, Magoose asked, "Are you feeling better children?" looking at Loora and Jai.

Loora spoke the first words in a long time, "Yes, Magoose and I thank you."

Kaylah and Kalub are sitting quietly, not knowing what Magoose was doing. But they could feel the love and the pain was gone. They were caught up in the moment, they burst into giggles and clap their hands in the excitement when Loora spoke.

Kalub yells "Yeah, "you can talk!"

Magoose in the private part of his mind thanks the Goddess and knew in his heart there was a lot more healing to do with these two.

Magoose spoke up, "Jai can you feel yet?"

Jai spoke, "Yes, I can feel the trees some, but they are not talking to me."

Kaylah piped up, "Did you say hello to them?"

Jai said out loud in an over dramatic voice, "Hello? Anyone out there?" Nothing answers.

Magoose started to laugh, walked over to Jai and pats him on the back for reassurance and said, "Do not worry it will all come in time. This is good children and it is not over yet. Now let's start walking again, we have a long way to go."

The children all stood and started to follow him again. This time with a new appreciation of the old wise man and the surrounding jungle. Magoose earned a great deal of honor and trust this day from the children. They walked most of the morning until the sun was high in the sky.

Magoose found a nice clearing and stopped and sat down. "This is a good place for lunch," Magoose stated.

He then closed his eyes, and tapped his walking stick for times on the ground. There was a lunch baskets that appeared out of no-where in front of them.

Magoose opened his eyes and said, "Well done, it is time to eat."

The children looked surprised and were going to ask how, but decided not to. They pull off their knapsacks and took out their plates and a rag for napkins. Each in turn took a piece of flat bread and some fish and they had a good lunch. Magoose took his and tore a piece off of his flat bread, places a small piece of fish on it, then gives it a silent blessing and throws it in the surrounding trees, then enjoyed his wonderful meal.

Magoose broke the silence, "Don't forget to drink lots of water children."

The children nodded their head with understanding. They took out their water bags and were surprised when they found them full of water. They drank and drank; they did not realize how thirsty they were.

"Wow Magoose, my water taste really good. Did you use more of your energy to make it taste good?" Kaylah asked.

"I agree," said Loora, "It is very refreshing."

"I sure does wash the thirst away," Jai added.

"I think Magoose did some of his energy stuff to make it taste good. Didn't you Magoose?" Kalub looking at Magoose for conformation.

Magoose smiled at them with a knowing smile and said, "It is good you like our water here in the jungle. It is time for more connecting. Are you ready?"

The children said, "Yes please!" excitedly.

Magoose nodded his head and said, "Lift your arms up high towards the sky. Picture in your mind that they are limbs of a tree. Your fingers are the leaves."

The children lifted their arms and closed their eyes. They began to feel as though their arms were branches of a tree. Their fingertips as the leaves blowing in the wind.

When Magoose sees all of their fingertips moving, he then said, "Very Good. Now picture your feet go deeply into the earth.

The children pictured the feet as the roots of a tree growing deeply into the earth.

"Very good." Magoose said. "Open your eyes and feel our jungles energy."

The children followed his instructions.

Then he stood and thanked the energy. He picked up his walking stick and tapped it on the ground four times and the lunch baskets were gone into thin air.

The children looked with inquiring faces at Magoose, but did not say anything. The children began to feel normal again, still feeling the connection of the trees.

Magoose said as matter of fact, "Energy my children. It is just energy. We must be going." He smiled and stood up and started walking again.

The children just looked at each other, and put their things away. Then stood up and follows him.

Loora asked, "Magoose, you talked about the Great Wheel last night. So are we like the four parts of the Great Wheel? I mean we are four children and there are four directions so, are we, you know, that kind of special?"

Magoose thought for a moment and then answered, "In a way child, yes you are. All human beings are very special and are part of the Great Wheel."

"Yeah, We are big and powerful!" Jai cried out.

"Yeah, now we can stop all the bad peoples that want to harm us." Kalub said.

Jai lifted his hands and pretends to fire shots at the enemy. *"Peeeow, Peeeow*

Kalub followed his friends' actions. *"bang, bang."*

Kaylah rolled her eyes at them and said, "We are not that powerful are we Magoose?"

Magoose was listening and spoke, "In time child you will be."

Loora and Kaylah just shook their heads at the boys, as the boys continue in their pretend energy fight.

Kaylah asked, "Magoose what kind of bird is that?"

"Those are Macaws," as Magoose, pointed up in the tree. "They are Green and Scarlet Macaws. You can tell because the scarlet is the red-headed one." Pointing up, "That one."

Loora looked up and pointed at the scarlet one and said, "I like the yellow and blue one; it has a long tail with blue shorter feathers."

Magoose said, "They can hear our voices and learn our language. You also can teach them tricks."

"That is wonderful Magoose," said Kaylah.

"I would love one as a pet," said Loora.

"I would love that funny looking ones with the long beak," said Kaylah.

"Those are called Toucans," Magoose said. "They can also learn to talk with us, and do tricks."

"Oh, that would be nice to have a pet that could learn to talk to me." Loora said.

"Just what you need!" Jai laughed. "A talking bird!"

The boys laughed and continued in their play as they walked. They pretended to fire shots at trees, flowers, and rocks.

The girls gave them a disgusted look. They continued to watch the trees and jungles treasures. "Magoose!" Kaylah cried out. "What is that kind of bird? I think it is the most beautiful bird I have ever seen!"

"That dear ones is the most sacred of all birds. She is the Quetzal," Magoose said.

"Oh, I love its sky blue feathers and its teal head. Hey Magoose, your feathers braided into your hair look like those." Kaylah said.

"I love it's red belly and long tail feathers," said Loora.

"Their tail feathers are the most prized and sacred, of all the birds. Only very important people can have one," said Magoose.

"You must be really important, you have many of them." Kaylah said.

Magoose smiled at Kaylah as said, "The Quetzal gave them to me. Do you remember what direction the Quetzal is in?

Kalub said, "Sure Magoose, the Quetzal is in the east."

"So you do pay attention. How many plants have you killed?" asked Kaylah.

"I am only pretending Kaylah. Besides I am feeling around me too as I shoot," Kalub said.

Magoose said, "Sadly children, I don't have time to take you back down the path to make you feel the energy of what you shot. To teach you how energy changed as you pretended to shoot. Can you not feel the sadness and pain you caused the plants and animals?"

The boys immediately recognized the change.

Together they said, "We are sorry plants and animals. We are sorry, Magoose."

Kaylah said, "I can fix it! I can heal them."

Magoose said, "We don't have time children. We must keep moving forward. Every action you take being special causes an effect. Remember this."

Magoose motioned to the children and said, "Let's keep walking."

They walk higher and higher into the mountains in till late afternoon.

* * *

The clouds started to roll across the sky and a light misty rain began to fall.

"What! What is that Magoose?" Kaylah pointed. "It has a head like a mouse, the body of a cat and a tail like a raccoon. There, looking at us Magoose!"

"That's a Civet cat."

"It's really big! Will it hurt us?" Loora asked.

"No young one, it will not hurt us," Magoose reassured her.

Loora looked up and laughed, "That's a funny looking monkey."

"That Loora is a Sloth. They move slowly to enjoy life more."

"There are a lot of different animals here," spoke Kalub.

"Yes, Kalub, there are many animals in the highlands of my home." Magoose whispered, "Look children, this is a rare sight." Pointing toward

95

the forest floor, he continued, "Do you see the yellow and ring-tailed animal? That's a Cacomistle."

"It doesn't talk?" Kalub asked.

"No, it's busy hunting." Magoose answered.

"What does it hunt?" Jai asked.

"They eat fruit, nuts, and bugs," Magoose answered.

"What kind of fruit?" Kaylah asked.

"There is a lot of different fruits here in the mountains. Let's walked over here and I will show you some," Magoose motions to the children.

Magoose reaches into one of the trees with long leaves and found a tan looking fruit. He pulled out his small knife and cut it open and handing a piece to each of them said, "This is a Breadfruit, come and try. This fruit is always to be shared. A whole one will make your tummy sick."

"It is not sweet like fruit back home Magoose," Kaylah said.

Magoose pulled a few green looking fruit off a bushy tree and said, "This is Guava.

"The children ate it.

"This is really good," Jai said.

Magoose pointed to some dark green bunches of fruit that hung way up in the tree. "That children is Papaya. Just like what you have back home. But this is a favorite nut one for most animals. "It is called Jocote. There are many different types of Jocote here on our mountain. Some are green, some are red and round. Some look like green and red bells. And this one," as he picked one up from the ground, "Is a nut. It is called Cashew." He pulls the shell off and to show the children how it is done, and popped it in his mouth.

The children copied him. "This is really good Magoose," Loora said.

"And this children, is the Monkey apple. You should have some in your home also." Magoose pointed to the tree, which was heavy with fruit.

As they continued to walk Magoose found another tree heavy with fruit. He thanks the tree and pulled off five pieces of Zapote and gave one to each of the children.

M mm, the children said.

* * *

They continued their trek into the late afternoon. Kaylah saw something familiar up ahead and shouted, "There!" she pointed, "blackberries!"

"Yes it is Kaylah very good," Magoose said.

The children all picked some blackberries and ate them. They feel refreshed after eating the berries and continued to walk.

Magoose feels a disruption in his energy field that he has been using around them all day. "Get off the path children and hide over there by the fallen tree. Stay put I need to go and check this out. No one should be this high up in the mountains," Magoose whispered.

Magoose walked ahead for a while, off the main path, to see what is going on. There is a small group of drones walking towards him.

Magoose telepathically called out to the children, *"Run away from the path and hide away from the path."*

One of the drones held a small black box to his ear, and talked into it, "We finished setting the road blocks, Captain. No one will get through this mountain pass." The drones laughed, and walked past Magoose without sensing him.

These must be worker drones or they would have felt me. We might be lucky this time.

Magoose walked back slowly to where he left the children keeping the drones well ahead of him. When he reaches them he calls out and said, "Come back to me now. We will need to find another path to our home. Trouble seems to be coming to our mountain as well.

* * *

The children run off the path to find a place to hide.

"Over here, I hear a stream," Kaylah said.

They all walk to the moving stream. There are many large rocks for them to sit on and old trees lying in the water. It was a welcoming place for them to relax as they waited for Magoose.

"This is a nice place Kaylah. I just love the canopy of trees and the wonderful sounds," Loora said as she takes off her knapsack.

"This place reminds me of our stream back at home. I love the elephant leaves and look over there I think there is berries," Kalub said.

They take their knapsacks off to explore the area.

"I am hot!" Jai exclaimed as he bent down to splashes water on his face, he heard "Be careful of the rocks Jai," Kaylah said just before his foot slipped on the rocks and fell in. The water is swift under him and carried him deeper into the water, as he tried to get back to his feet. As he struggled to get his footing back, his foot got caught between some rocks in the stream as he falls backwards. He yelled out, "Help my foot is caught!"

Kalub jumped down for the rocks and waded into the stream to loosen his foot. The water was moving faster in the deeper part of the stream. Kalub struggled to keep his own footing he bent down under the water to loosen Jai's foot. He discovered rocks were too heavy to move. So he goes to the other rock in the other side of his foot, which was in the deeper water so he had to dive under the water to see if he can loosen it.

Kaylah nudged Loora and said, "I think we better get some vines to help them out of this stream. I am really worried."

"I agree. Let's go and look."

Jai tried to pull himself up to help Kalub, but instead fell back down with a splash. He feels the water rushing around him. He tells Kalub, "Hurry Kalub, this water is cold. We need to get back to shore."

"I am trying Jai, the rock is just too heavy to move. It looks like the rocks moved and ate your ankle. I don't have the strength to move them."

He reached down with Kalub to move the rock. The two struggle until the rock moved and freed Jai's foot.

"Uh oh," Jai exclaimed as the water starts to carry him downstream. "Kalub I can't swim!"

Kalub is beside him and said, "It will be fine Jai. Just turn around so your feet are out in front of you. Like this," as Kalub puts his feet ahead of him. "Try to use your hands to guide you back to shore."

Jai followed Kalub instructions knowing this young boy knew a lot about survival. Instead of slowing down and getting back to shore. Jai began picking up speed. He is being carried downstream.

Kaylah and Loora watch the boys from the shore and run downstream to get ahead of them. As the girls get ahead of the boys, Kaylah said, "Stay here Loora and hold the vane really tight. I am going to swim out and meet them by that big rock."

"Please be careful Kaylah. I really can't swim and I will be of no help if you all get carried away."

"Don't worry, Mother taught us how to do this." Kaylah smiled and nodded reassuringly.

Kaylah took off her skirt. Her long cotton shirt was light enough for swimming. She tied one end of the vine around her waist. She waded into the water and swims to a large rock sticking out of the water. She waited for the boys to come.

Kaylah sees Jai first and she pulls on the vine tight. He caught the vine and pulled himself to the shore. Kalub followed close behind. Kaylah then swam quickly back to shore. Kalub and the twins helped pull her back to safety.

"You two are something!" Jai said out of breath. "I just don't understand how you two know what to do. You always know."

"Mother taught us this trick when we were four. Kalub fell into a stream and Mother taught us how to move so we wouldn't be hurt," Kaylah said.

"If you keep your feet ahead of you, your feet will hit the rocks instead of your head," Kalub added.

Kaylah laughed. "I remember that, Kalub. Oh my, you did have a nice goose egg, though."

Kalub couldn't help but laugh also.

Loora and Jai stood spellbound. They are amazed at what these little children knew.

Jai looked at the twins and said, "We better get back to our knapsacks. Magoose could be worried. I do thank you two for saving my life."

Kalub stopped laughing and walked over to Jai and said, "It is nothing my new friend. You said we are in this together. We need to trust and help each other so we can survive. And survive is just what we will do. Let's go."

"Yeah," Kaylah said as she walked over to the boys as she untied the vine from her waist. "Together."

They walked back up stream to find their knapsacks. They each pull out a towel to wipe some of the water off.

Jai said, I am going over to those trees to change clothes."

Kalub said, "Good idea Jai. My leather pants are really heavy and wet."

So the children change their clothes and met back up. They start walking down the path towards where they left Magoose. They saw

Magoose in the distance. Loora and Jai run back down to the path to where they were hidden. Kalub and Kaylah were close behind them.

Magoose smiles at them and said, "I have been looking for you. I do hope your adventure was fun. Follow me. We must very, very quiet the drones are close."

The children nodded their heads and tried to be quiet as they followed behind Magoose. It was not easy for them on the new trail. The Jungle floor had dry twigs and leaves everywhere. The branches and large leaves make a swooshing sound as they duck underneath them. Magoose sees the sun setting and knows he must find a place to camp for the night. He scans the area looking for the drones and the dangers of the forest as they walk. He encourages the children to keep walking even though they were tired. The stars and moon replaces the sun before they find a small clearing. Magoose once again walked around the little circle and sprinkled his tobacco. He very quietly sang the protection song and invited the children to in.

"Is it safe now to talk?" asked Kaylah.

"As long as we speak softly it will be safe this night," Magoose said, reassuringly.

"Why are the drones this far away from their camp?" asked Kalub.

"They are setting traps for travelers, so they can enslave more people. We must be very careful until we get to my home." Magoose said with a reassuring smile.

He tapped his walking stick four times on the ground and the baskets full of food were in front of them again.

Kaylah asked, "How do you do that Magoose?"

Magoose replied as a matter of fact, "It is just energy my child, just energy."

The children shook their heads and eat their fill. They were very hungry after their little swimming adventure.

After everyone was full, Magoose tapped his walking stick on the ground four times and all the food baskets were gone. The pot of Chukwah was being kept warm, as Magoose drew on the ground the Great Wheel.

Magoose starts to teach the lessons again. "This stone," as he pointed at the top-stone, "Is North.

In the North we learn lots of lessons. It is cold in the north; it is the time of winter. Here we find lessons to teach us wisdom. One of the wisdom's we learn is to honor our ancestors. We never worship them as some primitives say. Instead we try to learn the lessons they learned, so we don't repeat them over and over. We need to be thankful for our night stars that guild us and grandmother moon for keeping the cycles and light for our night. The Creator of all put them in the sky. Sometimes people forget to be thankful, then the evil one brings to them greed and fear. The evil one likes to play tricks on humans and tells them wrong is right and right is wrong. Be careful young ones to always keep your hearts clean with creators love, listen to the wise elders and always remember to give thanks to all things."

Jai spoke up, "Is that why you sprinkle the tobacco Magoose?"

"We always have to give thanks, and ask for what we need Jai. We are never allowed to forget to honor the Creators gifts. Tobacco is one of the sacred herbs that we use for offerings," Magoose said.

Kaylah spoke, "Magoose, will you help us not to forget?"

Magoose smiled big and said, "That is one of many things, I am here to teach you."

"Magoose, why do we need to know this?" Loora asked.

"It is part of my culture, which will soon to be yours. I need to catch you up to what the children in my village already know. Otherwise you will not be one with us. The outside people have forgotten the purpose and meaning of Great Wheel, that the Creator, gave us. They will change it and change it again. But truth is always and forever.

Some People have been chosen to remember the truth. So they can pass it on to our young people. These people are called keepers of wisdom, or medicine people. When you work with energy as we do, it is more important for us to understand. With this great gift, we have responsibility as well. It is called a heavy weight. Because we have to carry ourselves and the medicine for all living things. We never just flash the knowledge around. Instead use this energy to help, protect, heal and serve others."

"How come your people and ours do not use wheels? I learn all about them in school. There are carriages, and other things for transportation. Why is this?" Jai asked.

Magoose replied, "We do use the wheels for leverage, when building bridges. However, we found when we use carriages and rolling vehicles on wheels, we move to fast. Our people did not learn because they moved too quickly. Sicknesses and disease move so fast many peoples died. The great elders of my people and your great elders decided that we all were better off without them, until we are able to deal with those things better.

Sometimes turtle medicine is the better medicine path. When my people are ready. We will go back to the wheel. So for now as you need to catch up with our children they will also have to catch up to you. Does this now make since to you Jai?"

"Saying it this way makes good sense to me. Thank you for teaching us. I will work harder at remembering and understanding your teaching and ways. I think you will make a great father to me." as he turns away from Magoose not showing his tears.

Magoose paused and looked at the children's tired faces and said, "We have another long day tomorrow children, it is time to rest now."

The children put their away their cups and crawled into their bed. They all fell to sleeping thinking of lessons of the Great Wheel.

CHAPTER 6

The Jungles

Magoose awoke early and searched for any sign of the drones. They weren't close, but still around. He closed his eyes and called Norah, *"My dear, are you awake?"*

"Yes, I'm awake," said Norah.

"Are there drones around our village?" asked Magoose.

"No, we have no outsiders here. Why do you ask?" said Norah.

"The drones were on our path yesterday. They set traps on the main path, and they said they were working on the minor ones. Even our sacred bridge path, they were there. I am not sure why. It will not be easy to get around them without using my energy. I think we should send some of our scouts nd cheek on those traps and disarm them as need," said Magoose.

"Do you need my help?" asked Norah.

"Not yet, but soon, I believe. The young ones are learning to trust each other now. They took a swim yesterday in our river. They are forming bonds that will help them in their coming year." Magoose said.

"This is good news, my husband. It's important for them to learn to trust each other, and trust us as well. I am almost finished. Let me know when you are ready," Norah said.

"Thank you, my dear, they are almost awake." Magoose answered.

Kalub woke up and shouted, "Hush Monkeys! Why do you wake me up in the mornings?"

Magoose smiled and said, "Remember, they are telling you good morning, Kalub."

"Oh the lovely birds are singing too!" Kaylah said as she sat up and rubbed her eyes.

"Kalub you always yell at the monkeys. Why don't you just say good morning and not be so grumpy?" Loora asked.

"Because we boys are tired!" exclaimed Jai.

"Yeah," grumbled Kalub, "It's hard to walk up this mountain. I'm still tired!"

"You boys," said Loora.

"It is a long walk to my home children, but we need to keep going before the Drones find us." Magoose tapped his walking stick four times on the ground and once again their breakfast is ready to eat and the Chukwah is warm and already to poured. Fresh new bowls of water appeared by them so they could clean up.

"Thank you Magoose, This is really good," Kaylah said.

"I agree" Kalub said, "Thank you."

"Magoose, you said the Great Wheel is all around us and in us. So how does it flow in us? How are we special?" Loora asked.

"Everyone and everything that Creator has created, is part of this Great Wheel. You feel the energy around you. You can also work with this same energy. This is why you are special. Please finish now we have a long way to go," Magoose said.

When they finished Magoose stood up, "Please go now and stand outside the circle."

So the children got up and stood outside the circle and waited for the wonderful energy they experienced before.

Magoose walked again around the circle and clapped his hands four times at each of the directions.

Kalub and Kaylah put their hands outwards to feel the energy that Magoose has released. They feel the tone and giggle because of the way it tickles their skin.

Magoose walked over to them and asked, "What are you feeling little ones?"

Kalub said, "The energy tickles my skin Magoose."

"Yes and it sounds like music that makes me feel peace," Kaylah said.

"It is time to walk now, energy later. Come this way," Magoose said, as he points in the direction they will need to travel. "Today is a good day to look for a walking stick, please find one that calls to you." Magoose then spread out his energy to keep track of them and keep them out of harm's way.

Loora looked around her new home. The land was lush and green. There are many trees with large leaves, and some that tower over them. This place is not really heavily wooded. The birds, monkeys, and insects of the high jungle, are making a lot of noise. Loora thought to herself. "I ponder where I could find my walking stick?" As she continued to look as she walked.

Jai was also looking around, but he just is not really interested in finding a stick. He was capable of walking without a stick. So he just casually looks around as he walked. He looked around the jungle and was hoping they did not have to travel into the high rugged mountains.

Kaylah opens her heart feeling the trees. She asked the tallest tree "Do you know where my walking stick is?"

The Tree said, "Follow your heart, for it is not me."

Kalub also asks the energy around him to help guide him to his walking stick. He was looking around until he saw a snake. "Hello Brother Snake, how are you today? Do you like this jungle?"

The Snake replied, "Come-sss here young one. I have a sss-story to tell you."

So Kalub walked over to the snake. Snake put his tail on Kalub's back and slowly began to wrap his tail around him.

Magoose felt the danger and quickly said, "No! Stop!" Magoose hurried to Kalub's side. The other children stopped and watched what was going on.

Kalub said, "Don't worry Magoose, I speak to snakes all the time. They are my friends."

"Not here Kalub," Magoose said. "Here the snakes are not friendly at all. Are you Python?" As Magoose looked straight at the snake.

Python pulled his tail from Kalub's back and coils up around a branch of the tree and hisses at Magoose. "It-sss is-sss a fine child Magoose, One for enjoyment! I just-sss want to tell him a sss-story."

"Snakes here enjoy enticing people and then wrap themselves around them to squeezing the life energy out of them." Magoose said.

Kalub looked shocked and said, "Really, You mean I can't talk to my friends anymore?"

"I wish I could tell you they are your friends. Many things here on the main land," Magoose paused, "Many things are different. Snakes are one of those differences."

Kaylah walked over to Magoose and Kalub.

"You see, the animals and trees on your island are all peaceful. Everything lives in harmony. But here on the main land, we lost our harmony with nature. Some people like us, still remember the harmony, but nature is not as forgiving.

Some humans have hurt and still hurt our lands. You must be careful children, things are not as they were in your home."

He looked over at Python, "And you need to learn to search the hearts of humans and find the harmony in yourself. If a human can talk to you Python they are energy people, not food!" Magoose exclaimed.

The Snake spoke, "All thing in our jungles-sss is-sss food for us-sss great Magoose."

"You are a part of the Great Wheel Python, and with that responsibility," He squinted his eyes and talks more harshly, "You are to help the medicine people, Not Eat Them!" Magoose said.

Kalub is surprised at how stern Magoose was with the Snake.

"Children, this seems like a good place for a quick energy lesson.

Reaching into his bag, Magoose draws out a strange colored stone. "This is turquoise." He handed a piece to each child. "Go to your energy center and feel the stone."

"We have done this before with Toma!" Kalub and Kaylah said.

Magoose said, "Once you feel the stone and it sings to you, let me know."

Magoose took back the stones and said, "Remember how it felt. Have you ever blown bubbles before?"

The children nodded that they had.

"Blow a bubble around the snake," Magoose said.

As Magoose said this, the Snake angrily said, "That is wrong! SSS-Stop! Wait! Dont! It hurt-sss! My head Hurt-sss!"

Through quite laughter, Magoose said, "Think of your happiest thoughts and fill the bubble."

The snake started protesting and squirming even more.

Magoose said, "Now he can't lie to you. Turquoise is the color of truth my children. When you wrap anything living with turquoise and fill it with love. No matter how hard they try, they cannot lie to you."

Magoose turned to Kalub and said, "Ask the Snake what he wanted to do to you."

Kalub turned to the Python and asked.

Python replied hissing, "I want-sss you to come clos-ssser to me. SSS-So I could wrap-sss around you, crush you, and eat you. I would tell you anything-sss to get you clos-ssser to me. Any lie-sss I could think of. Just to bring you clos-ssser, and wrap my-ssself around until you until you could not breath. That is what I do. It is not as-sss painful when I let the turquois-ssse flow through me. However, my nature is always-sss to lie. If Magoose had not sss-stopped me, I would have a nice boy lunch-sss. Bad Magoose, you cost me lunch again.

Magoose said, "Exactly as I told you my children.

Jai said, "Why are you so mean snake? It is wrong to eat people."

Snake giggles, To me everything is food-sss if I can get-sss me tail around-sss it.

Loora said, It is really a different place here.

Snake said, "If you let go of zzat energy, I promise-sss to let you go and be good. For today anyway."

Magoose laughed and said, "I don't trust you."

Snake said, I can't lie in Turquoise Magoose, it hurt-sss to much. It feel-sss like sss-swallowing a sss-stick from zhee wrong end.

Fighting back Laughter Magoose asked, "You have tried?"

Snake said, I was-sss young. I ate too much fermented fruit. I no want to talk about this-sss now. As he started to slither away.

The children were so confused by the conversation, as snake started to slithering way, they lost focus and dropped their energy from around him.

Kalub said, "Magoose, how can a snake."

Magoose interrupt and said, "Another time children we must be going."

Magoose never thought that just looking for a walking stick would cause danger to the children.

"Kalub be very careful of this new land. Things are different here.

What was, in your home land, is not here on the main land. I will try to help you understand. But please be careful my little ones."

Kalub and Kaylah nodded their heads that they would.

Kalub yelled out after the snake and said, "Bad snake you got me in trouble!"

"I was-sss just hungries-sss" said the snake.

Kalub yelled back, "Then take a rabbit or a mouse, they were put on Earth for you to eat!" Kalub walked down the path still looking for his walking stick. Yet he was upset with the snake. As he walked he remembers his home and his mother and father.

As they continue down the path Kaylah continued to feel the trees for her walking stick, yet with more caution. Kaylah saw a nice walking stick. Its energy pulled her to it. It was by a lovely tall bush with many long vines growing out of it. It is not far from the path they are on.

She went to the walking stick and knelt before. She reached into her knapsack to pull out a crystal.

As she kneeled, the lovely plant wrapped around her ankle without her noticing. The bush choose this moment to tighten around Kaylah ankle.

Kaylah felt the grip of the vine around her ankle and yelled, "Ye-ow!"

The bushes vine pulled Kaylah off her feet and into the air. The bush started to violently shaking her and swings her around in the air.

The bush sings, "I got dinner!"

"Help! Help!" Kaylah cried out.

Magoose sprints like the wind to her. He yells out to the bush. "That is enough! Let go of her!"

The bush raises Kaylah higher in the air.

She screamed louder, "Help! Help! I don't want to be dinner!"

Magoose dives beneath the plants vines, filling his heart with the love of his first born son, his wonderful wife, and all the love he could find within him. He blasts the plant with all energy he could bring up within his being.

Upon feeling all of this. The plant is confused and overwhelmed with loving feelings. The plant forgot about the girl with this new emotion flowing through it. It lowered its vine that held Kaylah and slowly released her ankle and retracting its vines into it's self.

Kaylah lands with a -thump- and backs away.

The plant started to vibrates the energy Magoose is sending out.

Magoose carefully backs away. He gently pulled a few leafs off another plant with purple flowers that is growing close by.

Kaylah said "thank you for not eating me," to the bush.

She crawled backwards to her knapsack, then walked over to Magoose. She squatted down and rubbed her ankle. She looked up at Magoose and asked, "What was that? Do we have to be careful of trees and bushes too?"

Magoose looked down at her lovingly and said, "I am afraid so my little one. But only a few that are troublesome. That bush over there is called a Spike-yard. It grabs its food with its spiked vine's and pulls them slowly into its center of its body. Once there it digests them. We have another one also, it looks like a half-moon with little teeth, and it eats mosquitoes and flies. We call it the Venus fly trap. The ancients believed it came from Venus." He smiled and said, "Just be careful and watchful of your surroundings."

Kaylah looked at Magoose and said, "How am I supposed to watch out for danger, if I don't even know it is there?"

Magoose smiles down at her as said, "Well I guess that is one more lesson you have learned. I will teach you more my little one."

Kaylah nodded knowing he would, and walks with her head held down. Thinking to herself, *What kind of place will hurt people just for talking to them, or going by them? This is a bad place to be, this is not home.*

Loora and Jai found Sticks by the path. It did not talk to them, but then again, it did not hurt them, or teach them any lesson either. They were just sticks that they walked with.

Kaylah tried to talk to the trees again. She was feeling downhearted from all the that had happen so far today. This was only their second full day on the main land, Kaylah thought. "It is just not right! I miss my home, my mother and father."

Magoose felt the twins and understood their anger and sadness.

Magoose spoke, "If you took the owl and put him on the plains, would he survive?"

Jai said, "No it would be too harsh and without trees the owl would die."

Loora said, "I don't agree Jai. I think the owl would have to adapt. There is still a lot to eat and it would have to build in the ground instead of tree tops."

"Very Good Loora," Magoose spoke. "You came here to us, so that you might live. Although this land is not like yours, I have faith you will learn its laws and learn to love my jungle, as you do your home," Magoose said. "It is time to have some lunch. Come over here and sit down by these logs."

Once again Magoose tapped his walking stick four times on the ground and a basket of food appeared.

Kaylah and Kalub ate halfheartedly. They are sad to be in the harsh jungle where life is not friendly. They miss their home and the warmth of the plants and animals.

Kalub remembered his mothers and fathers faces.

"Kalub my son. Do not be heavyhearted. The jungles have many gifts and Magoose is their to help you always.

"Father? I really miss you and mother. I want to come back home." Kalub heard his Father say.

"You need to be safe my son. I sent you to Magoose and Norah. Grow strong. Strength will help you on your path. Don't be so harsh and judge. Every place on earth is a little different. Here you learned about the peace and harmony of nature. Now it's time to learn new lessons. In your life, you will learn many things, and through learning, you will find growth. We will always love you."

Kalub nodded his head in agreement and asked Kaylah, "Did you hear fathers voice?"

Kaylah looked over at Kalub with tears in her eyes and said, "We are connected silly. Of course I can hear."

Magoose spoke up, "Please finish up your lunch my children. We still have a long way to go before dark. Drink lots of water please. We need to travel faster." When he looked around and felt they were finished. He stood up and tapped his walking stick on the ground and all the bowls and food were gone again. "This part of the trail is very hard to climb."

Sure enough the path became very steep. Magoose walked off the little path and headed for a mountain path.

"Magoose why are we leaving the path?" Jai asked.

Magoose answered, "Are you ready to lose your life so young? I spoke yesterday about the drones setting up traps on the old path. It was safe and far from the drone encampment. But now we much take this path even although there is a drone encampment just up ahead. So we must walk and be as quiet as we can."

The children nodded their heads and followed Magoose. They walked through the jungle and step over large fallen trees and big rocks. The higher they climbed, the area around them became more rocky and woodsy. The rocks were now bigger and it felt very dry so they sweated more. The path became very narrow. One side of the path was a rock face and the other side was a ledge going steeply downward. They came to an open area where they could see for miles. It was truly breath taking. The jungle was far below them and the mist on the mountain was lazily moving over it. There is a large area where the mountain goes straight up for 100 feet. Magoose stopped, "Here is where we need to go up."

"Up!" Kalub asked. "How do we go up Magoose?"

"First, Kalub, take your machete and cut the long vine over there. We'll use it for a rope," Magoose said.

Kalub did as he was instructed.

Magoose looked at Jai and said, "You first please as he handed him the rope. "Do you see the grooves in the rock? This is how my people climb mountains. Through many generations they have created these grooves. Stay here a moment." He takes a few steps and grabbed a shiny black rock the same size as the grooves. He places the rock in a groove, and started to spin it sun-wise and counter sun-wise. After a minute he pulls the rock out and there was lots of powder.

Kaylah said, "Like a mortar and pestle."

Magoose said, "Yes and no, the shiny black rock is a diamond. It is much harder than granite. So it helps cut into the granite. With a mortar and pestle they are the same type of rock so they do not damage each other. Or one of the pieces could be wood, so it does not damage the stone. When we stand in our own personal power, we are like the diamond. We can move through anything so no obstacle can stop us." He drops the diamond and it shattered.

Kalub with a shock look on his face asks, "How did it brake? I thought when you stand in your powers nothing could break."

Magoose said, "Nothing could stop you. With everything there is a draw back. The diamond is extremely hard yet fragile. Just as we are very powerful and fragile when we stand in our power. Although if we go against the drones ray guns without understanding of protection and barriers yet. We would still all die. That is why we must take this path. Do you understand?"

The children nodded that they did.

Magoose said, "Jai carefully go at your own pace, take the rope and secure it, so if the young ones slip they have something to hold on to. We don't want anyone to fall and shatter like the diamond, that would be bad."

Jai said, "Oh great you want me to go first? How do you know I can do it?"

Magoose smiled and said, "Because I have faith in you. Please go now."

Jai started up and easily finds the toe and foot holes and makes it to the top of the ledge.

"Good work, Magoose yelled up." Tie the rope around the large tree to the left of you with the ancient symbols on it."

Jai looked around and found the large tree. After he tied the rope around it, he yelled down to Magoose, "It's tied."

Magoose pulled on the rope and make sure it was strong. "You next Loora, Magoose said and nodded his head."

Loora started to climb and finds Jai's foot and hand holds, and made it up to the top.

As Magoose looked around, he sees a large group of Drones heading his way. He knew they did not have time to get the little ones up the rope.

"Quickly now little ones, go back down the path and hide well. I will find you when this is over. Quickly now go!" Magoose whispers to them and pushes them back toward the path.

The large group of drones walked to Magoose and said, "What are you doing here old man."

Magoose said, "I live here in this area. What are you doing here is the better question."

"We are now your master under the authority of Altex," the drones reply.

"Ump, I don't think so," Magoose said. He taps his walking stick on the ground and said, "Sword!"

The drones are surprised at Magoose actions and some of them started to laugh and said, "What you fight us? One little old man against us? Are you stupid? Crazy?"

They did not know Magoose is a powerful Nebra. Magoose stands in his power while pulling the energy from all around him. Then he balls it up and sends it out over the area. The energy is so strong it blasts the drones off the face of the cliff.

Loora and Jai were lying down on the high ledge of the cliff watching Magoose. They felt awe and respect at what they saw.

After the last drone had fallen, Magoose looked up at them and said, "I need to go and look for the children. Do you want to come or stay?"

They looked at Magoose and Loora said, "I think I would feel better if we all stick together."

"Climb back down then and let's be off," Magoose answered.

So Jai and Loora climbed down and they all started looking for the twins.

* * *

Kalub and Kaylah run back down the path they find a small opening into the forest.

Hurry in here Kaylah," Kalub whispered.

Kaylah followed and they have to duck down under branches. The branches are thick and the little animal path is hard to see. Suddenly Kalub's foot gets caught in one of the roots of the trees and he falls.

"OUCH!" Kalub cried as he held his ankle.

"Oh no," Kaylah said.

She walked over and bent down to check his swelling ankle.

"We need to find a place to hide Kalub. Can you crawl?"

Yeah, I think I can Kaylah.

There is a little clearing just over there. The big tree is lying down off the path. It might shield us a little. Kaylah said.

Good idea Kaylah, but my ankle really hurts, Kalub said.

Kalub crawls over to the little area by a large tree that is lying down. There is greenery growing around it the area. There is a mossy smell that is welcoming to the twins.

Kaylah takes off her knapsack and pulled out a small bottle of white willow bark and skullcap. She fills the dropper ½ way and turned to Kalub. "Here this will help with the pain." as she puts it in his mouth.

"Yuck!" That will help with pain alright. It makes you think about the awful taste!"

"I am sorry brother, I am just trying to help."

"I know, that is the stuff mom uses. It is awful." Kalub grumbled.

Should we do as Magoose does and put a protection circle around us while we wait?" Kaylah asked.

"I can't stand sister, so I guess you better do it. Do you remember how?" Kalub asked.

"Well um, The Quaztal bird is in the east."

Kalub spoke up, "Quaztal bird please come and protect us in the east please."

They see a Quaztal Bird fly down from the trees and sit on a branch near them.

They both whisper, "Wow."

"Thank you" Kaylah said. "Um, Well Jaguar is in the south. So Jaguar please come and protect us in the south."

A real life Jaguar comes and stands above them on the tree log. Kalub backed away from the log and looked up. "Ah, are you friendly right? You won't eat us, right?" Kalub asked.

The Jaguar looked down at the children with an almost smile. The he laid down on the log and started making a purring noise.

"Thank you," Kaylah said.

"Do you remember the water animal in the west Kaylah?" Kalub asked.

"Well um, No. But, We could say please come water animal in the west and come protect us?" Kalub suggested.

As he finished speaking, a gush of water flows up from the ground. The twins look at each other with a shock look, then turned back to the water and said, "Thank you."

Kaylah said, "I am sorry we forgot who you are."

Kalub nodded his head and said, "Monkey of the north, please come and protect us."

A group of monkeys come and hangs from the trees around them.

Kaylah spoke, "I thought it was supposed to be spirit animals, not real ones."

Kalub spoke, "Well maybe we need more protection until Magoose finds us. As Kalub started yawning.

Kaylah asked, "How is your ankle?"

"It does not hurt as bad, thanks. But I am getting really sleepy now. I am going to rest until Magoose finds us. Alright?" Kalub spoke as he laid his head on his knapsack and went to sleep.

Kaylah sat down pulled her knapsack to her and placed it under his ankle. She looked around and tries to send a mental picture of where they were to Magoose.

* * *

Magoose saw where the twins left the path and found broken branches. "This way Magoose whispered to the twins. "I think they are over there where the tree had fallen."

They walked close to the circle, Jaguar started to growl. Magoose stopped and talked to Jaguar.

"My friend, have you seen two little ones close by?" Magoose asked.

Jaguar stands up on the tree and said, Great Magoose, you may not pass. The little ones you seek, I am now protecting with my life," he said as he bared his teeth.

"Very good Jaguar, you are a strong protector. Will you tell them I have come," Magoose said.

"One of the little ones are hurt, and they are asleep. They are truly the special ones you have been looking for great Magoose. You may not enter the protection circle they have cast. You know the law great Magoose," Jaguar said.

"I do know the law. I was unaware the little ones knew how to draw a circle. They have been watching me," Magoose spoke with pride.

Magoose looked around for a place close by for everyone to rest. Jai and Loora looked at Magoose with a puzzled expression.

Jai asked, "Why can't we just go and wake Kaylah up, they are just over there?"

"The little ones have been watching me Jai. They have asked the power animals to protect them. That is what has happened. If you go over there you will have to kill each of the animals before you could reach them. It is another law of the great wheel."

"They don't have any tobacco stuff do they? They could not do it right. You did not teach us how to draw this circle thing," Jai protested.

Magoose tapped his walking stick four times on the grounds and baskets of food appeared again. Magoose nodded at the baskets, smiled and said, "Eat, it has been a long day."

Magoose leaned over and filled a small basket for the twins. He walked to the east side of their little circle and spoke to the Quaztal Bird.

"I am Magoose the Teacher, Guide and protector of these little ones. It is time for them to eat. I ask the great power animal for permission to give them nourishment."

The Jaguar stretched on the log, watching.

Quaztal Bird looked into Magoose heart and found it true. The monkeys in the trees all started chattering and the waters started to splash a little on Kaylah, waking her.

"What? What is going on?" Kaylah asked as she looked around. "Oh Magoose you found us! Kalub! Kalub! Wake up! Magoose is here."

Kalub did not wake up. She tried to shake him a little but Kalub did not move.

Kaylah walked over to Magoose and tried to hug him but the Quaztal bird did not allow her to pass. "What is going on you silly bird. It is Magoose. He is with us."

Quaztal bird spoke quietly, "Ah little one, you have called us. You must give us permission before we allow entry, either in or out of the circle."

"Permission? Well ah, I give permission for Magoose, Jai, and Loora to enter our circle," Kaylah said in a confused voice.

Quaztal bird stepped aside and allowed Magoose to enter.

"Well done Kaylah, lets us not forget, you should show honor and respect to your protectors. If you ever need to use them again. It would be a wonderful idea." He said with raised eyebrows and a large loving grin. Magoose entered and put the basket down beside her.

Kaylah looked at the Quaztal bird and said, "I am sorry to call you silly. I thought we had said to protect us until Magoose found us. I did not mean to insult or dishonor you my beautiful friend."

The Quaztal bird said, as it displayed its plumage to her, "Thank you for the honor and respect my child. It is my honor to protect and help such human beings as yourself.

All the other directions nodded their heads in approval at the words. The waters flew upwards in a joyful manner and splashed them.

"What is wrong with Kalub," Magoose asked.

"He hurt his ankle so I gave him some medicine like mother has shown me." Kaylah answered as she nodded her head.

"May I see your medicine?" Magoose asked.

Kaylah lifted Kalub's leg off of her knapsack and digs around in it. She pulled out a glass bottle and handed it to Magoose.

Magoose looked at it and asks, "How much did you give him?"

"Um, about ½ a dropper full, Kaylah said.

"Oh my, Magoose said with a worried look on his face. "Little one, four drops under his tongue would have been better."

Kaylah looked at Magoose with a worried look and asked, "Did I hurt my brother more? I did not kill him did I?"

"No, No, little one. He will sleep along time, until the sun is high in the sky tomorrow," Magoose answered her reassuringly. "Eat little one, you will need your strength."

Magoose stood up and patted Kaylah on her shoulder. "We need to still travel this night. We must go up the cliff before the sun comes up. The drones will not be happy with me."

Kaylah ate a little from the basket, she looks down at her sleeping brother very worried. She goes to each animal and gives them a hug. She said "thank you for coming," then looked to Magoose for more information.

"Good job Kaylah, I did not know you were paying attention. You have done very well this night. I will carry Kalub you go and join the others," Magoose gave thanks to each of the animals as well and smiled big at the little one as she walked out of the circle to join the ours.

Jaguar looked at Magoose and said, "These ones are gifted Magoose, I will also protect you until you reach the end of your travels."

"Thank you Jaguar, You are a strong protector and I honor you, although we must climb the cliff this night. The drones arc around our mountain. You need to protect your young ones as well. They will kill all of you. You must hide your clan and tell all the animals to avoid these men."

Jaguar nodded at Magoose with honor and bounds away.

Magoose gentle bends down and picks Kalub up loving and placed him over his shoulder as if he was his own child. His sleeping head slides over his shoulder as he walked over to the others. He still walked well with his walking stick in his other hand. He asked, "Has everyone had their fill?"

They children nodded their heads and said "Thank you."

Magoose tapped his walking stick four times on the ground and everything is clean again. Then he motioned the children back to the path. They get back to the rope, which was left hanging. Jai climbs up first, and Loora is right behind him.

"You next Kaylah," Magoose said, as he tied the rope around her waist.

Kaylah finds it really hard to climb. She is smaller than the ancient people, so she has to stretch herself to reach the foot and hand holds while climbing up. When she gets to the top, Jai helped her and they waved down to Magoose and throw the rope back down.

Magoose ties his walking stick to the rope. He calls to the wind as it came to him. He floats up to the cliff ledge, still holding Kalub over his shoulder. Then he pulled the rope up and unties his stick. He gathered the rope, thanked the wind then tapped his walking stick again on the ground and the rope was gone. The children looked at him in awe.

Loora asked, "Why did you tap your walking stick four times to make the rope go away?"

Kaylah whispered to Magoose, "May I learn how to fly one day?"

"Come children we must walk fast. I will answer your questions as we go. This way please," Magoose motioned.

As they walk Magoose explains, "My walking stick is very special. I use my Walking stick as a portal or for things I need. When I do medicine work, I tap it four times to honor the four sacred directions. Although other times I do not have to.

As for you my little Kaylah, "With practice of using and calling energy. I am sure one day, as you grow stronger using your energy through heart, you will be able to do much more than just fly. With time and heart, wisdom and practice you can do anything. There is no limit of what you can do. Now we must be quiet please."

Magoose looked out and saw the drone's encampment. He walked closer to the mountain and motions the children to do the same. They walk around the mountain path until they found a swinging footbridge. It is a long bridge that crosses over the two mountain passes. It is made of wood slates and rope for hand holds. It looks to Kaylah that it was very old and barely hanging.

"Get across quickly the drones are close," Magoose whispered to them.

Kaylah looked at the bridge and then back at Magoose. "Are you sure it is safe?" Kaylah asked.

Magoose nodded his head with a reassuring smile.

The children cross carefully first. Magoose carried Kalub and crossed after the children were safely across. When he got to the middle of the bridge a group of drones came up to the bridge.

The drones shouted, "Halt!"

But Magoose did not stop he keeps on walking faster across the bridge.

Magoose yells out, "Run children, Hide!"

The drones realizing the old man was not stopping they run towards him. Magoose hurries across the bridge, carrying Kalub like a sack of potatoes. When he got to the other side he tapped his walking stick on the tied end of the rope and says, "Age!"

The rope holding the bridge together and to turn to powder. The drones screamed and fall down into the valley below.

The children were standing close watching what was going on with awe.

Magoose said, "Close your mouths, it is not safe we must keep moving now." Magoose thinks to himself, "It is sad I had to destroy such a wonderful bridge. I will need to repair that when this is over."

The children nodded their heads and they kept moving through the mountain jungle.

Kaylah asked, "Do you think they will stop following us?"

Magoose spoke, "Just up here young ones we will be safe. They will not cross the boundaries of my people."

Magoose hurried the children as fast as they could go. He did not stop to answer questions. It was almost midnight when they found the campsite. Magoose once again walked around and calls in the direction with his tobacco. He welcomes the children into the circle and everyone joins him.

"Magoose how did you learn to fly, asked Kaylah? Can I learn that too?"

"Yeah, I want to learn to fly!" Jai spoke up.

"Yeah, Me too!" said Loora.

Magoose smiled and nodded at them. He lays Kalub softly on the ground as he takes his bedroll off his knapsack and lays it out on the ground. He picked Kalub back up and lays him inside making sure he has his teddy bear close by. He then walked to the center where the stones outlined a nice fire ring and soon a nice fire is glowing in the night.

He once again he tapped his walking stick four times on the ground the hot Chukwah and the rest of the dinner is ready for them to enjoy.

Kaylah looked over at her brother as he rested. She pulled her bedroll off her bag and put her bag back under his ankle. She hugged his teddy bear goodnight and placed it back near him. She looked up at Magoose and asked, "Are you sure I did not hurt my brother? He is so still."

Magoose smiled at her and said, "I am sure you did not hurt him. He is resting very well because we have walked a long way. He will awake tomorrow," Magoose winked at her reassuringly.

One by one the children pulled out their bedrolls, and enjoyed their dinner. They fall to sleep as soon as their little heads lay on their pillow.

Magoose took a deep breath, clears his mind and speaks to his wife telepathically. *"Good job my dear wife. I am sorry for the lateness of the evening."*

Magoose heard his wife's wonderful voice of comfort come back to him saying, *"Are you and the children safe?"*

"The drones are everywhere my dear. They have put traps on the main path, and the cliff bridge I had to destroy it. Kalub has twisted his ankle and wonderful Kaylah over did the white willow bark and skullcap blend. But we are alive and well. I will keep the baskets and Chukwah here tonight just in case Kalub wakes up. I don't believe he will until noon day."

"Oh my, how much did he have?" asked Norah

"1/2 a dropper full. I am sure Kaylah was worried and tried to calm him down from the pain and she just over did it," Magoose said.

"Yes noon tomorrow he should awake. I don't think it will hurt him, but are you by the stream?" Norah asked.

"Yes, I am," Magoose said.

"You might need to remove some of the swelling, then wrap it before he wakes tomorrow. The cold water always helps," Norah instructed.

"I will do as you suggest in the morning. I am also very tired this night. Good night my dear."

Good Night my strong, brave husband." Norah whispered.

Magoose is asleep before his next breath.

Chapter 7

The Great Wheel

Morning came too soon for Magoose. He awoke to a brisk chill in the air. He thought to himself, "This day we will have more adventure I pondered what they will be. We are past the dangerous area now, so we take it slower today." He does his morning stretches, rolls his head around his shoulder's a few times. He gets up and starts the fire quietly, to allow the children to rest a little longer.

Magoose tapped his stick lightly on the ground and calls for bowls and towels. He walked over to Kalub and picked him up like a baby and carried him to the nearby stream. He gentle lays him on the grassy bank. He struggles a little to pull off his moccasin from his swollen ankle.

Then he places one hand inside the swollen ankle and the other hand on the outside of the ankle. He called lovely to Mother Earth asking for her help.

The bank of the stream slowly lower so his ankle could dangle in the cold water below. He asked the water to please flow around his ankle and to bring healing and restore it. The stream gave way to create a pool. The water moved in a sun-wise direction slowly into the pool to started the healing process. Magoose thanked Mother Earth and the water for helping him.

Magoose splashed water on his own face and thanked the healing water for his refreshment. He said his morning prayers and waited for the swelling of Kalub's ankle to release. Once his ankle was back to normal Magoose dried his ankle and wrapped it in some healing leaves. He carried Kalub back to the fire and laid him on his bedrolls. Then wrapped his ankle with strips of cloth to hold the healing leaves in place. He walked back to the fire and poured a cup of Chukwah, and sat on his blanket again.

"*Good Morning Husband,*" Magoose hears telepathically.

"*Ah my dear wife, good morning to you as well.*"

"*Did you sleep well?*" Norah asked.

"*As well as I could without my dear wife.*" Magoose replied.

"*I have some eggs today and I am just finishing the bread. It will not be long husband,*" Norah said.

Magoose tapped his walking stick four times on the ground and all the old baskets from last night were gone again.

Magoose spoke softly to his wife, "*I do love your cooking, but I don't think the children will be up to early this day.*"

Norah laughed, "*No that was a very long day yesterday. You pushed them well beyond what most children could do.*"

"*It was very important to get past the drones posts. They said yesterday, that they have taken over our lands, and our new master, is Altex*"

Norah gasped, "*They said what? Oh my no, It just can't be. Ouch! Just dropped that one, I guess I will feed it to the animals.*"

Magoose laughed a little and spoke, "*I do hope you are not hurt my wife. Burning one's self is not a good idea at this time. I would not be able to do this alone. You are truly my life line during this part of the journey.*"

"*Oh hush, I am fine my husband. Small burns are nothing in these difficult times. I have not sensed or seen any drones up this way. Our animals or children would say something if they had seen them. There is great worry among the people about the drones and you being so far away. They thank me often for staying behind to protect them. Although I am not sure what will happen if the twins cannot come to our village. I do not choose to stay behind for long time. Do you have any idea's what we will do?*" Norah asked.

"*Not yet my dear. The little ones will be fine. Kalub's ankle is healing and should be awake later. It is the older ones I worry about. Loora was damaged greatly in her young years of life. Jai is at the age of stubborn. It is difficult for him to be shown up by a younger Nebra's. They need a lot of healing. I do believe their hearts are pure, and they can be trained. But soon enough we will make the decision on what we will do. I do know this, yesterday when Kalub and Kaylah where on their own hiding in the jungle. They drew a circle, and physical animals came out of the jungles to guard them. The Jaguar told me they were the ones I have been waiting for."*

Norah gasped," *Physical Animals? That is unheard of husband. Maybe they were just around the area. Are you sure they were all protecting them?"*

"Oh yes dear. Real animals came and protected them. That jaguar would not let me close to them. He threatens me if I would try to break the circle. He reminded me of the law. Even the waters of earth mother herself came and protected them," Magoose spoke as he heard Kaylah rustling.

Kaylah sat up with a smile and said, "It's another great day Magoose. Do you think Kalub will wake today?"

Magoose nodded in agreement and said, "Good morning little Kaylah. You brother will be fine very soon."

"I am really worried Magoose. I did not mean to hurt my brother," Kaylah said.

"No my child. We all make simple mistakes. Through our mistakes we also learn and grow," Magoose said.

She smiled back at him and started to wash up. The warm water felt good on her skin as it helped awaken her body. She goes over to Kalub and tried to wake him. But he was still sound asleep.

Loora and Jai also awakened by their talking and started to wash up as well.

Magoose spoke to his wife telepathically and said, *"It is time. Have a good day my beautiful wife."*

Tapping his walking stick on the ground four times, the baskets of fresh bread, fruit and eggs with meat, appeared in front of them.

Kaylah said, I really wish I could do that," as she walked over to get her breakfast. "Thank you Magoose," as she returned to her bed rolls and began to eat.

In the distance a sound which is coming closer to camp they heard loudly, "ekk ekk ekk Kalub Ah ah ah ah."

Kalub awoke, pulled himself up and yelled, "Good Morning Monkeys!"

The monkeys replied, "Good Morning ekk ekk ekk Kalub Ah ah ah ah. Wake up!"

Magoose laughed then said, "Good Morning Kalub."

Kalub just grunted and said, "Good morning Magoose." His ankle was very painful when he tried to move and said, "Ouch!" and grabs a hold of it. He turned to the bowl of water and washed up.

"How is your ankle Kalub?" Kaylah asked.

"It still hurts a lot. But I don't want any more of your medicine." Smacking his mouth and making a face of disgust, as he remembers last night. "I want to eat and get your medicine flavor out of my mouth. I am really hungry," Kalub said.

Kaylah said, "You tummy still works you must be better than yesterday."

Magoose laughed and brought Kalub a bowl of fruit, with eggs and beans wrapped in a tortilla. "Here little one, I think you need to eat. You missed dinner."

"I missed dinner? I don't think I have ever missed dinner before, thank you Magoose," Kalub said. He reached out and took the bowls from Magoose. He started to eats like he was starving.

Kaylah was beaming at her brother. She is happy she did not harm him, as she ate a full breakfast as well.

Magoose looked around at the children and smiled and cleared his throat and said, "You missed our story time last night. Are you ready to hear one this morning?"

The children all nodded their heads and say, "Yes."

Magoose took a deep breath and started to speak.

One day Great Spirit was walking the earth. He had a problem that he was having trouble deciding what to do.

Quetzal flew to Great Spirits and asked if she could help.

Great Spirit said, "I have a secret that I don't want the human children to know. I am looking for the right place to hide it."

Quetzal said, "I will fly it to the farthest reaches of the universe."

"No," Great Spirit said. "Man will go there."

Jaguar was passing by and said, "Great Spirit I will take it to the deepest Jungle."

"No great Jaguar, humans will go there," Great Spirit said.

Little Ferret came along and started to jump up and down saying, "I know, I know!"

But Great Spirit did not hear little Ferret.

The Great Whale came to Great Spirit and said, "I will take your secret to the deepest ocean."

"No Great Whale, Man will go there too," said Great Spirit.

Little ferret jump up and down more with enthusiasm yelling, "I know, I know!"

Then Monkey came to Great Spirit and said, 'I will carry your secret to the highest mountain. Surely man can not go there."

"Oh yes Great Monkey man will go there also" Great Spirit said.

Ferret was just about to bounce him self out his skin and in a very large voice, with all his heart he said, "I know Great Spirit! I really, really KNOW!

Great Spirit looked down at the little ferret and carefully picked him up and asked, "What do you know little one?"

"I know where to put your secret Great Spirit, I really do!"

"Little Ferret, where do you think I should I put my secret?" asked Great Spirit.

Little Ferret whispered in Great Spirits ear, "Put it inside their hearts, they will never look there."

The Great Spirit thought for a moment and said, "It is done!"

Then returned to his place in the heavens.

What do you think this story means?" Magoose asked the children.

Loora spoke first, "I think the secret is the energy everyone has and the knowledge that we are all connected to the wheel of life, right?"

"Very good Loora," Magoose said.

Kalub spoke up, "Well I think it's about, we should never forget the small things around us."

"Very good Kalub," Magoose said.

"Oh yeah like remembering all the creatures great and small. That we should look everywhere before making a choice," said Kaylah.

"Very good Kaylah," Magoose said. "You children are learning fast about the Great Wheel and what it means. I am very proud of you."

* * *

They all rolled up their beds and are ready to travel when Magoose asked them to stand outside the circle.

Kalub tried to stand, but found his ankle was unable to support him and fell back down.

Wait Kalub, Magoose said. He walked just outside of the circle and finds a good walking stick, then returned back Kalub and handed it to him.

Kaylah went over to Kalub and helped him out of the circle.

The children waited outside the circle for the music of the energy.

Magoose walked again around the circle and claps his hands four times at each of the direction to close the circle to return the area to the original condition. It looked like no one was ever there. When Magoose finished this, he walked over to the children and says, "This way please."

They all begin walking again down the path towards their new home. Jai and Kalub started a new game. They made an energy ball and began to pass it back and forth to each other. Jai passed it to Kalub by using his foot. Then Kalub added his energy to the ball and pass it back to Jai with his elbow. Kaylah and Loora soon joined the play. As the children walk, they bounce an energy ball back and forth to each other.

It was almost noon when Kalub stopped and grabbed Kaylah, "Look!" Kalub pointed toward the thick trees. "There! Do you see her?"

Kaylah looked where Kalub is pointing. "Yes I think so, but it is blurry."

Magoose stopped walking when he felt an energy he knew and loves. He looked around to see where she was.

Kalub and Kaylah saw a light bluish-green mist appearing. The mist formed the shape of a woman. It was as though the wind was blowing, yet there was no wind. You could feel it flow like water, yet you are not wet. Indescribable emotions stirred in all of them.

Kaylah tries to talk to her. "Hello, can you hear me?"

"Yes dear children I hear you," said the voice. "So you don't like my beautiful jungle?"

Kalub answers first, "No, not really, it is not as gentle and um, what did Magoose say, in harmony like our home. Everything is mean and will hurt you."

Kaylah spoke up, "And it really doesn't like us either. It is not friendly. There are no little people."

"I love your birds. The macaws are very beautiful," said Loora as she was trying to see what Kalub and Kaylah were seeing.

The Voice lets out a small laugh and spoke sweetly. "We are different than your land yes, my children. But we are not mean or just want to hurt you. We desire to help you learn the good and the bad from nature. Just like in life, there is good and bad. Can you feel the tree you are standing next to?"

"Yes" Loora, Kalub and Kaylah said together.

"Who are you talking to?" asked Jai "I can't hear nothing."

Magoose tapped Jai on the shoulders and pointed towards the tree. "Do you see her Jai?"

"Oh, yes I can see her now, but I can't hear her." Jai said.

Mother Nature continued, "Do you feel her children struggling to live?" she asked.

Kalub shook his head no.

Kaylah said, "Yes, I can. We use crystals and place them near the roots of the trees back home."

Kaylah took off is knapsack and dug around it. "Here I found some. I was going to put one next to the place where I found my walking stick." Kaylah approached as she kneels and bows, holds up nine crystals in front of the lady in the mist.

The ladies voice spoke, "Those Crystals are the reason your home is in harmony. We here in the mainland don't have the healing crystals."

The twins spoke in harmony, "Don't have healing crystals?"

Kaylah spoke, "Why not?"

Magoose said, "Because the crystals do not grow around here."

The Lady in the mist smiled at Magoose and said, "Nice to see you again Great Magoose. It has been a long time."

Magoose nodded his head, and bowed low and said, "Yes my lady, far too long."

Loora questioned Magoose, "You know this lady? Who is she?"

Kalub was surprised and asked, "You can see her?"

"Yes young ones, I see, love, know, and honor Mother Nature with all my heart," Magoose said.

Kalub and Kaylah spoke in harmony, "Mother Nature?"

"You mean the "REAL" Mother Nature?" Kaylah asked.

"Yes" Magoose said.

The children stood wide-eyed just said, "Wow!"

Kalub asked, "Mother Nature, I understand life is both bad and good, well kind of. My Dad and Magoose told us about it yesterday. I mean no harm in your jungle. So why does your jungle want to harm me? I tried to be nice and talk like we do back home."

Mother Nature replied, "Some of my places are very harsh, and some of the Earth is very gentle. We need all kind of places in nature, to have balance on Earth. It is a great part of the Wheel of Cycles."

Kalub and Kaylah look at her and repeats, "The Wheel of Cycles?"

Magoose said, "Yes it is also part, of the Great Wheel."

Loora spoke, "So there are many wheels inside the Great Wheel, right?"

"That is right Loora," Magoose said.

Jai spoke up, "This way is so different than what we learned. I have never read about the many wheels of life. Why are these things not written? Why can't I hear her?"

Magoose answered, "Because things of the heart are not always in books. We learn about the Great Wheel through living life. Some people never learn about the seasons, and the cycles. They just take things for granted. Very few peoples understand and talk to the elements, and to Mother Nature herself. This is a great honor just to see the Great Mother of Nature. We believe, all life should be honored and kept in harmony. This is our main job, as energy workers." Magoose looked at Loora and Jai with a loving father type smile.

Kaylah took a crystal and dug a hole next to the tree and placed the healing crystal there.

"Thank you," Mother Nature said. "You truly are kindhearted. For this act, I have walking sticks for each of you."

The Children were surprised to see four wonderful knotted walking sticks laying there on the path. In their play they had forgotten about needing a walking stick. The children all spoke in harmony, "Thank you Mother Nature."

Kalub hobbled up to the sticks first. He chooses one of the shorter ones with 4 knots, picked it up, and then he handed a crystal to her and asked, "Mother Nature, where am I to put my thank you crystal? Who needs one the most? I don't feel, like Kaylah does."

Mother Nature asked, "My Kalub, may I touch you?"

Kalub nodded his head yes.

Mother Nature touched his chest over his heart, and he began to glow.

She guides, "Now Kalub feel with your heart and you will know where to put your crystal. Understanding this, my Kalub, for you are an animal talker. You have the ability to speak to my animals and find out what they need. You have the gift to manifest the needs of my animals as well. You are a teacher of wisdom of heart. You were born with this wisdom. You know things, sometimes even before you even realize that you know them. You are blessed with these gifts from the Creator itself."

Kalub closed his eyes and felt outward, while doing this, he feels an old grandfather tree. The grandfather tree is having trouble breathing and eating. There are some nasty vines that are squeezing and digging in so tight, it could not even pull the water and minerals from the ground that he needs to grow and live.

He started backing away as Mother Nature said, "It is good, and you have found your answer. The vines cannot hurt you, because you are using your pure heart energy. Do you know what you need to do my child?"

Yes, I think so Mother Nature, but I don't want to make a mistake in front of you. Could you please tell me if my feeling is right?"

Everyone felt a wave of joy and laughter over them.

Mother Nature said, "You are such a wonderful child." She released his heart and said, "Please go to the tree."

Following her direction. He walked over to the old tree without a limp and dug a small hole between the tree and the vine. He placed the healing crystal in the hole and covered it. He placed his hands on the ground and sent energy. He remembered what Magoose had done with the spike-yard plant. He took all the love that his parents, sister, homeland, and animals given him and allowed it to flow into the ground.

Mother Nature said, "I see Magoose taught you the first lesson I ever taught him."

Magoose's face becomes very red.

Mother Nature said, "Send the love energy through the roots of the plant and tree."

Kalub started flowing the energy through the roots. It goes up the tree and stopped where the vine is blocking the trees flow. He said to the vine, "Please let go of the old grandfather tree. Don't squeeze him so tightly. Can you not feel it is killing him?"

The Vine replied, "This is what I have always done, why should I change now?"

Kalub said, "You need the tree in order to survive don't you?"

The Vine replied, "Yes I do."

Kalub said, "But if you squeeze it as hard as you are now. You will kill the grandfather tree, then you will both die. I am learning the cycle of life from Mother Nature and Magoose. If you do not stop you will both die. Please relax your grip on the grandfather tree."

The Vine said, "Who are you to me? You are nobody! I will do, what I want, when I want, as I have always done. My mind is set and I will not be changed."

Mother Nature being rather annoyed at this speak softly said, "Hello vine, am I nobody to you?"

The Vine replied, "You are someone."

Mother Nature spoke, "I am just someone? The boy is speaking in my behalf to you. Will you stop now?"

The Vine chuckled and said, "Why? It is in my nature to do this."

Mother Nature walked over to Kalub, placed her hands on his shoulders and asked, "May I help you?"

Throughout the whole forest you can feel and hear…"Oh no," by all the plants around.

Jai looked up at Magoose and asked, "I just got a bad taste in my mouth. Is this normal?"

Magoose smiled largely and whispered, "Very normal son. All energy you can smell, taste, touch, hear, see, and sense it. Everyone has one or more of these abilities.

Loora whispered, "I can smell a change."

Magoose smiled and nodded, and turned his attention back to Kalub and Mother Nature.

Kalub replied, "Yes please." Kalub's' whole body starts to glow like Mother Nature.

As Magoose and the other children watched, they saw the bark of the tree get thicker, and the tree started to glow.

Kalub can feel the bark getting harder and harder, like the steal on the machete. He started to giggle, and said to the vine, "You are in trouble now, Vine."

Mother Nature spoke, "Don't lose focus. Arrogance is not becoming my child."

Kalub paused and felt his heart. She was right he was not sending out love. He changed his energy again and remembered the love of his family and home. He could once again feel the old Grandfather tree. It was growing stronger and stronger. He looked at Mother Nature with an I'm sorry look.

Mother Nature smiled down at Kalub, nodded her head and continued with the task.

The Old Grandfather tree finally spoke, "Thank you Kalub. Thank you Mother Nature. I can now feel my energy flow. It feels much stronger. I have not felt this way in many, many years."

Mother Nature removed her hands from Kalub's shoulder and backed away.

Kalub removed his hands from the ground, stood up and felt light headed. Then he turned and faced Mother Nature and asked, "Mother Nature did you do this to all the trees brother and sisters like him?"

Mother Nature said with a smile, "Of course." Mother Nature turned to Magoose and asked, "Try cutting it now with your blade."

Magoose tapped his walking stick on the ground and commanded, "Sword" then went to the tree and swings with all his might. His sword bounced off the tree with a ringing sound.

The Old Grandfather tree replied, "Oh my, that tickles."

The children stood wide-eyed at what they saw.

Kaylah asked, "What will the name of this tree be now Mother Nature?"

Mother Nature spoke kindly and announced to all the jungle, "This is now the Iron Bark tree."

"Wow!" The children all said in unison.

Kalub walked over to Jai and Loora and handed them each a crystal. "Here, the trees really like this offering."

Jai and Loora each hugged him in turn and said, "Thank you."

Loora walked over to the walking sticks that are lying on the ground. "I don't see you Mother Nature. But I do sense you. I can see the sticks. So why can't I see you?" She asked.

Mother Nature asked, "May I touch you?"

Loora shook her head yes.

"Close your eyes." Mother Nature said in a sweet low voice.

Loora closed her eyes and opened her heart.

Mother Nature touched her forehead. "My dear sweet child. You have chosen to suffer much in your short life. Know this young one, you are a great healer and seer now. Your suffering has allowed you to see into the hearts of humans. You may see what is unseen. You have the ability, because of your years of silence to hear what others can't hear. You will know when bad spirits are around. You may now speak to the ones that are unseen by most humans. With your love and experience you will heal many. Once you open yourself to your own abilities, you will find many more gifts. Open your eyes child."

Loora jumped back at the Beautiful sight of Mother Nature and exclaimed, "You are so beautiful Mother Nature," She said as tears of joy fell down her cheeks.

At the same time, Jai could also see clearly the beauty of Mother Nature.

Mother Nature smiled and gestured to the sticks and said, "Choose one."

Loora bent down and picked up one of the larger staffs with 7 knots on it. Then she walked over to a different kind of tree. It was very tall and had yellow bananas hanging from the top. She buried her crystal next to it. She could hear and smell the bananas tress thankfulness. This brought a smile unto her face.

Jai walked over to the walking sticks. He could now see clearly Mother Nature. He wished he could hear her. He bent over and picked up the other longer stick, which had 4 knots. He smiled at her and started to walk away.

Mother Nature stopped him and placed her hands over his ears. "You have the gift of hearing. You have the need to hear what can't be heard. To hear the Goddess when she speaks. To teach the lessons of strength of heart, honor, and to love...even what you hate. To humans Jai, you will need to hear their cries. Love and compassion is your gift. To teach trust. You mistrusted all your young life due to the unenlightened ones. Today you will trust with your knowledge of love. You will see the strengths and weakness of those around you.

Tears filled his eyes, for now he could hear her sweet loving voice. He became speechless for a while. Just gazed into her eyes. It took what felt like, along time for him to find his voice and said, "Thank you Mother Nature."

She whispered, "You are welcome."

He could hear the trees, and the buzzing, and all the things around him. He was so caught up with listening that he walked over to the trees and just sat down to listening.

Kaylah walked over to Mother Nature, her eyes where shining with wonderment and she opened her heart.

Mother Nature spoke to Kaylah in a very low soft voice. "I have given your friends a gift from both of you. You Kaylah, Your hearing, and from Kalub, his Sight. Both of you can hear, smell, taste, sense and see very well all my nature. From your friends I give you both, smell and taste. Now all of you will be in balance with each other. Your energy is connected with Kalub. So as one learns, you both learn. Sometimes you take your gifts for granted, be careful of this. Remember to say thank you. You are touched by the Universal gift of Love. You have the gift to love and honor even those not worthy of your gifts. So for you child, I give you Discernment. The wisdom to know right and wrong. You see clearly all situations. You will always have wisdom beyond your years. "May I touch you?" Kaylah nodded her head yes, and the Great Mother touches her at her solar plexus.

Kaylah felt a rush of warmth and energy go throughout her whole body. Kalub felt dizzy when Kaylah was touched, and he sat down.

Kaylah loved this new energy and after a few moments reached down and picks up her stick of 7 knots. She looked up at Mother Nature and said, "I thank you for all of our gifts this day. But how do I use it? If I could have a wish, I would wish this land to be more friendlier."

Mother Nature said, "You must learn the bad, before you can truly understand the good."

Kaylah just looked at her with puzzled expression. She turned around and walked towards the spike-yard bush. She knew she had to give it a crystal. As she approached, she asks to the bush, "May I approach? I have a gift for you."

The Bush grumbled at her and said, "Why would food give me a gift?"

"Because," said Kaylah, "You need love."

"What is love," asked the Bush.

"It is what I have in my hand. May I bury it by your roots?"

The Bush grumbled and but agreed.

So Kaylah went to the bush and before she could place the crystal near its roots.

The Bush attacked her. It wrapped its vine around her waist and pulled her up in the air. Kaylah started to Scream. "You lied, you lied"

Mother Nature turned and told the bush to let go of the human child.

The bush refused.

Kaylah found the mouth of the bush and throw the crystal into its mouth.

The Bush started to shake, and let go of Kaylah.

She backed away and asked, "How does that feel?"

The Bush still shivering grumbled and cried out, "It is awful, and you have poisoned me! My food lies! She lies!"

Mother Nature spoke, "Not at all, she has left a piece of love in you. Something you know nothing about. It will not kill you, but it will open you to a new life and a new life for your children."

Kaylah brushed herself off and skipped away, back to the group.

The Spike-Yard cried out, "Stop making me hum you bad crystal!"

Mother Nature motioned for Magoose.

Magoose said to the children, "Come to me. Stay here and don't go anywhere!"

The children shook their heads in agreement and stayed where Magoose asked them to stay.

Magoose walked over to Mother Nature and bowed low and spoke lightly, "My Lady."

Mother Nature placed her hands on his head and said, "You have all the gifts I could ever give one human. Today your job requires a great deal more. I honor you Great Magoose with patience, tolerance and wisdom beyond the stars. For today you care for the Great Star Children who will one day be known as the Guardians, elders, and head of the councils of this world, and spirit. You will need to be quick, know before they do, and see before they do. You have asked me why you were chosen for such great gifts growing up. Today, you now have the wisdom to know your answers.

You could have never understood when you were so young. You are great human being, and were chosen for the hardest job of all. I leave you with youth and dear sweet Norah as well." With this, she disappeared back into the mist.

Magoose stood and turned around, the children were in awe at what they saw. Magoose went from a withering old man to a young man again. Magoose walked over to the children and asked, "Are you all ready?"

The children nodded their heads. They were in awe, at the experience each of them had felt. They started walking down the path and they hear in the back ground, the Spike-Yard plant screaming, "Come back! Please come back! Take the crystal out of me. I will not eat you... much!"

* * *

Magoose started walking down the path again with a new understanding on what he was to do. They walked in silence; all lost in their own private thoughts of what has happened to them.

Magoose broke the silence and said, "Over here children it is pass time for our lunch meal."

The children followed Magoose to a wonderful clearing with a fire ring in the center. Magoose tapped his stick four times and basket full of wrapped beans, cheese, fruit and meat appeared. The children smiled at the baskets. They pulled out their water containers, and drank their water. Each one in turn gets their lunch.

The Quetzal bird flies to a tree by them as they are eating and started talking to the children. "You have learned much today, children. You have talked to our Mother Nature. We are watching you," then she flew away.

As they finished their lunch Magoose again tapped his stick four times on the ground and all the baskets are gone again. The children smiled at each other and continued to follow Magoose down the path. Then a Jaguar jumped out of the jungle and stood in the center of the path. He looked at Magoose and bowed.

Magoose stopped, "Hello my friend."

Jaguar spoke with honor, "Hello my old friend Magoose. We have been watching your young cubs. I remember when I was a cub. You saved me from the drones trap. You have always protected the animals here in our home place. I have a gift for your cubs."

"A gift?" Magoose questioned. "This is a good day. Your gifts are very special to my family. Please share with us your gift."

Jaguar sat down and spoke, "Long ago I remember from my ancient elders. The animals and humans use to be friends. We worked with each other, side by side here in our homeland. We learned about the Great Wheel together and how we were all connected. My people where given the sacred fire to share with the human children. We were the keepers of trust. The trust was broken by our elders. Our downfall came through greed and pride. I have two teeth and two claws for your cubs, so they will remember not to become greedy or prideful. Always remember to trust themselves and their Spirit Helpers."

The children are amazed at what the Jaguar was offering them. They walked up to where Magoose was standing and waited for more instruction.

Jaguar called, "Loora."

Loora walked to Jaguar. Jaguar hands her a claw and said, "This claw is for your strong heart. You are the carrier for the waters of life. Keep the flow of water always in her heart."

She said, "Thank you" and walked back to Magoose.

"Kalub come to me," Jaguar said.

Kalub walked to the Jaguar.

Jaguar hold out a tooth. "This is yours to remember to stand firm, with wisdom as your sword."

Kalub nodded his head and takes the tooth then said, "Thank you great Jaguar. I will do as you asked to the best of my ability." Then he walked back to Magoose.

"Kaylah come to me," The Jaguar asked.

Kaylah walked to Jaguar and bowed her head in respect.

"You have been touched by the Creators love. You carry within your very spirit, love and discernment. Always remember that everything is a lesson for your growth. The Good and the Bad," handing her the last claw.

She said, "Thank you Jaguar. I am not sure if I can accept all the lessons without being hurt or angry though. I can feel love, yes. To love all things is difficult for me. I am sure Magoose will help me learn more about my gifts. So one day, I can make this promise you."

Jaguar reached out and touched Kaylah on her arm and said, "I am sure when you are a woman you will be great. Learn and never lose your heart, Magoose's cub."

Kaylah nodded her head and she places her other hand on the Jaguars paw and said, "I will promise that." She smiled at Jaguar and released his paw and skipped back to Magoose showing him the claw she had received.

"Jai come to me," Jaguar called.

Jai walked to Jaguar and also bowed to him.

Jaguar gave Jai the last tooth and said, "You have the Jaguar's heart. You have strength and courage. You carry the fire of spirit, like we do. In your heart you carry the innocents of life's creation. You will become a great councilor and guide to your people. Do not forget your experience here in our homeland. Remember us, and the lessons you learned from Mother Nature and the Great Magoose. Carry your fire with pride, but stay away from being prideful." The Jaguar lifts both his paws towards Jai.

Jai put his hands on his paws. Jai felt the power, the energy, and the stories of the Jaguar clan flow into him. Tears of joy flowed from his eyes. He feels the added strength and courage. The life force energy bubbled up from the depths of his being. Jai spoke softly, "Thank you my brother. I needed your lesson this day. My doubts and fears did over ride my wisdom. Thank you for this great gift."

The Jaguar pulled his paws away from Jai's hand and stood up and bounded away.

Jai turned to Magoose and said, "I can hear and I have great gifts. What a strange and wonderful day."

Magoose smiled and walked over to Jai. He patted him on the shoulders and said, "You are an honored being, full of gifts that you do not realize you have yet. All of you children are very special. Come now we must get to our camping place, it is not far away."

They continued to walk down the path when a blue blur blazed past the children. The children dropped to the ground and shouted out at one time, "What was that?"

Magoose turned to the children with a large smile and said, "That was the greatest warrior of all time." While saying this, a blue blur circles Magoose four times up and seven times downwards.

The children watch in amazement. They hear a high pitch hum in their ears.

Loora said, "I can't hear you! You are talking to fast."

The other children asked, "You could understand it?"

Loora said, "It was too fast. I, ah, just too fast. As if all the words were spoken all at once."

Loora holds out her hand and said, "Please come and rest on my hand, I would love to hear what you have to said. Please just not so fast."

Magoose sat down chuckling, and said, "Good luck getting a hummingbird to talk slow." As the blur poked Magoose in the side, Magoose said, "Ouch." As the hummingbird lightly landed on Loora's hand.

The bird is huffing and puffing, and huffing and puffing.

The children said, "Please relax, slow your breathing like this." The children showed the Hummingbird how to breathe slowly.

The hummingbird flaps his wings and speaks very fast. Loora hears, "Creator of the Wheels of Life. Please allow me to slow down to the sluggish speed of a jaguar running. So that I may talk to Great Magoose and these special children."

Loora spoke excitedly up, "I heard him, I heard him, what a wonderful voice."

Magoose said, "I have never heard the hummingbird speak! This is a special gift."

Loora repeated back what the hummingbirds said.

Hummingbird rubbing its beak between its toes said, "I will do my best to talk as slow as I can."

Everyone's mouths open and are amazement that they could all hear hummingbird speak, even though it still quite fast.

"I saw you with Mother Nature today, you are truly the gifted ones, Magoose has been told about. This is for you special children. It is my story. Rarely do I take the time to tell it. However this one time for you special children I feel it is well worth slowing down for." She bowed to each child and Magoose.

A very long time ago, not long after the Turtle Islands were reborn. The Humans are learning about enlightenment.

There was a large group of warriors, who had helped defeat the monsters and Evil ones of mankind, and other evil beings from our lands. Being warriors, we had the hardest time, just sitting still and being people in our villages. As we would try sit and work our arm hands and feet would just start twitching. We finely realized that we were twitching because we craved war.

For as many generation as there are stars in the sky, we had been warriors. From mornings high sun until night we talked and thought about war. Everyday there was a battle to plan and fight. And then for two full moons there was peace. We were beside ourselves, fit to be tied, going crazy in our minds, waiting for the next war. All there was day after day, was the same peaceful days. We talked to other warriors from other villages, and decided that we would do training with each other and begin a kind of sport. We would wrestle each other, and see who could jump the highest, who was best with arrow and spear. Many things we tried to make into sport. Yet for a handful like me, it was not enough. We would met secretly and wage war against each other. To the point that we almost killed each other.

Mother Nature could feel the tension, and the unbalance in us. It was so strong, that she called all of the Great Spirit Beings together to discuss our problem. The council after several days, had decided, the only way to put us back into the world, and for us to be happy, was to put us into the animal kingdom. The wisest of animals and the most cunning animals where brought together to find out what animal we could become, to keep our honor, so we would never be bored again.

Ferret suggested to give us the speed of lightening.

Quetzal give us the ability to fly.

Jaguar suggested, to ability of stealth, so we could move quietly.

Monkey suggested, for us to still have heart connection to our people and still have lots of fun. Whale suggested that our food must be placed far a part and that we should be always hungry so we would not become bored.

The Great Spirits took their suggestions, they started by making the flowers have sweeter nectar. They asked the Flowers to spread out farther.

Then one day, when all the warriors where gathered that could not let go of war. A bright beam of light came from the moon, in the clearing where we were fighting. The light was so bright we could not see each other. We heard Mother Natures words and all the spirits council, ask us, if we wanted to be set free.

Many of us asked, "What do you mean to be set free? We do not want to die."

In a loving giggling voice, Mother Nature said, "Don't be silly. You are the bravest, strongest warriors in the whole world. We are so thankful and honored from all you have done. You sacrificed everything and did not ask for anything in returned. You are the embodiment of honor in all people. Because of this, the Great Councils, Spirit and Animals Councils got together to find a way to help you to be part of the Great Circle again. If you accept this great honor, we shall change you into Hummingbirds. You will be able to fly so fast no one can touch you. So quietly, no one can hear you. In trade for you speed, you must eat more often. You can only drink nectar from the sweetest flowers. We decided to give you a beak that can penetrate any armor and connect your hearts to all the woman and children of the world. You will be known as the protector of the innocent. The men will remember you as the greatest warriors that ever lived. Do all of you find this acceptable?"

The Hummingbird took a long deep slow breath, to continued her story. "This was the first time in my life and many of the other warriors lives we ever cried. As our tears fell to the ground, we begged on our knee's to the Great Council to make it happen.

Mother Nature said, "Close your eyes.

Father time said, extend your arms.

Grandmother Moon said, jump to me.

Great Spirit said, open your eyes children.

When we opened our eyes, it seemed as though everything around us was frozen in time. The only movement we saw was each other's wings. We started to fly around all the Great Council it seemed like an eternity. Then Mother Nature said, "Thank you."

After hearing her words we were so hungry we had to find food.

Over the years, we protected many woman and children from bad men. Whenever a woman or a child was hurt we could fly faster than lightening to them. We will always protect the innocents."

Hummingbird takes a long fast breath "I am sorry children and Magoose to be this slow. I must leave soon. Do have any questions?"

Kaylah said, "No, ah, not that I can think of."

The hummingbird replied, "Thank you for taking the time to hear our story. It is rare we can ever speak to people. Know that if you are truly in need while on our land all you have to do, is think of us, and call with these words, Hummingbird I need your help, or warriors, come to me. And we will be there. Faster than the lightening." hummingbird shots into the air, moving so fast around that children and Magoose that they could not see her, only the sound of the wind that she makes. Then she was gone.

Loora said, "What gift? She is gone!"

Magoose grabbed his hand feeling a twinge of pain. He looked at his hand; he saw the image of a hummingbird. With the words "We love you too Magoose." Magoose held his hand out-stretched so the children could see.

The children said, "Wow!"

Kalub said, "I want one too!"

As the children stood up Magoose looked at their knapsacks and said, "You have the mark on each of your knapsacks."

Kaylah said, "Here it is on your walking sticks too."

Everyone saw their new gifts and said, "Wow!"

Magoose notices the word speed on the end of his walking stick. He quietly said a prayer tapped his walking stick four times smiling to the children he said, "With what we have seen so far, anything could happen this day."

* * *

They began walking and talking about all the beautiful colors of their new hummingbird symbols on their knapsacks. The children agreed this had been a wonderful day.

Kalub said, "Nothing bad could possible happen today! Pausing for a few moments he asked, "Magoose who are the Sisters of Fate? They just told me I should not have said that."

Magoose's face goes pale and he said, "What did you ask?"

Kalub repeated what he said and Magoose said, "Oh Great," as he tried to smile. "They are wonderful, great, terrific, spiritual sisters, that influence peoples lives.

Loora with a joking voice said, "Do you really think they are wonderful and great? May I put turquoise around you."

Magoose feeling worried about the Sisters of Fate said, "What did you say?" with raised eyebrows and a stern look of steal on his face.

Loora said, "I said nothing, nothing. I am sorry Magoose." Knowing she over stepped her boundaries.

Magoose said, "We all get carried away at times and make mistakes when we are learning. I did it myself when I was learning. Remember there is always a price when we get overly confident.

Loora felt awful. She meant to say it lightheartedly, but that is not the way it came out. Loora kept her eyes to the ground watching the path as they continued on.

Magoose said, "Up ahead is a very long bridge. I need you children to be careful and step very lightly. There is a swift moving river below. This time of year it does not move that fast, but you do not want to fall in, because it is cold.

Magoose lead the way across the bridge. Kalub and Kaylah followed close behind, then Jai and Loora.

As Loora gets to the middle of the bridge, she thinks to herself, "Why did I say that? I am so stupid! I deserve to be punished!" She stomps her food on a board on the bridge and it gave way as she falls through, She screaming "Magoose!"

Magoose stopped and turned around when hearing her cry out for help as she fell thirty feet into the cold water below.

As soon as Loora hit the water, several frogs raced to her aid. Unable to swim, the cold water filled her lungs and Loora panicked. She began to lose all hope when suddenly; she was pulled to the surface. A frog rammed her in her stomach. The water released from her lungs.

The army of frogs shouted, "We will help you to the shore. May we take your shoes and knapsack so you can swim better?"

Loora cried out, "I can't swim!"

The frogs reassured her "We can carry you safely to shore. Don't be afraid, you are safe."

After hearing his sister fall into the water, Jai ran to where she fell through, panicked. The board next to the one Loora broke gave way under him, sending him to his sisters fate.

Many of the frogs just placed Loera's things on the shore and saw another child fall into the waters. Great Frog said, "Loora I guess it is time to learn how to swim. There are not enough of us to save both of you and your belongings."

Suddenly all but two frogs go dashing to save her brother. With a frog on each side of her they say, "See how we kick? Our legs Loora, watch us."

Loora started to kick wildly.

The Frogs said, "Relax Loora focus. Kick your legs smoothly up and down like scissors. Feel them push you throw the water slowly. The frog on her right said, I am going to let go Loora. Watch me. Your arms give you balance in the water. Brother frog has your other side. So you only need to balance on this side. Do you understand?"

Loora said, "Yes I think I understand but I am really, really, scared."

"Have faith in me and yourself and try," frog guides. "Try for me Loora please."

She agreed and the frog let go. She thrashes around for a little while until she could learn the rhythm. She said, to the frog on her left, "I think I have it now."

The frog let go and she quickly sinks into the water. The frogs push her back up. One stays beneath her while the other one faces her. "You must keep your head above the water Loora."

She cries out, "I am new at this! I have never done this before."

The frog said, "We will take turns underwater until you make it to the shore."

* * *

The frogs are doing the same thing with her brother. The two youngest twins, started racing for the opening in the bridge. Thinking quickly Magoose tapped his walking stick gently on the bridge and said "Restore." The bridge returned to the time when it was new and strong. The bridge began to glow.

Magoose hears, Mother Nature say, "Wood become as strong as the Iron bark tree. Share your strength with the vines. Be not broken and do not let them fall free."

Magoose tapped his walking stick and said, speed!"

The children heads hit the wooden planks where there had been a hole and tumble forward. Before the children could finish asking, "What happened? That hurt!" They were standing on the bank of the river watching the frogs save their friends. Magoose tapped his walking stick and whispered, "Speed."

The two children said, "Wow, Magoose you are amazing."

Magoose smiled at the children and said, "We need to stay here and not interfere. They need this swimming lesson. Also children, in order to be polite, we need to close our mouths so the frogs will not think we are stealing their fly's.

At this the children giggle. Still worried about their friends. Yet they know Magoose is here, so they know all will work out fine.

* * *

Loora and Jai, with the frogs help, finally make it to shore. They pulled out dry clothes from their knapsacks and put them on.

As soon as Loora saw Magoose, she broke into tears and runs to him crying, "I am so sorry Magoose, I am so sorry. It is my entire fault! I almost killed my brother too. Please forgive me Magoose. I could not live with myself knowing you hated me."

The other children and the frogs overcome with feeling her emotions and started crying too. The frogs hopped over to Loora and covered her. They started singing, *"We love you, we love you."*

Magoose takes all the love in his heart and let it flow into Loora.

The other children rushed over to help.

Jai said, "Magoose is not like the people in the school. He can feel our hearts, and he knew you meant no disrespect."

Magoose spoke in a soft voice, "Loora, I already forgave you. As I said before my wonderful child, we all make mistakes. This journey is hard on all of you. You are learning to trust and open yourself to others. If you did not make mistakes while learning new things, you will never become the great person that you are, inside. You would have never been given all the special gifts today. I promise to watch over you and protect you the best I can. I hope you believe me." He gently stroked her hair and kissed her forehead.

After a time Loora is able to breathe a little easier. She felt the love around her, yet she still kept sobbing. It was like her whole life came crashing in around her. The tears that flowed where healing to her very soul.

The children and the frogs back away. She started to take long deep breaths and said, "Thank you everyone, I can breathe a lot better now."

She looked at the frogs with so much love and started to cry again. She yelled out, "I did it again."

The Frogs asked, "What is wrong Loora?"

Loora said, "I forgot to thank you for saving me. You just sent me love like it did not bother you one bit. You still came over and comforted me. Even though I was rude to you."

The frogs started to giggle, "But, Loora," they giggling a little louder, "You did thank us with your love in your heart."

Loora started to smile through the tears. "Thank you my dear new friends."

Jai understanding what Loora meant, turn to the frogs and said, "Thank you for saving our lives and thank you for teaching us how to swim."

The Frogs smiled back at him and sent love to him, so help him know that it was an honor to help him as well.

Magoose and the young twins also said thank you.

A large group of bears approached as the frogs asked, "If we tell you a story Loora, do you promise to feel better? We do love you Loora."

Through her tears she said, "I will try."

From behind them they hear, "Can we hear the story too frogs? We have never heard your story before." The Bears asked the children and Magoose, "Do you mind if we sit and listen?"

Magoose and children smiled. Magoose answered, "I would be honored to have you as our guests."

Magoose telepathically asked his wife, *"My dear wife. Please prepare blankets for the children. Loora and Jai leaned how to swim today."*

Norah replied, *"Exciting day my husband?"*

Magoose said, *"I will tell you all about it soon."*

Magoose asked everyone to come and sit together in a circle and then he placed his hands on the ground. "Rocks please come forth in a circle. Wood please come to me." There was a pile of wood that appeared next to the circle of rocks. "Pele please, let your fire free to come to this circle and start my fire." The fire started to crackle with a soft hum. He tapped his walking stick four times on the ground and the blankets came.

The Bears said to the children, "Come and lay by us and get warm."

The children walked over to the Bears and crawled up on their backs. Magoose put blankets over them.

The Oldest Frog in the group spoke up, "I am called Great Frog. Our story goes back to the beginning of the Turtle Islands. At one time, mankind was out of balance with the Wheel of Life. He even stopped talking to the animals and plants. Man did whatever he wanted regardless of the price. Because of this the Great Spirit flooded all of the world. Magoose do you have five hours for the story?"

Magoose said, "No."

Then I will tell you the short version of the story.

Many of us animals while the two Great Turtles and the Grandmother moon was remaking the continents. Us frogs and many other animals, helped rescue the human that were good and kind. We taught them to swim like Loora and Jai, today.

Mother Nature asked Mother Earth if they could give a home to the good humans and their children. For not everyone was bad. There is always some good in with the bad. Knowing this, Mother Earth, created a place underground beneath the turtle islands and allowed the people who had done bad things but had good hearts to enter. She knew that many of them did not want to do what they did, but they did not want to be left out. It really hurts ones heart if you are caste out and do not do as the others do.

Mother Nature allowed us to bring the good people from the second generation, to re-enter the land after the waters lowered. She gave all the animals different assignments. We were responsibility for planting all the trees, flowers, and bushes around the rivers, lakes and streams. We were given the ability, that when we sweat the medicine could be used. I was given the knowledge," said the frog. "Since my clan is the one who asked for the human to be saved. Our medicine helped to open mans mind. Medicine people, come every now and then and take my sweat, and use it in ceremony to see their ancestor's and those that have passed, their future, and their past."

A group of tiny frogs, started to jump up and down and asked, "Can we go next?"

The Great Frog smiled and said, "Of course."

The colored Frogs lined up in a row. Speaking one after another, they began their story.

"Our name that man has give us, is arrow tree frogs. We make a poison that slows creatures and people down. We chose to be very close to humans, we taught them how to make bows and arrows. With the help of snake, they learned to use our sweat to coat their arrows. Humans realized that it was better for an animal to go to sleep when you hunt them and not feel so much pain."

A group of greenish yellow Frogs asked, "May we speak next?"

The Great Frog said, "Yes."

"We are called protector frogs. Our medicine gift is to kill off the bad stuff when you cut your skin. When you drink our sweat, we can help damaged parts of the body to heal. Unfortunately our medicine can't re-grow arms or legs.

All the different frog groups went through the same process teaching the children about their own medicine.

When they all had their turn, they thank the children for listening to their stories.

Loora forgot all about being sad as she listened to the stories. She was so happy and honored by hearing the Frogs stories that she forgot all about her worries and pain.

One of the Bears said to Jai, "If you don't mind I must stretch my legs." Jai and all the others had forgotten they were laying on the bears for warmth.

The mother Bear went over to great frog and said, "When I have a few days, to spare, may I bring my family back to hear the long story.

The Frog sticking his tongue out and said, "Of course."

Mother Bear licked Great Frogs back. As mother Bear entered the forest she said, "The trees sure look funny today."

Magoose thanked the frogs and told the children to come and follow him. They need to re-cross the bridge and get to their camping spot.

* * *

It was a little past dark when Magoose finally stopped and walked into a clearing, he sprinkled tobacco around and calling for the protectors in each direction. After he finished, Kalub and Kaylah also walked around the circle. At each direction they placed a crystal, and then joined the others.

Kalub set off for firewood and Kaylah began setting up the fire ring. Loora goes to the fire ring and helped.

Jai is still in a daze from listening to all that was around him. Not really saying anything, just listening.

Magoose pulled out a blanket from nowhere and placed it on the ground then sat on it near the fire ring.

When Kalub returned with an armload of wood, He said, "I could really use some help. It is really dark out there, and I can't see anything."

Magoose smiled at Kalub and said, "Put the fire wood over there."

Kalub did as he was instructed.

Magoose stood up and went to Kalub. He tapped the wood three times and the pile grew larger. There was enough for the whole night.

"Wow" Kalub said, "I want to learn to do that."

Magoose spoke, "In time you will. Always remember this; laziness is never a good thing. We need our bodies to match our energy. Never allow energy to make you lazy. Tonight I do this for safety, and your ankle. Not just because we could not do it."

Kalub nodded his head in a yes manner and said, "I think I understand that, Magoose. Thank you again for your teaching."

Magoose looked surprised at Kalub's remark, and then turned around and sat back down on his blanket. Magoose thought, "These children are growing every moment. From six years old in the morning to ten by nightfall. This will be an interesting journey with these young ones. Thank you Universal Life Force for all my gifts and my eyes to watch these children grow."

Magoose tapped his stick four times and again all the food and water they needed was ready for them to use and eat.

Kaylah lit the fire and started to search for something to fix for dinner.

Magoose looked at her and spoke, "Do not bother little Kaylah the dinner is already here."

Kaylah looked at Magoose and saw the wonderful baskets of food ready for them to eat. And again five wonderful large bowls of fresh warm water ready for them to enjoy.

"Wow! I really want to learn that," said Kaylah.

Magoose smiled and said, "Not all things are what they appear to be, my young ones."

Loora asked, "What do you mean Magoose?"

Magoose looked at all the faces starring back at him and said, "All I am doing is shifting energy. My wife has been cooking and preparing for us all day. My walking stick has a portal, which allows me to connect with my home and bring all you see here to us. Do you understand?"

The children looked confused and a little bewildered. They shrugged their shoulders and started wrapping the goodies into their tortilla and eat. They really did not understand what Magoose was saying. But Magoose knew in time they would.

The children were tired from all the things that had happened to them. After they ate they rolled out their beds and climbed in.

"Would you like to hear another medicine story children?" Magoose asked.

The Children nodded they did. So Magoose took a deep breath and spoke.

(Translated from Native speech.)

"A long time ago, Frogs lived in all of the streams, and rivers of our world. Just like they do today. They were happy singing their songs, sitting on their lily pads and laying the eggs that became pollywog's and then, became frogs. It was a good life, and most of the frogs were happy.

Then one day, one of the Chief frogs, whose name was Jumper, became dissatisfied. Everyday, from his lily pad, he could see something in the distance. This thing that he sees is larger than anything he had seen before. It was green most of the way up, and then became white. As he watch's, many of the animals go up there looking hungry. Then hours later, they returned looking like they had eaten a lot. He began to be dissatisfied with the flies, mosquitoes and water bugs that he usually ate. "On this large thing," He thought, "There must be delicious things to eat. That is why all of the other animals look so full and happy when they come down from it. It's not fair that we frogs have to stay in this pond always eating the same old things. I desire to go to this big thing and get some of the good things that they always have to eat."

One day he saw snake and called to him. Snake was slithering down the large thing and asked him where he had been and what he had eaten. "That large thing," said Snake, "Is a Mountain. Upon it are the biggest, juiciest, most delicious bugs I have ever eaten. They make the biggest flies here seem like gnats. UM, How happy I am that I can go to the Mountain."

Jumper thought about what Snake said, and he became terrible hungry for the Delicacies that the Snake described. He began to tell all of the other Frogs about them. He made them sound so good that all of the Frogs desired to have a chance to have some of them to eat. Soon the Frogs in that pond told the Frogs in the next pond about it, and so it spread until all of the Frogs in all the ponds, Streams and Lakes and Rivers all around the Mountain became dissatisfied with what the Great Spirit had given them.

Finally Jumper made a bold suggestion, "Fellow Frogs," He proposed "Since the Great Spirit is trying to keep us from all that is best in life for us. Let us set out on our own and Climb the Mountain and forget about the places where we live now."

Some of the Frogs agreed. They had really come to believe that they were being forgotten or ignored by the Great Spirit. Others felt that although those other bugs might be bigger, it would be difficult for them to live on a mountain, out of water.

"You are cowards," Jumper told the other frogs. "We frogs can live on land, we can do anything. Don't we sit all day on the lily pads out of the water? The Great Spirit just told us that we have to be in the water to keep us from all of the best things that all of the other Animals have. Let us set off for the Mountain." After he finished his speech, and while it was being announced to all the other frogs in all of the other ponds, Jumper heard a Voice in his mind.

"Little Brother," said the voice, "I have given you all that you need to live well. Don't be greedy for things that other Animals have. Be happy and sing your songs of thanks for the good things you have. Don't go to the mountain today. Things will not go well for you if you do go."

Although this made Jumper hesitate, he was so determined that he was missing out on something, that he ignored the warning the Great Spirit gave him. Soon he and the Frogs that followed him set off for the Mountain. As they started their climb, they noticed that all of the other animals who usually went up there to feed were busy running down, "Things aren't right on the mountain today," said the snake he had spoken to before. "Go back to your ponds"! The Frogs were determined. Jumper felt that the Great Spirit had told all of the other animals to act in this way to trick the frogs. So the animals had agreed because they didn't desire to share all of the food they had with the army of frogs marching up the Mountain. Up they climbed looking for the delicious bugs they thought they would find.

In fact, some of the frogs did find a few bugs and they were the biggest that they have ever seen and the most delicious. But most of the insects too, were flying in large Swarms Down from the mountain. As they climbed up they noticed that the white snow from the top of the mountain was melting and torrents of water were running down the mountain. Some of the frogs became sacred and desired to go back.

Jumper called them cowards and challenged them to continue. Soon large torrents of water were joined by melted Rock running down the side of the mountain. A Large cloud of steam began to envelop all of the frogs, causing their skins to burn. "Don't turn back now," Shouted Jumper, "If we show the Great Spirit that we will not fall for his tricks, all of this will disappear. " But it did not disappear; it became worse as the Volcano continued to erupt.

Jumper was not sure what to do. He realized, at the last-minute that he brought danger to many, simply because he felt what he desired was more important than what Great Spirit had given him. "Great Spirit," He prayed, "I will sacrifice myself gladly if you will save all of the Frogs following me. It is not fair that they suffer from my mistake. I should have listened to your warning and warnings of the other animals."

"Little Brother," He heard a Voice in his Ear, *"I will save all who follow you, as they now learned their lesson. Have them hop into the waterfall that you see ahead. It will safely carry them back into their ponds, Streams and rivers. But you must not join them."*

Jumper did as he was told. Soon all the Frogs were being carried safely home. Jumper sat there as the stream thickened, he was awaiting his fate, knowing that he had done wrong. Suddenly a Burst of wind came and blew him into a tree that was so high on the mountain the steam did not reach it. He was safe and watched as the Volcano finished it's eruption.

"Little Brother," Since you so much desired to live on the mountain, this is where you'll be from now on. You'll be smaller than you were before, and you'll no longer live in the water. The trees will be your home and the home of your Children for all generations to come."

So the tree Frogs, that strange, land borne relative of the water frogs. Now Jumper was a Happy Tree Frog."

* * *

They were dreaming of all the wonderful gifts they were given, and how beautiful Mother Nature was.

Magoose enjoyed the fire and telepathically told his wife, *"Thank you, my lady."*

Magoose heard a voice come back, *"Do you know I am young again?"*

"Yes", Magoose said. *"We were given youth from Mother Nature, so we can keep up with the children."*

"Mother Nature? Well did you thank her for me also?" spoke Magoose's wife.

Magoose told his wife all the events that happened this very long day. To Magoose it felt like a week instead of just a few days. *"These children are full of life Norah, they have so many questions, and are learning quickly. I ponder if they can fit into our culture? I am just not sure if they will be ready."*

"We could keep them out for a few more days, Norah suggested.

"I have been working with them on the Wheel, but to be ready for our culture? hmmm," Magoose thought.

"You are worrying Magoose," said Norah. *"These children are not just special, they will be the ancestors of tomorrow,"* Norah continued. *"I have seen visions."*

"I know we are all the ancient ones of tomorrow. But to fit in? Thank you my dear for all your help lately. I know it is a lot of work I have asked of you." Magoose said. *"I am going for a walk to think, I will talk to you later."*

"Good night my husband," Norah said.

"Good night my dear lovely wife," Magoose replied.

Magoose placed a shield of protection around the circle. Then he went for a walk to think about the coming challenges.

Magoose looked at the moon and he started to pray. *"Dear mountains of my homeland, how are we to prepare these children of yours? To fit into a primitive culture with their abilities? I doubt it is possible. They learn so quickly and feel so deeply. To bring them to my people, I feel would stop their growth. To hide them away from people is wrong as well. They have seen more than any of our children. Oh, grandmother moon help me in my quest, to find answers for these children. Help me to heal the wounds of these young ones past. Allow me to choose my words and guide them to their future, with open hearts. Thank you, Mother Nature for all your gifts."*

He walked and thinks until the moon is past the top of the mountain.

When he returned his wife was sitting in the circle waiting for him. He opened the circle and stepped through and closed it behind him. He looked at his wife and thought, *"She is so beautiful."*

"Why thank you my husband," she said softly. "Did you have a nice walk?"

"I guess so, it is difficult to put together lessons and plans for these children. They truly are special. Like we were," he said. "I guess you used your walking stick to find your way to me?" Magoose asked.

"I was in dream-time when Mother Earth came to me. She told me it was time to join you. So I picked up my walking stick and my bag. I awoke Deerah and asked her to watch our home and to help with meals," Norah explained. "It is time to rest, or we will not be able to teach them, come morning."

Magoose laughed, "You are right."

They laid out their bedrolls and slept in peace, with more questions than answers about these wonderful children.

⚜

CHAPTER 8

Learning New Ways

The sun was starting to rise when Magoose opened his eyes. He looked around and saw everyone still sleeping. He sat up, stretched and started the morning fire. He said his morning prayers and tapped his walking stick four times and all the water in the bowls lay beside the children again. His wife awakened and started to prepare breakfast. It is was a lovely morning the air was crisp and clear. The birds were singing their songs, and the monkeys are coming closer to the camp this morning.

The chattering of the monkeys woke Kalub and Kaylah up.

"Hush you noisy monkeys, and good morning! Sheesh," Kalub said as he rubbed his eyes.

Kaylah turned and said, "Who are you?"

"I am Norah, Magoose's wife."

Loora was waking and said, "I thought you were at home, helping with the wonderful food?"

"That is correct, I came to help Magoose prepare you for our village," Norah said.

Norah was a beautiful woman. She is tall and slender with a heart-shaped face with large blue eyes that shone like crystals. Her hair was blue black with shades of gray running through it. Her skin color is a reddish dark tone. She has a natural soft-spoken voice almost a whisper.

Jai awoke with all the chattering and looked over at Norah and said, "You are very beautiful. Who are you?" Jai asked.

"Norah young one, my name is Norah, I am Magoose's wife. Well children, breakfast is almost ready, so go ahead and clean up."

154

Norah finished stirring the pots of grain cereal and poured it into bowls. She heated up the flat bread, as the children finished cleaning up.

Kalub took the old wrap off his ankle. "Magoose, my ankle still hurts some. I wrap toward my heart right?"

Magoose nodded his head and said, "Good job remembering. That is right young one. You learn quickly."

The children one by one stood in line getting their breakfast and going to the large basket for their flat bread.

Kaylah asked, "I don't understand how you got here Norah. Will you explain it to me?"

Norah smiled and explained, "It is easy young one, I just thought myself here and I am."

All of the children looked mystified at her.

Loora thought about what she said. Then asked, "Is it like seeing a place in your mind's eye, and really wanting to be there and then you are?"

Norah looked surprised and replied, "Yes, that is right."

Loora nodded her head understanding as she smiled.

Jai spoke up, "You mean we are allowed to do that here? Then how come you did not just do that to get us to your village?"

Magoose said, "Sometimes, Yes. You were not ready to just walk into our village. You are not primitives and you are not Mayan. It takes time to learn the Great Wheel and to change the way you think. Our children do not speak or think like you do. We speak in stories, and give ideas. You were not taught like this. Even now if I speak as I would to my own children, you would be lost by my words."

Jai nodded his head with understanding and continued eating.

"Were you able to do this when you were young, Loora and Jai?" Norah asked.

"Ah, well yes. When we were very little we were late coming into the house," Jai said.

"So we just thought about our Buka and we were there," Loora spoke.

"But we got into really big trouble," Jai said.

"So we never did it again," Loora said.

Kaylah and Kalub just look at each other and shrugged their shoulders and continued to eat.

Magoose and Norah looked at each other with a knowing that they have special children.

Magoose took a deep breath and said, "This morning, we need to find out what you all know, and can do, on an energy level. This is very important if we are to join the village. You each are special and with being special there are things you can and can't do. Also you need to learn to develop all your gifts. When you are with us anything's is permitted for the next few days. You are allowed to be yourselves. It is very important to know this and to trust us. I know we have not known each other very long. I want to be more than just your teacher. I desire to be your friend."

The children all shook their heads up and down and smiled big.

"Wonderful, I am very happy you all approve," Magoose said.

Norah spoke up, "Put you bowls away and come and join us around the circle."

The children all stood up, put their bowls away, walked over and joined Magoose and Norah.

"Form a circle little ones," Norah motioned them.

"Today, I am going to start with Jai. Jai can you produce an air bubble?" Magoose asked.

Jai shook his head no and said, "I don't work with air."

"Alright," Magoose said. "What element do you work with the best?"

Jai was a little scared and looked over at Loora.

Loora nodded her approval so Jai felt for his energy. He knew where in his body to find it. Magoose taught him a few days ago how to bring it up. The energy flowed into his heart area, then out to his hands. He concentrated on this energy found that he could easily produce his fireball. It was blue in color, and he held it out for everyone to see.

Magoose was impressed. He nodded his head and said, "Very good Jai that is a wonderful fireball. Can you use water to put it out?"

Jai thought for a little while and tried to bring water up from his solar plexus and out through is heart. The fireball became a water ball and bursts all over the ground.

Everyone clapped their hands and said, "Great Job! Way to go!"

Next was Loora's turn. Magoose asked, "What element do you work with?"

Loora thinks for a moment and found her energy in her solar plexus and thought about the water that she loved so much. She pictured it flowing in her mind's eye. Remembering the way it flows and the sound it made in the fountain back home. She brought it out from her heart center and she added the love of wind into her energy ball. Then she showed everyone her ball of energy, of water and wind.

Everyone clapped and were feeling excited that now they could use their energy freely.

This feeling brought so much joy in Loora's heart, knowing there was no punishment anymore from using her energy. The ball of energy grew very large and started to spin.

Norah noticed right off, and pulled up the energy of stillness. She walked over to Loora and placed stillness in the ball of swirling watery wind. The ball stopped swirling and Norah spoke, "This is good that you can create Loora, I am so proud of you. Remember you can do great harm with water and wind. You must always be aware of what your energy is doing. Do you understand?"

Loora looked at her with a puzzled look. She is not sure if she should continue or stop. She looked into Norah's eyes. There was no anger or upset feeling in Norah's face. Unlike what she felt and saw in the people back home. She said in a questioning voice, "Not really. Normally when I am angry, the wind blows everything around the room. It has never really harmed anyone but the water in the energy, just gets things really wet."

Norah smiled the gentlest smile Loora has ever seen. "Watch this my child. Magoose please put up a shield around the circle. We need to cheek that nothing on the outside of our circle will be hurt."

Magoose raised his hands and set a clear bubble around the circle, then nodded to Norah.

Norah removed her stillness from Loora's ball of swirling watery wind. Norah stepped back to allow Loora to control her ball. Norah spoke, "Do you see it swirling?"

Loora nodded her head and said, "Yes I do."

"This swirling could become out of control," Norah said. "It is your job to keep it just in your hand."

Loora being confused with all the emotion of the past and what she is learning now. She began having trouble controlling her ball. It was swirling so fast that it started to become a funnel. It spun around and went high into the air. Loora thought about peace and the love in Norah's' eyes. She placed all the love into the funnel. The funneling wind started to calm down. Then Loora asked her ball to calm down. With a great deal of convincing, it then became a ball of watery wind again.

"Well done" Norah said and started to clap her hands with excitement. Everyone else joined in and yelled "Well done!"

"You both are very talented indeed" Magoose spoke, nodding his head in approval. He looked over at Kaylah and said, "It is your turn now Kaylah."

Kaylah looked into her solar plexus and thought about an element. Hum, well she is not fire, water and air is not right either. Well that left Earth she thought to herself. She could remember what earth felt like. She remembered the mud bricks her and her mother made. A mud brick was not a ball. She looked up at Magoose and said, "I don't think I have an element Magoose. Is something wrong with me?"

Magoose smiled and said, "No Hun, not everyone can produce balls of elemental energy like Loora and Jai can."

Norah smiled big, "Well you can think about the herb and the grasses right?"

Kaylah looked at her in surprise and said, "Yes, yes I can remember that energy. I love gathering herbs for mother. And you helped me identify the mushrooms on your last visit."

Norah said, "Yes, I remember showing you the mushrooms and herbs near your home. Reach inside yourself and feel the energy."

"Yes, I think I can do that," Kaylah said. "Like this?" She closed her eyes and thinks about the herbs she gathers for her mother. The wonderful smell of thyme and rosemary during the starry nights when her and her mother gathered the herbs. She remembered the smell of the fresh scents filling her up. The energy started to form a ball in her hands. It was green colored and rotating around between her hands. Everyone could smell the aroma of the herb flowing out of the ball.

"Wow, that is great Kaylah," Kalub exclaim.

Kaylah opened her eyes and looked at the energy. She was surprised to find a sparkling green ball of energy in her hands. Then she remembered the spike yard plant and the ball started to have points on the outside of it. She remembered all the plants she worked with. The ball changed with her thoughts.

When she looked up at Magoose and Norah, they are looking quite surprised at her. "That is really good Kaylah," Norah spoke.

"But what good is this ball?" Kaylah asked. "What can I do with it?"

Norah smiled and spoke, "There are many things you can do with the universal Love little one. We need to learn to create before we learn what to do. Love is a wonderful gift from the universe. It is the Love of life, and the herbs to heal with. With Love you can heal all the pains of humans. With the stars, moon, and planets you can bring the universe into yourself. You bring the Creators love and give it to others. It is Love in the purest form."

Kaylah nodded her head with understanding and then told the ball to stop and go away. It did, but left her hands tingling.

"How did you do that?" Loora asked.

Kaylah shrugged her shoulders and said, "I just asked it to stop and go away, and it did."

Loora looked down at her ball and told it to stop and go away, and it did.

"Wow that was very helpful. Thank you," Loora said. "That means I can control my energy," and smiled a big smile at Kaylah.

Everyone laughed in the excitement of learning, the ways to control their energy.

"Very good children, now it is Kalub's turn," Magoose said.

Kalub looked at Magoose and stated, "I don't have an element. I have been looking. I don't really care for the plant peoples like Kaylah does."

Norah asked, "Well Kalub what do you like?"

"Well, I love animals. Mother Nature said I was an animal talker. I don't think I can create an animal that talks right?"

Norah lightly laughed, "No, we don't create talking animals."

Everyone started to giggle at Kalub statement.

So Kalub just stood looking around at the others, feeling out of place.

Magoose said lovely, "Enough children. Kalub, you and Jai were playing with an energy ball. Do you remember?"

"Yeah, I remember. It was just a clear ball nothing special. Not like we are doing today," Kalub said.

"I understand," Magoose nodded his head. "You put your energy into the ball, as you were walking also, Right?" Magoose asked.

"Yeah, it was just energy. Nothing special, just energy. It was just a game. I don't do elements or Creators Love, or anything special. It is just energy," Kalub said.

"Kalub, look in your center and just create a ball of energy. Nothing special, just your energy," Norah Guided him.

So Kalub looked within himself and began to feel his energy. It felt warm and tingly. He brought it up through his heart and out to his hands. It became a smoky white ball of light. It tingled his fingers as he held it. Kalub asked, "What is this Magoose?"

"That dear one is energy in the purest form. Very few can bring up pure energy."

"What is it for?" Kalub asked.

"It is for anything you want to make it" Magoose said.

"Anything?" Kalub asked.

"Anything!" Magoose answered.

"Wow," Kalub exclaimed.

Then Kalub asked it to stop and it did. His fingers still tingles. Kalub asked, "How long until my fingers stop tingling?"

Magoose laughed, "Just a few minutes the first time. Your hands will not tingle after a few times of working with pure energy."

Kalub shook his hands up and down really fast, and in a few minutes it did stop.

"Well done everyone," Magoose said. "I am very proud of each of you. Your lessons are going very well."

Norah started to clap her hands. She looked proudly at the children. Soon Magoose joins in chapping.

Loora asked, "How will this help us fit in when we are in your village Magoose?"

Magoose looked over at Norah, and then took a deep breath. "We have people that are used, to help build our pyramids. They help lift the stones into place. They must learn to control their energy to do their jobs. Just like each of you," he pointed his fingers at each one of them. "You must also learn to control your energy and your emotions" Magoose encouraged.

Norah piped in, "You girls will be trained to do healing work with me.

Everyone has a job in our home. The boys can learn how to work with stone and help with the lifting. It is a starting place for young ones."

Magoose spoke up, "Today we are going to set up shelters to protect us from the storm that is coming. Jai and Kalub will come with me. Loora and Kaylah you will go with Norah. We will be gathering today to set up a home for us, here in the jungle." Magoose said.

The children all nodded their heads and everyone started to get busy.

Magoose brought down the shielding, so they could gather the trees and branches needed. Magoose and the boys went into the jungle to look for large trees that are lying down. It was against nature to cut a live tree for their shelter. Magoose saw many long poles, lying in an area. He asked the boys to help gather the poles and place them in a pile and the boys did. They pulled and tugged on the large poles, putting them in a pile.

Kalub asked, "How are we going to get all these heavy poles back to the circle?"

Magoose smiled and said, "Energy."

The boys raise their eyebrows at Magoose.

Magoose asked the boys, "Are we alone?"

The boys said, "Yeah."

Magoose continued, "Are there people around us that do not work with energy?"

The boys said in unison, "No."

"Do the people where we are going with these poles, all use energy?"

The boys said "Yes."

"Then either we can pull and struggle these poles back to camp, or teleport them."

The boys looked at him, "Teleport?"

Jai said, "Oh teleport, I understand."

Magoose winked at them. "Then come here boys and I will teach you to teleport," Magoose said. "Reach down into your center."

The boys did as instructed.

Magoose spoke, "Put your hands on the poles, close your eyes and picture the poles."

The boys did.

"Very good!" Magoose said. "Now picture the poles in the circle."

The boys did.

Kalub heard a slight popping sound. He opened his eyes and Jai and Kalub were standing looking at each other.

"Where's Magoose and the poles?" Kalub asked.

Jai said, "Back at the circle I bet."

"Maybe," Kalub said.

"I think we forgot to see ourselves there too, Jai suggested.

"I forgot to do that too. It sure is difficult to remember how to do all this energy work," Kalub said. "So now what do we do?"

Jai shrugged his shoulders and said, "I guess we start walking, or..."

Just then Magoose appeared before them, "You forgot to picture yourselves with the poles," He said with a big smile on his face. "Come over here and hold my hand," Magoose guided.

The boys walked over and each held one of Magoose's hands.

"Now close your eyes and see yourselves back at camp," Magoose instructed.

The boys closed their eyes and then heard the popping sound. Their stomachs started doing flip flops. Then they hear another popping sound.

"Well done you two." Magoose said.

When they opened their eyes they were back at camp with the poles.

Kalub looked a little pale and said, "My tummy does not feel good Magoose. Toma used to do that to us."

"It will pass in a few minutes Kalub. It happens only in the beginning of teleportation. You will get used to it with time." Magoose said with a smile.

They all heard another popping sound. Norah and the girls were back from gathering the branches, and vines.

"My tummy hurts Norah, Toma used to do this kind of traveling." said Kaylah.

"It will pass in a few minutes little one," Norah said smiling at her.

"That was fun!" Loora said. "Can I do it again?"

"Not now Loora, we will later," Norah said smiling.

"It looks like we have enough poles and branches to get started after lunch," Magoose stated. Then he tapped his walking stick on the ground four times and the food baskets all appeared again.

Loora asked, "But how can you do that? Norah is here with us?"

Norah smiled and said, "I left a friend of ours in charge of our meals."

"Oh," Loora said.

Everyone sat down, as Magoose said the prayer and they all began to eating their lunch.

While they were eating Norah started the instruction: "I would like to speak to you children about what is happening, why you are here, and why you are being instructed the way you are. I realize you are very young and there is a very little time to prepare you for what will come. As you all know the earth changes are coming. Some of you dreamed about the horrible things that will happen to your home island."

The children all nodded their heads frowning at the memory.

"Magoose and myself," she pointed to Magoose and herself, "We do energy work. We are the special ones of our village, just like you." Norah sat down on her blanket as the children were listening intently. "It is important for all of you to understand that we are allowing you to use your energy, because nobody here is watching us. We always have to be mindful of others that don't choose to find, use, or know how to use their gifts."

Loora spoke up, "Norah everyone is taught how to use their energy. Right?"

"Not here in the main land," Norah said. "Here in our jungle home, Magoose and myself have found peace and harmony, using our energy freely. If a stranger comes along, we do expect you to stop doing energy work immediately. We cannot allow anyone to see us using our energy. We can not use our energy because there are some people that would harm us for using energy. Bayon spoke of you Jai, but not of you Loora, do you know why?"

Loora said, "Yes, My mother did not want people to know I existed because I was, too special. They called me a Nebra."

Norah nodded to Loora at the hearing of the words. "I understand" Norah said. "You are very lucky to be with us today. That word is no longer used on the main land. We call this kind of energy people, Medicine People or Spirit Workers. Which is not considered to be a bad thing here anymore. Most people would love to be one. We have just changed the words to be accepted by those that don't like energy."

Kaylah asked, "Why is being a Nebra or even saying the word such a horrible thing? I have just learned this word from my father, and then heard it from Loora and Jai. Every time I hear it," pausing to think of the right word. "It makes me shiver inside."

"Dear Kaylah a long time ago, a Nebra was a person that won wars. They were the ones that brought so much energy to a fight that they could bring down fire or water or any element they wanted and turn it against the ones they were fighting.

They were more powerful than the best weapons. They were loved if they were on your side, and greatly feared and hated, if they were on the other side. There is no stopping a Nebra when they are in full power."

Loora sat wide-eyed with her mouth opened at hearing these words.

"Loora you are a great person on the wheel, I am glad you are on our side," Kaylah exclaimed.

Loora looked up at Norah and asked, "But I thought it was a bad thing, and we are beaten for being this way and you call it good? I don't understand Norah, Jai and I have always been treated differently. We could not play with other children. We could not learn like the other children. They told us our energy was a bad thing. Mother said, that we used really bad energy. Everyone that spoke to us, told us how evil we were! I remember when I was eight, I wanted a book from the shelf. I called it to me and it came. I was discipline for doing that. So now, how can this be good?"

Norah giggled and said, "Please understand young one it is only bad if you are afraid of it. People are still afraid of Nebra's and the power they have. Magoose and I are also Nebra's and we are not afraid of any of you. All six of us are Nebra's with different gifts. Magoose is a fully trained Nebra. He is from many generations of Nebra's. Magoose is the most dangerous person walking the area at this time. He can kill as well as heal."

"Wow!" the children said in unison.

Magoose smiled, and winked at them and said, "Don't be fooled my children. Norah was highly trained with stars knowledge as well.

Norah nodded her head at Magoose and continued. "With just a thought he can bend trees, cause earth shakes, dry up waters, or bring rain. There is not an element or an energy that Magoose can't use. Yet, it is his choice to harm none, and his willingness to train you to do the same."

She pointed to each of them. "Magoose uses his heart and love of all things to do good with his gifts. You will never have to worry, we will never do anything to harm you. Our job is to teach you to the best of our ability to use your energy. All we expect from you four is to respect, come from heart, and learn to do what we ask of you. Then when you are finished with your training, you will be expected to pass this knowledge down to the next generation. This is what we do to trade for learning the medicine path."

"Everything is balance, even your training. Mother Nature, may she always be blessed. She brought us youth, so we will have the strength to teach and guide you. Do you all understand this?"

The children nodded their heads that they understood.

Magoose spoke softly to the children, "Let me tell you this. If you were not Nebra's, I would not have come to the sky-ship to meet you! The earth changes will be very difficult for all peoples. Many all over this world will die and we can not do anything to help them. Death is a part of life. It will not be easy for those of us left living. It is part of the cleansing process of the Earth. We can only help those that do survive and you will feel the Earth peoples pain and losses. Together we will be strong. This lesson is for tomorrow not today," as he winked at them.

The children nodded, with sadness in their hearts, because they could not help the other peoples who will die. In dreamtime the children have seen the pictures of their homeland being destroyed.

Norah spoke up, "We need to gather a lot more big branches and wood this day, so we will have enough to start building our shelter."

The children agreed and everyone went back to work gathering large poles, branches and vines.

* * *

The sun was setting as Norah prepared the evening dinner. Magoose tapped his stick to bring the nice bowls of water and towels. There was a cold chill in the air, here in the higher mountain pass.

Norah told the children, "Please clean up now children you don't want to eat with dirty hands," as she smiled a loving smile.

After cleaning his hands, Kalub pulled some fruit from his knapsack and gave it to Norah.

"Here, I brought this for you. I climbed the tree and everything!"

"This is a wonderful gift," Norah said with a smile. "Do any of you children have food in your knapsacks that might go bad?"

Loora and Jai said, "I don't know, it has been so long since we even looked." They dump all their things from their knapsack and looked.

"Our red berries have green stuff growing all over them, is that good? Will it make medicine?" Jai asked.

Norah yelled over to him, "Don't open that! Just hand it to me please.

Jai did as he was asked, and handed he green sandwiches as well.

Norah holding the clear packages in her hand is amazed by the stuff they call plastic.

She closed her eyes, and the children hear a popping sound as she said, "Eat well Pele, I hope you enjoy your gift."

Loora sniffed at the meat roll and said, "I don't know if this is good or not. This log of meat looks like a rainbow."

Norah said, "Close it up please and bring it to me, Pele will eat well tonight."

Loora and Jai stack their survival bars still in their wrappers. Then they lined up all their crystals and the rest of their gear. They look at Norah and said, "We have it all organized for you to see."

Norah asked, "That in the black plastic?"

Loora replied, "They are survival bars. One bar gives you enough energy to make it through a whole day. Mom said they are good for 50 years. But, they taste like paper bark."

Norah replies, "50 years? They could not come from nature. Why don't you keep a hold of them just in case you ever have need of them." She thinks to herself, "Those things will still be good when she is 60?" as she shutters inside.

Kalub and Kaylah how on Mother Earth, did you fit all that stuff in your packs?"

With huge smiles they said, "Because it all fits?"

Norah said, "Well then I guess we could use, the smoked boar first." She is amazed how fresh

the boar smelled. It is like it was just cooked today. She asked, "Kalub and Kaylah, what type of knapsacks are those? I have never seen meat go this long without going bad."

The children looked down and said, "Our friend made them for us?"

In the distance you can hear Magoose chuckling at the trouble Norah was having getting information from the twins.

Norah prodded, "Mmm, ...what is the name of your friend that made them for you?"

The children look up smiling, "Toma made them for us. He is our friend." Then they look back down again.

Norah asked, "Alright children I have never heard a name like Toma before today. Didn't you mention his name earlier today?" Nodding at Kaylah.

Before Kaylah could speak Kalub bursts out, "He is a wild elf and we are not supposed to say anything about him or our secret," then covers his mouth with his hands.

His sister poked him and said, "You weren't supposed to, oh, ah, say anything."

Jai and Loora asked, "You had wild elves as friends?"

Norah asked, "Um... well... I have heard of many hidden creatures of this world. Wild elves are ones I have never heard of."

Kalub and Kaylah said, "We are sorry, we are not supposed to tell."

Jai and Loora put their hands over their mouths and looked at the ground.

Kalub said, "I am in trouble. I am sorry. Mother and Father told us to never talk to anyone about them. If we did, people would say were crazy. The people would do mean things to us. Please don't do anything mean to us. I am sorry, I did not mean to tell you."

At this Norah hid a laugh. With a compassionate voice Norah spoke, "Just because I am old, and from the stars. Does not mean I know everything children. Please tell me more. I would be honored to learn about your friends.

Kaylah said, "You want us to teach you about Toma? Really? We are not in trouble?"

Norah said with a loving smile, "No one is in trouble. You have done nothing wrong. We are not in your homeland. You are safe with Magoose and I. We are special just like you. Let us not keep secrets. Please share with us."

All four children say together, "Really? Anything?"

Norah replied, "Anything."

Jai stood up places his heels together and his hands behind his back, closed his eyes he began to speak, "Wild elves are a sub class of normal elves. Regular elves formed on earth before humans or star being arrived. They are kind and noble. Their spiritual ability is unknown. Even with our best probe and technology Lemurian's have never been able to find a single elf village.

Many elders believe they possess a cloaking device and their gold bracelets are the secret to their ability and technology. Their intelligences is rated 8.5 on the Nebra scale. While humans are rated .1 to 1 on the Nebra scale.

Wild elves intelligence is believed to be between human and regular elf. We know that on the main island of Lemuria must be a wild elf village. Since many of the gifted children have seen them when they were young. Official orders."

"If you ever see a wild elf, you are to capture it. You are to bring it back to lab building 7. Once it is there we will dissect, and find out their secret powers. Test the content of its stomach in order to understand these lower class creatures better and locate their home. Failure to report an encounter is considered a high crime against the state. All law breakers will be punished accordingly, that is all." Then he sits back down.

Kaylah and Kalub cried out, "NO! They would kill Toma if they found him?"

Loora nodded fighting back her tears.

After a few minutes of silence. Norah begins to smell the food burning. She ran to the cooking area, clapped her hands and yelled, "Restore!" She called them all over to the fire and said, "Let us start eating as I finish cooking the rest of the meal. She turned and saw Magoose smiling at her just feet away.

Magoose spoke lightly, "May I help you get caught up, my dear wife?"

They talk quietly as they finish cutting the fruit for the evening meal.

The children talk to themselves as they enjoy the meat. They are so caught up in talking, about the wild elves they did not notice Magoose and Norah had brought them fresh fruit and water.

Magoose and his wife sat a few feet away, listening to Kaylah and Kalub's adventures and enjoy the stories they told.

Kalub looked down and saw the drink and fruit. "Thank you Norah."

He turned and saw Norah and went pale. Not feeling how close she was and was listening to the stories.

The other children chime in and repeated, "Thank you," as they go pale.

Magoose and Norah smiled at the children and said, "What wonderful adventures you have had. I have learned so much listening to you.

"I have also enjoyed your stories," Magoose said.

Kaylah and Kalub "Could you please, tell me about your knapsacks?" Norah asked again.

The children all smiled with bright eyed.

Kaylah told the story of the village, and the vision Toma had. She told them about the special knapsack that only weight one stone, yet she could put her whole room in it and it would still only weigh one stone. She added, "Toma said, that we could never fill them up." Brother and myself have noticed whatever you put in them, never goes bad. It is like time stands still while it is in the bag.

Norah smiled and said, "Thank you children for telling me your secret. I understand it is a great secret. I promise to never tell anyone."

Magoose piped up and said, "You can count me in as well. Toma must be a great friend to make such wonderful knapsacks. I will not tell your secret."

Norah passed around their hot Chukwah as Magoose started to speak.

This children is one of our known medicine stories. Medicine stories are told all around the world. Sometimes a little different, yet the same is the meaning. It may help you to understanding why we need to stay in heart and give. This story all medicine people all over our land knows. We learn this story when we are around 3 years old, sitting around the circle during, Gathering the Field Time.

It is called Jumping Mouse with Heart.

(The following story is translated directly from Natives speak.)

Once there was a Mouse. He was just the like the other mice doing busy mice things. Sometimes when he was doing mice things, he hears an odd sound. He would lift his head and listen very hard. "I ponder what that sound is?" he thinks to himself.

One day he asks his friend mouse, "Do you hear an odd sound? Like a roaring?"

"No," his friend said. "You must be hearing things my friend."

Mouse goes back to his mouse things and tries to ignore the roaring in his ears.

The more he worked the louder the sound became. He could not block it out of his ears.

One day, he decides to investigate the sound he hears in his ears. He sneaks out his village and walked down the path towards the sounds.

As he listened he heard, "Hello! Hello, little brother.

Mouse looked around to see who was calling him. "Oh it is you brother Ferret."

"What are you doing so far from your village, little brother?" asked Ferret.

"Well, um, lowering his nose to the ground, I hear a roaring in my ears. It is an odd sound," Mouse said.

Ferret walked over to mouse and sat down. He said, "I know what the roaring in your ears is."

"You do?" asked mouse.

Ferret said, "Yes, It is called a river."

Mouse repeated, "A river? What is a river?"

"A river is a very large amounts of water flowing down the valley. Walk with me I will show you."

Little Mouse agrees and they walk to the great river. When they get there Ferret said loudly, "Come over here! I have a friend I would like you to meet."

Little Mouse goes with his friend to the edge of the river. It was very, very large. It has rocks sticking out with the water rushing around them. The water moves very fast down the center. Little Mouse sees a large green frog sitting on a green lily pad. There is beautiful flowers around the edge of the river. Ferret said, "This my friend. His name is Chief Frog,"

"Hello," said Little Mouse.

"Hello, Little Brother. What bring you this far from your village?" Chief Frog asked.

"I heard the river roaring in my ears. I wanted to see this beautiful place." Little Mouse said.

"I see," Chief Frog said. "What do you think of our medicine river?"

"Medicine River? I did not know it was a medicine river," Little Mouse said.

"Oh yes, I only live in the medicine rivers, streams and lakes. You are a brave little mouse to come this far from your village. Would like some medicine?" Chief Frog asked.

"Medicine for me? Yes!" Little Mouse said.

"Then climb on that rock over there," as chief frog points to a large rock.

Little Mouse did climb on the big rock. It was a very difficult climb for a Little Mouse.

Chief Frog yells at Little Mouse, "Jump as high as you can!"

Little Mouse jumped way up high and saw the Great Sacred Mountains. When he come back down he fell into the river. He is soaking wet and scurries to the bank. He walks over to Chief Frog and yells, "You tricked me! I am all wet! I do not have new medicine!"

Chief Frog said, "Oh my friend, you are mistaken. You saw Sacred Mountain, which is a great gift. And you have a new name."

"A new name?" Who me?" Little Mouse asked.

"Oh yes, your new name is Jumping Mouse with Heart.

"Oh, thank you. It is a great gift to have a name." Jumping Mouse with Heart said smiling.

Jumping Mouse with Heart, runs back down the path to his village. He gets home and runs to his friend's house.

When he finds his friend, his friend is afraid of Jumping Mouse with Heart and said, "You are all wet little mouse. Did you get eaten by an animal? There has been no rain here for a long time."

"No, No my brother. It is the great river. I fell in and got wet. I stood on a rock and jumped and saw Sacred Mountain."

What is this babble? You were spite out by a wild beast. You must be poison! You were not good enough for the wild beast. So it spit you out. You are not my friend anymore!" He scurries away quickly.

Jumping Mouse is sad and goes back to his house. For three days nobody in the village would talk to him, or even look at him. He goes to sleep every night and sees visions of Sacred Mountain.

On the forth morning he decides gathers his things and leaves his village. It takes him all morning to gather his courage and heart. He walks a long way to the edge of meadow. He looks out and sees the Great Plains. He sees many spots in the sky. He knew the spots were eagles because of the many stories he had heard as a child. Jumping Mouse with Heart gathers his courage and heart and starts to run across the grassland. He finds a grouping of sagebrush and stops to catch his breath. He had almost caught his breath when he hears a voice coming for the sage. He turns to see who it is. There before him is a very Old Mouse with a missing toe.

The Old Mouse said, "It has been a long time since I have seen another mouse. How are you this day Brother Mouse.

I am great, I finally worked up courage to go and see Sacred Mountain. When you called to me I was just taking a rest."

"Oh come inside, please eat, drink, spend some time with me Brother Mouse," the Old Mouse said.

Not wanting to be rude to his elder, Jumping Mouse with Heart joins him.

As they sat and ate, the old mouse told him the story of how he lost his toe. He said when I was younger, much younger, I heard a loud noise and followed it to this large rushing water. I saw several large animals. I was so scared I cut my toe as I scrambled back to my home. When I returned the other mice saw I was injured and had assumed a larger animal tried to eat me and I tasted bad. They refused to talk to me after many nights, with no one to talk to I packed my things and left, I was to sad to stay there. I ran across a ferret and a frog that wanted to talk to me. I was so worried they would eat me. That I ran and ran until I got here. With all the eagles above me I was too sacred to go anywhere else. So I made my home here. I sleep during the day and at night I gather food from all around. It would be so wonderful to bring this knowledge back to the mice. Sadly with this missing toe, I would never be able to stay in the village long enough to teach them. They would surely chase me away. So here I must stay. The Old Mouse sighed.

Jumping Mouse with Heart was so moved by his story, that he made a decision. Since the village would never take him back in the morning he would give the old mouse his toe before he left. He knew the wisdom this mouse had is greater than his own wisdom. He believed he was just a little mouse with a dream. The Old Mouse said I have extra bedding for you over there" pointing to a large pile of grass. You can spend the night with me or stay as long as you like. I love having guest.

Jumping Mouse with Heart agrees and stays the night with the old mouse.

The old mouse leaves to gather food. When Jumping mouse with Heart awakens he see enough food to last five days, and five days' worth of drink. When he finishes the meal with the Old Mouse. He asked him to close his eyes. With great heart he removes his pinky toe and places it on the Old Mouse's foot. The mouse seemed to lose many years and the toe fits perfectly.

Feeling this the Old Mouse jumps around and sings and dances. Thank you, thank you Jumping Mouse with Heart, I can finally go home. He is so happy and honored he puts all the food and drink into a bundle for Jumping Mouse with Heart to take on his journey.

As Jumping Mouse with Heart is leaving, he says a prayer to Great Spirit and sending blessings to Old Mouse. Please protect me on my journey. And guide me on this path to the Scared Mountain that is calling me.

He takes off with all of his might toward the Sacred Mountains. It is very difficult to run, missing a toe. By midday he finally balances himself and runs very well. He finds a bush of chokecherries. Lying beside was a great animal.

Jumping Mouse with Heart says, "Hello there, can you hear me?"

The great animal that was laying down said, "Yes I can hear you."

Jumping Mouse with Heart asks, "Why are you laying here?"

The large animal says, "I am sick. I was told that the only thing that can cure my sickness is a mouse's eye. In all my years, I have never seen a mouse. I am told they all live in the meadows and never come close to the mountain. It makes me sad because mouse has such great medicine. A mouse eye can cure any sickness. Where will I ever find a mouse that would give up an eye."

Jumping Mouse with Heart thought about was this great animal. He asked, "What is your name?

The great animal says, "I am the Great Deer. What are you? So I may know before I die. It is only polite to tell your name. When someone is this close to death and cannot see."

The Mouse said, "I am Jumping Mouse with Heart. I have thought long and hard. Since frog gave me special medicine. My eye must be medicine also. I am just a tiny mouse heading to the Sacred Mountain because it calls my heart. You are a mighty creature. You are in great need. Since I have learned to live without a toe, what is a mere eye compared to a might deer." At these words his eye left his body and went to the great deer. Instantly the deer was healed.

The Deer jumps around and dances. She thanks the great mouse for his eye. Since you have helped me, I shall help you. Stand under me and I will keep you safe you from the eagles.

Jumping Mouse with Heart runs underneath the Great Deer until they get to the jungle.

At the edge of the jungle the Deer says, this is as far as I can go. Good luck my brother on your journey. The deer goes back to the grassland.

Jumping Mouse with Heart looks around and continues to walk towards Sacred Mountain. Soon he finds a great Jaguar. Jumping Mouse with Heart becomes scared. Then he hears, "Mommy, mommy, I am hungry! said the little cubs.

"I am sorry little ones, I am blind I can't see to hunt. That awful skunk took my eyes and only a mouse's tail can save me." Hearing this sad story, greatly touches the mouse's heart. He begins to cry out of his one eye and thinks. "If she cannot see her cubs will starve and die. I am one small little mouse, who am I to allow seven cubs to starve, and a mother to die. For the cost of one mere tail."

It took the small little mouse several minutes to gain the courage, to approach the family. As the little mouse gets close enough to speak to the mighty Jaguar, her nose starts to twitch.

She said, "Little cubs I smell something I have never smelled before. It is a new scent. I don't know if it is food or friend."

Upon hearing this, the small little mouse says, "I am friend great Jaguar. My name is Jumping Mouse with Heart. I have thought a long time about this. If my small little tail can restore your sight, and help you feed your cubs tonight, it is yours." As he said this, his tail flew off and healed the Jaguar.

The tired worn out mouse falls to the ground. Jaguar picks up the tired mouse and bring him back to her den. She instructs her children to not eat this mouse. Protect him with your life. Because of his medicine we will all eat well tonight. At that jaguar disappears into the jungle.

Jumping Mouse with Heart awakens in the morning. Feeling the warm sun upon his back. He looks around and sees the jaguar family. He asked, "Did it work Mother Jaguar? Do you have your sight? Did you feed your children last night?"

Mother Jaguar said with a loving smile as if he was her own cub, "Oh great and wonderful mouse. Your medicine was so strong that I could see as clearly at night as though it was day. Thank you great mouse. For your gift of medicine to me."

Jumping Mouse with Heart said, "It was my honor because you are much more worthy than me.

For the cost of my little tail. All of you are strong and healthy."

Jaguar asked, "Where will you go next?"

Jumping Mouse with Heart tells her his tale and how he got here.

Mother Jaguar said, "My wonderful friend. Climb upon my back, I will take you to the edge of the forest. You still have a long journey ahead. With my help we will shorten the distance for you."

Jumping Mouse with Heart was so excited he ran up her back and said, "Thank you, this means the world to me."

As they traveled through the forest, he said a prayer to Great Spirit. "*Oh Great Spirit, thank you for allowing me to help such great animals. Even though I am not worthy. I have made so many friends. And traveled so far. Please continue to guide me to the sacred mountain.*"

He felt his heart grow warmer inside.

They reach the edge of the forest. Mother Jaguar said, "This is where I must leave you. I am sure you will get to where you are going."

Jumping mouse with Heart says, "Thank you my new friend." He jumps off her back and rolls in the dirt. Without his tail he finds he is out of balance with his little body. He takes off running towards Sacred Mountain. In a little while he stopped tripping and falling. He finds his balance to run smoothly.

He ran until noon then he stopped to drink and eat. As he was eating lunch he sees the Great Ram. Hello Great Ram, Jumping Mouse with Heart said.

The ram shouted, "Ram! Ram! Yes I am a Ram!" Then quietly sat back down and laid his head on the ground.

Jumping Mouse with Heart asked, "What is wrong with your Great Ram?"

The Ram stood up again and said, "Ram! Ram! That is what I am!" then his eyes become dim again and laid back down.

Jumping Mouse with Heart felt the Ram has lost his mind. He knew what me must do. He thought, "If I give him my last eye, I will be blind. I will not be able to finish my quest. This is such a great animal. I know I must."

Jumping Mouse with Heart said to the Great Ram, "I give you my eye so it may restore your mind and spirit." Just as he said it his other eye flew out of his head and the Ram is healed.

The Ram spoke, Jumping Mouse with Heart, "Thank you for healing me. I know of your quest to Sacred Mountain I will take you there."

Jumping Mouse with Heart said, "I am blind I will not be able to continue my journey."

The Ram spoke, "I will carry you there. You do not have to worry. The Great Waters by Sacred Mountain will restore you to perfect health."

Jumping Mouse with Heart felt his way to Rams head. Ram carried him up to the Mountains Sacred Lake.

"Here my friend. We are here. Just listen for the water and go in, you will be restored."

Jumping Mouse with Heart climbed down from the Rams head and said, "Thank you my friend." He listened for the water and found it. He got in and splashed the water around. Jumping Mouse with Heart is healed. He stood by the bank when he felt a shadow on his back. He is hit before he could react.

He woke up when he hears Chief Frogs voice. "Jumping Mouse with Heart my friend, you have made the long journey."

Jumping Mouse with Heart said, "My friend yes, it was difficult."

The Chief Frog said, "I have new medicine for you."

Jumping Mouse with Heart said, "Medicine for me?"

"Go and stand by the rock," Chief Frog said.

Jumping Mouse with Heart was very unstable but got onto the rock.

"Jump as high as you can."

Jumping Mouse with Heart did as he was instructed. He jumped as high as he could! The wind caught him and carried him higher,

"Do not be afraid!" The voice said. "Hang onto the wind and trust!"

Jumping Mouse with Heart did. He closed his Eyes and hung on to the wind and it carried him higher and higher. Jumping Mouse with Heart opened his eyes and they were clearing. The higher he went the clearer they became.

Jumping Mouse with Heart saw his old friend on the banks of the beautiful Medicine Lake, It was Ferret.

"Ferret calls to Jumping Mouse with Heart and said, "You have a New Name!"

"You Are Eagle."

The children thought about the story for a long time.

Then Jai asked, "Magoose, the Mouse had to sacrifice everything to get his gifts. Do we have to give up everything for ours too?"

Magoose took a long sip of his Chukwah and said, "To be a trained Nebra is a heavy weight. To follow the love of the universe can be difficult sometimes. We all have to make sacrifices along the way. Sometimes is it easy but most of the time it is difficult. You are so young, yet you have made many great sacrifices so far.

"I don't feel like I have made any sacrifices Magoose. I feel lucky to be here and to learn with you and Norah," Loora said.

Magoose thought about what Loora had said and replied, "For some the path is easy. For others the path is very difficult. It was easy for Jumping Mouse with Heart because he was ready to follow spirit with all his heart.

Kalub yawned and asked in a sleepy voice, "Magoose is sacrifice and service the same thing?"

Magoose thought about the question and answered, "Sometimes."

The children yawn and nodded their heads. As they went into dream-time they thought about Jumping Mouse with Heart, and how we can help others with their gifts.

CHAPTER 9

Their New Home

The next morning Norah and Magoose were up at sunrise. They enjoyed a cup of Chukwah before they woke the children.

"It is a beautiful sunrise." Norah commented.

"Yes it is. I enjoy looking at the pinks and oranges," Magoose said.

"There is a storm coming. We need to build a shelter today." Norah said.

"I agree. I know Kalub and Kaylah understand how to build a temporary shelter. Maylah did not miss anything, with those two." Magoose smiled as he remembered.

Norah smiled and said, "She was a wonderful mother for those two. I really enjoyed our time with her."

"Do you know what we will try to make today?" asked Magoose.

"I had a vision last night. I feel we should try to make a step pyramid." Norah suggested.

"A Step Pyramid? Our children are good, but do you really think we should try something that large?" Magoose questioned her judgment.

"We could start with a few small shelters, to help them hold the energy for a long time." Norah suggested. "Or we could just let them hold the energy for as long as they can for our home."

"I think it is risky to have the children hold energy for that long of time." Magoose said. "Burn out is possible."

"If they are Nebra's, then they can hold the energy," Norah reminded him. "How long did they hold the energy of the ball when you were walking?" Norah asked.

Magoose looked at Norah and said, "All day but, they took turns while we walked."

"I am young again, full of energy and life." Norah said. "I know I can help the children when they need it."

Magoose thought about what Norah suggested. "I agree, I am also full of energy and life. We did create our home together a long time ago," Magoose said.

"Good then it is settled," Norah spoke happily.

* * *

Kaylah and Loora woke up first. Kaylah got up and started to roll up her sleeping blankets and went to the fire. Loora followed her with her cup in her hand.

"Good morning Norah and Magoose," Kaylah and Loora spoke.

"Good morning girls," Norah and Magoose said.

"Did you sleep well?" Norah asked.

Jai was waking and said, "Those owls were noisy last night."

The girls laughed and said, "I did."

Kalub awoke and said, "Hush monkeys! You are always too noisy in the morning," as he sat up rubbing his eyes. He yelled, "Don't you know people like to sleep?"

Everyone laughed at Kalub.

"They just want to tell you good morning Kalub," Norah said.

"I know, but they are so noisy doing it," Kalub said.

Magoose tapped his walking stick four times on the ground and the mornings breakfast appeared.

Magoose gave thanks and after everyone's bedrolls were put away and they all have a good breakfast.

Norah spoke up, "The time has come now, please stand around me. I will show you what we need to build and how we will be doing this." She drew a step pyramid on the ground four stories high and four stories below ground.

From the picture the children could see it a Diamond shaped picture. The middle of the diamond was at ground level. Norah continues to speak, "This is called a step pyramid."

The children bent down and looked closely at what she drew on the ground.

"We need to build it close to the ground, not high like those from our home. But we will dig into the ground for the extra four floors, so that it will blend into the jungle and not be seen."

Jai looked up uncertain. "How are four children and two adults going to build such a great place?"

"Energy young one, Energy," Norah smiled and winked at him.

The children looked at her with doubt in their eyes and shook their heads in disbelief.

Kalub said, "That is impossible, we don't have that kind of energy. Do We?"

"I don't think so," said Jai, "I have great power with my fire, but nothing like what you are asking."

"A step pyramid is very large and will hold a small community. We are just children. Just children!" Loora stated.

Magoose spoke, "What is the difference between this dirt circle and a hole in the ground?"

"Um m" Kalub said.

Kaylah replied "A lot of work!"

Magoose shook his head no. "Little one that is not the answer I was looking for."

Jai looked up and said, "Um, well emptiness. A hole has no dirt or rocks. It is void of space."

Magoose said, "Well done Jai. How and or what could make a void space without shovels or work?"

Kaylah and Kalub were truly puzzled at his answer.

Loora and Jai thought more about it.

Loora was speaking out loud, "Void of space. To not be there. Empty. Um, I guess wind could blow it away. That is a lot of dirt to be blown away and would cause harm, to where ever it went. We could just ask the earth not to be in that place, right?" Looking up at Magoose and Norah.

"Yeah!" Kaylah said "And the earth could be hardened to make the bricks to steady the walls."

"Yes," Kalub speak up, "and the poles inside the bricks to re-enforce it right?"

Magoose looked at Norah with a pleased look, and whispered in her ear. "You thought this would be easy, right?"

Norah laughed low. And then said "Sure."

They both giggled and looked back at the children.

"Very good children, now where should we put our pyramid?" asked Norah

Jai looked around the area and pointed and said, "Over there, Norah. It is close to the stream so we can bring water inside the house. Yet in the jungle enough so that anyone walking by would not see us."

Magoose raised his eyebrow in surprise and said "That is a wonderful spot Jai, well done."

"Let's go over there and find out if we can build our home," Norah spoke, as she stood up.

The children followed her lead and walked over to the place Jai had suggested.

Magoose raised his walking stick and called out to the jungle. *"Oh, Mighty Jungle, we need a safe place to grow and learn. May we have our home under our mountain canopy. Four times under and four times above, so we can keep your sacred love?"* Magoose told the children to picture in their minds their home.

So each of them did, with little differences that made their home their own.

There was a hum each of them felt. It filled them up with a peaceful feeling.

"Wow, this feels really good Magoose, what is it?" Jai asked.

"That children is our answer." Magoose said.

"If you get a good feeling then the answer is yes. If you get a bad feeling then the answer is no." Norah said.

"You mean by just asking the Jungle, then feel for the energy, it will tell us wither it is alright or not?" Kaylah asked.

"That is right Kaylah," Norah said.

Magoose lowered his walking stick. He reached out and held Norah's hand. Norah reached over and took Kaylah hand. Kaylah held Kalub's hand. Then Magoose reached for Loora's hand, and Loora held Jai hand.

Magoose said, "Just like the poles, concentrate on the step pyramid like Norah showed you. Picture the hole in the ground large enough to hold our pyramid."

The children picture the great hole and the picture that Norah had drawn.

"Truly feel it children! It is time to bring forward the energy of our home!" Norah said.

Magoose started to sing the power song,

"Nay yah, Nay yah, Hay nay yah,

Oh hey ya, ma koo dath dos, Praj gar jay doth,

Nay yah, Nay yah, Hay nay yah,

Oh key ya, ma koo dath dos, Praj gar jay doth".

The children start to sing with him, the tone starts to vibrate the whole area and soon the earth started to shake and made a great noise. The leaves move around them swirling. The trees uprooted themselves and moved from the meadow exposing a great canyon deep in the earth

Each of them was in awe of what was taking place. The dirt rose into the sky in suspension.

Magoose yelled to the children over the noise the earth was making. "Children use your energy, produce your balls of energy, but this time just allow it to flow."

The children reached inside themselves, found their energy and brought it up and out their hands. One by one the children's energy blended together with Magoose and Norah's. Their energy arched upwards and down into the earth.

Norah spoke out, "Loora help hold the dirt up!"

"Kalub and Kaylah think of bricks for our new home! Form them clearly in your mind."

Bricks started to form from the suspended dirt and move easily into the great canyon to start the foundation.

Magoose called to Jai. "Use your blue fire energy to dry the bricks!" Jai focus his fire energy into the canyon. Blue and red flames rose high into the sky all around the hole.

Norah spoke, "Jai lower your flames!"

Jai pulled back some of his energy.

Norah spoke, "Poles enter our home!"

The poles leaped off the ground and flew high into the air and disappeared into the great canyon.

One by one the bricks fell into place and the timber filled the great canyon. The pyramid started to grow out of the canyon and into the air.

When the sun was high in the sky their creation lit up the entire sky.

They heard a woman's voice that sounded like it was coming from all around them. She said, "Children make your personal desires for your home." They each sent their image of their hearts desire for them new home.

Kalub spoke up, "I can't hold any more! I am out of energy!"

Kaylah spoke up, "Me to!"

The Children then fell to the ground in exhaustion.

Magoose spoke up, "Sing children, and sing the power song!"

They each sat up and re-balanced themselves. They started to sing again and see the picture again in their minds.

"*Nay yah, Nay yah, Hay nay yah,*

Oh hey ya ma koo dath dos, Praj gar jay doth,

Nay yah, Nay yah, Hay nay yah,

Oh key ya, ma koo dath dos, Praj gar jay doth".

Slowly they regained their energy and they beamed their energy again towards the canyon.

Again the energy arched and went into their new home. The children had to concentrate and closed their eyes.

Each level one by one started to form upwards. Magoose and Norah were also starting to feel weak from the energy they were using.

Magoose looked at Norah and said, "It is time to allow the Mother Earth to finish our home."

Norah agreed and they both joined the children sitting on the ground.

While they were sitting they all witness the completion of the brickwork four stories high. On each level there was beautiful shrubbery and foliage that re-rooted themselves. It began to look like the jungle again. The vines grow strong around the outside of the pyramid.

The leaves placed themselves around the jungle floor. The jungle replanted itself so well that it did not look like anything was touched. The ground started to shake, Loora and Kaylah crawled to Magoose's lap.

* * *

Jai and Kalub sat with Norah. It felt as if time stood still. Then with another earth shake, the Pyramid settled into place. Mother Earth in her infinite nature came forward to finish the final touches.

The Pyramid stood that stood before them was just like the pictures they had seen in their minds. There was enough room at the top to plant the gardens and for a mother sky-ship to land.

At the base of the pyramid two beautiful figures stood by the front iron wood door. One was dressed in brown like the rich dirt of the Earth and the other was misty greenish blue.

The one dressed in brown spoke first. "Well done my children this is your new safe home and learning center," as she looked down lovely at them.

The two figures walked out of the door and stepped down. Each step led outwards like a cobble road. Each new step a jade colored stone stair forms under their feet. Seven times they took a step until they stood in front of Magoose and Norah.

"I am Mother Earth, and this is my twin sister Mother Nature which you have already met."

Kalub spoke first, he could not believe what he was seeing, "Did, ah, did we create that?"

Magoose was speechless and just nodded his head up and down his eyes were wide at the awe of it all.

Mother Earth spoke softly, "Your combined energy helped us to see your deepest desire was to learning and growth. We have used the knowledge that flows from each of you. From all the different places you are from and combined them together. This is The Land of Nebra."

She motions with your arms towards the pyramid and all around the area. "Only the ones that should be here, will be allowed to see it and to step on these pathway stones. If one does not have the sight they will not be able to step on the stairs, unless they can touch their energy. If you attempt to step on the stairs you will receive an electrical shock as a warning. Then if you continue to do so your spirit will go back to the spirit world and so will end your life cycle here on earth."

Mother Earth continued speaking, "Those that have been blinded but are Nebra's, will need to be guided to the stairs. Their sight well be restored instantly. All Nebra's will be free to come and go on these premises. We took some of your healing crystals Kaylah for this first bottom stair. We placed a healing crystal beneath the stone. If you are injured all you need to do is get back to this step and you will be healed. We have placed for you a healing center in your new home. Mother Nature has set up everything for each of you so you will feel at home when you enter."

She walked to the circle they made the day before and continued to speak. "This circle will be your new temple. Since Kalub and Kaylah placed the sacred healing stones around this circle, Mother Nature and myself have used them to create this temple and your home."

Mother Nature spoke, "There is a price to pay, once you cross these stairs you may not go back into the world until, you have learned to use your energy with heart. Developing your energy is very important. The dark forces will always try to find the Nebra's and use their energy for bad. They will not pay the price of heart. Only a fully trained Nebra may come and go off these grounds, as they need. This will be the place of all energy learning."

Mother Nature continued, "There will be four places throughout this world for Nebra's to go. This is the first place. There will be another manifested in the middle of the next earth change. Then the third will be right after the next earth change. But I am getting too far in the future for you. For now we need to learn about this one."

Mother Earth walked over to Loora and asked, "May I touch you dear?"

Loora nodded her head yes, and Mother Earth placed her hands over each of her temples and said, "It is not a bad world Loora and you were damaged by the unenlightened. They do not understand how special you are."

Loora looked into Mother Earth's eyes and immediately understood, and her eyes started to flow with waters of joy, and was fully healed.

"Loora you will heal all the wounded people who come here. For the pain and suffering that you under went you are now a great healer. All of the scars that on your body are gone, you are healed!" Mother Earth spoke.

Norah was very excited and let out a little sound; her hands cover her mouth, slightly clasped together.

Mother Earth walked over to Jai and placed her hands on his temple and spoke, "Jai, because of your wisdom and bravery, you have been gifted with strength of heart to love. You have learned to trust through the trails of life. You will guide my people to their gifts and bring peace. You are now a mighty peaceful warrior."

Mother Earth went back to the bottom step of their new home and stood by her sister and spoke, "This night is a special night. You have one full moon from this night. No Nebra will be harmed here on this land! This will be the First Home for the Energy Workers on earth."

Mother Earth then clapped her hands four times. A great blue and white light with sparkling green lights, lit up the whole area where she stood. It looked as if these sparkles went everywhere at the same time. It was truly beautiful sight to behold.

Mother Nature giggles and said. "Yes, sister from the earth you came and from the earth you return. She does make a glorious exit, Yes?" She looked around and saw the awe of each face.

A golden glow began to form next to Mother Nature.

Mother Nature let out a sigh, then takes a few steps backwards and said, "It is about time you came, Father Sun."

A golden tanned male figure appeared, dressed in leather pants with a necklace of gold. His eyes were blue like the sky, and his hair was long and black like the night sky. There was a streak of white on each side of his temples.

Magoose and Norah go to their knees and lower their heads to the ground and started worshiping him.

"Now, now there is no need for that my children," Father Sun said. Father Sun walked over to them and then went down on his hands and knees. He places his head on the ground.

When Magoose and Norah looked up they could not believe what they were seeing. Norah went into tears.

Magoose and Norah looked up. Father Sun had bowed *to them*. Norah cried. Father Sun sat up and said, "It's you. All of you." He looked at each of them. "We need to thank you for your present work and choices, and for the work and choices you will do. Each of you shall be remembered as the ancestors and the grandparents of the Wheel of Life. Because of each of you, many gifted humans will be saved from the hands of the unenlightened."

Father Sun leaned back on his heels, than sat crossed-legged. Magoose, Norah and the children did the same.

Father Sun continued, "This is a good day, for you are the chosen ones from the Gods and Goddesses themselves. Each of you have more to learn and we are here to help. Mother Nature, Grandmother Moon, and I will be guiding you. You need to learn the fullness you gifts as a Nebra."

He looked over at Kalub and Kaylah and spoke, "You two are very special, I have watched over you since before you were born. You both have gifts that are very rare indeed. Pure heart and love was given to you two. Use it well. Listen to your elders and know that you will always be loved."

Kalub and Kaylah nodded yes they would.

Then Father Sun looked over at Loora and Jai and spoke, "You two were born Nebra's. You had to go through the hatred and pain so that you could understand what the new children will have to go through. Learn to have heart for the next generation. Learn well your gifts so you can teach them.

"And as for you two," pointing at Magoose and Norah, "You," nodding to Norah, "You are the star that fell from heaven." Then nodding to Magoose, "This is the man who was kissed by Mother Earth herself. What a wonderful pair you turned out to be."

The children looked at their elders with new respect and said very quietly, "Wow."

Father Sun continued, "You both are lights in the world. Magoose you have all the abilities of the Nebra. You my wonderful lady have all the abilities of your home, The Dragon Planet from Light, right?"

Norah spoke, "The Dragon Council Planet, Yes Great Father Sun."

"I have placed blue crystals from your home planet on all sides of your new home. I used Kaylah's night stone and created many night stones. With this light you may find your way to all the wonderful places in your new home. Each of you have now been aligned to your direction," Father Sun said.

Kalub whispered over to Kaylah, "Just like in the story that Magoose told us."

Kaylah exclaimed, "Wow!"

Father Sun hearing Kalub's whisper, whispered back to them, "Magoose is a great teacher children. Norah and Magoose will guide each of you to your own greatness."

The children looked over to Norah and Magoose and just said, "Wow!"

Father Sun continued, "I have also used Kalub's fire crystals, and embedded them into the hearth of each fireplace to keep the winter cold away. There is a never ending supply of wood in each living area. All things are in harmony in this area. It is all of your jobs to keep the harmony. Your water and food for this winter is already in place in your home. There is water that flows to each room and waste areas."

"We did hear your request little Kaylah," as Father Sun looked over at her lovingly. "This home is like your home Kaylah for all your needs. For this was your concern, what you call bathrooms? Your pictures and your heart were seen, and placed throughout the Pyramid."

Kaylah turned red and looked downward and said, "Thank you Father Sun."

"Kalub, every room is big enough to learn and grow. Your hunger for knowledge is impressive. We have taken books and scrolls of knowledge from all over the known universe. We the elders will always be adding world book and scrolls to your libraries. This way you will always know what is going on in the outside world and the universe as required. If anyone has a need for learning supplies it will be manifested. And you will find a friend who is in charge of all this.

It was good to have many different age groups and interests so we can know, how best to serve you."

"Loora your requests brought joy to us. We each put it in to our hearts. Beauty and comfort is everywhere in your home. From the floors to your ceilings. We have enjoyed giving you all the beauty for your new home."

Tears rolled down Loora face. She tried to give her best smile to Father Sun. Loora tried to speak but only squeak out a sound.

"Jai, your concern was warmth, and safety. Trust me when I say, all is safe here. You have the protection from Mother Earth, Mother Nature, and myself. You will be a great Nebra. For you will be a great protector and always connected to your first home."

Jai through great effort said, "Thank you."

"My Norah the faithful, a kitchen is what you called your cooking area. You were mostly concerned with the proper care and feeding of all the children. You have hot and cold water, cooking stoves and ovens enough to feed armies. There is enough food for all of you and a never ending supply of clean water. All the supplies have been placed, from kettles to the last fork your needs are filled. You have no worries my child."

Norah was in tears at hearing this and bowed down and said, "Thank you Father Sun."

"Magoose, my green thumb, Gardens. Oh yes, so many! Many gardens are here in your home. Magoose, we have gifted you help to care for, love and teach all the wonders Mother Earth has to share. There are even cave areas for your love of things that don't grow in the light. Your wonderful Mushroom and healing plants are ready for your loving touch. The children will always know, Mother Nature. From the paths they walk, to the jungle they will grow and learn in. All of Natures animals are here. All living in harmony with you forever.

If I had a word to describe all of you, it would be simple. Although your home is not simple, your lives will be. Enjoy, learn and be happy. For this is a new day."

They were amazed and joy filled in their hearts. All they could do is mumble out loud "Thank you Father Sun."

Father Sun walked over to the South entrance Magoose, Norah and the children followed. They walked out to the massive field.

Father Sun Spoke, "Let there be play in our new home." The ground opened up and many bricks fell from the sky to form a long playing field shaped like an I. The bricks lined themselves up to form angled walls that went 11 feet into the air. There was 6 foot wide path down the center of the court and on either side was stone hoops angled sideways. One was only 4 foot high off the ground, the other was 9 foot high off the ground. Places to sit were all around the ball field. Then suddenly many balls fell from the sky. Big ones and small ones some that bounced back high and some that only bounced a little. The balls bounced around just bagging to be played with. All the gear was placed on the stands that surrounded the large ball field. Father Sun said, "Let the cheering and the sport of play be here now!"

The children all clapped their hands and cheered.

Father Sun just smiled then glowed so brightly that they all had to cover their eyes from the glow until he disappeared.

Mother Nature said, "That my children was impressive. Father Sun to come and gift you all, is a great honor. He has never manifested on earth, at least not to my memory anyway."

"That was great!" Jai said.

"Yeah!" Kalub agreed.

"Those balls just fell from the sky!" Kaylah said. "Magoose, do you know how to play this game?"

"Magoose was the best when he was young," Norah said smiling at the remembrance.

Mother Nature spoke, "Well now it is time to gather your things and enter your new home."

So they all walked over towards the East entrance to the temple area. Each pick up their knapsacks and put them on. Then they picked up their walking sticks and walked back over to where Mother Nature stood.

"Come now, over here and let's get you safely into your home." Mother Nature said as she motioned them.

They formed a line in front of the stairs and Magoose and Norah took a deep breath, paused and then stepped on to the first stair.

A voice they never heard before spoke, "Welcome home Twin dragons. One that is Blue and one that is Green. In their heart they knew which was they were."

Upon hearing this, Magoose started to glow a soft gentle green. Norah started to glow a light blue.

The children looked with awe said, "Wow!"

Mother Nature smiled at them and asked, "I felt you both afraid of your home you created?"

Magoose answer, "I felt. Is the deeper question. If I really was, really worthy if this great blessing."

Mother Nature just shook her head as in disbelief and said, "The wheel is yours Magoose to form and shape it for the next generation to come. You can now breathe the peace you have always searched for."

Next was Loora and Jai turn they took a deep breath. They stepped together onto the step and smiled at each other.

The same voice they have never heard before today spoke, Welcome home Fire and Water.

They were excited that no harm came to them, the felt their element deep inside their heart. They rush up to Magoose and Norah who is standing on the top stone waiting for the children.

Kalub and Kaylah did not move to the stairs.

Mother Nature tried to encourage them, but they shook their head no. "Why will you not come?"

Kalub spoke first, "Magoose and Norah are old medicine people, and they are Nebra's! All of you great peoples said so. Loora and Jai were born Nebra's you said that too."

Kaylah spoke, "We have been told for many days now, we are special and gifted, but we are not Nebra's. We don't want our lives to end. Father said we were their life blood! Whatever that means."

They both look at each other and shrugged their shoulders.

Mother Nature walked over and sat on the stair. "Do you think I am a Nebra?"

Kalub and Kaylah thought about it. "Well no," they said in unison.

Mother Nature spoke kindly, "I am sitting on the stair and I am not hurt."

Jai from the top of the stairs said, "But you are not human!"

All of the Adults looked at Jai with an angry look. Jai sat down on the top stair wishing he had not stated the oblivious fact.

Mother Nature looked back at the twins with love in her heart and asked, "If I am not a Nebra or human how can sit here untouched? Did we not all make this home together? Who do you think I am?"

"You take care of the land with energy, and you look after the gnomes and fairies," said Kaylah.

Kalub piped up, "And the Elf kingdom and brownies too."

Mother Nature looked surprised and asked, "How do you two know about the little peoples?"

"They are our friends," they both spoke together.

"The High elves don't like humans though, I think they are afraid of us," Kalub spoke.

"But the wild elves like to play hide and seek, and tag," Kaylah said.

The children giggled at the remembrance.

"You two are very rare. No human! Not even children, do the little people talk to," Mother Nature said.

The twins look at each other and then look at Mother Nature, with a puzzled expression.

"Well I don't understand Mother Nature, they" (pausing) "little people as you call them, have always talked to us and played." Kalub said.

"I have not seen any here on the main land, but sometimes they like to play games and not show themselves. It is there way, that's all." Kaylah said.

"They have councils like we do, and they have children and toys, and homes just like us. The High elves think they are in charge of all elves. If you knew the wood elves they will tell you different. The wood elves help us to learn more about the arrow and bow that Magoose showed us. They taught us more how to use them. Not to kill but to hit a target." Kaylah said.

Kalub spoke up, "Yes, that is right. We dragged heavy dead trees to make a target that is what the wood elf called it. The brownies would laugh at us when we missed. But I guess in the main land they have all been killed. This land is out of, um m, balance."

Mother Nature was shocked at what she was hearing from these two young children.

Kaylah piped up, "I like the sprites the best of all the fairies. They like to play in the flowers and they are really beautiful. They can change into butterflies too, did you know that Mother Nature?"

Mother Nature nodded her head that she did.

"Of course she does silly she takes care of them," Kalub said shaking his head.

The moon is starting to peek over the high trees when Mother Nature spoke, "You two need to come with me up to Magoose and Norah."

"But we can't!" they cried, "We are not Nebra's."

"Nebra's dear ones, are the special, gifted, energy users. These are the ones that can touch their energy, and choose to use it with heart and love. There will always be those that keep the balance and use darkness. These are the normal type of Nebra's. Good and bad."

"But you have other people too. These people don't believe in silly energy. They just live life and try to ignore the seasons, Creators love, and gifts. These people are not bad or good they just are. They have the gifts in them, they just ignore it. If Creator tried to show them they become very afraid and they talked themselves out of what they felt or saw.

They teach their children not to touch their energy. They tell made up stories that they heard and pass it to their children. But some of their children do find creators gifts and walk away from their parents teaching. Most of them turn dark, and follow a made up power, that the bad energy teaches them.

There are a few that do find the love and Creators truth and light. Those become Nebras too. We who know the energy and those that choose to use it, or choose to touch it are called Nebra. The people who do not want to see the energy came up with that word and other bad words for the same thing. So they can hate it.

Nebra is a word that means: energy workers, Medicine People, light bringers, special, healers, herbalist, and the gifted ones, and more. These words are the ones that the unenlightened ones and the evil ones what to hate or even kill. They are scared of their own energy and gifts. Oh my, I am getting far in the future for you two, that is not of your concern today.

You will need to understand all this later in your lives. Now I need you to know that you are worthy and have full rights to come and enjoy your new home. You both made the choice of being here at this time. Please take my hands both of you."

So they did. They stepped on the first stair and took a deep breath waiting for the electrical shock. Instead they felt joy enter their bodies.

The strange voice spoke, "Earth, Air. Welcome home." Each of the twins felt their element in their heart. They walked with a bounce in their step, as she took them to Magoose.

"Come everyone, for it is late, as she motioned them into their new home. You will need to find your space to live and eat. I leave you now with the peace, and if you need us, just ask and we will be here at your side." With those words she was gone.

Kalub and Kaylah said, "Goodbye and thank you Mother Nature."

Jai and Loora said, "Thank you."

One by one they stepped into a great gathering place. This is the largest room they had ever seen. It was bigger than many houses put together.

Magoose spoke, "This is larger than any great pyramid I have ever been in."

Jai and Kalub went to the center of the room and found stairs. All 4 of them could stand side by side and go up together hand in hand. In the south, were two great stone fireplaces that 2 full size adults could lay down in.

There were many very long couches forming a horseshoe around each of the fire places. In the North where are many long tables. Along the wall there is long tall bookcases, it is well lit with crystals. When they stepped on the floor they feel warmth, but odd as there was warm air rising gently through the gaps on the stone floor. The ceiling was wonderfully decorated with the universe and the stars in the heavens. All of the planets of our solar system were there, and the moon, sun, and every star lit the room.

Norah walked to the south part of the room, to the beautiful carved door, made of iron wood tree. The woodwork was delicately carved and rich looking, all around the frame. She opened the wonderful door and saw bookcases that were carved out of Teak wood with colorful books they could not count. There were cupboards with many shelves and doors. Everywhere they looked the delicately carved wood surrounded them.

Magoose followed her and said, "Stay here until we come back."

Everyone nodded their head and said, "Yeah." They looked around with in awe. They found a place to sit down near the warmth of the southern most fireplace.

* * *

Norah saw a bathroom at the end of the hall. She walked the other way and followed the hall around. She saw many cupboards with drawer and shelving along the hallway. There is a door going outside and one going back into the large room in the middle of the hall. At the end of hall is another bathroom. She decided to go back into the large room and Magoose followed. Norah and Magoose walk back in and started for the great stairs and went down.

Soon, Kaylah stood up and said, "I really need to find a bathroom."

Loora spoke up, "Me too! You boys stay here and we will just go out the west door, we won't go far."

The boys nodded their head that they would. The girls walked to the west door and decided to turn right. At the end of the long hallway they found a bathroom and were very happy. The girls came back through the door and the boys were relieved to see them.

"Is it very far?" Kalub asked.

"Not at all," said Kaylah, "Just turn right and it is at the end of the hallway."

Kalub stands and Jai followed. They both go out the large door.

Kaylah was getting tired and laid down on the couch. Loora found another couch and laid down also. Loora spoke, "It is nice to have a home isn't it?"

Kaylah spoke up, "Yes it is. But I miss mother and father, do you?"

Loora spoke, "I don't miss my home. I think I am home for the first time in my life."

The boys came back into the room. They look around and see the girls lying down on the couches near the fireplace.

Kalub spoke up, "That looks like a great idea." Kalub got on to the couch with his sister and laid down and Jai got into one of the other couches.

Kalub looked around and said, "I have never seen such a great place like this before."

"Me either," "I can't wait until tomorrow so we can look around," said Jai.

"It will really be fun," said Kalub.

"I love the stars and the wood carving they are so nice," said Loora.

As the children were staring at the ceiling they fell into a deep dreamy sleep.

When Magoose and Norah came back with plates of food in their hands. They found the children fast asleep.

Norah asked, "Ah, they look so sweet. Should we wake them?"

Magoose said, "It is best to let them sleep. We will put these plates on the tables. If they wake up late tonight, it will be ready for them."

After Magoose and Norah ate, they also look around the room and found a couple of couches near the other fireplace closest to the East, and they laid their heads down and were off to the misty land of dreams.

❧❧

CHAPTER 10

Learning about their new Home

They awoke late the next morning. The softness of the couches was enough to take away all their worries. The comfort of their home created a feeling of safety, so they all slept very deeply. As they awoke, they found warm soft blankets over them and the fire was just a soft glow.

They looked around and found on one of the tables had large stone pot with bowls and spoons. There is fresh, warm bread wrapped in a towel. The smells from the freshly baked bread invited them to the table and they all sat down. There was butter and stone mugs for each of them. Each found they had hot Chukwah and milk. There were different kinds of fruit, just waiting to be tasted. The plates from last night were gone.

Norah looked over at Magoose and asked, "Who do you think did this?"

Kalub piped up, "I thank who ever, it smells and looks good."

Kaylah gave him a glare and said, "You are always hungry."

Loora said, "Yes, well Jai is always hungry too."

Magoose said, "They are growing boys, they always eat a lot more then you pretty girls." Magoose cut the bread and passes it around.

Norah laughed and served up the corn cereal.

As she did he gave thanks to the God and Goddess and he gave thanks the ones who prepared this wonderful meal.

Norah spoke, "So mote it be," which meant she agreed.

"This is really good," Kalub spoke up.

"Yes it is," Kaylah agreed.

After everyone was finished eating their fill, Jai asked, "Can we go explore?"

"Well as long as you stay in the pyramid. This place is very large, so watch the sun, and before it gets too low in the sky we will all met here. Agreed?" Norah asked.

Everyone agrees and the children took off up the stairs to the second floor.

There was room on the stairs for all four of them to go up together. It had beautiful stone steps with nice twisted cedar railing on both the upper and downward staircase.

On the second floor upward they found many rooms. There were hundreds of them, all looking like classrooms of some kind. Nothing seemed really interesting, each one have nice desks and crystals to light into the room. All the classrooms near the outside walls have wonderful windows were they looked out to see the area.

In one room there is a large maple desk with books on it.

"Well this is scary you know. All these rooms and nobody here to fill them," said Kalub.

"Yes it is. There is a lot of books for learning it looks like," replied Kaylah.

"But there is no teachers for all these rooms. I don't understand why they are already set up. There is only four of us," Loora said.

"Yeah but there was a lot of desks and books. Why would there be so many for only a few of us?" asked Jai.

"I don't know," said Kaylah.

"But look over here, each classroom had the teacher's bedroom also," Loora said.

"If every classroom is supposed to be a teacher, then that means Mother Earth must think that we will have over hundred teachers coming here. That must mean there are over a hundred Nebra's," Jai said.

"Don't you think that is strange? I thought there were only a few of us." Kaylah asked.

"I think there will be a lot of subjects all these names of different subjects written on the doors are strange. But I have heard of this one Alchemy," Jai said.

"I have never seen these kinds of classes," said Loora. "I have never heard of a lot of these classes, like medicine herb, spiritual arts? I guess we will know in time."

"Well I like the benches and grass here by the stairs. This is nice," said Kaylah.

"Yes we could play ball right here," said Kalub

"We don't have one, Kaylah rolling her eyes at Kalub.

"If we did we could," said Kalub. "There is a lot of room."

"Yes there is Kalub and it is strange that there are so many playrooms with only a few of us," said Loora.

"I think there will be more of us," said Jai. "I think we are just the beginning of whatever Mother Earth and Father Sun wants, or has created."

"Look at all these windows. You can see out to the temple area!" Kalub said.

"Wow, you really can," Kaylah said.

"Let go, I would like to see more," Kalub said.

On the third floor was sectioned off by four great rooms. Each great room has many small rooms. Each small room has four beds in them, and a little private dressing area for each bed. The dressers were rich dark wood that held wonderful new clothes. In each great room there is a fireplace with couches and chairs. There were tables and chairs placed around the room also. There was a note on the doors about girls and boys areas, and to the south a note for Magoose and in the north a note for Norah. There are great bathroom areas that held a lot of toilets and very large baths and a whole row of private showers too. They found each area to have a grand bathroom.

They did not touch the notes, because they knew it was private. They went back to the central great stairs lending to the top floor. When they arrived on the fourth floor, they found six doors and four of them look like large green houses. The ceiling had pictures of Father Sun and Mother Earth holding the Earth. There were two dark empty rooms. All round the outside area were windows. They looked out each one to see the outside. There is a small ladder that goes all the way to the very top of the school. They climb the ladder and stood looking around.

"We built all of this?" Kaylah asked.

"I just can't believe this pyramid with all this beauty was built with our energy," Kalub said in awe.

"We did have help from the God and Goddess," Jai said.

"Father Sun was impressive and Mother Earth really is beautiful too," Loora said.

"Well I love Mother Nature. She is wise and beautiful, Kaylah said.

"Let's go I want to see everything," Kalub said.

They all agree and climbed down the ladder and went back to the grand stair case and went back down to the main floor. They went out of the great room and found a large hall was that went all round the great room. In the large hallway they found many cupboards with drawers and shelves. They found two large rooms with lots of bed in the west part of the hallway.

These look like hospital rooms, Loora said.

As they walked around they find outside doorways leading outside in each direction. Where they could see the jungle, which surrounded their new home. They looked to see the special trees, animals, and the many beautiful birds. The heard the wonderful music of the jungle.

Jai said, "Look at the ball court. I can see it from here. I just can't wait to learn to play the games.

They ran to the west doorway and looked out where they could see the stream with the clear water running over and around the rocks. There were many fish jumping and playing in the stream as it ran down the mountain. It was almost hidden in the wonderful jungle surrounded them.

Then they ran to the north door to see what was there. The monkey greeted them cheerfully as they played in the trees. They swung on the vines and chased each other around in the trees. They greeted the children again with many joyful sounds. One playful monkey tried to pull the tail feather from the great macaw. He was scolded severely by the bird.

They heard the bird say, "Don't pull my tail." The monkey ran away holding it's a sore finger.

They saw Father Sun smiling down on them from over head.

Then they returned to the great room and to the center of the room to the great stairs and heading downwards. The first below ground level they found Magoose and Norah and told them of the notes upstairs.

This level opened up to a grand kitchen. Where they found large barrels of wonderful fruit that Kalub and Jai grabbed. They found storage for the grains, nuts and cocoa for their Chukwah. They found a place where Magoose could keep his wonderful mushrooms. There was trough of running water flowing for cleaning and preparing all the food.

It looked like it came of the wall and ran out of the trough through a pipe and down through the floor of the kitchen. There was grand wooded tables for making bread and ovens that were big enough bake bread for an army.

There were small rooms that had fireplaces in them with comfortable couches and chairs. Each room had a bed with wonderful quilts and dressers. They looked at the great stoves that they could prepare food for many people.

There were many cookies laying out on one of the grand tables.

There were so many different kinds they could not try them all. So they grabbed many of them and put them in their pockets.

"Don't eat too many children, it will spoil your dinner," Norah said smiling.

"There is always room for cookies Norah. Honest!" Jai said with a grin on his face.

Loora never tasted such wonderful cookies in her whole life. She is amazed at the different flavors each one had. There is chocolate, peppermint, cherry and so many different flavors she did not even know existed.

Norah said, "Go down to the next level children you will find interesting things there.

"Wow really?" The children said as they ran to the grand stairway and headed down.

When they came to the bottom of the stairs they looked around and saw.

They see a large rectangular open area with large wood doors facing each direction. There were large tables for studying and comfy chairs as well.

In each direction there was a large wooden door with notes on each common area door for which was address to each of them individually.

They each saw their door and Kalub went to the North, Kaylah to the East, Jai to the South, Loora to the West. Each of them stood and stared at their door in amazement.

Loora while standing at her door with her name and note on it said, "I ponder what the notes say."

"There are two pages!" Kaylah spoke up as she looked at her note.

All of them look at each other and agreed that they should go into their rooms and read them privately then met back in the common area by the stairs. So each of them open their doors to their separate common rooms and sat down at the large carved table, to read their notes.

* * *

Kaylah began reading:

"Kaylah you are the Spirit Guide of the East, leader of the Clan of the Quetzal.

Welcome Kaylah Spirit Guide of the East, your gifts are the power of Love, lighting the path and you are a Seer. You have many more gifts you must find as you grow. Think of the Quetzal and allow Quetzal to guide you. You can also call upon all winged creatures to help you.

Your element is Air.

Your Sense is Hearing

Your colors of the East are Yellow and Gold for Illumination. White for Purity of spirit. Peach for New Vibration and connecting to the Star Nations. Turquoise Blue for Awareness and the connection to the Universal Life force and the Rainbow.

These are just some of your gifts. Look forward to your lessons.

You are blessed.

Love from, Mother Earth, Mother Nature and Father Sun. Enjoy!"

* * *

Jai began reading his:

"Jai you are the Spirit Guide of the South, leader of the Clan of the Jaguar.

Welcome Jai Spirit Guide of the South, your gifts are Trust and Innocence, Leadership, keeper of truth and protection. When you are ready think of the Jaguar. Allow him to guide you to all your gifts.

Your element is Fire.

Your Sense is smelling.

The Colors of the South is Red for Protection. Orange for Courage. Scarlet for Passion, and Love. Green for Growth and Healing. Yellow for the Warmth of Heart and the Warriors Heart Beat.

These are some of your gifts. Look forward to your lessons.
You are blessed.
Love, Mother Earth, Mother Nature and Father Sun. Enjoy!"

* * *

Loora began reading hers:

"Loora you are the Spirit Guide of the West, leader of the Clan of the Whale.

Welcome Loora Spirit Guide of the West, your gifts are to looks within, the Flow of breath and Healing. As you grow ask the Great Whale to come and help you. Talk to the Dolphins and the Great Ocean, they have many gifts for you. Grandmother Moon will help you in flow.

Your element is Water.

Your Sense is taste

Colors of the West are Blue– Green Traditional Healing Colors, Indigo For Dream Work, Black to find the Void within, and to pull any Color you need, White to pull Sea Foam at Moonlight.

These are some of your gift. Look forward to your lessons
You are blessed.
Love, Mother Earth, Mother Nature and Father Sun. Enjoy!"

* * *

Kalub began reading his:

"Kalub you are the Spirit Guide of the North, leader the Clan of Monkey.

Welcome Kalub Spirit Guild of the North, your gifts are to Guide with wisdom, creation and vibration. Ask the great Monkey to help you with your gifts. You may also call on the monkey.

Your element is Earth.

Your Sense is Touch

Colors of the North are Green for healing. Violet for looking within visions. Brown for the Earth. Blue for the healing the Spirit. White for wisdom and purity.

These are some of your gifts. Look forward to you lessons.

You are blessed.
Love, Mother Earth, Mother Nature and Father Sun. Enjoy!"

* * *

Each of them came out of their clan room silent as what they had read. The doors change as they walk out of them. They became wonderful carved and colored doors.

The children looked around at each of the doors with amazement.

"You have a Universe with stars and planets. Wow, look and the great Quetzal on your door," Loora pointed to Kaylah door.

"You have a Jungle with tall trees. Hey there is the iron wood tree, with the family of Jaguars. Just like we saw Jai," Kalub said.

"Loora you have a great waterfall with all those lovely Macaws we saw. Look there," Kaylah points. There is a Whales see the water coming out of his spout? I see dolphins in the pond too," said Kaylah.

"Kalub I love your door" said Jai. "The Planet Earth is in the background. Look here there is a group of Monkeys reading a books."

"We have our clan animals on our doors now this is exciting don't you think?" Loora said.

"Yeah it is so wonderful," Kalub said. "I love my room it has a fireplace and the floors are warm and there are lots of bedrooms but I don't understand half of these words on my paper."

"I don't understand mine either," said Kaylah. "It is just a lot of words."

Loora and Jai agreed.

"I can read and write very well. I can read some of this, but some of it is way above my level, Loora said.

Jai said, "Well let go ask Magoose he would know. Maybe he could explain what all this means.

They all agree and went up to the kitchen area. They all look around but did not find them. So they went to the Great room sure enough they found Magoose and Norah are holding their own notes.

"Magoose, Norah, I am happy we found you. We have a lot of question about the notes." Loora spoke up.

Magoose took the notes and said, "Yes the notes are very interesting I believe."

"What do they mean, I can't read half of mine," Kaylah spoke up.

203

"Neither can I," said Kalub.

Come over here children and lets read them together and we will see what they all mean," Norah spoke.

So the children walked over to Magoose and Norah and sat down.

Norah began to speak, "These notes are what you need to either learn or what you already know. They are guides to help you, so you can teach others."

"Teach?" Loora spoke up, "I can't even understand these things. How can I teach them?"

Norah said, "alright, let's look at the top place on your notes. These are the gifts and the attributes of your gift."

"What is an Attribute?" Kalub asked.

"It means the characteristic, quality, or feature of this direction on the wheel. Each direction comes with qualities to help each person. It can also help you understand your traits or what makes you who you are."

"So you mean each one of these is in me?" Kaylah asked.

"Yes they are Kaylah," Magoose said. "Everyone starts in a direction on the wheel of life and learns about what their natural gifts are."

"Or what makes us special." Norah added.

"But what if we don't understand one of the things on our list," Jai asked.

"Well it looks like on your note they gave you ways to connect with whatever you need. You have special rocks, plants, animals, vibrations and tools that will help you," Magoose said.

"You mean we need to learn all of this?" Kaylah asked.

"Yes you do," Magoose said. "It is part of the Learning here."

"That is why there are so many classrooms upstairs right Magoose?" Kalub asked.

"That is right," Magoose said.

Kaylah asked, "But I am not sure if I am the East. I love the plants and water. How do they know what direction I am?"

Magoose answered, "It is very easy little one. Each direction has an energy that you start with and do naturally. Loora in anger used hurricane forces, it is natural for her. You little Kaylah have the ability to see what others cannot. Such as the little people. Only those in the place of the Universe Love and Kalub being in the North the place of creation can see and use the love of all things to play in the little people kingdom. You two are very special, although you need Loora's energy to cleanse yourself by using her water. Jai's fire to light the way or for protection. It takes all four of you to complete the Great Wheel, just like the story I told you."

"Well when do we have to start all this training?" Jai asked.

"I am not sure of that," Magoose said. "I do know this, each of us is important in the Great Wheel, and we need to learn and pass on this knowledge for those that come. The Atlantain's are looking for us. They will try with all their might to destroy this learning center."

"But they can't Magoose," Kalub stated. "They have to pass the step first."

"Oh yes there are those that can pass the step and they will. It is just a matter of time," Magoose warned.

"The Atlantain's want power, and they will do anything to get power." Norah said.

"Yes I know that" Loora spoke up. "I heard my tutors talking about them and how they created drones and weather machines to destroy Lemuria."

"Oh they want more then to destroy Lemuria," Magoose spoke, "And they want complete control of the entire world. They are moving to the main lands in order to control them first. They are not Gods but they will appear to be to the primitives and they will do great damage to the cultures of the people there."

"But," Kalub spoke up, "That is why our people closed the boarders, so we could not do this. Why can the Atlantain's do this?"

"Because they have no morals Kalub," Norah spoke.

"That is not fair!" Kalub exclaimed.

"So are we at war Magoose?" Jai asked.

"Not yet son, but soon, Yes," Magoose said. "The earth has not shifted yet, but it will and with that shift they will find us and try to destroy us."

"But you are a great Nebra Magoose, and Mother Earth put protection around us so no one could do us harm," Loora said.

"Yes and no," Norah said, "You see the unenlightened can not enter this area that is true. They do have some enlightened ones, ones with the gift, also. Enlighten people hold the gift of love in their heart. There are also he enlightened ones that hold darkness in their hearts and work for evil."

The children looked at each other with a scared looks.

"Magoose?" Kalub asked, "There are over a hundred class rooms upstairs all empty. Where are we going to find the teachers to help us learn everything on this list?"

"If we are to fight, then we have to learn," said Kaylah in a worried voice.

Magoose agreed, and answered, "Yes, after the next full moon we will be able to find the teachers and children. We first have to begin to understand our gifts, and accept the notes that are given to us. This home is grand and it is full of great things. Not even I, know how all this work. I do know this, everything on your list can be learned, and it is not a bad thing. The Wheel of Life will continue and we will find our balance and protect our home the best we can."

He winked at the children and continued. "I know the ground outside has a barrier as well. We are in a large bubble of protection. It must be at least 12,000 hectors surrounding our land here, so we can grow and learn what we need to."

Kaylah said, "We climbed the ladder and looked around. It is beautiful with the ball court and our temple. The jungle is all around us. It is so breath taking Magoose. I would love to go and see at night all the wonderful Stars."

Magoose smiled, "Maybe one night we will do that little one. It does sound like fun."

Norah asked, "Do you know the names of the stars?"

"Not yet," Kalub and Kaylah said. "We are too young to go outside at night."

Loora asked, "Do the Nebra children of Atlantis know about their government?"

"I am not sure," Norah spoke. "We can pray they do not. For if they are unaware they can be trained and grow in peace instead of hate."

Magoose said, "Well it is time for us to clean up it is almost dinnertime."

"Alright Magoose. But where do we clean up?" asked Kaylah.

"In your own clan house," Norah said. "Each of you has your own

Clan room to use and take care of. It is a big responsibility but I am sure you all can do it."

"You mean all of that area is mine?" Kaylah asked.

"Oh yes. Yours and who ever joins your clan."

"Oh, you mean the other children that Altex hates will come here?" Loora asked.

"I am not sure what will happen at the full moon. We can only make guesses," Magoose said.

They all shook their heads in agreement, get up and went down their stairs to their rooms.

"I just can't believe we are going to be learning all this." Jai spoke up.

"I don't really know if I can," spoke Kaylah.

"What do you mean you don't know if you can Kaylah?" asked Loora.

"Well some of this is really hard and I don't even know the words." Kaylah said.

"Well I know Magoose will help us he is really smart." Jai said.

"See you all in a little bit." Waved Kalub as we walked into his room.

Everyone said, "See you at dinner."

* * *

In each of the clan rooms the children found a door with their engraved name engraved on it.

Inside their room they found a special bed and a dresser full of nightclothes. Their closet area is full of wonderful day clothes. Each set of day clothes sitting on hangers and there were shoes sitting on racks. There was also soft towels, wash clothes for their baths and shampoo, soap, and bath items they would ever need.

Magoose and Norah went up the stairs Norah asked, "Do you think there is quarter for us instead of each of the Main Clan rooms? We are married you know."

"Everything here is so well planned, I am sure there is a wonderful room for us."

They turned and walked down the hall toward the east. They walked hand in hand past many doors before they came to a larger heavier wood door with their names beautifully carved into the wood. Magoose and Norah beautiful carved into the wood with their spirit dragons—one blue, one green was beautifully carved below their names. They open their door they saw their clan colors decorating the room.

Carved dragons adorned the wood furnishings. The fire place glowed softly in the part of their room. The saw another door to where they did not know. The canopy bed was large enough Magoose could truly stretch out his long legs and was soft as a pillow.

Norah skipped to the bed and jumped landing softly on the wonderful quilts. It felt as soft as a feather pillow. She did not desire to get up but there was so much more to see in their wonderful bedroom.

Near the fire they found an inviting love seat and two comfortable chairs with tables carved with dragons as legs. Reading light crystals hung from the ceiling over the love seat and chairs. Other lighting crystals hung near their bed that lighted the rest of the room.

Norah found the closets and where filled with every day and ceremonial clothes. They found racks wonderful shoes of style and colors and boots for hiking.

Magoose opened his closet and found wonderful everyday clothes with racks of comfortable shoes and boots that fit perfectly. There were many shelves of ceremonial things waiting to be discovered.

Magoose and Norah held each other, thankful for their new thing the spirits provided, this day.

* * *

They clean up and each of them found wonderful clean clothes to put on. The boys had black and white pants hanging in the closet, many forest green tunic shirts with half and some with full sleeves. In a carved box on top of their dressers were arm cuffs, and a nice choker made of hair bone pipe wrapped with copper. It had jade beads between the each section of hair bone pipe. Each stone that hung down from the center of the choker had their clan animal carved into it.

They had wonderful clean moccasins that fit perfectly with a nice wool layer inside them. Each of them found pajamas in their Clans color.

* * *

The girls look into their dressers and closets. There are white and black flowing skirts and tunic style shirts with half and some with full large sleeves. They find white and black pants hanging on hangers as well. Each of the Tunics were flowing and with hand-embroidered designs of forest green thread. They found beautiful Silver necklaces, with Jade triangular pieces place delicately opposite from each other all the way around their necks like a choker. They found ankle high moccasins that were lined in wool and fit perfectly on their feet. They also have wonderful simple pajamas in there clans color neatly folded in the doors. On the top of their dressers were hairpieces some are gold, some with feathers flowing downwards, some have beads with beautiful Onyx, Jade and some were silver. They have all kinds of different things to make them look nice.

* * *

Loora had never seen such wonderful things and enjoy putting everything on and danced around, humming to herself, and feeling wonderful with the beauty and peace around her.

Kaylah liked her hair the way her mother showed her how to braid it. She decided not to use anything of the new items. She just re-braided her hair and put in her beads like her mother showed her.

* * *

Kalub on the other hand loved his long hair, and he had troubles washing it. He did not undo all the braids that his father did and a lot of pieces of strands of hair were sticking out of his once neatly braided hair.

* * *

Jai enjoy his shower and put on his new clothes, just combed his long straight hair and went to the great room.

* * *

Norah and Magoose loved their new clothes and they fused over their hair and clothes until they are just right. It felt very good to be clean after the difficult journey here. It has only been five days since he met the children at the sky-ship. It felts like a long time had passed.

They walked hand in hand to the great room to join the children, who were sitting down in front of the fireplace talking about all their wonderful new things.

"May, don't we all look extremely nice tonight," Magoose said with a big smile.

"I love my new clothes," Loora said. "I have never seen such beautiful clothes before."

"You do look lovely Loora," Norah said with a smile.

"Well Now, lets us go down and find something to eat shall we?" Magoose said.

They all went downstairs to the large dining area. They found a meal fit for royalty waiting for them.

"What is this? Or the better question is who did this?" Norah asked

"I don't know," Magoose said. "Maybe our needs," (pausing,) "All of our needs will be provided for?" He questioned.

"I don't know, but it sure looks good to me," said Kalub. "I am just glad there is a lot of food I am hungry."

"Me too," said Jai and they went to the table and sat down.

"Wait now children!" Magoose said. "We must be thankful for what we have and were given. Saying thank you is very important or else our hearts will become dark." Magoose stood at the front of the table and offered the food to the four directions and to Mother Earth and Father Sun. He spoke, *"Thank you for what we have and to all who prepared this food. We also give thanks for those that provided this meal. We bless you and honor your presence in our life." "So mote it be."*

Everyone followed and said, "So mote it be."

There is a brisket, corn with peas, rice with mushroom, and butter with sweet bread, lots of different kinds of fruit and rice pudding for desert.

They all ate well this night, still not understanding how the food was prepared or who prepared it. Norah is very thankful for the wonderful meal.

It is late now Magoose said. We will be off to bed and tomorrow we will start your lessons on reading and writing.

Kaylah and Kalub are very excited with the news and they smiled and their eyes beam with the wonderment of what they will learn. Loora, and Jai you both will be working with Norah with your gifts. You will need to find out what you have on your list and what you need work on. This way everyone will be working for the next few weeks and getting ready for the next event."

"Next event?" asked Loora.

"Yes," Magoose said, "Mother Nature said this coming full moon something will happen. We need to be ready for what ever that is."

"Oh," they all said.

The children got up from the table and hugged Magoose and Norah and send their good nights.

Kalub and Kaylah went into their separate clan rooms. Each of their bed area had a sliding wooded door that opened to each others room. It was nice to sleep near each other for comfort in their new home, Then they drift off to dream-time and dreamed about the weeks ahead.

Loora and Jai went into their clan rooms and find their room also adjoin to each other. It was a strange thing that their rooms were separated by a sliding door. For the twins where not ready yet to be alone.

* * *

Magoose said, "I think you better go and relieve your friend."

"Oh my you are right! I had almost forgot with all this excitement about my friend," Norah said.

Norah went over and picked up her walking stick. She thought of her homeland and she teleported back to their home. When she arrived back she finds Deerah, waiting for dinner to be called for. Norah walked over to her and said, "Thank you my dear friend."

"Norah! I am so glad you are back. I have missed you a lot. What news of the children do you have?"

"I am sorry to tell you that they will not be coming to join our village. Mother Nature has decided to give us a new home. We are going to go and live their."

"New home? Are you really going away forever?"

"I am sorry Deerah, it is our calling." Norah said.

"I understand Norah. Magoose and you are truly special. What am I to tell the elders?"

"Tell them Father Sun has called us away," Norah replied.

"Thank you Norah for coming to our village. May the Good Spirits always be with you," Deerah bows her head and walked away.

Norah went to her daughters pyramid and went in. She saw her beautiful daughter dressed in her medicine dress. She was wearing a hand embroidered dress that fits her well on top and flows like the river at her waist to her calves. Her hand beaded moccasins almost touches the hem of her dress. Her brown eyes and warm smile is a welcoming site to Norah.

"Good evening Mother," Joy said as she welcomes her mother into her home.

"Good evening my dear Daughter. You knew I was coming?" Norah asked with a smile.

"Yes Mother, I knew it was time. I had the vision from the Great Bear. He told me to pack my medicine things. I am to teach now the gifts of the west," Joy said.

"Our new home is wonderful. It is full of the Lemurian beauty. The children are gifted my child. The little ones Kalub and Kaylah, who you met a few years ago. Do you remember?"

"Oh yes, mother I remember them. They were very smart and seam to remember everything we taught them," Joy said.

"There are two other twins named Jai and Loora. They are little younger than Earis. They are learning to trust us," Norah spoke with a smile. "Has Earis shown any signs yet?"

"Only when he is upset. He throw a rain cloud the other day at Elder Tabora. It was not really a great situation, but he seems to forget how he did afterwards," Joy said.

"I see. Well Mother Nature has put a protection stone in front of our new home. If you step on it you will get an electrical shock. If you stay on it, you will die. Do you want to try and see if Earis is ready?" Norah asked.

"I don't really want to leave my only son. I would like to try if you think we can," Joy pleads.

"It would be wonderful to have my family in our home. We will not be able to come and go for long. We only have until the full moon before something will happen," Norah said.

"I will wake him," as she rushed in to Earis room. Earis is awake and dressed with his knapsack on ready to go in no time. Joy picked up her pack with her walking stick and they follow Norah out the door.

"Grandmother, you became young," Earis commented.

Norah smiled, "Yes Earis I have. So has your Grandfather."

Norah looked over to Joy, nodded her head. Joy held Norah's hand and took a hold of Earis hand. With a step they are standing outside in front of the steps leading to their new home.

Earis said, "That was a strange feeling.

Norah asked, "What do you mean Earis?"

Earis said, "Well...it was like I was pulled through a wall and it kind of hurt a little. If I was not hold on to your hands I bet something bad would have happened.

Norah said, "Well that answered one of the questions I had."

Joy asked, "What question mom."

Norah replies, "Nothing Joy it is going to be fine. Let us continue.

Earis asked, "This is a wonderful place Grandmother. Where are we?"

"It is a secret Earis. Now it is time to step on the stair. If you feel anything bad step off quickly," Norah guided her Grandson.

Earis stepped on the stone and a voice started to speak. "You Earis are a storm maker. You will have the ability to create and stop all storms in this world. When you are grown you will create helpers. You are very tall because of your abilities. You have very special gifts that even the Great Magoose does not know about. You need to be Tall and strong, yet understand gentleness and love. Your clan will be, over the next six years, in the south. Although once you are grown, you will be in Norah house. Welcome home Earis."

"Awe! Did you hear that?" Earis asked.

"You next sweetie," Norah motioned to Joy.

Joy stepped on the stone and felt the love of the universe. She hears the same voice. "Our dear sweet Joy. You were named correctly. The Great Bear walks beside you and you listen with your heart, and you have patience within you. You will bring the knowledge of the people you have learned from, to this your new home. Only a short time will you stay with us. During your stay you will have a place in the teachers area. You will be teaching many peoples throughout this world. Learn to teach the young ones. So gather your knowledge quickly. Know you are loved always. Welcome home."

Joy looked over to her mother with tears running down her cheeks.

She said, "Thank you." and walked up the steps towards the door to join her son.

Norah stepped back on the stone and it hummed then walked up the steps to join her family. They walked inside and are amazed at the beauty they see.

"Oh Mother this is wonderful place. Thank you for bring me," Joy said.

Norah guided Earis, "This way child. You will be with Jai tonight. Your room is just down these stairs." Norah tapped on Jai's door and leads Earis in.

Earis asked, "Where do I sleep?"

Norah looked around the room and saw his name on the door next to Jai and said, "Find your Name."

Earis looked around the room and saw his name one door. He ran to his mother and gave her a goodnight hug and said, "Good night mother."

"Good night my little one," Joy smiles proudly.

They leave the room and go back upstairs to the classroom area. They look around for Joy's room and found it. They say good night and Norah went to her room where Magoose was waiting for her.

* * *

"Is everything alright?" Magoose asked.

"More than alright my husband. Our daughter and grandson are here with us." Norah said.

"Our Grandson? The child showed the signs? That is great news! What clan did he fall into?" Magoose asked.

"Yes. The voice from the steps said he will be in the south for six years. Then to come to my clan. He is a Storm Maker. A new kind of Medicine." Norah said with a big smile.

"This is wonderful news," Magoose said as he yawns.

Norah put on her night close and Magoose joined her as they climbed into bed.

They are all happy as they dream about tomorrow.

CHAPTER 11

The Preparation Begins

"Wake up Kaylah it is time to go to school," Kalub said.

"Yes that is right Kalub, we get to start school today, this is an exciting day." Kaylah said.

"Hurry lets get ready Kaylah," Kalub said.

She walked to the door she said, "I will meet you upstairs for breakfast alright?"

Kalub answered, "Alright."

Kaylah closed the adjoining door and started her morning and they begin to get ready for their day.

* * *

Loora and Jai were also awake Loora closed their adjoining door and gets dressed.

Jai walked out of his room looked around and the door next to his has a long name carved into it. It reads, E-a-r-i-s-i-a-t-i-a. Jai tried to pronounce it. "Ear is iatia, Ea ris I a tia, Um, Eari siatia, Ear isia tia, um. That is a long name. Who would ever give someone that kind of name?"

The door opened and a boy stepped out and said, "E-air-us-I-Ay-sha. My Grandfather calls me Earis. Earis means a Healing Wolf Cub. The Golden Iatia is a Golden Jaguar with rainbow colored wings. It is a bringer of life or destroyer of life." Earis took a deep breath and smiled at Jai and continued his story.

"Grandfather said, the night I was born he was first introduced to the Golden Iatia. He said he would come for me. Grandfather did not understand what the Golden Iatia meant so he prepared for battle. He said the Cat just started to giggle. It sat on his hind legs and using his wings for balance. Grandfather said, the Cat told him I am here because of your grandson. I bring him a special gift and it has to be given on the day he is born.

Grandfather then said to the Iatia, I have never seen or heard of your kind. Are you from the light? Or do you dwell in darkness?

The Cat smiled and said, "I am a creator and a destroyer Great Magoose. I am a Star Being that needs no ship to travel. Do you understand?"

"Before my Grandfather could even answer, the Cat started to glow so brightly that he could barely see. The rainbow colored wings, looked like gems circling a golden ball. He said it zipped faster than lightening. It paused in front of me, as my mother was holding me. From this being came a gold ball with lightening coming from the ball. It entered me and I began to glow a golden color.

The Cat whispered back to grandfather, as the Ishia left. "He will become like me. A bringer of life and a destroyer of life. He will heal, and he must learn to balance his heart. By the end of his life, he will evolve back into a star being like me. Good luck with this one he will be a handful."

The next thing my grandfather saw, looked like a spiral bean stock starting from the ground, reaching past the sky into the stars. The leaves where every color of creation. Then it disappeared as fast as it appeared then it was gone. Grandfather does not know much time went by."

"I just thought it is a cool story. Until I got in trouble for throwing a rain cloud at the elder the other day. But he never should have never taken my fish and said it was his. I am really glad I am here. Because now I don't have to rebuild his house. Man, is he going to be really angry that we are not there. Come to think about it."

Jai looked at large boy, he was almost as tall as Magoose. He has dark black hair, and brown eyes. He is wearing a smile from ear to ear.

"Who is your grandfather? I am Jai. When do you get here?" Jai asked.

"Oh, Magoose is my Grandfather? The voice said last night I was in your clan! Are you a Storm Maker too?"

"A what? Jai asked.

"Well the voice last night said I was a Storm Maker. That is why I am so tall and big," Earis said as he nodded his head.

Jai thinks about the story to himself, *"I better not make him mad."* Then asked, "Did you find your clothes alright?

Earis replies, "Oh yes, and guess what? They really fit! It is difficult to find clothes that fit me. And look, I have really comfortable moccasin now too."

Jai smiled at Earis and was glad he had come, for the company. He said, "Come on, you need to meet everyone."

"Do you think they will like me?" Earis asked.

"Yeah! I am sure. Kalub and Kaylah are great people. And my sister Loora is wonderful," Jai replied.

"I have met Kalub and Kaylah when they came to our home with my Grandfather. They are really nice. Kaylah really does love everyone," Earis said.

"Awe, you have met Kaylah and Kalub? When... how... did you met them?" Jai asked.

"They came our village a few years ago. We played together for a few weeks, while grandfather and their dad had to go on some business," Earis tells him.

The boys finished get dressed and met everyone at the stairs.

Loora sees her brother and a new boy and said, "Who are you?"

"I am Earis. Who are you?"

"I am Loora. How old are you?" Loora asked.

Earis replies, I am just twelve. How old are you?"

Loora blushed and said, I am ten almost eleven."

Jai looked over at Earis and says, "Only Twelve? You look really look much older."

Kalub and Kaylah came out meet them by the stairs. When Kaylah saw Earis, she ran up to him and gives him a huge hug.

"Earis, Earisiatia! Wow! When did you get here?" Kalub asked.

"Kaylah! Kalub! I got here last night. I am so happy to see you two again. It has been a long time."

Kaylah said, "Yes it has. You have really grown!"

Earis laughed and said, "Yes, Grandfather calls me his little giant."

They all started laughing with joy in their hearts.

Kalub tapped Jai on his shoulder yelled, "You are it" and ran up the stairs with Jai just a few steps behind him. Earis followed in the chase. When they get to the top and Jai caught up with Kalub and slapped him on his shoulder and said, "Now you are it." the boys went over and sat down by Magoose.

Earis hugged his grandfather and said, "Good morning grandfather." Magoose smiled at his grandson and said, "Good morning my boy.

Kalub poked Earis and said, "You are it now."

"Hey, That is not fair! We are about to eat, Earis said.

Kaylah and Loora giggled at the boys and sat down by Norah and Joy.

Loora asked, "Who are you? You are very beautiful."

"My name is Joy. I am Earis's Mother, and daughter of Magoose and Norah."

Jai looked surprised and said, "Magoose and Norah had children?"

"Of course, isn't she beautiful?" Magoose said proudly.

"She did not get her looks from you." Norah said smiling at Magoose. "Did you sleep well children?" Norah asked

"Oh yes Norah," Kaylah piped up, "It is very warm from the floors and the fire was really nice last night."

"We did too," Loora spoke up, "I love my room, and my clothes. I really like it here in our new home."

Everyone gathered at the table for breakfast. There was grain cereal and bananas, with fresh bread and butter on the table. There was milk for the children and large mugs of Chukwah.

Jai asked, "Have you found out who has been fixing our food yet Norah?"

"Not yet Jai, I do thank them before I eat," Norah said, as she looked around at the children.

"You are right Norah we forgot," Loora spoke softly.

So the children stopped eating and gave thanks and started eating again.

* * *

Magoose spoke, "Good morning children, today we are going to start your schooling."

The air vibrated with excitement, as the children's eyes beamed with joy as they looked up at Magoose.

"Kalub and Kaylah you need to learn to read and write and do more energy work. Loora, Jai and Earis need to learn more about your skills as energy workers.

So please go with Norah and Joy this morning. This afternoon after lunch, you all will meet me down at the circle temple for more energy training. This evening you will learn how to make bags for keeping special things in.

We will need to start making your medicine things. Every evening we will work on your crafting skills. You need to know about incense, candles, talismans, time and calendars. You must know how to defend yourself and to protect yourself, from what is to come. I have been told through my dream-time guide, that the earth changes are about ready to happen. The Atlantain's are already preparing their people and drones."

Kaylah raised her hand, "Magoose, what about our people? Will they also come to the mainland?"

"We don't know Kaylah," Norah said softly. "Your government does not feel that the primitives are ready for their advance knowledge and skills to join them. They don't want to upset the balance. Your people do have drones also, however, they are having trouble with them due to emotions? Isn't that right Magoose?"

"Yes that is right." Magoose answers.

Earis asked, "Grandfather who are the Atlantain's? How come I don't know about them?"

Magoose answered, "Change of plans, Earis come to the library with me first. I thought I had more time. Unfortunately, I have been so busy of late, that I have not been able to sit down and have that talk with you."

Norah spoke, "It is all about free will with the Lemuria's, they always are looking for things that might cause or be out of balance and fairness rather than power. Once a people start making people it is never a good sign. Both cultures have worked against nature herself."

"Kalub and Kaylah, we will work upstairs in the great room and start our reading and spelling lessons. When I am finished talking to Earis." Magoose said.

Kalub and Kaylah said together, "YEAH!" and ran for the main stairs and tried to see who would get to the top first. Earis saw the twins playing, so he hurries to catch up. Loora and Jai just walked up the stairs, they are not excited about school. Schoolwork was never fun, and they doubted Nebra school was any different. Magoose, Norah and Joy followed.

The books were already on the tables and their names written on yellow plaques and placed by each of the books. Magoose and Earis went up another level to the Library and have a talk. The other children all sat down and started to learn the best they could.

In the Library Magoose pulled out a chair for Earis, as he entered the Library his mouth dropped and his eyes looked around and saw small blue chips on the many tables in bowls. He saw books that that made his mind race with thoughts. He shouted, "Grandfather there are more book in here then ants in the jungle. I know I messed up an elders home, but are you going to make me read all of these? I don't think... I... I...can.

Magoose chuckled, "My wonderful boy, not today do you have to read all these books. Come and sit down in this chair. I will bring a few books I want you to study. I don't know what the blue chips are for here on every table. Come sit down so we can start."

Magoose placed four small books on the table in front of him. The first is titled, *"Everything you wanted to know about Atlantis but never bothered to ask."* The next book was, *"A story of joy and sorrow. The raise of Atlantis and how they are destroying themselves."* The next book is titled, *"The wonderful maps of Atlantis."* The final book was, *"The complete guide to the Land of Nebra, your new home."*

Magoose said, when you are done with these, come and meet up with us in the great room. This is all you have to read for today. Other books are for other days. Any questions Earis?"

Earis asked, "I understand grandfather. Are you mad at me?"

Magoose said through loving eyes, "No my little giant. Things happen. If there are no more questions I must go. Behave yourself you never know who is watching."

Once Magoose leaves, he picks up the first book and began walking around the library as he read. What seemed like minutes he was done. He picked up the next book. When he is ½ way done he heard a soft voice. "If you could hear me, I would help you read those faster."

A smile formed on Earis face, "And what if I like to read at my pace. I am the fastest reader in my village."

Toma asked, "You can hear me?"

Earis continued walking and smiling.

Toma thought to himself, "Is he playing with me? Or did he really hear me."

Toma grabbed a few books and sat at the same table Earis was at. Picked up one of the blue chips, places it on the book and runs energy on it. He repeated this on all the books. Putting them back on the shelves and grabbed more and did the same.

Earis comes back to the table and get the next book. And said, "I am not reading all those books. I only have to read these few." Earis continued to read, while he walked, and smiled.

Toma walked behind Earis and said, "I am the Librarian here. My name is Toma. Can you hear me?"

Earis spoke, "Would it not be great if there was a Librarian in here who could help me read faster."

Earis started to walk faster.

Toma sighed and returned to the table with more books. He continued to run more energy through the crystal, placing the crystals on each books.

Earis returned to the books and said, "I said, I am not reading anymore books today. Please quit putting more books on my table."

Toma said, "This is not funny. Don't you know it hurts someone's heart if you ignore them? I thought Mother Nature said only the enlightened ones, you know special children would be coming here. Kalub and Kaylah never treated me this way. They are my true friends." He looked down as if he was going to cry.

Earis looked straight at Toma and spoke, "You are friends with Kaylah and Kalub? You are not just pretend? You know like my imagination?"

Toma almost fell off his chair, "Yes, little people are real, and we have feelings too."

Earis said, "Back at my village, all the other parents and kids said that if you see a talking creature, then it is just your mind playing tricks on you. Or a bad medicine person trying to steal you, or trick you. I never thought they were real. I am very... very... sorry Toma."

Toma's eyes brightened. He lovingly said, "I was just playing back at you."

Earis said, "Oh... That was good. By the way Toma, what are you doing with the blue things?"

Toma said, "They are called crystal wafers or chips. They are very small flat crystals that hold a lot of information. You run energy through them when they are on a book. They learn everything in the book and store it. Remember knowledge is power Earis. It is like food and gives us strength. To get the information out," he stood up and pointed to his belly. "You put it here, and run energy through it. And you are able to read all the books stored inside the crystal in your mind."

Earis said, "Really? I know how to do energy work in my mind. Sometime I could put my hand on a person and heal them. That was until a few day ago. Before then I could see what is wrong with a person. Open up my heart and then my hands become really warm. Sometimes in minutes, sometimes in hours, the person or animal would be healed."

Toma said, "That is wonderful. Natural healers are very hard to come by these days. When you are done reading. Could you please help me with my back."

Earis replied, "I would be honored."

Earis goes to another table and begins to unfold the map. Toma continued to gather books and putting them into the crystal.

About an hour passes.

Earis said, "I am finally done." He put the books he read back on the shelf. He then helped put away the books Toma had pulled out. Once they are done.

Earis said, "When you are ready put your hands on the table and I will work on your back."

Toma turned so quickly he knocked the crystal wafer onto the floor. Earis came up behind Toma not wanting to break the chip, picked it up and put it in his pocket. He placed his hands on Toma's back and started saying his name. Then said, "From me to you." and began to humming those words.

Toma's back became warm. He felt so relaxed and peaceful that he fell to sleep standing up. He looked around and Earis although was gone. He said to himself, "Awe, I feel so much younger now. I feel like I am only 400 again. He looked around for the crystal because it was not on the table. He thought to himself, "Oh well I must start again." He began scanning all the books on hand to hand combat, advance weapon techniques, and the 400 book series called, A*dvance energy and you, a complete guide to becoming a master Nebra's,*" a long with the other books Magoose requested.

Just in case Magoose did not pick up the crystal wafer when he was sleeping.

Earis returned to the Great Room and said, "Sorry It took me so long."

Magoose smiled at him and motioned him to go with Norah and Joy.

Kalub and Kaylah are writing out their alphabet and are smiling.

Norah and Joy are working with Loora and Jai on the other-side of the room.

"Joy said, "Very good you two. You are holding energy very well."

Kaylah and Kalub said with their hands raised, oh.. oh... lunch is ready! Can we go?"

They all look at the time and realized the their tummies were rumbling and grumbling.

Magoose, Norah, and Joy said, "That smells good. Let's go and take a break."

During lunch Magoose said, "I am very proud of how well everyone are doing. I am also, very proud of you Earis, who would of thought, just 3 days after your medicine came in. You would have such great focus and control.

Earis said, "I guess all the healing I have done has helped me."

* * *

After lunch they all headed to the circle temple area.

"It is time children to learn about your bow and arrows." Magoose said. "This is how we pull the string and tie it to the top of our bow."

They held their bows between their feet and bent the bow to meet the string. It was really hard but they did it. For Earis it is an easy task. Magoose taught them how to shot and started to roll a hoop along the ground and the children were to shot their arrows through it. Each one tried to do as Magoose instructed, it was not as easier said, than done. Earis put his through every time. Then started to help Kalub and Kaylah.

"How does this help with our energy Magoose," asked Jai.

Magoose instructed, "Feel the Hoop with your energy Jai, then let your arrow fly it will find the hoop. Soon your arrows will fly right were you need them too. Not everything can be won by using fire balls. You must use all your skills not just energy. These lessons are also important because, they will help you balance with everything around you. From using your energy, sticks, arrows, and rocks, everything is important."

By the end of the lesson, they were getting more than half their arrows through the hoop before it rolled past them. To the children it became a great game.

* * *

The children follow Magoose to the library to check out more of the school.

Kaylah and Kalub looked all through the books, looking for words they recognize. Jai and Loora went looking around for silly stories, so they have something to read before bed.

Earis went with Kalub and Kaylah and asked, "What kind of books do you like to read."

Kaylah and Kalub answered, "We are just learning to read. I am not sure what there is to read.

Earis spoke kindly to them and said, "Sit down I will get some easy books to read for you. As he returns with almost 30 books.

Kaylah and Kalub looked at each other and breathed deeply.

Kaylah said, "That is a lot of books to read before dinner. I am still having a hard time, with my letters and numbers."

Kalub added, "Me too."

Earis said, "I have a cool trick for you."

They both say, "A Trick?"

Earis said, "Yep a trick." He took one of the blue wafers from the bowl. Placed his hand over the Crystal wafer. The first book was, "ABC's, for age 2 and up." He scanned the first book. He goes through all 30 books. Then said, "Did you see what I did."

They both smile and said, "Yeah we understand that."

Kaylah continued, "We have gone through picture books like these with mother. But we did not know that there were teaching books like this."

Earis frowns a little and said, "Of course you would, know how to use these crystal wafers. I am sorry for assuming you did not know."

Kalub and Kaylah chime up, "Earis...we have seen other people use them. But ours are a little different. Thank you for showing us. Now we know how to put stuff into them."

Kalub asked, "Do you still put these," he points to his belly, "Here to read them?"

Feeling better Earis said, "Yes my friend. Come with me and I will show you where the children's books are. So you can do some reading tonight."

After several minutes of helping them. He looked over at Jai and Loora's table. It was almost as if they made a fort out of the books on their table.

Earis thinks to himself, "I need to start filling up my crystal. Or they will start out reading me. I am older than they are and they know so much more than I do."

Earis hurries and started choosing books. Some on building and construction, a huge thick one that says, *"How to fix anything Atlantain."* He spied another one for Lemurian. He saw some interesting titles on the top shelf, he had to get the ladders and climbs up. There is a whole series on *"Building, and flying sky-ship's."* The next shelf down had books on *"Building fixing and using energy weapons."*

Earis realized he can't bring all the book down at once. He remembered he had the crystal wafer on him from earlier. "I better get to work on scanning all these books. It will take me a few days to read all of these. Upon finishing them, he climbed down.

He looked around the library and saw Kaylah and Kalub talking. They are talking about how neat and wonderful to finally be allowed to read books, like mother and father did.

This helped to drive Earis's search for books. He found a section of books on healing. He is really curious about the book titled, *"Micro-cellular regeneration How to rebuild anything with common atoms."* Being in a hurry he decided to scan the whole section.

Jai and Loora noticed Earis running around like a hummingbird. Scanning all types of books.

Loora decided to see what he is scanning. She walked over to Earis and said, "Hi Earis."

"Hi Loora," Earis replied.

"Have you ever used one of those before." She pointed to his crystal wafer which is now purple.

Earis said, "No. Why do you ask?"

Loora said, "We have only been using them two years. But these are a lot like the ones we had in school. Our's at school get deeper in color, once they become black they are completely full."

Earis asked, "Oh, They can fill up?"

Loora said, "Yes Earis they can fill up. I bet these will turn black if they ever fill up all the way. You can also take one and transfers it to another one the same way."

Earis said, "I don't think I will be able to catch up with you two, ever."

With a confused look Loora said, "Why do you say that?"

Earis stares at the ground and said, "Earlier grandfather had me read four books. They were simple learning books on Atlantain's. Your people are able to do things I could never image. The Atlantain's are so much more advanced, then my mind had ever dreamed. I really...really need to catch up on what your people know! I realized today, that I am one little grain of sand. In this giant library."

Loora softly smiled at him while gently rubbing his shoulders. "It is alright Earis. I feel the opposite way you feel. I always wanted to leave my home. I desired a simple life. Hoping and praying for it with all my heart. One day, I could use my gifts and not feel bad or be beaten for it. Your Grandfather, and Grandmother, has helped make my dream come true. My brother also felt the same way.

After our exercise with the hoops today. Me and My brother spoke telepathically, which means my mind to his mind. And we were glad that we could come to the library. So we could read up on all the things you learned and have been practicing for years in your mind.

Jai said, "Your one of the most wonderful children we have ever met, other than Kalub and Kaylah. You have a stronger connection to the Great Wheel, which was our hearts desire. You know how to use your energy and were allowed to use! You are very special to us."

Earis almost broke into tears upon hearing all of this.

Kalub, Kaylah and Jai, feeling so many emotions coming from Earis, they head over to comfort him. Before Earis knows it, he is surrounded by warm hugs. He looked into Loora's eyes, and noticed she was blushing. His heart started to fill with love and joy.

Kalub jumped on his back like a monkey, and started tickling him. All the children join in and had fun tickling Earis. Loora and Kaylah are laughing so hard at Earis snorting laughter they started doing it too.

Kalub and Jai, ran to the other-side of the library shouting, "Boar attack run away."

Kalub also started to sing, Boars are free, the boars are free. No Boar can catch me.

Jai started singing along.

Earis and the girls stopped tickling and laughing at hearing this, and shouted. "We can get you!"

Kalub said, "I am a monkey you can't catch me."

The children race all through the library. Singing and shouting with squeals of delight.

Earis realized his crystal is not full and went back to work. Upon scanning a book, Earis crystal goes black and started to pulse a little in his hand. He put it back into his pocket, grabbed a few more crystals and continued scanning more books.

Joy hearing strange noises, went to the grand staircase and walked upstairs to the Library. She found the voices were coming from the library she went decided to take a looked. The moment her foot hit that last step she knew the children were up to no good.

She slowly and quietly approached the library. She leaned her back against the wall near the libraries door. She thought to herself, "This was the first time she can remember Earis truly fitting in.

She listened to the wonderful sounds of children playing. After a time, she heard a loud crash she jumped from her hiding spot, into view of the library. She pointed to Kalub and asked, "What did you do young man?"

Kalub with a look of shock, said, I am so sorry Joy. We were reading our books and... Earis... got us excited and... We started to have fun. I am sorry Joy; I should have not jumped from table to table like a monkey. Joy locked eyes on Earis who appeared to be the only one studying.

She looked a Jai and asked, "How did all of this start."

Jai looked down at the floor and took a deep breath and said, "I am sorry Joy. Loora went over to Earis and was explaining how to use the library tools. And he was looking really, really sad. I was just talking to Loora before she walked over there to Earis. About how cool, neat and wonderful your son was. And how wonderful it would have been, if we had a parents like you and grandparents like Magoose and Norah.

When I … he took another deep breath… saw Earis looking at the floor so sad. I kind of told all the other children telepathically, let go cheer him up. I kind of told Kalub to jump on Earis back and tickle him.

Joy interrupted him and said, "Thank for clearing it up. So let me get this straight. My son, looked sad, you all went to make him feel better, and the next thing you know. So you children started to act like animals. Tarring up the library and my son at some point," In a questioning voice, "Went back to reading while all you continued to play?"

The children all nodded their heads.

Joy said, "That sounds like Earis." The children were very confused. All of them but Earis stared at her with a dazed confused look.

Joy's smile grow bigger and she said, "I am not like my Mother and Father. I remember what it was like to be a child." She lowers her voice and went to the children. "I will not tell on you this time." She turned around and told Earis, "Keep your nose in your book." Then said, "I will fix the bowl that Kalub knocked to the floor."

Joy picked up the bowl did a little energy work and fix it. Joy asked, "I need you four to do something for me? We have traveled so much with Earis he has hardly ever had friends. If you could sneak up on him again and tickle him again so I can see it happen?"

The children slowly sneaked up on Earis like Jaguars. As soon as she finished restoring the other items, that were broken. She saw Earis jump out of his chair, then was tackled to the floor. The children tickled him until he was giggling so loudly it made Joy laugh as well.

Earis yelled, "Mom!"

"I told you, being serious too much, would get you into trouble. Tomorrow I want to see all you children playing in the ball field. Too much work and too little fun is not a balanced for your Nebra energy."

Earis put his arms out and yelled, "Roar!" Joy does the same. They all gather in a circle and hug each other.

They heard a tapping sound behind them. They see Joy shake from a cold chill that goes from her head to her toes.

They heard Magoose and Norah's voice, "More rocks Joy?"

Joy remembered the sweat lodge and started to laugh.

They look around and saw a smile on Magoose and Norah"s face. Play time is over children. It is time for dinner. There is a new rule for our new home. No running and playing in the Library.

* * *

That evening during dinner.

"Wow did you see that?" Kaylah spoke. "I know who is preparing our dinners," she giggles.

"What?" asked Norah.

Kaylah jumped from the table and ran down the stairs into the kitchen. "Ticky tack, ticky tack, I see you!" she exclaimed.

"Know you don't," said the gnome.

"Yes I do, I see all the little peoples," said Kaylah.

Kalub entered the kitchen and said, "Wow, there are gnome here and fairies too." Kalub said with excitement.

"Oh yes I see them too," said Kaylah, "Thank for helping us."

"You can't see us," the Fairy said as she stomped her foot.

"Well we could at home too. They played with us all the time," said Kalub.

Kaylah spoke, "The wild elves are in danger please help them."

"What do you mean in danger?" asked the fairy as she pointed her stick with the five pointed star on top.

"The volcano is going to burn up Lemuria and the waters are going to rise and sink the whole island," Kaylah said.

"Yes we saw it, that is why we came here," said Kalub.

"Oh my, if what you say is true then we must warn them," said the Fairy.

"I did before we left," said Kaylah. "Toma said he would tell everyone. I am so worried about my friends."

"Not to worry little Kaylah," Came a voice from the other room. "We are here with you. Mother Earth asked us if we would like to come, and help you? I offered to help quickly, so I could be near you. I get to work in the Library!" Said Toma the wild elf, excitedly.

It will be wonderful to help all the children learn and grow. We can help when we have time, in the Gardens, the Library, and even help you learn how to work with the herbs! We are not bond to this place, we have just come to help. We have to rebuild our village and homes here."

"Wow Toma you are here! I am so happy," said Kalub. "Now we can play like we used to and learn even more!"

"Yes I would like to know more about the herbs, that you were teaching us," Kaylah added.

Earis from the far end of the room waved to Toma. As Toma started to wave back.

"What is this racket going on," says a Fairy, with a teal dress, and a golden crown on her blond colored hair. "Human's? You are talking to Human's?"

"They are my friends Queen mother," Toma said.

"We are not friends with human's," the Queen spoke in a ruff voice.

Kalub spoke, "We are not normal human's, we are special, sent by Mother Earth."

"We know what you are," the Queen spoke.

"I am sorry you feel that way," said Kaylah, "We love Toma very much. We were very worried that they did not make it off the island. I am very glad you are here!"

Kalub walked over to the Queen and bowed, "My name is Kalub queen fairy. I only want to play with my friend."

"You can't see me!" She sticks her tongue out and pointed her little royal wand at Kalub.

Kalub spoke in a giggle, "You are funny Queen Fairy."

Kaylah looked over at Kalub with a mean look. Then looked at the Queen fairy and said, "Yes we can. Because we are connected to the earth and the Great Wheel of Life."

"You four, can you see or hear me?" Pointing at the other twins and Magoose and Norah. They did not reply. "Hump," said the Queen. "I suppose it is only special ones, very special that can see us.

The Queen Fairy looked over at Earis and asked, "Are you a boy or a man?"

Earis walked over to the Queen Fairy and bowed. Just like he saw Kalub do. He said, "I am also special Queen Fairy and I am a boy still, in human years."

"Well, I don't like the idea. You are welcomed to talk to Toma if you like. But I don't want this friendship to hinder your work or schooling. Do you understand?" the Queen Fairy said.

"It will not Queen Fairy," they all answered in agreement.

"Then stop looking at me! I will go back to my tree, if you keep staring at me." The Queen Fairy warned.

Kalub, Kaylah and Toma all danced around in the joy of reuniting.

"It is time to finish dinner you three," Norah said.

So Kaylah, Kalub and Earis waved back to Toma, as they walked back up the stairs to the tables.

Norah spoke softly, "Thank you dear small world ones. We truly need your help if we are to prepare these young ones for the fight ahead." Then she walked back upstairs to the table to finish her dinner.

"It is so exciting that Toma is here don't you think," Kaylah said.

"Yes, I am so glad one of our friends made it off the island." Kalub replied.

"How do you three see those people?" asked Jai.

"I would love to see them," said Loora.

"I don't know," said Kaylah, "They just appeared to us one day as we were playing with the monkey's. I got my foot caught in the branches. Toma came and helped me get back down. He has been helping Kalub and I work on his identifying herbs skills." as Kaylah took another bite

.

"We have played together for a few years now," Kalub said.

"There can't be anyone else around when we play. Cause Toma said that our people will think we are not right in the head." Kalub pointed to head and circled his temples.

"Well I really like the Sprites," said Kaylah. "They help me with my herbs and making medicine."

Loora asked, "You know about the herbs? And making medicine? How can someone so young know about the herbs and medicine?"

Kalub said, "I am not young, I am almost 7."

Loora, Jai and Earis started to giggle.

Kaylah added, "Our mother taught us. She uses the herbs in cooking and helping us if we get sick. I can read the herb names and I know what they look like. We can't read the big names, but we can read a little. Things that are important to survive we can read and know how to do it. It was father that was beginning to teach us to read. He would leave simple notes and we both struggled to figure out what it said. Sometimes Nicky my sprite friend, would tell us what it said. Then when he came home we could read it back to him."

"It always made father smile," Kalub giggled at the memory.

"Yeah, he thought we were really smart," Kaylah also giggling.

"Hey Kalub I have an idea," said Kaylah.

"What is that," asked Kalub.

"Well do you remember the teal dress that the Queen was wearing?" asked Kaylah.

"Sure I do," said Kalub.

"Well we are making our pouches tonight why don't we include her dress color and Toma brown vest and pants he always wear?" Kaylah said.

"That is a great idea," Kalub said.

"I really like the red cap the gnomes wear and the green dresses," Kaylah said.

"I think we should include the little people's colors in our bags because we can see them. Like to... honor them... right Magoose?"

Magoose smiled and spoke, "That is a good idea, and little people are a part of the Great Wheel also. It is good thing that you are thinking of including them."

Norah spoke, "Maybe you should find one color that fits the whole kingdom."

"But they are all Mother Natures children," said Kaylah. "What color would all the different peoples be? They are all so different you know. The wild elves are nothing like the gnomes, and the sprites are nothing like the fairies. The tree nymphs are nothing like the brownies."

Kalub giggles, "If they even heard you comparing them. They would probably pock us with their little spears."

"You see Magoose and Norah, all the little peoples are different, like your culture and the other primitives, or even us. We are all human, but not alike at all," Kaylah said.

"Awe but, little Kaylah, we are all alike. We all breathe the same air, we all have energy, we all have ideas, and we all have families too. We have the same fears, and worries," Magoose said.

Kaylah argued, "But they do too. We all have the same emotions, but they are a different kingdom!"

"Yes," Norah said, "Still they have different energy then we do, same but different. They come from the Earth herself, and come from the Universal Life Force. They do not die like humans, they are Immortal Ones. That is the main difference Kaylah."

"Really? I did not know they could not die, wow, that is wonderful don't you think Kalub?" Kaylah asked.

"I don't know Kaylah, to not die, to live forever, is a really a long time, I am not sure if I would like that," said Kalub.

"Maybe so," Kaylah added.

Joy asked, "How long have you seen the little people Earis?"

Earis said, "I have seen them off and on, as far back as I can remember mother. I have never said anything before today. Because as we had to traveled so much, many of the people say if you see them, then there might be something wrong with you. With such a powerful mother and grandparents, and people always on guard around me, I did not want to make our lives more difficult."

"Well children it is time to sit by the fire and make our bags," Magoose said with a smile, to lighten the room.

"Yes I am ready for that," Loora said. "It will be nice to learn how to do things like Kaylah and Kalub can."

"So they all went upstairs to the great room and walk over to the great fire place. They found the couches and sat. Then started to cut out a large rectangle from the paper. Then they add another rectangle that was shorter than the first, so that the top of the first rectangle would fold over to create a flap.

"Wow, we can have it any size? Asked Kalub.

"Oh yes any size you would like and any color you would like as well, said Magoose.

"But why do we need to cut it out on paper first Magoose?" Kaylah asked.

"Because you can use the paper to form the pouch like a pattern. If you would like many colors of fabric, you can, as long as it fits the pattern. Then we will sew the sides up and have your flap to fold over and keep you things safe. Magoose instructed.

So the children finished each of their paper patterns. They walked over to the table with all the fabric and leather. They make choices from what they have learned so far. They picked out the clan animals, colors and things in which they felt connected to.

They each tried to tread a needle, which is a difficult thing to do. They started to work the thread along the side of the bags. It is hard to make even stitches, with the different pieces of material. After a few hours of working the children were tired so they got up, put their things away and said goodnight. They went to their separate clan room.

Kalub and Kaylah opened their adjoining door and laid on their beds. They put their wafer on their tummy and run their energy through it. They read until they finally fell asleep.

Earis took out his wafer set it on the bed. He climbed in and before he can do as Toma instructed him to, he fell fast asleep.

Joy collected the scraps of each of the children's bags. She started sewing little bags for the fairy kingdom. Each one she made was decorated with beads, feathers, and fringe laces. It was late when they all went to bed.

CHAPTER 12

Gnomes of Tech-nock-row-see

Magoose wakes up to begin his new day. He looked out the window and saw the rain was truly pouring down outside. He was disappointed seeing all the rain. There will be no ball playing today. Rain would make it impossible to work the slanted walls to get the balls in the hoops. He started to plan a new day instead.

Kalub and Kaylah wake up and started to prepare for a new exciting day.

Kaylah said, "What do you think we will learn today?"

"Maybe we can learn to play the ball game. Oh that would be fun," Kaylah said.

"Hope we get to work with Joy and learn how to work with our energy better too!" Kalub said.

"Kalub do you feel like you learned last night with the crystal, like we know how to read?" Kaylah asked.

"That is strange question. Yeah I think the words make sense now." Kalub said.

"I would like to scan more books tonight and see if they really do work so we can learn faster and more." Kaylah said.

"I agree. We better get dressed and get to breakfast. I am getting hungry." Kalub said.

Kaylah closed the adjoining door and gets dressed.

* * *

Jai and Loora wake up. "Good morning sister." Jai said.

"Oh yes, It is a wonderful morning. I truly enjoy using the crystal wafer to learn while I slept. It is so amazing." Loora said.

She closed the adjoining door. As they get ready for breakfast.

The children meet at the stairs and go up together. When they saw Magoose, Norah and Joy the children ran over and join them.

Magoose said the Morning Prayer before they all eat.

"What are we doing today?" asked Jai.

"We are going to work more with your energy. It is very important that you children are connected with your direction."

"How do we do that," asked Kaylah?

"We are going to learn to dance and become one with each of your directions and know your power animals."

"That sounds really interesting," said Loora.

"What will it do?" asked Jai.

"Well Jai, it will prove to you, that the Wheel of Life does exist and you need to know for yourself, what animal you are connected to."

"I so believe now Magoose, ever since we made our home," said Jai. "I do believe we are a part of something great. What it is, I don't have a clue."

"I am so proud of you Jai. Believing is a big part, of how energy works." Magoose said.

"It is good to see each of you growing stronger in your energy and beliefs," Magoose smiled.

After they finished breakfast, the children ran upstairs excited to learn and start dancing. They go to the fireplace area and wait.

"Alright everyone I have placed the rattles here on the table before breakfast. Everyone one gets one for each hand," Joy said.

Norah entered room and brought with her a nice hand drum.

Magoose said, "It is time for each of you to listen with your heart and ask for your power animal to come to you. You must halfway close your eyes and just feel the rhythm that Norah and I will keep for you. It is important to ask the directions to come and assist you before your dance comes to you. You already know the east is Quetzal, the south is Jaguar, the west is the whale, and the north is Monkey, and Mother Earth is Crystal, and Father Sun is Dragon. The seventh direction is the Universal Life Force also known as our Creator.

The Universal Life Force Being, is the one who created all things.

Make sure you are using your heart and be in the Love Energy when you calling to them. Any question?" He looked at each of children waiting for any reply. "Are you ready?"

The children began to center themselves with the lessons that Magoose had taught them before. So they feel for their energy and bring it up through their solar plexus to hearts and each in turn said, "Yes."

"Alright, One more instruction. When you here Norah beat the drum four time, then a really fast beat. This sound means for you to stay goodbye to your animal and stop dancing," Magoose said.

Norah started to rhythmically beating the drum. Magoose joined in shaking the rattles to what felt like the heart beat of the Earth Mother.

Joy is close by watching for any signs she might see so she could step in. So if in the dance they might do anything to might hurt themselves.

The children called to the direction as Magoose said. They felt inside them and they started moving, with the rhythm of the drum.

Then the energy shifted and Magoose could see the animals in the room. All the children stated acting like their personal animal.

* * *

Kaylah started to hop up and down like she is a baby Quetzal. Her arms are spread and she looked as if she is almost ready to fly. She started to feel the clarity of things around her. The Quetzal started to teach her.

* * *

Jai is walking around like the Jaguar looking around with the eyes of the predator. He began to understanding the balance of nature. The Jaguar started to teach him.

* * *

Loora felt like a huge whale. She sat breathing with her eyes closed, learning the flow and breath of the ocean. The Great Whale started to teach her.

* * *

Soon Kalub also started to Climb up on the tables and felt the joy of the jungle. Then he sat watching everyone with great curiosity. The monkey started to teach him.

* * *

Earis walked around like a wolf. He is beginning to understand the teaching of the wolf. He saw a Golden Iasha come and enter the wolf. The wolf started to teach him.

* * *

After what seemed like a long time, Norah hit the drum quickly four times and then paused. Then again hit the drum quickly four times again and paused. Then she quickly beats the drum to bring them back.

The children felt themselves returning to normal.

Magoose said, "Well done you all, well done. You did a great job calling the direction and being your animal. It is time for lunch," He is very happy they were able to let go of all fear and allow their animal to show themselves.

Kalub said, "Monkey come and talked with me Magoose! He taught me about the wonders of the jungle. He talked to me about the importance of family and connecting to all things around me."

"This is good Kalub. Monkey has many gifts and lessons for you, I am sure," as Magoose motioned to them to the stairs.

Each of the children start talk about what they saw and experience in their dance, as they walked to the eating area.

* * *

After lunch they all returned to big room upstairs.

"Now I would like for you to get your pouches again and put on your animal on to your pouch," Magoose said.

The children excitedly run over to their boxes that had their pouch in it. They went over to the table and found all the different things that that felt would best show their animal on their pouch. Then one by one they sat on the couch and started sewing and or placed a bead and chose colors that represented their animal on to their pouches.

It is good to learn about their abilities. They worked all afternoon then Magoose spoke up, "We will learn to play the ball game tomorrow while Norah goes back to our home and picks up a few things."

"Ball game," asked Earis?

"Yes it was blessed by Father Sun, so let's all go and enjoy our new play area also" Magoose said.

"That sounds like fun," Kaylah and Kalub whispered to each other.

It is late in the afternoon when Earis asked, "May I go to the library now?"

Joy smiled and nodded her head.

Kalub asked, "I would like to look around some more. We have not seen what is beneath our area yet."

Magoose and Norah smiled knowing what they will find. They nod their heads in approval. The Children put away their medicine bags back into their boxes and head off.

Earis ran up to the Library. He opened the door and saw Toma and a Gnome sitting at the table. He went to the table and sat down near Toma.

Earis speaks to his new friend, "Hi Toma."

Toma looked at Earis and said, "Good afternoon Earis. This is my friend Ralphis. He is from the Gnomes of Technockrowsee. He is one of their crazy inventors.

Ralphis chimes in, "I have just invented the most wonderful marvelous gadget that the world has ever seen. Nothing in the world can compare to my marvelous gadget. It has a five hundred quad ninety processor, two hundred and thirty core processing chip. This baby can spit out information at two zillion tubanons. I don't even think Great Spirit can think this fast," said Ralphis.

Ralphis was talking so fast it makes Earis's head hurt. In his hand he is holding what looked like a bracelet that did not look like anything special.

Ralphis continued, "With my newest masterpiece, one simply needs to place this so the metal touches the neck. Then place ones of these simplistic chips," pointing to the bowl of crystal wafer on the table, "And my wonderful device will transfer the information instantly into ones memory. Here watch." Ralphis grabs a wafer, and ran around scanning books in the library.

Earis looked over at Toma and asked, "Is he... you know... and circled his finger around his temple."

Toma smiled gently and answered, "No Earis he is not crazy. He is just a gnome of Technockrowsee. You see, all they can think about, are Alchemy, Science, Electronics, and building things. They have a hard time with anything else, including brushing their teeth and tying his foot wear. Just bare with him for a little while. He will remember something, running somewhere, or what not, and run off and check on it and you will not see him for awhile."

Upon saying this, Ralphis runs back and slapped the device around Earis neck. "Hold on Earis this should not hurt too much. The Ogre survived my last test.

Earis feels the device squeezing around his neck. Before Earis can even grab his neck the necklace band is gone.

"Quit moving around," said Ralphis. To activate this just say, "Greatest thing in the world. And Tap twice here on the back of your neck." Ralphis tapped the spot two times. And places one of the crystals inside. He tapped it two more times and said, "Best thing in the world."

Earis suddenly see's and tastes colors.

Ralphis yelled, "Human, Human can you hear me."

Toma said, "Ralphis, "Why are you talking gnomish? He will not be able to understand you."

Ralphis said, "Just you wait Toma... Just you wait."

Earis said in gnomish, "Yes I can hear you. Why? Is this thing going to make me deaf?"

Ralphis said in odd dragon tongue, "Have you ever heard the story of cheese? Say Yes if you have heard it please."

Earis said in the same language, "Have you ever heard the story of cheese? Say yes if you have heard it please. What is this weird device supposed to do anyway?"

Toma shuddered, "I don't believe it How... what... did you do to my friend?"

Ralphis started laughing, "I improved him silly elf. Now if I could only figure a way to take it off without removing his head."

There came an odd chirping sounding from his waist. Ralphis pulled a strange piece of metal that has words moving on the surface, Earis noticed.

Toma said, "That looks new."

Earis said, "What is going on? My head feels like it is on fire. My ears are ringing, and I now taste colors."

Ralphis laughed and said, "Simply a bug. I am sure you will learn to live with it, or it will fade, or... well... ah... never mind. It surely could not kill, you could it?"

Earis screamed, "What?"

Before Earis could finish yelling it. Ralphis is gone and a ring of pink powder is on the floor, where he last stood.

Toma sighed deeply and said, "I am sorry Earis it is just the price of being around a gnome of Technockrowsee."

Toma walked behind Earis and said, "Please close your mouth before you bite your tongue off. I don't know what reaction this will give you." Toma tapped two-times, on the spot the gnome pointed to. Pulled out the crystal wafer, that is now orange with blue spots. Takes it to the recycling can and drops it in. "I don't even want to know, what effect that device had on that poor Innocent Crystal wafer." Toma sighed.

Earis asked Toma, "What just happened?"

Toma scratches his head for a few minutes and said, "I think... well... Raphis thing takes all the information from the crystal wafers. And might put it directly into your brain. I don't know what the side effects might be."

Earis pushed his chair back to stand up. He started to feel a little dizzy he said, "I think I am going to"... as he falls on to the floor and goes to a deep sleep.

Toma sighed. He places an empty crystal wafer, into the slot tapped it two time crosses his fingers and said, "Greatest thing in the world." Earis continued to sleep. After a few minutes he tapped two times and pulled the crystal back out. Sat down and tried to read the crystal. It did not change colors, nothing happened to Toma, and the crystal wafer is empty.

Toma sighed with a smile on his face of relief. He thinks to himself, "This is the best one yet. Ralphis really out did himself." He telepathically asked the other little people for help. He wrote a long note to the Adults explaining what happened to him.

Then sat waiting for them to come.

Magoose, Joy and Norah saw a note floating in the air followed by Earis also floating in the air. The note kept brushing Joys hand until she grabbed it. They all follow and watch Earis as he floated down the stairs and into his room and lower onto the bed.

Magoose and Norah saw two more notes appeared on the dresser. They all sigh and groan when they read their notes.

Magoose said, "Poor Earis. Joy remind me if I ever learn or able to talk to gnomes. To always first ask if they are from Technockrowsee."

They all nodded their heads in agreement and laughed.

Toma sighed as the Fairy Queen continued to yell at him. "This is what happens when you talk to Humans."

Toma thought to himself. "I am curious what Kaylah and Kalub are doing."

* * *

While the children ran down the stairs. Jai and Loora get to the bottom first followed by Kaylah and Kalub.

Kalub yells, "No fair you two, your legs are longer. You can take four stairs at once."

Loora laughed, "Fair? You two slid down the railing. How is that fair."

Kaylah protested, "We had to! It was the only way to keep up with you," she said with a big smile on her face.

Jai said, "I bet it was fun too."

The children started to look around the floor. It was kind of dark and a little scary for the youngest twins. Loora accidentally bumps into a glowing crystal on the wall. Instantly the room was bright as day. It was a massive room. The children could see four hallways that looked like the go on forever. There are crystals on the ceiling, and walls light the area like a sunshiny day.

Jai said, "Which direction should we start in. I am not sure where we should go first."

Kaylah went to the left and saw the door on the right it said, "Keep out." she turned to the left and saw another that door said, "All-purpose water room." Kaylah asked aloud, "What does purpose mean?"

The children look at the two doors.

Loora said, "I think like our rooms, when we need something or some place the school builds it. Like it just appears. With the help of the little people, Mother Earth, Magoose, Norah, and Joy or I don't know. Some how they... well...I not sure."

Jai chimed in, "None of that bothers me and in fact I think it is really neat. I have been thinking all morning that we need to learn to swim.

Loora nodded her head.

Jai continued, "The all-purpose water room, must be for us.

Before he could finish speaking Kaylah had already opened the door and walking inside. The other children followed.

Kalub said, "Hello anyone here?" His eyes are drawn to the first moving and glowing statue on the wall. "Wow! It is moving."

The children were all amazed. They saw three large still ponds. On the walls are many different swimming animals. Doing their natural motions of how they swim. The waters are crystal clear. Kalub noticed platforms with many different levels. On the top was a long board. It is made out of strange material.

Loora looked in the small shallow pond to the left at all the different movements of the frogs.

Jai saw in the center pool, on the bottom are many different colors, then he looked harder and found they were different sizes of balls and nets. All the nets have wooden hoops that are angled.

Loora said, "How is it that all of this fits in this tiny room? I just ... Wow!"

A sign flashes behind them drawing their attention.

Kaylah reads it out loud. "Please use soap before entering pool." She saw arrows pointing to two doors. One that said boys, and the other that said girls.

The children went into the shower rooms. Inside there were towels, many drawers with numbers on them. They contain small light weight clothes. There were many boxes on the wall. There were showers with soap. And many toilets, changing rooms and sinks. One wall had a long mirror, brushes, and many other items.

Kalub is the first to come out, still pulling up his clothes as he ran. He stopped dead in his tracks. "Wow!" he yelled. There are balls in the center pools. That must pool for games. On the other end there are all types of round rubbery things with air inside like balloons and long pieces of wood tied with rope. They all hung down from the ceiling waiting to be used.

The children came out hearing Kalubs voice.

Jai said, "I saw the balls before we changed into our swimming clothes."

As he ran Kalub shouted back, "I am going to go dive off the platforms."

Loora and Jai turned to Kaylah and asked, "Could you please help us with our swimming."

Kaylah smiled big and took a deep breath and said, "After wards? If we have time can we please go down to the other end of the room where the slides are at."

Jai and Loora laugh and said, "Yes, that is the second thing we wanted to do."

As Kaylah taught Jai and Loora the tadpole swimming style, as she saw her brother jumping off the platform into the water, like a big rock.

Jai and Loora asked Kaylah, "Which one do we do next. I think we mastered the tadpole it is easy.

Kaylah replied, "I guess... we should follow the pictures on the wall. That is kind of like how mother taught us, when we first learned.

Loora said, I have part of the frog down but how do you keep your head out of the water?"

Kaylah smiled and said, "The trick to the frog, is when your arms go from your head to your legs in the water. You lift your head up and take a breath. When you kick your legs and move your arms forward you hold your breath. Mother always said, "If you don't want to eat water, you need to keep your mouth closed with you kick.

Loora and Jai laugh.

Jai said, "I want to learn how to do the Otter. He just laid on his back and kicks his legs, after the tadpole anyway.

Jai and Loora practiced the frog stroke for a while.

Kaylah while doing the jellyfish, asked, "Do you two think you have the frog down enough that we can go a little deeper in the water."

Jai quickly said, "I don't think I am ready for the dolphin yet. I would rather stay above water."

Kaylah started to slowly move to the deeper part of the pool. She called to the other children and said, "Keep swimming slowly to me. Remember breath when you pull, and hold your breath when you kick."

Jai and Loora promised to do their best and slowly swim towards Kaylah.

Kaylah looked over her shoulders, and see her brother climbing his way to the top of the platform. She thought to herself, "I hope he does not land on his belly this time. It will really hurt."

Jai and Loora slowly swam to Kaylah. And heard a loud splash! They tried to look over but ended up sinking in the water. Kaylah shouted, "Focus! Kick, Kick, Kick. Pull your arms and breath." Upon hearing Kaylah yell, Kalub quickly swam to their side of the pool and made his way to Kaylah.

Kalub jumped into the pool and said, "Look at my arms and legs, stay focused."

Jai and Loora finally get the rhythm of the frog.

Kaylah circled Jai and Loora to her brother.

Kalub said, "Focus on us and lets go back to the shallow end now."

Once they made it back to where Jai and Loora can stand. They all make their way out of the water.

Kaylah turned to her brother and said, "From the sound of your dive brother I thought you went in belly first. But you are not all red."

Kalub replied, "I know better than to do a belly flop from that high of a platform. He turned to Jai and Loora and said to them, "Do you think you are alright to go down the slides and stuff? I think you should be tall enough to stand over there. The deep end is only on one side of the pool."

Jai and Loora look at each other.

Loora said, "If we stay out of deep water, we should be alright? Right Jai?"

Jai nodded his head and agreement.

Kalub started to running to the slides.

The other children all started laughing. The back of Kalub's legs were all red and looked sunburned.

Kaylah said, "I guess he miss judged how many times he could twist."

Loora asked, "I thought you and your brother where masters of swimming and diving."

Jai said, "Yeah, I thought both of you know how to do everything in the water."

Kaylah smiled brightly and said, "Well you see, if you don't know how high you are above the water and practices a few times. It is hard to know how many twists and turns you can do before you hit the water. It is kind of like when you throw a knife. You have to know how many times the blade will turn before it hits the target. It is very hard to master throwing a knife. The same is true of diving. Swimming is easy once you learn the strokes. I also would never call me or my brother Masters! We are still learning just like you. We have just been doing it a longer time. Did I say that right? And do you know what I mean?"

Loora said, "I think so. But we have never thrown a knife before. I guess it takes a lot of practice to learn to dive then."

Kaylah smiled and nodded. She adds, "It will be a little while, before you two should even try it. You can get hurt bad if you don't know what you are doing. Can we just worry about getting you two to swim? And learn your animals first?"

Jai and Loora reply together, "Agreed."

Kaylah tag Loora and said, "Ticky tack, ticky tack one, two, three. Jai is frozen you can't catch me."

Kaylah took off running, while Loora counted to three, Tags Jai and they race after Kaylah.

* * *

Joy looked up from her sewing and said, "Do you think we should go and cheek on the little ones?"

Norah said, "It would be nice to soak in the hot springs a little. They are playing in the water play room."

Joy asked, "How do you know where they are?"

Norah said, "I always follow those children! They are young and full of life. Kalub and Kaylah are so innocent and curious, trouble always find them easily."

They walk to the bottom of the stairs and find the water room and walk in.

Joy saw the two oldest children running to the slide play area. And shouted, "Do you really think you should be running around water?"

Jai and Loora slow down and greet them and said "We are sorry!"

Joy and Norah go to the center of the room to find the adult changing and cleaning rooms.

Norah said, "It is nice the woman is opposite of the mans."

Joy nodded her head in agreement.

Once they are done changing into their swimming clothes and washing up.

Norah said, "It is just as I hope it would be."

On the wall nearest the woman's room, is a large waterfall. Many different colored stones cover the entire wall on that side. She saw the steam coming off the water. Some of the many pools have more steam then others.

Joy loves the fact that there is a higher pool labeled teachers only!

They make their way to the teacher's Hot spring. The teacher's Hot spring was located in the center of the Hot Springs. Water runs down on many sides. There were as many colors as crystals and gems, as a rainbow.

Joy saw a small panel of different colored crystals in the smooth marbled edge of the pool. All around the edge just above the water are many flat clear gems. She notices that each child has their own gem and underneath each gem has the word rescue with a button and a crystal on each side. Joy went over to the crystals picks up the blue chip and puts her feet into the warm perfect temperature water and started to read.

Norah gentle slides into the pool. The warm water surrounded her. She felt the gentle pulse of the heat on her skin. Norah closed her eyes for a moment and said, "Thank you, all of you wonderful creatures and beings that have helped make this possible. Mother Earth, I am so blessed that you have allowed us with the help of all the other Guardians. I do not feel worthy, of such great gifts. Yet every day I gain a deeper understanding of why this is necessary. From the deepest parts of my heart I thank you for all you have and may grant us in the future. So mote it be."

Joy said, "So mote it be. Mother, I can keep an eye on the children as you relax. If you would like that?"

Norah said, "Thank you so much my wonderful child. Sometimes it is hard to remember that you are all grown up. A very powerful being and wonderful mother and teacher. I am so very glad we will see more of each other."

Joy smiled and said, "I love you too Mother. It looked like all these different crystals are some how watching each child. The red crystal will start to flash if it senses trouble with that child. The button seems to be a rescue device.

It said, *Fully tested and functional, The Greatest system ever built.*"

Provided under the strong urging of Mother Earth by the Gnomes of Technockrowsee.

"Mother I am happy about this and scared at the same time," Joy said nervously.

Norah sat straight up strait and asked "Who built this?"

Joy cleared her throat and passed her Mother a chip and said, "Go to the last book mother, it is funny."

They both watch a moving book. That the gnome called a Vit-Tee-O. This Vit-tee-o shows brownies and Ogre's being bounced off walls, ceiling and floors. One image is of an Ogre being eaten by a giant squid. With the head gnome commenting maybe it would not be a good idea, to put all the creatures of the oceans in here.

As Mother Earth and Mother Nature sigh rubbing their temples. At the very end they see everything working in perfect harmony and balance. No one is hurt and everything worked as described in other books. Mother Earth and Mother Nature thanked the gnomes and other creatures that helped build the water room.

Father time who came to help build the room said, "I am going to rest," as he teleported away.

As the two of them are going through the other books they hear a quiet beep, beep, beep. They look at the two crystals beeping and see Jai and Loora near the deep end of the slide area.

Joy pushed the button to see what would happen. A pair of dolphin rush into the deep end and pull Jai and Loora back to the shallow area.

Then the dolphin suggested the children go on the moving water around the outside edge of the water room. They tell them there is a wonderful small water fall and some rapids ready for them to try.

Jai and Loora do as the Dolphins suggested and went to the area.

Joy looking at this and was relieved that nothing horrible happened to them. Then saw Mother Earth's stamp of approval on the button.

Joy and Norah heard, the two dolphins speaking throw the crystal, the Dolphins said, "Disaster diverted. Is there anything else dolphin team two can to do for you?"

They replied, "Thank you for showing us how this worked. Have a great day, you are released."

The dolphins said, "It is a honor and privilege to help the Nebra's." as they disappeared.

Jai and Loora approached the water falls. As soon as the warm hot water hits their skin they let out an "Aww! That feels strange."

Kalub and Kaylah looked around for them. They saw the top half of Joy, sitting in the high Hot Springs. They grow very worried and start calling out for Jai and Loora. They are worried they went under the water. That had been so caught up in all the fun, they forgot about Jai and Loora. They never even noticed or heard anyone else come in.

The children shout together, "Where are Jai and Loora? We don't see them anywhere. Help us find them please!"

Joy smiled at them to reassuring them that all is alright. "They are fine" she said. They decided to take a trip on the lazy river water.

Kaylah shouted back, "Oh, that narrow water that circles the room is a ride?"

Kalub speaks up, "Can we ride it too? I am tired and I am getting really hungry."

Joy said with a laugh in her voice, "Behind you two there are some circle disks that float. All you need to do is get one put it into the water, get in and it will carry you around the room. You will find, many surprises as you go. You are very smart children."

The Young twins shouted back, "Thank you."

When they get back to where they started, Magoose had came in. He found a shell next to the door. He lifted it up and spoke into it. "It is dinnertime if any of you water children are hungry."

Norah said, "Does that include us adults as well old man?"

Magoose blushed when he saw his beautiful wife and said, "You are a child at heart right?"

Everyone got out and went into the changing-clean up rooms. They all met back up with Magoose at the entrances door.

Joy asked, "How Is Earis?"

Magoose said, "Hungry, he is up in the eating room waiting for us."

"That is wonderful news Father. Thank you for healing him." Joy said.

Magoose replied, "I could not take the device off of his neck. But I did stop his headaches."

They all went up to the eating area. The children ran over to Earis and started asking questions about what happened and why Magoose needed to heal him.

Earis explained, "I ran into a strange gnome, and got a bad headache. Next thing I know I woke up in my room with my grandfather there and my headache were gone. Everything is still a little fuzzy as to… about how I got back to my room.

That night as the children were going to bed.

Earis thought to himself, "I might as well use this thing while I can, before it puts me to sleep again." He inserted the crystal he had scanned at the library into the gnomes device embedded in his neck and said the words, The Greatest device in the world and tapped on it twice. Which started the flow of information into his memory.

CHAPTER 13

The New Comers

The next morning everyone was up and ready to play the ball game Magoose talked about.

"Good Morning Children," Magoose sang out.

"Good Morning, Father Magoose," The children sang back.

After breakfast Magoose spoke, "let us go out to the ball field, so we can learn how to play our new game."

The children were excited and run out the door, across the field, down to the ball court and looked around.

They found steps going down in to the playing field located at each end of the ball court.

There was a door off the bottom stair with a sign on the door that said, "Team preparation room." The children walked in and saw strange padded clothing placed on shelves along the wall. There were more balls in boxes far on the other side of the wall. Sticks and Bats were placed on the back side of the wall. Each shelf was labeled for different sizes. Down the center of the room were benches for lots of people to sit.

Magoose and Norah walked into the changing area. Magoose started to go through all the different shelves. He took off different sizes of protective pads for each of the children and passes them to the children.

"This my children is how you put them on. He carefully wrapped a protective leather padded skirt around his body that fit just under his waist to just below his bottom. It was cut so that the skirt part flowed past his bottom in the front and back but the sides were cut higher that was just below the hip. Then Magoose put on a sash that wrapped around his hip area many times to hold up the skirt and protecting his hip area.

He spoke to the children, "Please be sure you have your padding on your hips because this is where you will hit the ball."

The children followed Magoose's direction and did the same. The sashes were strange to tie. They wrapped the sash many times around them to hold the skirt in place.

Magoose then put on padding on his elbows, knees and shins. The children followed his direction.

Magoose put on a protective hat so that the ball would not knock him out. The children did the same.

When that was done they were ready to go out and learn how to play the game.

The ball field was shaped like a capital I. It has a long dirt field about 10 meters wide and 30 meters long with a knee high step full length along both sides. At the top of the step was a slanted wall that went up for about 4 meters at a 30 degree angle. Above this area was another wall about 2 meters straight up and down. This was out of bounds all around which protected the watchers above. There were benches all around the ball field so people could watch the action down below.

On the tall vertical wall was a goal hoop. It was mounted in the vertical position so the ball had to pass thru horizontally through a small hole. 2 meters above that hoop was another hoop of the same shape and size. The lower hoop was good for one point, the higher one scored 5 points.

They all gathered to the center of the field.

There were many balls lying around the ball field. Magoose started picking some up and teleported them back into the preparation room. When most of the balls were picked up Magoose went to each person and handed them a hollow ball to play with.

Magoose tossed a ball into the air and said this is the ball we will use to play the game. This one is much lighter than the bone breakers used in competition for the real games.

It is normally made of solid rubber with morning glory mixed in, to give the ball the right bounce to play with. This one is hollow and weighs about 3lb so we will use this to practice with. This ball is the same size as the bone breakers and will help us to learn about the game and how to control the ball with our bodies and our energy forces.

We don't have enough players for a full team on each side but we will have fun anyway.

You never touch the ball with any part of your body except your hips area. You may only use energy if you are a Sky man.

With a full team each team chooses two who are the "Sky man," they try to score points when the ball is passed to them. Sky man can use only use their hips to score points. They bounce the ball back and forth until a goal can be made. All missed tries cost them a point. If the ball goes back to the playing area the ball is then played by the under man. In Nebra game they can only pass the ball thru the goal using their energy. That is their main strength to score points. If the ball is lost and bounces out of their area again the play will continue with the under man.

We will talk about the best plays to score points later.

The next two to four players are called "Steppers." They can go anywhere on the step area. They can either score solo points in the lower hoops or pass it to sky men. They may only use their hips to pass the ball. In children's play they only use the lower hoops to play with.

The final two to six players are called the "Under Men." Their job is to get the other team to create a foul. The first player tosses the ball to the opposite side of the ball field to the waiting team. The ball may only bounce once. If it bounces twice you lose a point. If it bounces more it is a foul. If they ball is rolling on the ground you can try to pop it back up for continue play. If it stops rolling it is also a foul. The other team then hits the ball using only their hip to the other side of the court. This continues until one team fouls the ball. Fouling area is any wall area around this court. They also try to get the other team to hit the lower wall with the ball. This is known as a "foul," when they do they lose possession of the ball. The ball is then thrown to the step men who work it to the sky men.

You will lose a point every time you foul and miss the hoop.

"Can you remember all that" Magoose asked.

They all nodded their head and said, "Yes!"

"The first thing you must learn to do is to pass the ball around and try to hit your ball high up the wall where the step man will be."

Magoose dropped his ball and on the first bounce he hit the ball with his hip towards the steps. The ball bounced back to him and he hit it again using only his hip area. The ball went high up the wall each time he hit it. When the ball came back to him he caught it and asked the children if they would like to try.

The children said together "We can do that easy".

It was not as easy as it looked when Magoose did it.

"When you are ready we can learn to pass the ball to each other," Magoose said.

It was not as easy as it looked when Magoose did it.

"All of you must practice this until you can do it well," Magoose said.

After practicing for a while, Magoose said, now you need to practice moving the ball with your energy only.

Hit the ball with your hip up toward the hoop then change it's path using only your energy to make it go thru the hoop. Do you understand, he said?

Watch each other to see who is best on your team, they will be the sky man, Magoose said.

The children said they understood and began to practice.

As they practiced they saw that Kalub and Loora had the best energy control of the ball.

It was difficult to choose step man because they had all learned to move the ball with their bodies very well.

Magoose said, "Because we don't have enough people for a full team. We will use the second best ball controllers as forwards. They will help the sky man with energy as well as being step man.

Joy and Earis were chosen as step men. This left Magoose and Norah as, the under men.

They practiced the combination moves to make a score until lunch time.

Magoose asked, do you think you are ready to try to play a real game after lunch? They all said "yes, Yes, Yes!

How would you feed about the Boys against the Girls Magoose said?

"Yeah, that sounds good!" They all agreed.

They raced back to their home to find a wonderful lunch waiting for them in the dining hall.

Everyone was excited to play the game and they ate their lunches quickly and hurried back to the Ball Court.

* * *

Magoose and Norah stood back to back. Magoose held out seven fingers, Norah guessed the number.

Jai spoke up, "If the girls go first then we boys get to choose the Goals. We want the Jaguar rings. The girls can have the Macaw rings."

Everyone agreed.

Magoose spoke up, "We all have 4 players so I am changing up a few rules just for us to play today. Norah and Joy are the under man and Earis and I are underman. We will try to foul each other. One of us under man will need to help the step man to get the ball to our sky man."

Joy spoke up "I will help Kaylah with that."

Magoose nodded his head. I will help Jai. Earis my wonderful grandson would be too tall to help Jai. Now there needs to be a step man to help our sky man. So Jai you will need to help Kalub and Kaylah you will need to help Loora. The Helpers may not make the Hoop only help. Agreed?

Everyone agreed.

Earis throw the ball to the girls and the game began. Earis was the first one to foul the ball so the girls got to start inching the ball to the sky man. Norah was able to pass it to Loora she passed it to Joy who passed it back to Loora. Loora could not yet pass it to Kaylah so she passed it back to Joy. Joy hit it harder and Loora was able to pass it to Kaylah. Kaylah worked her energy as the ball came to her. She tried to put it through the hoop but it missed and went back to Loora. Loora tried again to pass it to Kaylah who this time was able to push the ball throw the hoop. The girls all cheered.

"Five points for us," Kaylah yelled out.

"Minus one for a missed try!" Jai called out.

The ball was now in the boys court and Magoose hit it high to Earis who bounced it high into the air near the goal. Kalub connected with the ball and guided it smoothly through the hoop.

"Nice shot Kalub," Magoose yelled out.

The ball went back to the girls side of the court and this time Joy hipped it to Kaylah who bounced it to Loora who guided it smoothly thru the hoop for another goal.

The ball then returned to the boys ground man Magoose. He had a clear easy hip shot it to Jai who passed it to Kalub but this time the ball bounced back to Jai who took a wild shot with his hip and it went through the lower hoop for 1 point.

The ball was returned to the girls and Joy passed it to Kaylah. She tried to use her energy on the ball like Loora did but instead she made a strong wind which blew the ball back to the boys side where Jai quickly passed the ball into Kalub's waiting energy stream and thru the hoop for five points. .

The boys cheered at the goal and double possession. Earis bounced the ball to Jai who also tried to use energy to put it in the top hoop. Loora deflected the ball with her energy and it bounced back to Earis who passed it back to Kalub who had formed an energy funnel to guide the ball easily thru their hoop for another five point score.

STOP Magoose said, "I think I was not clear enough with the instructions.

Sky men are the only ones who can use energy to put the ball in the hoop or block the other team from making a shot. Understand?"

"You mean Jai and I can reach out with my energy to block a shot or stop the ball, Kalub said?

"No only Kalub can, that is what I mean." But remember Loora can block as well, she is a sky men too, Magoose said.

That made the game more interesting.

Norah passed the ball to Joy who was not ready and she missed the ball and it bounced back to Norah. Norah did not expect the ball to return and she missed the ball as well and it went to the boys side of the court.

Magoose quickly passed it to Earis, he was not expecting the pass and missed as well. The ball bounced back to the girl's side and without any guiding energy went thru the lower hoop for one point for the girls team.

Norah used her hip the ball to Joy who passed it quickly up to Kaylah. In the excitement Loora added her energy to the ball in play. The two energies collided and in the excitement Loora lost control of her energy and it rained very hard on the court for a moment. The shot was missed.

The ball was made of smooth rubber and a little water makes it difficult to control . Magoose tried a hip pass to Earis, it was slightly off and Earis tried to correct its path but it flew out of control. Jai tried using his energy to control the balls flight, he did pass it on to Kalub but it had burst into flame. Kalub, in control of his energy, guided the flaming orb thru the center of the hoop.

"Time out everyone, it seems we need a new ball" Magoose said as he put out the flames.

The game continued.

Norah bounced the new ball to Kaylah but she missed it. The ball bounced off the wall to Joy. Joy hit the ball high into the air and near the goal. Loora surrounded the ball with her energy. She concentrated very hard but Jai on the other court was trying to block her shot. Kaylah saw Jai working his energy and put up a blocking shield against him so Loora could stay in control of the ball. Loora, carefully this time, made a tunnel of wind and placed the ball in the center which carried it thru the hoop.

Magoose passed the ball to Earis who bounced it to Jai. Loora sent her energy to Jai to make him lose his connection with the ball, Jai felt her energy effect his, and passed the ball to Kalub who found it easier to control. Kalub focused on the ball and guided it to the wall, it bounced and went thru the high hoop.

Norah tried for the ball but she slipped and it bounced to Joy who passed on to Kayla. This time she was prepared for Jai's energy, and added some of her own, then sent it back to the boy's side of the court. The boys scrambled to get out of the way of the incoming fireball. With the distraction it was easy for her to put the ball thru their goal hoop.

Magoose slipped and fell on the muddy field and missed the returning ball. The ball bounced off the step back to the girl's side of the court then bounced again out of play. Magoose won the number guess this time and took back control of the ball. He passed it hard to Earis, whose muddy feet slipped sending him down the slope, across the step and face down on the muddy ground. The ball bounced back to the girl's side, again.

Joy recovered the ball and passed it, too hard, it hit the wall hard. Kayla managed to get control again and passed it on to Loora but Loora was laughing so hard at Earis that she lost control of the ball and it bounced away back to the boys side of the court.

The Earis took control of the ball this time and he was able to pass it back to Jai who held the ball in mid air as he passed it to Kalub. Kalub missed the ball, it struck the wall and bounced back to Earis. Earis tried to pass to Jai but missed and it bounced away to the upper wall near Kalub again. This time he controlled the ball with his energy and made the goal.

Girls side again; Nora slipped in the mud as she passed the ball to Joy. The pass was to low. Joy was barely able to get underneath it to push it up. Kayla was ready she controlled the ball with her energy and slid it through the hoop.

The game continued until the sun was starting to set.

Magoose stopped the game and said, "we can not play at night it is taboo. The girls win by three points. Good Job ladies. Please put your gear back on the shelves in the preparation area, but first, line up gentlemen we need to congratulate the ladies before we clean up and go up for dinner."

So the boys lined up and put their right hand out as the girls ran past them slapping their hands. It was a good game.

They washed up in the preparation area before they went back inside for another wonderful dinner where the laughed and shared their thoughts of the game and their energy "play".

After dinner Kayla asked, "May we go to the hot water area now Magoose?"

Magoose looked at his wife and everyone was in agreement. The game had created sore muscles and a few bruises. They could use Earis healing hands and a good hot soak. They all went down to the water room and enjoy the evening.

* * *

A few very busy days passed in their new home. Earis had really surprised everyone. He had passed every test, both mental and with energy, on the first try. It was as if he had done it many times before. None of the other children understood how or why he was able to learn things so fast. They either forgot or never knew about Ralphis's "Greatest Invention Ever".

Kalub and Kaylah started going to bed earlier, with their memory chips fully loaded, than they normally did. It amazed everyone how quickly they are able to read and write in many languages. They are reading books beyond even what the older twins could read.

One day, while Jai and Loora spent the day learning about herbs and plants, they formed a plan to find out how, Kaylah and Kalub were learning so fast.

They would use the young twin's love of candy to find out their secret. They found out they were using the crystal wafers in their sleep. The crystals were a wonderful tool for them. They learned faster and remembered what they learned.

The children's thirst for knowledge during this time was unstoppable. Toma was very busy keeping the library organized. The library tables were covered each day with books the children scanned and studied. They learned about different cultures, their languages and stories, about history and strange words they had never heard of. They learned much more about their energy and how to use and control it. The use of the crystal chips helped the adults and little people brush up on and expand their knowledge. Kaylah had taught the adults and the little people Tomas secret about using the crystals to learn while they slept. Kaylah had traded Toma's secret for the lessons on how to make her favorite candy.

They enjoyed learning about the ball game and were getting good enough to start small games against each other when they had time.

* * *

It was almost lunchtime when they heard a voice, which thundered through the whole school. Welcome Home Master Druids. Your clan is the Green Dragons.

The Master Druids looked at each other and walked up to the large iron wood door that was at the top of the entrance steps. They opened the door and said in a loud voice, "Hello? Hello," is there anyone here?"

"We are in here," said Magoose.

They heard footsteps and then they saw Magoose and Nora. They were dressed in long robes that nearly touched the floor with hoods that covered their heads. As they approached Magoose said, "Welcome Master Druids, I am called the Magoose."

"Welcome Master Druids, I am called Norah, and who are you, where are you from?" Norah asked.

"I am Elder William and this is my wife Elder Ann." They said as they pulled back the hoods from their heads which showed their long blond hair and fair skin.

Under her dark robe Elder Ann was wearing a blue skirt with another blue wrap around her waist with a long end hanging down in front. Nora had never seen shoes made like the ones Ann was wearing, *"very different,"* she thought. On her top Ann wore a brilliant white shirt over her strong chest.

Elder William spoke first, "We were, hiding from the Atlantain's in the black forest, when Mother Nature found us. She said it was time for us to go home, then surrounded with a ball of light and sent us here. We were standing on your first step with the crystals on either side. The steps led us to your door. No one greeted us so we came inside out of the rain."

Norah and Magoose, followed by everyone else, slightly bowed their heads but kept eyes on the elders. They formed a diamond with their hands, touching first finger and thumbs together as a sign of greeting and respect, and then said together, "Blessed be the Elders. May you live long and well."

These are our beloved grandchildren" Norah said, touching them.

The twins here are Kalub and Kaylah, and the older twins are Loora and Jai, and this tall handsome young man is Earis, our grandson".

"Hello," said the children.

Norah said, "Please, come sit by the fire and warm yourselves," motions them to the couches by the large fireplace in the great room.

William and Ann enjoyed the fire for only a moment when there was a very loud bell that chimed for the first time. It was loud enough to be heard everywhere, with sound to spare. They all jumped as it was the first time it had rung.

"What was that and where did it come from," Magoose said.

Toma showed himself to Kaylah and said "That is the lunch bell, clever right?"

Kaylah and Kalub laughed and said, "Yes that is very clever."

Then Toma disappeared back down the stairs.

Kalub walked over to Norah and said, "Toma said it is the lunch bell."

"The what," Norah looked puzzled.

"The bell is to tell us it is lunchtime," Kaylah spoke up.

Jai said, "I don't need that, "My stomach tells me when it is lunch time."

The children all laughed at Jai's words.

Magoose and Norah let out a heavy breath. "Well then I guess is it time for lunch children, let us go," said Magoose.

"Please join us Elders," as he motioned for them to follow.

They all went downstairs to eat. On the table were many new kinds of food. There was stew with lamb, carrots, and potatoes in a tomato broth. There was rice with mushrooms, and corn with butter dripping off of it. There was hot round bread and a large picture of hot Chukwah with milk.

Magoose stood and gave a blessing to the Four Directions and to Mother Earth and Father Sun. Special thanks was given for sending them new friends, and new foods. He thanked the little people for their time and energy to prepare everything.

Norah asked the elders, "What do you teach?" William said, "I teach astronomy, and my wife teaches alchemy."

"Alchemy? What is that," asked Loora.

"Alchemy is the making of medicine, and oils, incenses, potions, and things of that nature. I teach how to combine the essence of different plants and minerals together to create what I need for nearly anything. I also teach how to produce alloyed metals and how to grow crystals."

"Wow" said the children. Kalub said, "I want to learn all that stuff."

"Me too" said Kaylah.

Loora, Earis and Jai shook their heads in agreement.

"What is this Norah?" Kaylah asked as she pointed down to her food.

"I am not sure," Norah answered.

William answered her question, "It is called lamb stew where we come from."

"Oh," said Kaylah, it sure tastes good. They all agreed and enjoyed their lunch.

Loora broke the silence of eating and said "We saw some class rooms on the 2nd story upstairs. They have living places attached to them too."

"Really," said William, "and you have no teachers?"

"Not yet," said Norah, you are the first to arrive.

"Mother Nature said that there will be many children and teachers just before the Earth changes," said Magoose.

Ann looked up from her bowl and gasped, "You know about the earth changes?"

Magoose answered, "Yes, the youngest twins had dreams and warned their parents."

"Our children are," Magoose paused, "Very special."

"They are energy workers and hold great places on the Great Wheel of life. Kaylah can create pure love and star energy. Jai can create a wonderful fireball. Loora is wonderful with weather, she can create a hurricane, if she really gets mad."

Kaylah interrupted and said, she "Needs a little work at controlling it though Magoose" she said with a lowered voice.

Magoose nodded in agreement, while Loora blushed.

Magoose continued, "Little Kalub over there can use the pure energy to do many things. I never in my life saw anyone create pure energy like Kalub can," Magoose said proudly.

"Earis can do many things, shielding people from harm and healing the sick and injured were the things he showed us first".

William looked up at Magoose. "I have seen the signs in the stars about this earth shift". The planets are lining up to cause this shift of energy," he said.

"There is a new set of stars in the sky that I believe it is part of this shift. We already know about the weather machine created by the Atlantain's. They have been causing a great deal of trouble with it. They have created a massive amount of ice in both Polar Regions. That is causing this planet to cool down. I believe we could go into a massive ice age."

Kalub spoke up, "Well I know the volcano is going to blow up our island."

Kaylah added, "And there will be a great wave of water that will sink it."

"Island?" William asked, "What Island is this?"

"Our old home Lemuria," Kalub and Kaylah both said in harmony."

"That was our home to," Loora and Jai said together.

William and Ann looked at each other and turned to Magoose.

William said, "Lemuria was said to be myth. We thought that island was gone a long time ago." "Magoose spoke, "I visited there a few years ago, and the children were there few weeks ago."

"Are the Lemurian's as advanced as the Atlantain's?" Ann asked.

"Oh yes, but they live with nature not against it. Lemurian's are a peaceful people for the most part." Magoose said.

"Not all of them are", Loora said,

"Most of them are good people who love nature. They are very kind and work in harmony and have developed great skills for using energy. They are not seekers of power, they are just like the rest of us primitives, just loving nature and living a good life to the best of their abilities. It will be a great loss to all of humanity when it sinks. They have beautiful music and libraries greater than ours here. Their crystals will be lost and only a memory. I would be happy for Atlantis to sink but the two islands are somehow connected, what happens to one will happen to the other." Norah added.

"What is a black forest?" Jai asked.

"It is not really black, it is a name of a place on the other side of the world. We have many people that work with magic and we worship the Gods and Goddess of earth and sky. We are called Druids," William answered.

"Wow, I have never seen Druids before, but it Sounds like what Magoose and Norah are. We call them Medicine people or Nebra's." Jai said.

Kalub asked, "What is magic? And how do you use it?"

Ann spoke, "We use all of nature's energy, and then we focus it and use it to do what we need to do."

"Oh, I understand that," Kalub giggled, "You are energy workers like us."

William and Ann looked at each other and nodded their heads, yes, Kalub I guess you could call us that. We have special Gods and Goddess that we work with.

Kaylah asked, "Oh you mean like Father Sun and Mother Earth?"

William answered, "Yes, I think we use different names but it sounds the same.

"Loora asked, "Do you believe in the Great Wheel too?"

Ann looked surprised at her knowledge of the Great Wheel and said, "Why yes, the Great Wheel is the basis of all our beliefs.

"Oh, Jai said, "So why do you call it by strange names, if you are just like us?

"Probably because we did not grow up here." William said.

"On our side of the world it is called by a different name. I think you are right it is all the same," he said smiling with a new understanding.

"Well it is time for us to go back to the great hall. There is more to learn today," said Norah.

"I love learning," Kalub and Kaylah said together.

"Us too," Loora, Earis and Jai agreed.

This is the first time in their lives Loora and Jai's life they truly do love learning and they had never been trained with so much love before.

"Are we going to work more on controlling our energy? I really need to work on controlling that ball." Jai asked.

"Yes we are Jai, it is afternoon now, and I think it is time to learn to control some of your energy." Magoose smiled and winks.

"Energy?" William asked.

"Yes we all have energy in our bodies which we use to heal, sense the things around us, for protection, and to fight off enemies to, if we have to," Magoose said.

"You mean use Magic and you teach these children how to use it? William asked.

"I don't know what Magic is, we are learning to use all the energy that is in and around us which is given to us by Mother Earth and Father Sun. We have ceremonies, dances, journeys, and learn to live with nature and use Her power. It has been our way for many, many generations."

"Everyone here can use energy," Norah spoke. "It is a choice that people make. You can either flow it, or bury it deep inside you, but you still have it."

"Mother Earth called this, the Land of Nebra," Loora spoke up. "It is place for us special energy people, who choose to use our energy with heart for the good of everyone. Here we are learning to control it and use it for the for the highest good."

"Nicely said," Norah commented, smiling at Loora.

"Alright now children it is time to go upstairs." Magoose said.

The children got up and ran upstairs looking forward to a new lesson.

Magoose was right behind him. "Alright now, over here please. That right, now everyone hold hands and form a circle," Norah said.

"Today we will be learning how to pass our energy balls safely. It is important to learn all energies so that you can be ready for anything that comes at you. Are you ready?" Magoose asked.

The children were excited and said, "Ready."

"Alright, Jai you first," Magoose said.

So, Jai created his fire ball. Then passes it to Loora. Loora passed it to Kalub

and Kalub to Kaylah. Kaylah passed it to Professor Williams, and He passed it to his wife, she passed it to Magoose and He passed it to Norah and Norah passes it to Joy who passed it to Earis. Earis passed it back to Jai.

"Well done everyone. Now, Jai make it stop," Magoose guided.

Jai had trouble putting it out until he remembered what Kaylah said, and just asked it to stop, it did.

Everyone worked with the energy balls they created and passing them around until it was dinner time.

Then in the distance they heard in a loud voice speaking. It echoed through the whole school. It began to speak, "Water, Fire, Air, Green Dragon, Earth, Fire, Air, Blue Dragon!

They all looked at each other in surprise and ran to the entrance door where the sound had come from.

When they opened it they found a line of children followed by adults on the entrance steps with the voice calling out their personal elements.

"Oh my, it looks like we have a few more children now" Magoose stated.

"A few?" "There are a lot of children!" "We are not alone anymore", Loora said.

"Yeah," Kalub and Kaylah said together.

"This way" Loora said and motioned to the children. "Come on this way we have plenty of food and a warm fire."

So the children eagerly followed her into the great room.

"Kalub Kaylah," Loora asked, "Would you please show our new friends the way to the dining hall?"

"Kalub and Kaylah hurried to the stairs and said "follow us" and waited for them to follow them to the dining room.

"This is going to be more fun now, don't you think Kaylah, said Kalub?"

Kaylah said, "Yes I like the idea of having a lot of friends to help us fill our lonely rooms."

"We can still be together right Kaylah?" Kalub asked.

"Sure we can. I know there will be a lot of children that would like to stay with each other," Kaylah said.

When the children arrived in the dining hall they found steaming pots of stew and loaves of bread waiting for them on the large tables. Small bowels and with silverware were set for each child.

Go ahead and sit down Kalub said. "There is room for everyone."

It did not take them long and they began to eat as if they had been starved.

There were a few grownups and children alike in the hall.

It looked like the school could really begin; they had teachers and now students.

Magoose and Norah sat back down at their table and the children follow them.

William and Ann had a look of shock on their faces. Not believing how easy everything was being done. It is as if these people knew what was going to happen.

"This is so excited don't you think?" Kalub said.

"Yes I do," Jai said as he looks around. "They are all here or at least most of them are, it looked like, teachers and students both. Today is a great day," Jai finished.

Loora is just beaming at everyone.

Some of the children looked scared, and some look happy.

Magoose stood on the bench part of the table and said, "Welcome everyone. I am Magoose. I am the head of this Learning center and your new home."

As Magoose looked around and said, "I will assume that the adults here are teachers."

The adults started to nodded their heads.

"That is wonderful. All teachers after you finish eating will go to the 2nd floor and find your classroom and living quarters."

"All children if you were called an element will go downstairs and find your clan room. Clan rooms are the following. East is Air, Quetzal is your animal, your head of your clan is Kaylah." Magoose Pointed to Kaylah to stand.

Kaylah stood and sat back down.

"South is Fire, Jaguar is your animal, your head of your clan is Jai." Magoose pointed to Jai.

Jai stood up and sat down.

"West is Water, the whale is your animal, your head of your clan is Loora,"

Loora stood and sat back down.

"North is Earth, Monkey is your animal, and your head of your clan is Kalub."

Kalub stood and waved to everyone and sat back down.

Green dragon and Blue dragon is up on the third floor with Norah and myself.

"All clan rooms are down these stairs please take time to get to know everyone. This place is your new home. We would like you to feel comfortable and truly welcomed. Once you are settled in, we will take tomorrow to allow all of you to get used to your new home. Once again I would like to welcome you all to the Land of Nebra."

Everyone clapped and finished eating.

Soon people were standing and going to their area. The children followed downstairs.

Kalub and Kaylah hugged each other and went to their clan room.

Kalub walked into his clan room and there were a lot of scared faces. "Hello everyone my name is Kalub."

"Hi Kalub," the voices came back in harmony.

"Do any of you have brothers or sisters in another clan?"

Three children raised their hands.

There was one about 4 years old that walked over and said, "My twin sister is water. I don't want to be away from here!" as her eyes water up.

Kalub looked down at this scared wide eyes little girl and said, "Then go to your sister and tell Kaylah your twin is in her house. I said it would be alright."

The little girl smiled really big and ran to the water clan.

"Anyone else? Alright, This area is the comfy room where we can gather and study. Then all girls are to the right door, boys are to the left door of our clan. You will find our bathrooms in the corner. You will need to find a room and just relax and rest tonight. I know this place is very large and can be scary. But just remember we are all family here," Kalub is trying to be reassuring.

Kalub looked around and now there is a room with a monkey on the door and his name. He sees many different names on the doors around the big room.

* * *

Kaylah in the water clan room was also talking. A little girl about 4 went to her and stared at her. Kaylah looked down and said, "Yes little one?"

"My, um my sister we are twins is in your clan."

"Kalub said I could be with her please?"

"If, um m, it is OK with you?" The little girl was full of nerves and scared.

Kaylah bent down and said, "Sure little one what is your name?"

"Um m, well, um m, my name is Zara and my sister is Tara."

Tara ran to her sister side and they hugged.

Kaylah bent down and said, "Welcome both of you. Kalub is my twin brother."

"Really?" The girls said.

"Yes really." Kaylah said. "We understand what it feels like not to be with each other for even the shortest time." And she smiled at them. "Alright everyone, find their room the boy's door is on the left and the girls is here on the right. When Kaylah looked around she found a door with a Quetzal Bird on it. It was to the right at the end of the row of doors, and it had her name below it. Zara and Tara found another bed on the other side of their room. She walked over and saw a door to the other clan. It was Zara's room they were very happy. They could each be in their clan but stay close together. This was a great new home.

Loora and Jai found there rooms were connected also in the long row of doors with their clan's animal and there name on it.

After a few adjustments for twins and brothers and sisters, everyone settled in and found their rooms. The children all cleaned up and get ready for bed.

268

Magoose and Norah pop into each of the clan rooms to be sure the children were able to fit everyone, and made sure there was no problems with the new children.

Magoose was really proud of the children and how they fixed a few things. "I think they are naturals don't you Norah?" Magoose said as they walked back upstairs.

I am very proud of the young ones, it was like they understood what they needed to do and just jumped in and did it. I do hope we have enough inspiration to do the same," Norah said.

After long chattering the children went to bed and dreams of their new friends and safe home begins.

❧❧

CHAPTER 14

New Friends

As the children awoke the next morning they all found a dresser full of new things. Everyone found the school clothes all neatly folded in the draws, and hanging in their closets.

The girls all had their flowing white skirts with a half sleeved white tunic with their clans color embroidery on it. The boys and men found black and white pants and nice white tunics with their clans color embroidery on it. What they were wearing last night seemed to be gone. So the children all dressed and looked alike.

The adults found black and white tunics like the children but not colored, except for their silver or gold necklaces.

As the children hurried up the stairs for breakfast, they saw wonderful tables full of fruits, hot cereal and hot bread, ready for them to eat.

They all went to a table and sat down.

Magoose stood and looked around at all the wonderful faces of all the children. He noticed they were all wearing the same outfits and so eager to learn. He said the prayer of thanks over the food and then sat down. Everyone started to eat and the chatter was wonderful to Magoose, Norah and Joy. They really felt like they were home.

Magoose and Norah were talking with the teachers about the new school programs during breakfast. Norah is concerned about the different ages of the children and if they should separate them in the schooling or keep them together and work on each of their skills in groups.

"No," said one of the teachers, "I feel age is a good thing for learning.

We will say 4-6, 7-9, 10-12, 13-15, and 15-18. This should work for schooling."

"Anyone know how many teachers we have?" Magoose asked.

"Yes sir," William spoke, "There are 270 teachers here."

"270 oh my, that is a lot." Magoose said.

Professor William spoke "Not with all the different ages Magoose. We could use a few more really."

Has anyone counted the children? Norah asked.

Yes I have one of the older teachers said, there is 674 children right now.

That number went around the tables like hot cakes. 674 children, can you imagine.

Oh my, I knew there was a lot, but I never thought it was that many.

"All energy workers?" Ann asked.

"Oh yes," Magoose replied. Then he stood up and spoke, "I would like to see some age groups please.

For the first group will the 4-10 year old's please stand and go and sit by the SW fireplace upstairs and please use the tables, and please sit until I get up there. Thank you."

It sounded like a great army getting up and going upstairs. There were at least 600 children standing up and walking to the stairs. They all started talked as they went up. It was an incredible sight.

Next I would like to have the 11-15 please go to the SE fireplace.

The children all stood and went to the fireplace. There was not as many in this group.

Most of the student left there was now only a few left. Magoose starts to count. There are only 25 of you.

He said. "Oh my I thought you would be the biggest group. Well I guess you will be the helpers to the teachers and will be working with me privately outside starting tomorrow."

They all clapped at Magoose words.

Magoose asked them to help the little ones with their pouches this evening. They said they would.

He thanks them and releases them to go upstairs also.

Magoose and Norah went up the stairs. They told the children to go and explore the Grounds and their new home. "Enjoy your free day, But do NO harm to anything or Each Other!" Magoose spoke firmly.

The children all nodded they would and started to look around and explored their new home.

* * *

Magoose and Norah set up the great hall this day for everyone's pouches.

It seemed like whatever they need, seemed to manifest for them.

The Teachers went to the great hall and all sat at the tables and start to discuss what should be done with their new life and all these children.

Magoose and Norah walk over and sit at the front of the table.

"Well I guess we found out the age group of the children," Magoose said as he is turning toward the teachers.

Everyone nodded.

Ann spoke, well the 4-10 looks like the largest group of children. This is a great age for teaching. They are so hungry for knowledge.

"Well," Magoose said, "I will leave the teaching up to you teachers. But one more thing, I want all the students in the great room every evening after dinner, no exceptions. All punishments will have to be at a different time." With that he turns and walks to the stairs and was gone. Norah was close behind him.

The teachers just stare in amazement at Magoose. "He must have patience of gold," Ann spoke.

They all nod their heads in agreement.

Elder William spoke, "Well we are all teachers here, and I do hope you found your rooms as comfortable as we did."

Everyone nodded that they were.

"The classroom seems to grow and everyone has their perfect amount for what they need. So I feel that we need put together a schedule for the children, so they can learn from as many as possible. The more a child can see the world from different eyes, opens their hearts and minds wider. It will make them better teachers later. We need to see how many of you are willing to teach math?"

Their are 32 teachers raise their hands.

"Next will be Language skills? How of you know how to read and right?

two people put their hands up.

"This we can fix this easily. All of the first student and teach here can all read and write very well. There is new ways to learn, and we have a few things that will help you learn. An hour before Sun we will meet in the Library. No exceptions. Next is Alchemy?"

There are 2 hands that went up.

"Cultural Learning awareness teacher will be selected tomorrow in the library, right before breakfast. How many Astronomers, truly understand the working of the stars. Not just their names and meanings?"

As he spoke, 200 hand shot up, when he finished only 2 remained. It looks like we will be spending more time together.

"Gardening, Herbology, and soils knowledge? How many people have farmed before?"

78 hands went up. Out of you who still have their hands raised.

He continued, "Understand soil conditions, weather patterns, storm conditions and drought cycles, Insect control, and natural plant balance." While he spoke this time, almost half of the people lowered their hands.

At the end 15 hands remained.

"What about Animal knowledge? How many animal talkers do we have?"

43 hands went up.

"How many people truly understand the life cycles, herd movement, training, life cycles, and animal behavior both domestic and wild?"

There are quite a few that understand animals. There was 19 teachers.

"Any one teach complete Survival training? Meaning, making sure someone with basic tools, can survive weeks on their own, with no assistance.

One of the teachers said, "May I ask a question."

"Of course," Professor Williams says.

The teacher asked, "I only know how to teach desert survival. I have never been in the jungle until last night. As he points to another teacher, "She knows water survival. Last night, I became educated on wave movements, animals, and all types of new things. Involving the water. Knowing this sir, could we get together, as teachers, and do classes, so everyone can know the different environments?"

"Excellent Idea! Mother Earth has chosen well," Professor Williams said.

He continues, "How many of you, understand my definition of my survival training. From the place you grew up in?"

Nearly everyone raises their hand.

"Wonderful!" he exclaims.

During Lunch we will get together and work out which environments, and who is best with each.

Last but most important. How many of you know how to stand in your personal power, and in balance with the Great Wheel"

17 hands shot up.

How many have done this more then 3 times. 9 hands stayed up. I need to see all of you after we are done."

A couple of side notes and questions, "How many of you feel that you are full or Master Nebra's?"

3 hands goes up.

"How many of you feel that over the next few month you could become one?

73 hands shoot up into the air.

"On to the fun stuff. We have a great ball field anyone know how to play?"

The teachers all looks at him and shook their heads no. Alright, How many of you would like to learn the ball game from Magoose and teach it?"

Slowly 8 hands rise.

"That is great." Professor William said. Well Magoose said, That Father Sun placed the Game field here on this land and wants us all to play.

Professor Ann spoke up, "We will set up our children in groups. 4-6 year old's then our 7-8 year old's. 9-10 year old's, and so on.

The teachers like her idea and started their lessons plans.

Ann stated, "And for all you who did not raise your hands for any thing. Are now part of the elder students. Until you Master a subject that you would like to teach. Mind you, you will be assistance to other teachers. Agreed? I think it is important to know that most of these children have been surviving with their parents in the woods. I know Kalub and Kaylah have reading and writing skills. They can put up shelters, fix any medicine, hunt, tan, bead, make their own clothing, and cook and they are only 6 going on 7 this winter solstice. Most of this army will need some basic schooling to start with."

One of the teachers spoke up, "What about art, dance, and music? My door to my room is labeled culture. This is something I can do well."

"Yes I can do this as well!" Another teacher spoke up.

"Oh with everything going on you are right. We always need culture although which culture should we pick?" Asked Ann.

The First teacher said, "Why limit the children to one culture. We, at least I can teach many cultures.

"I agree," said Ann. "Thank you."

Elder William spoke, "I know Loora and Jai had a lot of schooling they were being forced to learn and work with the government for, well training to be killers. They did not know that. But Magoose told me. So they have a lot of book knowledge and basic energy knowledge. We have a many different kinds of children."

"That is a good idea," spoke an older man with gray hair. "We could set up testing to see what each one knows. This way we could have a place to begin."

"Who agrees?" William asked.

"Everyone agree to that? Everyone raises his or her hand to agree. "Majority rules so we will test to see where the children are at, and we will have another meeting at the end of the week?"

This is good. Professor William says. Then he stood and went to his area and the others follow.

When they got upstairs they found all the doors had their name and were labeled with the subjects, and the age of the children that will be in the room.

Professor William looked around and said, "Well I guess we did not need to have a meeting. Everything is already set up for us."

"This is a really strange place we have come to. Although I am happy we are safe at last," one of the teachers said.

* * *

Ariannah is scared the bad people had come back again. She is hiding in the place of safety her parent's told her to go to. Even though she had done this many, many times her stomach hurt and she was worries. Her head hurt. Her ear's had a humming and ringing sound in them. The other children were even more scared then they normally are.

Outside were the yelling and screams of the adults demanding to know where there children were at. She could hear the bad people walking over the stones above her head. It was dark, hot, and smelled real bad in their safe place. 4 large crystals are in each corner, they are told by the good people that the crystals help make it hard to find the hiding place.

Ariannah knew something was different; she was not sure what it was.

HUM, HUM

"What was that? She thought too herself.

HUM! HUM! Kurtrank I Have a hit on the locator. . .

What does that mean she thought. It sounds bad too, she thought her self.

Ariannah heard, "I have a hit but can not seem too get a exact location on it."

The boss said," if we do not find children this time we will pay for it with our lives." Slowly the hiding place got brighter and brighter. The Humming got louder.

"Push Your Energy Harder Stupid Pawn. Let me put it this way if we fail the Last thing you will have to worry about is eating and breathing do I make myself clear you stupid PAWN!"

"Yes sir My scanner say's they are right here in the center of there dance circle somewhere around this portal." spoke the drone.

"That Cannot be Pawn" Thundered Kurtrank, "there is no sign of a hidden place noting is different. Nothing …. Nothing At All GERRR" (she hears a smacking sound) "Push the energy harder in that thing."

HHUUMM HHUUMM EEPP

The 4 crystals started to glow brighter and brighter. There hiding place felt so so hot all the children's skin hurt and there head's felt like they were going to explode.

Wepetshu Yelled, make it stop for the love of mother earth make it stop!

Suddenly the crystals shattered and all the children screamed.

Did you here that Boss there under us, yelled pawn.

Shut up and grab the pry-bar's or something before I get real mad.

Ariannah whispers, "I think they are going to get us this time I will not go with them no matter what. How many of you can use or are trained to use your energy?"

Wepethu raised her hand and says, "Before they took dad last moon. He taught me to move myself with my mind. He said just close your eyes feel your heart energy and think of where you want to go. I can only go a few miles though."

Wampiuth said,"I can make lighting tornadoes. They are small yet they do pack a punch."

Burtus said, "Serah showed me how to use a shield last summer. I have been practicing in the center of the river."

"The Center Of The River WOW!!!" cried out the children.

"I Know I can shield us all for a while. Remember it takes a lot out of me once we are safe I will help getting around. I may even need to be carried," he continues.

Tink tink tink "Put Your Back's In to It Pawn's If theses primitives could put theses stones here It could not be that hard. Drone's ready the nets and gun's. Energy Scum Worker's do what you do and take them down if they fight back. If they get hurt that what the healing and brain washing chambers are for. Worst case we can use them to make more Energy scum. Ha Ha Ha Ha, I kill me. Ha Ha Ha Ha."

Yah we can always make more. We are coming to get you children fight back and you will be punished." Kurtrank said.

Ariannah asks, "Did you here that?"

They all nodded their heads.

Burtus said, "OK I am almost 14 and probably the strongest energy worker here.

Wepetshu and Ariannah When we get out of here I need you to get too either find Serah or her parent's. There are no more safe places in our land. As soon as we step out of here I will shield us. Look and see where there are no bad people and all of you run till you are safe."

The last stones above them started too lift.

"9 8 7 6 5 4 3 2 1 Push a little bit of your energy too me and keep touching till it is time," Burtus shouts.

Silver and gold swirling colors of light started to form around the Children.

Popping and humming sounds filled the air.

Burtus said, "Mother earth, Eagle, wolf, bear, Buffalo, Father sky, Grandfather sun, Grandmother Moon, and Mother Nature" (as he point's in the direction of the names) "Please I ask of you fill me with your love and strength as I do what must be done." A solid egg shape of energy almost 1 foot length thick forms around the children.

Kurtrank said, "It is a trap there must be an adult in there group Fire at will MEN! Do not let anyone escape. If you do them it will be upon your head not mine.

The children stayed in a tight ball noise came from all directions. Beam weapon's, net's, Swords, and energy ball's. There are energy balls bouncing off the shield and back to the bad men around them. The children are very scared yet they know not to run. After a few minutes of fighting... the shield becomes thinner.

Burtus Yells, "I am having a hard time keeping this up get ready."

Kurtran yells," He is going to drop any second everyone to this side. Everyone but the energy scum stop attacking. Energy scum get ready to drain his shield. They are just kid's what can they really do? Alright energy scum go go go."

Burtus said softly," As soon as I drop the shield to my back run for it do not look back and forget about me. I have been training for this day. I knew they would find our spot one day. Mother Nature told me in a vision."

The shield opens up in the back.

Wampiuth throws 5 fast energy tornado's over the shield as he runs with the rest of the children. Wampiuth sees the shield form gray and black band's as they are almost out of sight..

They all hear Burtus yell, "I will never give up, Star's Lend Me Your Strength, Wind's Howl, Lightning Strike, and Please Help Me Protect My Friend's...... I will not stop. I stand in my Heart and power." Burtus's voice fades in the distance.

After what seemed like days, yet was only a hour, the children see a sky-ship. Wepetshu and Ariannah shout, "This way in the cave east go east."

Arianna starts to tear up she can no longer feel Burtus.

Wepetshu draw's a circle around them and said a prayer too Mother Earth. The other children said one as well. They hear the sky-ship land and voices grow louder. Wepetshu asks Arianna if she remembers what she said earlier about teleporting.

Ariannah nodded her head.

"Good,Wepetshu said "We will have to try there does not seem to be a choice. OK Clear your mind everyone on think of Mother Earth fill your hearts with all the love you can. Grab a hand No matter what happens do not let go of the circle or you may be lost."

Wepetshu sits behind Ariannah and places her hands on her shoulder's.

Just like I was shown she thinks push my energy through them and hope Mother Earth can guide us to a better place that is safe. A quiet popping sound is heard.

"Get the net and net them all, "A voice cries out.

Ariannah feels a pull forward as the pressure on her shoulder from the hands disappears. She cried, "Mother Earth with all of her being."

Carved stone, a warm glow of light, and couches are all around them. The children look all around them in disbelief. Ariannah Stands up Yelling" WEPETSHU I cannot loose another friend today." She is so tired and drained from the Teleport she drops to the floor, as her voice fades.

The next thing she thinks, "I am so dizzy. Why is it warm? Why is the ground so soft?" Arianna thinks to herself. She opens one eye scared of what she might see. Many voices she knows well filled her ear's. Ariannah jumps too her feet shouting, 'We did not make it NO, NO, NO, We were so so close." Saying this she falls too knees in tear's.

Burtus voice fills her ears," Silly billy, billy, we all made it. I was told from the teacher's here, it was your will to save all the other children that helped you get here. I have no idea how you were able to stand with all those nets on you before you fainted. Mother Earth hand delivered Wepetshu. She had all kids of metal stuff in her arms and legs. I just visited her after lunch. The people taking care of her are named Magoose and Earis. They spent all night healing her.

Sunlight was shining in a window on Ariannah. She knows she was safe so how come she could not stop crying.

A sound came from the hallway. "She is a wake Earis are you sure you are ready?"

"Yes we need to help her get to the entrance and her friends too."

Joy said, "Why are you so focused on Ariannah?"

Earis, "Mother I have had many dreams about her. I love her like she was family maybe more."

"Alright I trust you son. I just worry about you. I am your mother and you mean the world to me. I will go clear out the room so you and Father can take her there." Spoke voices from the hall.

The door opened a Beautiful woman walked in and said, "I am sorry children lunch is almost ready. Please get ready as we will take great care of your friend I promise."

The room emptied as they all wave good bye and gave their heart-felt thank you's.

A face from her dreams appeared, "Yes it was him. The boy from the pyramid how could he be here it was just a dream right?" She thought.

Magoose will be here shortly to gather we will take you to the Entrance," Earis said in a kind voice.

A tall man with kind eyes entered the room. He told her, "You are safe here Ariannah. We will help you"....

Jaguar clan, the strange voice called me a jaguar. "I just can't believe this." she thought. "I was just in a room seeing a person walk out of my dream's next thing I know. I am standing on a stair hearing a strange voice and all of my sadness and pain gone. I know a lot about this place and it is a school. People walking around me saying strange words. Now are taking in the same way I do. Can this be a dream? I even know my teacher's name's, classes, and none of this is feels weird. I feel at home, for the first time, since my parents were taken. Will the wonderful and exciting new event go on forever?" she continued thinking.

"Ariannah?... Ariannah?... Are you ok?" Magoose gently asked.

"Grandfather I thought this was supposed to restore her and help her understand the school?" Earis asked quietly.

Ariannah blushed as she looks into Earis's Eye's and said, "I am great. I am … well... I... am just taking this all in. I am so, so, so, thankful, you, both of you. Thank you, O Thank You. …. Such a long time has passed since I have felt like I was safe and at home anywhere. O my I did not really…

Hello, Everyone and thank you all so much I am honored and feel so blessed to be here. I am thinking and talking about myself so much. Before I ended up here somehow, it was like a unending nightmare. Right now it feels like a wonderful dream that I could not bear to see the end," she spoke as turned around addressing the huge crowd.

Many people, ever so many people are around her. More people then she had ever seen are here in one place. It is like the biggest city in the world all inside this one single building.

"Earis I have seen you in my dream's. You are the boy in the Pyramid. Can I really do all the things you have shown me? You are like the calmest caring boy in the world and so so handsome and tall." Arianna said.

Earis starting to look almost sun burned replied, "Thank you, I must say you have the Beauty of Mother Nature yourself..... um .... well Yes, Yes, you can do everything we did together in your dreams. My understanding is we are connected in our dreams so we could help each other. I feel as close to you as I do my own Mother ... maybe more even."

Ariannah grab's his hand and said, "I feel the same way my brother, my friend, my teacher. Ouch Oh, Oh, Oh, My stomach hurts. Lunch ...Lunch someone said lunch is almost ready? Can we, may we please eat I am suddenly starving."

Magoose said on the way to Dinner, "Ariannah only you and your friends have come here without using the Front door since my grandson arrived. Only difference is he had help. All of you arrived here on your own. Sometime when you feel up to it would you mind telling, One of us about it. I am sure few here will ever forget it. Net's all over you and you were able to stand up with all that weight on you and your friends."

Ariannah nodded. Her eyes grew wide and she asked, " My friend I heard you and Earis healed her and that would be alright. Thank you so much. Could you tell me what happened to her?" Magoose replied, "Well as you all made it here safely."

She was grabbed by the drones. Their leader had starting making her into one of them. Mother Earth said your friend was able to teleport with most of the people on the ship holding her down into the ocean. Then she still had the strength to teleport herself once they let go. Mother Earth found her and put her directly in the healing rooms. Your Male friend, once he felt all of you were far enough away to be safe he dropped his shicld. Well, when he opened his eyes from what he said. He looked around and he was near the Main Entrance.

I would rather allow him to fill in the rest of the detail's. It is not my place to tell his story." Arianna agrees as they sit down too eat.

After a wonderful dinner Norah stood and says, "It is time for everyone to make pouches for their medicine things. We have all the supplies upstairs in the great room. Please join us for this new project."

The children are excited and hurried with dinner. One by one went up the stairs to start their pouches.

Everyone learns the basic of pouch making. The older children help the younger children it was really a nice evening.

Everyone was busy making their pouches and helping others make theirs. As Magoose and Norah looked around they felt a lot of happiness and peace. This is everything they ever dreamed about. They have a wonderful home and lots of children. Magoose was working on his rattle and Norah re skinning her drum.

One of the older children stood and went over to Magoose and said, "Excuse me Father Magoose, We are done sewing our pouches." "May we go to bed now?"

Magoose looked up smiled and said, "Please our children, when you are finished you may go to your rooms. Have peaceful night sleep."

They all spoke, "Good night Father Magoose." "Good night Mother Norah."

Norah with tears in her eyes spoke, "Good night children."

She was so filled with joy, thinking of all these wonderful children loving her it was almost overwhelming.

"It is late my dear, I think we should turn in ourselves," Magoose said.

Norah agrees. "We should visit our new children before bed."

Magoose nodded and they walk and cheek on the new children before heading for bed.

❦

CHAPTER 15

Surprise Attack

Morning came and everyone was rested and come to the great eating area. The children sit and waited for father Magoose to come down so they could eat.

Magoose and Norah said, *"Good morning children."*

The children sang back, *"Good morning Father Magoose and Mother Norah."*

Magoose said the Morning Prayer.

"Thank you great spirit for waking us up on this wonderful day.

We give you thanks for the little people who prepared this lovely breakfast for us.

I ask you to help the children remember all that they know, so that their new lessons can build on that knowledge. May we all have wonderful lessons this week. So mote it be."

The children sang back, *"So mote it be."*

After breakfast, Professor Williams stood up and said, "We offer a "Heart Felt Welcome" to you all and thank you all for coming to join us.

Today we will be getting to know you and begin to find out who you are and what you can do with your energy. That will help us to know what classes you need to help you grow. Testing, will be done with your teachers of the subject. You must not judge yourself. None of these tests carries a personal grade for others to see. This school is not like schools out in the world. This new home is only teaching you what you want to learn. We do encourage you to read and write and do math. We, the teachers, need to know what you know and what you don't. Each of you are on the path of becoming a Nebra. Each of you will learn what that means and who to become what Mother Earth and Mother Nature desires of you. We are only Guides."

The children all nodded, that they understood.

"I would like all 4-6 year old's please stand up." Professor William said. After the count, there were 274 of them. "You will go to your basic schooling with your new teachers to the 2nd floor Professor Williams smiled and said "Welcome to your first day in the land of the Nebras."

They all sang back to him, "Thank you." The children's eyes beamed at him as they waited for their teachers to lead them to up to their classrooms.

130 teachers had come with the children and now directed them to their class rooms. They were separated into smaller groups and then into the classes for the subjects they wanted to learn.

"Thank you all for your patience today children. There are a lot of you, and we need to find just the right classes and make a schedule for all of you.

First of all we will be doing language, which will include reading and writing. All higher knowledge begins with these skills. Learn well in these classes as your future depends on your skills in these classes.

Math is also a very important skill it will be very important in learning all other things like building thing and Astrology.

The study of the planets and stars is called Astronomy, and to achieve great things in the future, it is very important. Our understanding of time and the calendar is found in this study. Your ability to align yourself with nature depends on your careful study of this subject.

You will be using astrology to help you align yourself with nature and your abilities using energy.

Herbology will teach you how to grow plants for food and medical plants. You will learn everything from growing, to how to use them. You will start with basics then on to the advanced classes.

Classes on healing will include both plants and animals. Human first aid will teach you how to deal with the small bumps and broken bones. You will learn to use your natural energy to perform hands on healing. One of your classmates helped to heal a grandfather tree on the way here.

History may be the most important lessons of all. History will show us the good and the bad things our great grand parents did so we will know what to do, or not to do, in the future.

Lessons of the Great Wheel will help us to know about the different levels of life and the animals that help us thru life. In these lessons we will learn of Vibration and Tones and Music and how the help us.

Last but far from least, Alchemy, this will teach us of important Rituals of our culture and the rituals and cultures of other lands. In this class you will also learn Survival Skill which you will need after the earth changes that will come very soon. We also need to know how to guide others to our school who have not arrived yet. There are many other children still out there in the world that need our help.

Each of these Lessons will help you grow. We have basic classes for the 4 to 6 year olds. For our 7 to 10 year olds we have more advanced classed. 11 to 15 year old have more advanced classes. For the few of our 16-18 year olds we even more advanced classes to help you in your preparation for your Mastership. At that point you will be welcomed as teachers. Each age group will be in a different area on the floor where the classes are. Classes for ages 4 to 6 will be held on the east side of the hall. 7 to 10 year olds will be held at the south end of the school. Classes for 11 to 15 year olds will be on the west side of the hall. Classes for 16 years old and up will be held on the north end.

Some of your teachers are very young. Don't mistake age with ability as they are very good in their chosen field. Treat them with respect as you do our elders. That is all for now the professor said. "Please take a schedule from the table, it will tell you your schedule for the classed you will go to first, and where they are located. If you cannot read yet, ask an older student where to go, and when. We will now take a 15 minute bathroom break, after that, please go directly to your assigned class room. Every one picked up their schedules and looked them over carefully.

Loora shot up her hand and ask, "Professor what if we fail?"

Professor William looked shocked as he said, "My Child there is no failing. You will advance at your own speed. There is no such thing as failing, Professor William shook his head.

Then continued, "We will all learn what we need to. If it takes only a day or the rest of your life. There is *no failing*. Only life itself can grade you. You will advance at your own speed and achieve your goals whatever they may be. Study hard, be kind to your teachers and you will advance when you are ready, there is no failing. The energy I feel from you tells me that you will advance quickly beyond your years and have very few problems" the Professor said. "Everyone here needs to learn something."

Loora looked surprised at the answer and said, "Thank you professor."

Kalub looked at Kaylah and said, "Wow! This is exciting did you hear all the things we get to learn?"

Kaylah said, "Yes they are going to teach us everything, this is so wonderful."

Everyone picked up their schedules, and their new life had begun.

"What classes do you have Kaylah?" asked Kalub

Kaylah shows Kalub her schedule and Kalub showed her his list of classes..

"Wow, we have the same classes this is great," said Kaylah.

"Yeah we have to study Language, Astrology, Alchemy and Math every other day. The other days we have Herbology, and then Survival. After Survival we get to learn about the Stars and Planets in Astronomy class. The Wheel Of Life classes on the other days. This might be confusing," said Kalub. "We need to go to Language class right now" Kayla said, and they ran up the stairs.

* * *

Earlier that morning.

Commander, Commander! I think we have figured out where the Nebras and children are located. We picked up a brief message that was sent by a girl that escaped yesterday. We traced it to a place on the mountain that has no signs of life, none at all, nothing but rocks to reflect our scans. That is odd as there is always some kind of life, trees, squirrels, deer, something, the Machine Operator said. The computer says that those evil, vile, Lemurian scum must have built something up there and have a cloaking device to hide it. The only other possibility is that some how that area is absorbing our scan pulses. "None of the other possibilities that the computer suggests are remotely possible", the Operator said.

Altex replies, "You may be correct! Our scientist, number 42541, will be here tomorrow.

Altex thinks to himself, "How dare they interfere with my plan? All they have are those rotten crystals," he thought to himself. "All that bunch is good for is being chomped up and made into parts of my army."

He took a deep breath and spoke again, "Drone Commanders! Prepare the sky-ship's, basic energy drones, the basic energy scum. "Let their own kind destroy them. How dare they think they can live their own lives, not under my control."

"Do it now! Altex screamed," The rest of his words are drowned out by the sounds of the drones and his underling barking orders, for the preparation and launch of the Sky-ship's.

Within minutes the Sky ships are in the air, heading their sky-ship's to the location of the void in their scanners patters.

The commander began to lay out the plan of attack. He barked "pay attention now, look at the scan map, this is the exact location of where the scan signals were lost. We will be landing further to the east, here he said and pointed at the spot."

Team one; you are going in first to draw the enemies attention and fire.

Team two, one minute later you start. You will push past Team one, to this location," he said while pointing to the map.

"Team three, you are our strongest and the most advanced in our force. You will hold and stand ready for exactly six and half minutes from the start of the attack, set your timers don't be early, or late! At that time, you will move forward and destroy anything that is not ours. "All of their defenses should be weak or destroyed by that time."

Wave two should be able to take out all of their remaining Nebra's and you are there to insure that nothing is left alive, understood."

"Sir yes sir!" yelled the team of drones.

"When that is done, your orders are as follows, "First, anything and everything that grows is to be smashed, broken or poisoned. Anything that crawls, will be crushed. Anything that thinks, will no long be allowed to think. Anything that moves on its own, shall no longer move. If any of these orders are not done, you will no longer need to worry about eating or sleeping ever again. Do I make myself clear?"

An ear splitting roar from the drones, "Sir, Yes Sir!"

Each sky-ship captain confirmed that their orders are clear and understood. In just under two hours they will arrive at the target.

As the sky-ship's land, and to every sky-ship at the exact same time, the information officer yelled, "scouts down, scouts on the ground."

"The entire area is being protected by a shield with an un-known power source, the leader of the first team reported to his commander."

"We are unable to penetrate! Can you detect their shield generator source?" The commander said, "Hold your position. Then he gave an immediate change of orders. "All attack pilots, lift off and prepare to deploy shield depleters, Fire when ready."

"That will punch more holes in their defensive's than they can handle."

"All drones, put on your energy absorbing armor immediately!"

He shouted, "Stop looking at me you scum! Move, Move, Move!"

Within minutes, hundreds of strange devices covered with black metallic crystals, were on the Nebra's home shield. A thunderous roar, exploded on the outside of the shield with no effect.

"All advance units, deploy Shield Depleters at ground level on the east side of the shield. It seems we have under estimated the strength of their shields!"

* * *

There is an energy shifts like a great Arctic wind through the entire learning center. A hush fell all over the expansive grounds, everything is quiet. Everyone felt the shift.

They stop and run to the great room. They stand there waiting for Magoose and Norah to find out what is going on.

Earis runs up to the top floor, and up the ladder to the top of the pyramid. Standing on the flat top of the roof, he cries out *"Mother Earth, please hold well to my feet. For you shall be my rock. Great Quetzal to the east, Grant me your enlightenment, Energy, and protection. Great Jaguar to the south. Please grant me, your stealth, your energy, and your protection. Great Whales to the West. Please grant me, your wisdom, your strength, your endurance, and your protection. Great Monkey's of the North. Please grant me your wisdom, your heart, your balance, and protection. Father sky, I call to you with all my heart. Grant me your strength, your wisdom, and your protection. Grandfather Sun and Grandfather Moon, I humbly ask, for your energy, and protection. Please watch over my friends, my teachers, and all I love, below me."* His voice sounds like thunder and lightning with each call, then says, *"I shall begin."*

Magoose and Norah also starts running to the great room. They meet the teachers at the stairs as they hurry them down to the Great room.

They all felt the energy of the learning center being hit by something bad. Some of the children and adults remember this feeling. Panic and fear raises in them. Everyone looks at Magoose and Norah for instruction.

Magoose standing there with a worried look on his face he says, "All you children stay inside here. You will be safe. Adult please come with me."

Two little voices from the middle of the great room says, "No Sir. They have come for us."

The two little twin girls stood up and walk to Magoose. They looked scruffy even with their new clothes on. They walk together hand in hand with fear written all over their little faces. They are only about 4 years old. They are small with big brown doe eyes, and long faces.

Norah goes over to Magoose and looks at these little ones and asks, "What do you mean little ones?"

The little twins spoke, "It is the drones,

Second ones said, they have found us."

First one said, "It is because they want to kill us."

"There will be no killing of children today," said Magoose firmly. He began to shake his head No, to reaffirm the idea.

The first one said, "But they are sir! They have been hunting us along time."

The second said, "Ever since we were born."

The first one spoke, "Our parents took us off the island of Atlantis and hid us with the old ones."

The second one spoke, "We have the gift of the crystal planet."

The first one spoke, "Our mother was a Nebra slave from Lemuria and our father was an Atlantain." Second one spoke, "We are wrong, we are bad."

First one said, "should not have be born."

They says together, "We are a mistake."

First one said, "But we were created out of love mother said."

Magoose is shocked at the idea little children would believe such a horrible thing. They are not worth of being born? What kind of people would tell little children they are bad or being a mistake.

Norah asked, "How did you come here."

The first one said, "The drones killed our parents."

The second one said, "We ran along time."

The first one spoke, "A woman dressed in a beautiful brown flowing dress came to us and asked."

The second one spoke, "if we wanted to be safe."

The first one said, "Never be harmed again."

They both said, "We agreed!"

The first one says, "We held her hand and came here. But we were put in different clans."

The second one said, "Kalub allowed us to be together in Kaylah clan."

The first one said, "Kaylah is very nice and allow it. But the drones hate us."

The second one said, "They can follow our energy."

The first one said, "Some of them are breed and trained Nebra's."

They both shivered at the word.

Magoose lets out a little laugh and went to one knee and looks at the little girls with big eyes and dark skin. "Young ones," he says, "We are all Nebra's here."

The girls panic and fear over came them. They hold each other close trying to protect each other from Magoose.

Norah spoke softly, "So are you two. You see little ones, there are Good and bad Nebra's."

The girls look back at her with a large question on their faces. They says together, "There are?" as some of their panic and fear leaves.

"Yes," speaks Norah. "But the drones will kill all Nebra's. We threaten them because we can do the," Norah pauses.

The girls look at each other and spoke, "Energy."

Norah looks at the trembling girls and closes her eyes and thought of a rose. She pulls the energy up to her hand and creates a rose for each of the girls. "You see children we all can use energy. Our home is a safe place that we can learn to control our energy. To focus it, and learn to use it, with love not hate. Do you understand?"

The girls nodded their head and begin to feeling better with this new idea.

Norah hugs each of the girls and tells them to go back to their seats.

Magoose stands straight and tall and in a deep tone says, "Our Home is under attack. All children will remain inside, Teachers and all expert energy workers will need to come with me to stop some drones.

Burtus upon hearing this teleport's as did Serah, Tenip, and Tabieya, to the four corners of the garden area. They call their protection as Earis did. Then they stand ready, as Mother Earth instructed.

Magoose continues, "I am sure with all of you coming at one time the energy was noticeable. Our light is so bright, that those that would want to destroy us saw our lights. So we will just have to slap their hands and tell them they can't come join us. Sometimes children we have to stand and fight. But even with the drones, we fight with love in our hearts. Never raise your energy in hate. Not even for those that want to kill us. Love is the only way to fight. So let's go teach our friends, that this is sacred land. I think they need a good spanking, yes?"

Norah and the children all giggle.

Magoose took the fear from the room and turned it to a positive energy. He turns and goes to the main entrance.

All the Adult teachers follow Magoose out to the entrance and formed a straight line all the way around the outside ledge of the pyramid. Many voices from outside calls the older children to the second floor ledge.

Kalub, and Kaylah hear along with the other younger children Earis voice. *"Come to the gardens quickly, you can help also."* So they all run up to the gardens to help Earis.

When Norah really takes a look around, there is not a piece of the pyramid they could see that did not have a person standing there. It is quite a sight to behold.

Magoose starts by taking a deep breath. He calls in protection then raises his hands toward the drones.

A pink ball of energy starts to expand around the school and soon everyone is standing there holding their hands out, with their palms out beaming the same pink love energy.

This starts to reinforce the barriers from the first wave of drones.

Earis energy touches Magoose's energy until it reaches the bottom of the pyramid. The teachers energy re-enforces the energy they are creating. Earis thinks, "Nothing can enter our learning center now!"

* * *

The informational officers scream, "First wave forward, the shield is broken, repeat the shield is broken."

The first wave of drones attack on all sides. Moving step by step forward. The ground almost thunders from the thousands of drones marching in straight lines forward. The rabbits, guinea pigs and ground burrowing animals hurry into their homes underground and call to Mother Nature. Any more soft creature the drones see disappears from the flashes from their energy weapons.

One, two, one, two, this is the drone core.

One two, one two, this is the drone core, they continuously shout. The first wave of drones upon reaching the half way point. Have broken and destroy everything they had seen.

Magoose hearing their chanting starts his chanting. Soon all the teachers and children chant their heart chant. They lift the vibration of shield around them.

"Second wave! Attack!" The informational officers scream, to the second wave. They moves at a much faster pace. They ground begins to shake. As they chant, one two three four, you will be gone by this drone core. Five six seven eight, no more food for you, you are late. Upon each time this is said, for many feet around the energy drones. Black waves of energy rush forth. The green plants start to shrivel and become yellow.

The moment they reach the first wave, the information officers, all scream as one voice, "No one shall survive first wave! Fire, fire, fire! Second wave defend! Third wave ready! Full speed charge!"

The moment their voices stop you hear loud blasting sounds.

Like thunder in every direction. The second group of drones forms a black energy wall 7 feet high. That the first wave is firing through.

Earis upon hearing the informational officers words, cries out, "Stars lend me your strength! Mother Earth I ask of you, Raise your energy from the ground and extend your protection all around. Storm clouds form. Lightning strike, My heart is pure I will and must fight. I stand in my power, nothing shall pass."

All the children in the gardens see the windows disappear. The children are surrounded with empty arch ways.

They hear many voices singing to them as if one voice. "In your hearts feel our love, except the energy from the stars above. We grant you strength in this fight we remove all your fear and fright. Use your energy, pure and true, allow your love to hit their wall and pass on through."

Upon hearing this, the children do as they are asked. They pull love energy, all that they can. Bringing it through their hearts and out into their hands.

They beam it towards the black wall, and what looks like fireworks. Thousands of colored lights all move out from the top floor of the pyramid in straight lines, hitting the black wall of energy, passing through it.

It hits the first wave of drones and passes through them, and into the ground. The drones armor starts to glow. They are unable to move or fire their weapons, because of the energy the children are beaming through them.

Burtus, Serah, Tenip, and Tabieya, are amazed that the accuracy of all these children. It is as if, they are guided from the heavens above. They notice, from each child's hand and heart, comes a beam of energy.

Magoose lowers his hands, took off his headdress and creates a sword of lightning bolts.

Professor William creates a sword of blue flaming fire.

Norah stands in her power and calls her blue dragon to come forth. Huge Twin Dragons forms above Norah made of pure blue energy. Fire came out of one of first twins mouth, and sparks of lightning from the other twin.

Joy stands in her power and calls her power animal and a misty like bear, made of pure energy came. The huge bear stands with tornado's forming in its paws.

Professor Ann stands in her power. She calls her energy forward, and it starts to form around her hands and starts to flow out from her hands and goes in all direction twisting around each other like hundred a pieces of string. The string like energy is silvery pink.

Magoose smiles over to Professor William and He nods back at Magoose. Each one ready for the next step.

He yells out! "All those that are shielding. Focus with all your might. Mother Earth is here. Push your energy towards the top and the bottom. All those in power do not attack until they are in casy striking distance. From below a rumbling is felt through everyone's feet, that is around or in the learning center. Above everyone can hear the cracks of thunder.

The drones in the first wave, cry out to the intelligence officers, "Sir, we are unable to see. Many of us can't fire our weapons. It is like we are frozen in place. What are your orders?"

* * *

Back in Atlantis, Altex is screaming words of anger. He is so angry with the fighting going on, he said, "It is just a bunch of stupid children and a few Adults. How can this be difficult for you? All odd numbered drones break rank and reform in the east. We will show them how mighty we are. Stupid children, stupid Nebra's how dare you belittle me! You are just parts, for my war machine, if I lose a single drone you will pay dearly."

Commanders, is the shield broken?" Altex asked in a commanding voice.

The Commanders from all 4 battle groups reply at once, "All outer shields are completely taken down sir. However, the building in the center is heavily reinforced. What are your orders sir."

Altex commands, "Take the shield group back to their fighter sky-ship's, have them load projectiles. You should have something that will go through their shields."

"Sir, yes Sir!"

* * *

Moments later, there is over two thousand sky-ship's, the size of blue whales take to the skies. Each one has 30 odd shaped balls spinning around it. They all head toward the learning center. Several of the children in the gardens look up. The children see a gold figure and a white figure. The white figure has blue and gold energy lines extending all around them. They disappear into the cloud Earis has formed. Not understanding why, all of the children, throughout the school, feel their energy grow stronger and stronger, they have been beaming energy for several hours, yet they keep feeling stronger and stronger.

Earis, cries out, "Do not, if you can help it, allow any of those balls around the sky-ship's enter the building.

The Twin Dragons, Bear, the energy lights and Magoose start shooting at all the balls on the sky-ship's.

Magoose cries out "Pure energy at the highest vibration destroys them."

As several of the objects explodes from one of Magoose's lightning flashes.

The air starts to hum, the sky's start to grow dark, everyone in the battlefield looks up.

The moon has moved directly over the sun, and a beam of colorful white light hits the cloud above Earis. In seconds lightning erupts from the cloud. Gold beams of light flow into all directions. Tiny white colorful animals the size of a person palm, came out from the cloud. They hit the sky-ship's with such great force. The sky-ships are completely covered with the energy. Then they disappear from view.

The balls move in all directions, and one moves towards the top of the learning center. The great twin dragons grows as big as the pyramid and takes all of them out on her side. The great bear tornado's pulls the balls towards the bear's paws where they shattered and black dust fall to the ground.

The green string like energy wraps around the balls, like a ball of yarn pulling them to the ground. One ball makes it through, it hits the potato crop. A black energy forms over the potatoes and leave a light dust covering the potatoes.

Kaylah looks over and said, "Lucky no children were near those."

Kalub nodded his head in agreement.

The special Nebra drones, leap over groups one and two. Some of them taking to the air, some staying on the ground. Large black crystals extend from their hands. The ones in the air, and the ones on the ground are working together like they are one unit. They start pushing their crystals against the energy shield as everyone is working with the balls.

Magoose yells, "Everyone who is not, fighting, push all the love you can! Think of your happiest memories, your greatest joys, push them into our shield!" Magoose is firing beams of lightning from his sword at the special Nebra drones. He looks over at Professor Williams and said, "Nice job with your blue flame."

Professor Williams said, "Thank you. You said we needed to spank them not kill them right?"

Magoose laughs with joy as he fires more beams of lightning.

At this moment the commanders see's that all the odd drones have reformed on to the east side of the pyramid. He orders the drones to ground the energy that they are being hit with. They continue to move forward. There will be no prisoners today.

All of the drones start screaming as they push a piece of metal into the ground as they run to the learning center.

From the sky above, you can see metal wire that drags in the ground behind them. The grounding wires are trailing behind the drones. The ground is truly trembling under their feet. Behind the drones, the land is like a desert. No animals are left in sight. It is completely barren.

As the group of drones run into firing range, Magoose and the other defenders, unleash. Bolts of fire, water, earth of the purest forms blast the drones. Then bolts of lightning, blue, white and gold, sprang forth from the cloud. It looks like millions of raindrops.

Magoose and Professor Williams stop and look up. Then all heads turn towards the advancing drone army.

There were gold bolts of energy that hit the black crystals. They were all shattering on impact. The force is so powerful that it knocks the drones holding the crystals, back into the advancing drones.

The blue bolts of energy, strike every drones that could use energy.

The white bolts of energy passed through the energy using drones, into the first wave of non energy drones.

The teachers and the students and the commanders of the drones watch as the entire army bursts into a white power. Similar to sugar grains, and float back down to the ground.

The earth roars louder than an exploding volcano. Then the earth opens up where the white powder fell and swallow it up. Then the earth closes again, as if the powder was never there.

Deer, wolves, bears, jaguars, squirrels and rabbits, appear all around as if the beams never hit them.

In the mist of all the fighting, Altex is informed on his screen, that the fighter sky-ship's that were the size of blue whales, are back in their hangers, the pilots are missing.

He starts smashing the screens and screaming at the top of his lungs he says, "How can this be? The Mayan's will pay for this. If their technology is greater than mine, none of them will be able to survive in the end. I am the most powerful being on this planet. This world is mine and mine alone.

Any one who stands against me will not or can not survive.

Commander, commander, comes through one of the speakers, "All of our soldiers are gone.

Some type of massive energy attack came from the top of the building. None of our great army of drones survives. They have became white powder and it looked like the ground swallowed them up.

What are you orders sir."

In a cold unfeeling voice "Program the sky-ship's to return and everyone else on the ground attack that building!"

The Commanders reply, "Are you telling us we must... sac..

Altex interrupts, "That is correct. If you fail to do as ordered. If you come back I will not... It would be worse than... It would be better to attacking that building. Is that clear?" In a tone that could shatter ice.

In a quite whimpering voice the commander voice says, "Sir yes sir."

All the remaining commanding troops form into one large group, as the sky-ship's lifts off the ground heading for home.

They scream at the top of their lung running to the learning center as they fire their weapons.

The beings, upon the cloud, appear to be walking in thin air, down towards the ground.

It seems like they are heading towards where Magoose is standing. Light returns and the moon starts to move. 5 beings, one by one stand in front of Magoose with their back to him.

The weapons and items being fired from the soldiers pass right through them. The shield absorbs all the fire and projectiles. Almost everyone that is able to see this is in awe.

They truly are immortals as they stare in amazement. In a slow gentle motion all 5 of them raise their hands to the sky. They say in unison singing "It is done!" as their hands drop.

The gigantic sky-ships that were left, line up in a row. They were aiming directly at the island Atlantis. A beam of energy created from all 5 of the beings, starts to pull back the sky-ships a little towards the learning center. It is as through, a giant hand and scooped up the sky-ship's and put them in a sling shot and fired them. Right before the sky-ship's took off in a blur. Millions of colors of energy sparks surrounds them. And before one could blink they were out of sight.

The still advancing solders saw this, they grab their communicators trying to inform Altex of what they see. To no assistance, the airway was empty. For the first time in any of their lives they truly knew the meaning of fear. They started to run in every direction, but before one could blink all 5 of the beings, circle them it is hard to describe what truly happened next.

You could feel what happened, but you could not see it. The earth started to rubble, and a large mass of white powder came from the ground. They spoke in a tongue that almost no one could understand.

Magoose is one of the few that could repeat it word for word. Some say those men after a brief encounter; they just ran into the jungles. Nobody really knows what happened to them.

The five said, "You poor creatures, you were once living and alive. That out of balanced being Altex did this to you. We have released you from your pain, and imprisonment. Come forth as you once were, before Altex changed you."

The 5 were instantly in line. Hundreds of wispy images where in front of them as if in formation. Atlantain's, Lemurians, and a few strange beings no one recognized, the rest looked like human, somewhere the in this wispy images. It really strained your eyes to see. For they appear like reflections, in a waving crystal that is shaking.

A Voice spoke that no one had ever heard before, *"IT IS FINISHED! No More is on this Land! Now that you are free and your pain as been released. You have a choice, your original bodies are no more, yet your pure essence has been restored. Those that came from the stars may go back and be reborn. Those of the earth, have many choices. You can become helpers, of anyone of the beings in front of you, or you can be reborn in an aspect of nature. And help strengthen what you were once forced to destroy."*

People from far away could hear the voice. It was as through, it was everywhere at once.

Around the world all that could hear the voice felt peace and harmony throughout their being. Sibling that were arguing, began to hugs, old family and villages, arguments, seemed pointless, several moments of silence happened.

CHAPTER 16

Lessons of war

Mother Nature asked, "Who desires to come with me, or become part of nature." Several of the star beings, and a little over a hundred of human started to float above the others. As she touches each one, she uttered different words like, Sequoia, oak tree, redwood, ferret, corn maiden, etc. When she was done all of the beings disappeared.

Mother Earth said, "Who here desires, to be my helper?" Almost 30 of them floated up. Mother Earth said, "Thank you" and reaches forward, and touches each of them. Guardians of the fire, holder of truth, protector of the gateway. Of the earth kingdoms. Water sprites, as the list went on.

Father sky, the man with the flowing colored energy says, "I am Father Sky, I help the balance from above who would like to be my helper." 4 people floated up one appeared to be Lemurian he lean forward and touch each on. "Keeper of star knowledge, mountain secret keepers, night dancer, and gateway keeper. Are now your new names and jobs. Thank you for offering your help."

Grandmother moon says, "How many of you desire to be my helpers? For I am grandmother moon many more of them rose above the rest." She leans down and touched each one. "Moon keeper, star keeper, truth talker. Buffalo woman," and the list went on.

Father Sun starts to glow brightly as he says, "How many here desire to be my helpers?"

The rest of the humans rose up. Father sun smiles even brighter, "I am so honored you have come to help, move into two groups please." He extended his hands and touched one group. "Sun workers." Scoops the other group in his hand, and brings them close to him. He spoke so quietly no one could hear him.. Then one by one the wisp disappears. The 5 turn towards Magoose and with one step, they are back in front of the learning center.

Father Sky said, "We have much to do and are very busy. We are so happy and honored that you have done such a wonderful job protection your home."

Mother Nature and Mother Earth steps forward and spoke together; "It fills our hearts with joy. That almost all of you used pure love and joy when you fought. Almost all of you released your fears, and became stronger for it.

Mother Nature said, "During this time of conflict I was not able to help you at first. When Earis called us all here. We each had many jobs to do. I promised all the living creatures that would be safe here. No one would hunt them, unless that creature allowed it. I am a bit sad we were unable to save all the plants and trees."

Mother Earth speaks, "I have never had my own energy used against me. And it took a little while to figure out what to do. Those large machines, where taking my energy and giving it to the drones. They changed it into something awful and made me fill sick. Because of all this it took me awhile. I had to find energy that I could send around the learning center. That they could not harm with those machines. I took the powder, left over from the drones, and all that are part of the sacred wheel worked together, to restore them. Because of so much damage and machines smaller then grains of sand in them. We were not able to restore all of them. There was just not enough left of who they once were.

Earis, thank you for going up top like I asked you too. For you held the point of the pyramid for us.

Magoose, the stones on this building, are very rare and special, they absorb all kinds of energy. So even the wildest of energy worker, cannot harm them. We only ask Earis for his help, in case they had some way of harming them. Thank you everyone, shortly I must release all the borrowing creatures. That we protected.

Grandmother moon, lovely spoke, "I am so proud of all of you, it is rare for me to be called down to the earth. I flow and move energy with Father Sun to the earth every day. Yet visits are rare.

Father sky smiles at everyone and said, "I am Father sky, I am honored all of you that called me here. Seeing so many stand in their power, fills me with great joy. He bows his head slightly to everyone in the learning center.

Father sun starts to glow bright as he speaks, "Shortly the Golden Iatia will arrive and take who he needs. So worry not to all of you who have been restored, you are home."

He looks at Magoose, "Great Wonderful Magoose, you have honored me with play. Never have I seen so many filled with joy as they play my game. The love of you and my Dear Norah, you both have flowed well into all that are here."

He looked at the school and said, "I am proud of almost everyone those that we are not proud of. We know who you are. If you do not learn to work with your heart energy instead of emotions, you will not be here anymore. I am sure you will understand. We are great beings and can't be fooled so easily. On this world and throughout all the Great Wheel, there is something that makes us strong, or makes us weak. We call this free will. It means, anything you do is by choice. No being or person, with rare exceptions, can make you do anything. You are responsible for your actions. Every choice you make is your own. There is an old story about two wolves. One wolf is love compassion, blessings and joy. The other wolf is self-doubt, anger, controlling others, and not of ones heart. With your actions, and choices, you feed one of the two wolves. Sooner or later, one wolf will take over. That is free will."

All 5 of the Great beings start to step up to the cloud, as they do, a gold cat with rainbow colored wings appears he says, "To those that were saved, climb on my back as we travel we will find homes for all of you. Four of them begs to stay. The golden Iatia asked, what is it you desire. They reply in harmony "To help this land and these people. May we be allowed to assist in some way." The Golden Iatia turns to Magoose and bows his head he asked, "Do you allow these 4 to stay and help you. They are restored with pure heart and can do no harm."

Magoose said, "It would be our honor to have wonderful beings to help us. And to help us remember what has happened this day."

He bows his head and said, "It is done. Thank you Great Magoose."

The cat with rainbow colored wings said, "I am the golden colored Iatia, I can create and destroy. I leave these 4 and I am on my way."

He smiles brightly and continues, "Watch."

Upon saying this he moves like a beam of light through the cloud, over the learning center. All 5 of the beings, standing on the cloud and Earis disappear in a flash of light.

The shield starts to fade around the learning center. And the windows reappear. The windows now are so clear, you almost can't tell they are there. All the children in the garden, agrees it looks even brighter now. As everyone's eye return to the ground, they see Mother Earth and Mother Nature talking to the 4 restored spirits.

Mother Nature and Mother Earth calls to everyone in the learning center I asks, "Anyone willing to help of their own free will come down to us. So that we may restore this land and its protections?"

Mother Earth turns and walks away with the 4 star beings. She heads to where the barrier once was. You are now the east.

She walks with each of them placing them in each direction until she gets back to the east.

She calls to all of the teachers in a loving voice that slightly tugs on their heart drawing them to her. Who would like to help?"

Everyone that has chosen to help was instantly there.

Mother Earth guide the people around the inside shield and stop and honor each of the four star being in the directions. They stop and thank them for helping. The people see that the rich dark soil has returned.

Magoose, Norah, and many of the others walk with Mother Earth around the protected barrier and walking spiraling to the learning center. They reset it with the knowledge they have learned this day.

Mother Nature calls to everyone else in a loving voice that slightly tugs on their heart drawing them to her. Who would like to help?"

They feel it and instantly they are there. The children are filled with joy and wonder. They all realize that everywhere Mother Nature walks after the battle; everything is green and lush and became the jungle again.

Mother Nature asked all that are there, "Please open your hearts feel all the love of Mother Earth below you. Feel her energy connect to your heart. Hold hands and walk with me. The children start walking where Mother Nature directs them to go.

Kalub and Kaylah sees the little peoples villages, avoiding the home of the Gnomes of Technockrowsee.

Mother Nature said, "During the battle, poison fell upon this spot. Mother Earth has removed the poison. Because she has done this, we can re-grow here without worries.

Had there been plants growing, when the poison feel... Let's just say, it would have been much more harder to fix." with a loving smile.

Kalub and Kaylah said to Mother Nature, "During the battle, one of those strange balls hit our potato crop.

Mother Nature asked, "Inside the learning center?"

They nodded in agreement.

Mother Nature said, "Kaylah and Kalub, please stay with me."

To everyone else, "Thank you so much for helping. You have helped restore the land. Everything that grows, and all the different crops and fields outside. The love you have given has helped make the plants, tree, and animals stronger."

The children all hug Mother Nature spreading out in many directions.

Mother Nature says in a firm and loving voice, "Children, please go back to your home." She bends down and talks to Kalub and Kaylah, "I have a bad feeling about the potatoes." She reaches down and takes their hands.

The children feel slightly dizzy and see a strange Gnome standing in the middle of the poisoned potato crop. Crystal and wires of all types were buried in the ground.

Mother Nature gasps her eyes almost closed she focuses on the strange Gnome and said, "Ralphus, you were not given permission to use or test any of this. You know not what you have done! This was very bad."

Ralphus smiles brightly and says, "Good day to the Lemurian children who can't see me. And to the lovely Mother Nature, nothing to worry about. I am the greatest inventor in the world, and a few sub galaxies. I have fixed the problem. My wonderful, greatest invention in the world has taken away all the poison. I was just about to test to see if there was just a speck left."

One of the machines behind him started to make whirling land popping sounds. A very thin piece of paper-bark came out of the machine, followed by the word, UT OH in large print. Ralphus kicked the machine and said, "Quiet you."

Mother Natures said, "Please read that entire thing out loud."

Kalub and Kaylah asked each other, "Why did the Gnome kick the machine?"

Ralphus grows slightly pale and asks, "You children can see me?"

The twins smile and nodded their heads and said, "What is all this stuff."

Ralphus thinks to himself, "Do I answer their question and run away in the confusion, or should I just run away."

Mother Nature speaks up in a very stern voice, "Don't you dare leave Ralphus! I know that look."

Ralphus's eyes grow wide as he stares at Mother Nature.

She claps her hands together and said, "Stay!"

Ralphus yells, "EKK, Ouch!"

To the children it looks like there are thousands of Ralphus suddenly. The next second his feet are planted in the ground like roots. And his upper body is twisting around in a circle like a punching bag.

Kalub exclaims, "Did he go away and leave one of those punching bag things in his place? Did he? If it is a punching bag can I keep it Mother Nature?"

Ralphus Gulps.

Mother Natures replies, "I just may give him to you for that. But first we have a bigger problem. Ralphus read that note now!"

Ralphus gulps as he grabs the piece of paper.

"Soil test complete.

Soil has no poison remaining.

Plant test complete.

All potato on south turtle Island are now...slightly toxic.

UhtOh. Mother Nature will be mad again!

I told you it was a bad idea.

To set up multiple tests.

On all the potato fields on South Turtle Island.

Stop kicking me! I will tell!"

Mother Nature lets out a long sad sigh. She walks over to the Machine, as she does she kicks Ralphus and starts pushing buttons.

The twins are amazed.

Ralphus keeps appearing all over the top of the potato crop yelling, "Ouch each time."

The twins can't help but laugh; this is the funniest thing they have ever seen.

After a minute or so, Mother Nature lets out a deep sigh. Walked over a kicked Ralphus again. This time he starts spinning around where his feet are planted saying, "ah ah ah ah."

Mother Nature sits on the ground and asks the twins to come sit on her knees.

As the children sit Mother Nature says in a sad, yet loving voice, "Thank you for telling me about this children. I was able to stop much of the damage. Unfortunately Ralphus... well... his actions has made it impossible for even me to remove all of the poison. Fortunately" She says with a smile. "The planet is still here, clouds don't breath fire, or any other of his crazy actions did not happen. His machine shows, that if you boil the potatoes the poison cannot harm you." She sighs deeply. "This is a good lesson for you. The lesson is, always be careful and try to avoid Gnome of Technockrowsee."

Ralphus loudly protests, "Why do people keep saying that? We are just here to improve your lives. Accidents are just part of the process. My inventions have made the universe a better place. You don't become leader of the Gnome of Technockrowsee by accident."

Mother Nature starts laughing.

Ralphus continues speaking "457 have gained that title because the former blow up, became insane, or other not my fault reasons... well... the point is the universe could not live without our inventions. By the way, since it was not that bad, May I go now?"

Mother Nature laughs harder and shakes her head and snaps her finger and Ralphus is gone.

She said, "Well we need to clean his mess up again. Two large bags appear, with the words, "Technockrowsee equipment Danger!" in red letters.

Mother Nature said, "Please hold the bags children. For this stuff is too dangerous for you to touch."

She collects all the parts and pieces and places each into the bag.

She states, "It appears we have gotten them all."

When she finishes a large purple and blue pock-a-doted Ogre appears.

Mother Nature says, "Tie the bags and back up children."

Kalub and Kaylah run to the far wall and watch this strange creatures that is so brightly colored it almost hurts their eyes.

Mother Nature smiles lovely at the Ogre and says, "Candy time!"

The Ogre grabs the two large bags, and starts chomping down on them.

After nearly a minute the Ogre finishes. With a large burbs and fart at the same time. The Ogre created a purple gas that came from both ends at once. Then he says in a sad voice, "Candy all gone."

Mother Nature says in a comforting voice to the Ogre, "Don t worry my child. You will come with me to day and have a full meal of candy."

Mother Nature walks over to the twins she whispers to them, "This was Ralphus's attempt for a garbage disposal. He is harmless unless you are one of those bags. The twins breathe a great sigh of relief.

Kaylah asked Mother Nature, "Ever since he did that thing there, I can taste color."

Kalub said, "Me too. I just didn't want to say anything."

Mother Nature giggles, "It is simply the cost, of dealing with Gnome of Technockrowsee. It will pass, as did the trash. It all goes away in time. I must be off to teach the people of South Turtle Island, how to use their potato's again. Once again I must clean up Ralphus mess." Mother Nature lets out a big sigh. "One of his accidents did great rainbows."

With that she was gone.

The children sat for a few minutes staring at the strange creature. Suddenly it just up and down saying, "Candy time," and was gone.

The children stand up and run to Magoose to tell him what happened. Hopefully Magoose, Norah or Joy will believe them.

One of the teachers is still in the far corner of the garden making mumbling sounds. Pointing to where the creature once was.

Mother Earth is walking with Magoose, Norah, Joy, and the teachers back to the stairs of the learning center. Kalub and Kaylah come running down the steps yelling, "Magoose! Magoose! Mother Nature, Ogres pretty colors, and beware of Gnomes of Technockrowsee!"

It takes an hour for Magoose, Norah, Joy and the other teacher to figure out what they are trying to say. Upon figuring it all out, Magoose turn to Mother Earth and asks, "Is there a way to protect us from the Gnomes of Technockrowsee?"

Mother Earth starts laughing with tear in her eyes and says that reminds me. "Come with me Magoose, Norah, and Joy please." They take Mothers Earths hand and Joy asked, "Where are not going to the home of those strange Gnomes are we?"

Mother Earth laughs louder when they disappear from sight.

The teachers and student are all daze and confused from the day's events.

Professor Williams guides everyone into the Learning Center. "Come everyone, it is over! This way please," Professor Williams Guides.

They enter the learning center as a bell rings. Everyone goes to the eating room.

Jai goes to Professor Williams and asks, "What happened to Earis, that strange cat when right through him. He disappears and I have not seen him come back yet. He is my friend so I am concerned."

Professor Williams he brings Jai to a couch and says, "I know a great many things. I have traveled far and wide. And in these few days, I have learn and seen more than me and my wife together had experienced in our long lives. I have learned to trust Magoose completely. The Great Gods and Goddess, do everything for a reason. All the ones I have ever seen or meet are guided by love. Keep this in mind; I am not sure their plan for your friend. I know all the little world people helped make this learning center possible. They know much more than we do. I am willing to bet if you cheek his door that should give you some clue if he will return."

Jai asked, "It was Magoose, Norah, Kalub and Kaylah and My twin Sister and Me who created this Learning center. We did not know all the little people, or other helpers except for Mother Earth. Mother Nature and Father Sun. I trust Magoose and Norah with all I am. But they are gone also. Do you know when they will be back?"

Professor Williams's eyes widen with a smile he said, "Had you told me that when I first arrived, I would have walked out the front door. Thinking you ate something that was not right. After today, and that Ogre, Not much should... surprise me."

"I have learned to trust, in Mother Nature. She picked Magoose to run this Learning Center. Magoose is still the father of our school. Do you understand?"

Jai nodded his head and said, "Thank you Professor Williams. For your knowledge, each of us where giving a clan room to be in charge of. Even Kaylah and Kalub are blessed by Mother Nature and Mother Earth. Each of us four has the responsibility of each of the directions.

Professor Williams smiles upon hearing this and says, "Go cheek Earis door. I will cheek the others doors.

They each walk away and cheek the doors. Jai is relieved to find Earis door still with his name on it. The top of the door reads, Earis Iatia No one else may enter. Were the door meets the wall, Steal bars have made it impossible for anyone to open.

Below his name is a note that reads.

"I will be back, when my work and travels is through.

Thank you everyone at the learning center, for allowing me to be part of your lives.

Hopefully, I can visit from time to time."

He also notices a note from Mother Nature reading,

This door is guarded by equipment from the Gnomes of Technockrowsee. Touch at your own risk.

Upon reading this Jai runs very fast upstairs away from the door. Jai gets to the eating hall where Professor Williams is waiting, and explains to him what he saw.

Professor William also spoke what he saw. They are both relieved and sit down to eat.

During the meal Kalub and Kaylah go table to table telling all the other children about the many little people homes located around the learning center. One of the teachers decides to ask the twins why they are telling everyone about this, because no one else can see it.

They think about the teacher words after a minute Kalub says, "Well... maybe... if we are lucky...one of the strange gnomes can make glasses that others can see them."

The teacher smacks his palm to his forehead and says, "I pray not... sorry to trouble you two. Go on."

Toma give a note to the professor and his wife and both sets twins from Earis and Magoose. It was a wonderful meal. Many of the children and teachers could not stop talking about the day's events.

During the meal Magoose, Norah, Joy and Earis are speaking with the Gods and Goddess. During this time, Earis is informed of his destiny, and is allowed to write notes for his friends. Joy and Norah are granted secrets about the learning center, and knowledge those at the school where not in heart.

Magoose is taken aside, and showed a great many things. In the end Magoose was given an object that allows him to speak anywhere, as he was actually there. It was described to him, that this device allowed the user to see everything in the place it showed them. The device made an image of him that looks exactly like him yet he could not touch or pick up anything. Magoose instantly new his first use of this device as asks to use it.

⁂

Altex is smashing and destroying things in his command center. "What good is sky-ship's with no one to fly them. My clone factories have nothing to build with. All of my parts are gone. There is less than 50 Atlantain's left in my command center. How could such primitive people do this to me?

We are so much more advanced. How..." he screams.

Kicking and smashing everything around him. He goes through a list of Atlantain's, and sends orders for them to report to the cloning stations. He makes another list of Atlantain's, to report to the learning tubes. While thinking to himself, "This army will be unstoppable." He commands everyone at the command center, that it would be to their best interest to have his new army ready in a week. As he paces back and forth.

Magoose stands before and said, "Hello my old friend."

Altex became completely enraged. He grabs his weapons and starts blasting Magoose. They simply pass through him and started destroying everything on the other side. He demands Magoose to tell him their secret.

Magoose simply looks around and said, "What lovely place you have here. Don't break it up on my account.

Altex sits in his chair still kicking and growling. And said, "What do you want scum? You do realize you can't leave here alive."

He starts slapping buttons as the entire command center doors and windows shut and lock and a force field surround the command center.

Altex starts to smile and laugh. "Not even the Great Magoose can get out this one alive."

Slowly he walks towards Magoose and said, "Come to think of it I have always like you Magoose. Your stupid trusting nature always helped me get the upper hand."

He then Jumps at Magoose and passes through him and hitting his head on the wall behind him. He wobbly stands up and faces Magoose.

Magoose simply smiles and said, "Are you done yet?"

Altex screams at the top of his lungs, "Fine say your words. They will be your last."

Magoose said, "Thank you for allowing me to speak my friend, you are so kind. I have a message for you. This message comes from the depth of my heart. I am sorry to inform you that your drones have all been reclaimed. We have no use for your inferior sky-ship. So they were returned to you. Do you like how well they were upon return my friend?"

Altex goes on a rampage kicking, smashing everything in sight. He spoke words so vile; I could not in good conscious repeat them. After what seemed like eternity, Altex finally straitened up adjusted his clothing opened a door and pulls out a bottle.

He sits back down at his desk, pours himself a glass and said very politely to Magoose, "So my friend, with an icy chill to his voice. Why do you honor me with your presents?"

Magoose's eyes grow serious and said, "I have come to bring you a message. Are you finally ready to hear it?"

Altex says in his polite icy voice, "Of course Great Magoose. What feeble words of wisdom could possibly mean anything to me? As you know, you and all your people will be part of my machines."

Magoose replies, "I give you this message spoken with words and truth. From this day forth neither you nor your army will ever be allowed to come near my home or harm anyone there. You simply are too full of hate to realize there is nothing you can do. We will thrive and you will simply disappear."

Magoose bows slightly and adds, "If I ever see you in person, and our eyes meet again. You will be no more my friend. This is the last time we shall ever speak. Choose you closing words very carefully."

Altex burst into laughter he looks at Magoose and says, "You are the inferior one. I would never fall or bow before someone as worthless as you. If you simply give me your secret, I may spare you and your stupid children."

Magoose locks eyes with Altex he said, "You are not worth my time!" he then disappears.

Altex explodes into anger again. He starts chasing several of the people in the command center. Like he rabid mongoose. Thankfully for them, his temper-tantrums had already warn him out.

* * *

Magoose finally meets back up with his family. They give Earis a loving farewell Earis reaches into his pocket hands Magoose a beautiful gold inlay box and says, "I felt you should have this Grandfather. After great discussion it is decided that this was best kept in your hands.

There is an information crystal that explains all about the item. And the improvements that Mother Nature, Ralphus, and Myself have made.

I have no need for it anymore. I have literately become a living library of all knowledge that the learning center has. In the last few weeks, I had been giving permission to visit with all the little peoples. They were kind enough to grant me their knowledge.

Thankfully Mother Earth did not grant me the arrogance of some gnomes. I hope this gift honors you and server you will."

"Grandmother, I love you so much. You and mother have always granted me the greatest gift of all. Total love and compassion. Even when I caused trouble, and did not think things through. Grandfather has always given me this, and his gentle wisdom."

"Mother, Thank you for everything. I will never forget our travels. Each place we went taught me something new. It helped me understand myself better. You are the greatest mom I could have ever hoped for. Please do not worry about me. I will visit you as I can. I also give you my word; I will completely test all devices before giving them out." He gives a gift to his grandmother and mother and said "Goodbye."

Magoose, Norah and Joy found themselves back into their rooms. They hear the dinner bell put their gifts in a safe place and begin to wash up and changing for evening meal. By the time they arrived almost everyone was finished eating, and telling stories of the day.

Magoose asked for everyone's attention please and said, "Children and teachers, I could not be more proud of you then I am today. Even with everything that has happened today, you stayed in love and heart. Almost all of you have released your fear, anger, and hatred. Everyone here has learned which wolf they feed. Our school and protections, are stronger then I could have ever dreamed of. Sadly during today's events, someone who I dare not mention has given us a price. The potato's where saved," he lets out a deep sigh, "from now on anyone working with potatoes must boil them first. The wood nymphs, have created a new drink, for the Adults. It is called Manieyock. New rule only adult teachers may have or use it per Mother Nature."

* * *

It was almost bedtime. The little twin girls, Zara and Tara sat by the fireplace, worried.

Kaylah and Kalub felt their hearts, and sat next to them.

Kaylah said, "Don't worry little one, the drones were after us too. They have been looking for Kalub and me for years. You are not the only ones the drones wanted to kill."

Kaylah reached out and held one of the twins. Kalub held the other.

Loora and Jai saw Kaylah and Kalub with the little twin girls.

"That was great, wasn't it?" Jai said.

"Yes, it was interesting," Kalub said, "and to think, we had to be able to fight like that."

"Yeah," Jai said.

Kaylah spoke, "Well, we better start thinking about that. We are all like these children. The Atlantain's want all of us dead. Only here in our school, will we ever be safe."

Kalub agreed.

Loora and Jai sat with them next to the warmth of the fire, and thought about the future.

Loora said, "Just think, the earth changes have not started yet."

Kalub and Kaylah looked at her and asked, "What do you mean?"

"Just that," Loora said, "We are already at war, fighting for our home, learning about our new friends, and the earth changes are yet to come."

Jai added, "Don't forget about Altex wanting to kill us all too."

"That's not funny," Kaylah said.

"Well, it's true you know, he will find a way to get to us, he's not dead yet," Jai said.

About the Author

I am Cheecowah Jack.

My life has changed and shifted enough to know the great workings of Nature.

I met Kalub and Kaylah during a difficult time in my life.

I love this story very much, and after a few people asked for copies of what I wrote, they also fell in love with it. I decided to put this into print to share with you.

I love hearing stories from the elders and the teachings of tribal minded people.

I have been to the Mayan Lands and traveled around the country, searching for ancient knowledge.

I am in love with Lemurian culture, the way they live and the small pieces of their stories I have found.

I love the Great Macaws. While in Mayan country, I was able to study them. Upon my return home, I learned how to work with, and train them. Now I share my home with a wonderful blue and gold, which fills my life with joy every day.

I love nature, spirit, music, animals, my green house, learning ancient tribal ideals and traveling.

Have an awesome day.

www.ingramcontent.com/pod-product-compliance
Lightning Source LLC
Chambersburg PA
CBHW061557190726
48288CB00007B/2066